ESCAPE FROM BAGHDAD!

ESCAPE FROM BAGHDAD!

Saad Z. Hossain

The Unnamed Press
Los Angeles, CA

The Unnamed Press
1551 Colorado Blvd., Suite #201
Los Angeles, CA 90041
www.unnamedpress.com

First published in North America and the United Kingdom
by The Unnamed Press.

1 3 5 7 9 10 8 6 4 2

This book was originally published in 2012 in Bangladesh
as *Baghdad Immortals* by Bengal Publications.

ISBN: 978-1-939419-24-8

Library of Congress Control Number: 2014948158

This book is distributed by Publishers Group West

Printed in the United States of America by McNaughton & Gunn

Designed by Scott Arany

This book is a work of satirical fiction. Names, characters, places and incidents
are wholly fictional or are used fictitiously. Any resemblance to actual events or
persons, living or dead, is totally coincidental (mostly).

CONTENTS

A Note on the Glossary at the End of this Book

A NOTE ON THE GLOSSARY
AT THE END OF THIS BOOK

There is a glossary of mostly factual terms and names at the end of this book ("factual" being a relative idea open to loose interpretation ("loose interpretation" meaning we're aiming for a 50% chance of something on the page tallying with someone else's verified opinion.)) So, if you find yourself wondering: What's a Druze? Or who's Moqtada Al-Sadr again? Or what does JAM stand for? Or IED? Just refer to the helpful, mostly factual glossary at the end of the book.

★

1: SOUTH GHAZALIYA

"WE SHOULD KILL HIM," KINZA SAID. "BUT NOTHING TOO ORTHODOX."
Silence then. A kind of scathing, derisive, stifling silence expanding to fill the room, crowding out the detritus of previous conversations, leaving two blackmarketeers drinking in a darkened space, in the back of a battered house, with nothing much to say. The room was dark because they had used foil paper to blacken the windows. The lights were off because outside, the JAM militia, known as the Mahdi Army, had just torn through 13th Street, which was rare, because 13th Street in Ghazaliya was a dead-end nothing suburban thoroughfare.

"Out of principle alone, it should be done," Kinza sipped his Jack Daniels, which he had bartered from the US Marine Ted Hoffman for a piece of Chemical Ali's skull. "Not because I hate this man. It is nothing personal for me. I am merely an agent of fate, like the Count of Monte Cristo."

Kinza's partner Dagr received this comment without surprise or apparent concern. Though he had once been a professor of economics, it turned out the wartime shift in profession had been ridiculously easy for him.

The JAM normally preferred 14th Street, as it allowed them access to the northern Shi'a neighborhood of Shulla, but in this excursion they had run into the South Ghazaliya Defense Brigade, sworn to defend South Ghazaliya. The JAM often won these encounters, but recently their firebrand Shi'a patron, Moqtada Al-Sadr, had cut down their bullet rations, and today the SGD had produced a black-market US army M60 and risen to their youthful promise. All this defense had forced the JAM into Kinza's street, a hail of smoke and diesel and bullets, AK47s popping. Kinza had brokered the sale of the M60 to the SGD in the first place, *provided they fought on 14th Street.*

"My friend, we have a moral duty in this situation," Kinza said.

The situation was indeed demanding of their attention, moral or otherwise. Two days ago, Kinza and Dagr, purveyors of medicine, gossip, diesel, and specialty ammunition, had inherited the living person of Captain Hamid, formerly of the 8th "As Saiqa" Special Forces Division, of the Republican Guard. He had been the chief savant of interrogators, vigilant against traitors to the party, known especially for his signature style and a certain personal flair to the work—an artistic flourish to the branding, undoubtedly the star striker on the torture pitch, the number 10 of all 10s, the 23 of all 23s. Now this Mother Teresa of black holes, this living spit of Torquemada, belonged to them.

This inheritance had come to Kinza and Dagr by a circuitous route. Kinza's cousin twice removed, Daoud, had been a second lieutenant in the All Martyrs of Anbar Army, an offshoot of retired Republican Guard types who had agreed to shelter the notorious Captain Hamid. This brave battalion had lasted for all of two weeks before a combined (but wholly coincidental) US and Shi'a pincer attack had fulfilled their dearest wish of martyrdom. Both wounded, Daoud and the captain had taken refuge with Kinza. The captain had survived, Daoud had not.

"Morality is for the Aztecs," Dagr said. "We should sell Hamid to the Americans. We could probably retire on the reward."

"Was he on the deck of cards?"

"He almost made it," Dagr said. "I think he was ranked 56th. There was some talk of putting him in the second round, but I guess he just slipped through the cracks."

"Funny, I thought he would have ranked higher," Kinza said. "Not the face cards, maybe, but in the deck, at least."

"We could just let him go. In Shulla, maybe," Dagr offered quickly. "Let nature sort it out."

Kinza made a face. That was not a solution he favored.

"We could sell him to the Mahdi Army," Dagr scratched his head tiredly. "Sadr might have put him on *his* deck."

"Sadr has a deck?"

"I think he made one," Dagr said. "But he left out the queens and changed the hearts to little crescents."

"I hate dealing with the Mahdi Army. Last time they made me pray all day and then woke me up at night to pray again," Kinza murmured.

"You're a product of your race. Self-loathing defeatist," Dagr scraped back his chair. "You hate everyone. You hate the Sunnis for killing Hassan. You hate the Shi'as for breaking up the Ummah. You hate the Americans for being crass. You hate the Palestinians for being beggars. You hate the Saudis for being cowards. And because of this, you piss on rational self interest."

"Thank you, professor," Kinza saluted him with an empty glass. "Condescending as usual. You still live in a tower. A shitty tower, but a tower nonetheless. Hatred is a physical thing. It comes from the gut. I physically need to kill Hamid."

"Because he is a torturer."

"Yes."

"Then you become a torturer as well, and therefore you deserve a similar death, by virtue of your own logic."

"Which is why I am hesitating," Kinza refilled his glass. Next to the bottle was a 38 caliber revolver, police issue, now black-market issue, soon to be Shi'a or Sunni or Coalition issue—so many issues it was impossible to decide. These days, every house in Ghazaliya had a confused gun. "Would it fundamentally alter our relationship, professor, if I tortured and killed Hamid?"

Dagr smiled sourly. "I am a market parasite. I help corrupt soldiers steal medicine from the Thresher, our friendly neighborhood American military base so I can sell it at huge profits to needy people who were once my friends. I have shot at a 14-year-old boy who was probably related to me, just for jumping out of an alley. I have…"

"Ok," Kinza held up a hand. "I am not speaking of you now. I am speaking of the professorial you. Would the man who taught economics at the Abu Bakr Memorial have a problem with what I want to do?"

"That fool would have shit his pants."

"Yes, but the problem is, when normalcy returns, then the pants shitters are all back on top, and I would probably have to answer to all of them for everything I do today to survive. And in that time, my friend, I would hate to have you pointing a great shitty finger at me."

"Today, I would help you kill Hamid," Dagr said finally. "Tomorrow I would hate myself for it. The next day, I would hate you for it as well."

"Then what do you suggest for comrade Hamid?" Kinza asked. "Seriously, I want to know."

"He should have a trial," Dagr said.

"A hanging trial or a firing trial?" Kinza asked.

"A fair trial."

"What the hell is that?"

"I'm not joking," Dagr shrugged. "Give him a trial. Round up a few dozen people from the neighborhood and try him."

"I like it, a kangaroo court."

"A *fair* trial."

"How do you give a torturer a fair trial?" Kinza asked. "What possible judge would be predisposed to favor him?"

"He followed orders didn't he?" Dagr shrugged. "Everyone followed orders."

"Look, he didn't shoot a bunch of random Kurds," Kinza said. "He killed our own people. Academics, professionals, businessmen. People like you, in fact. What if it was your father he had his cigar into? Wouldn't you like to be the judge then?"

"I agree with you," Dagr said wearily. "It's just that in passing judgment, in executing that judgment, you become tainted yourself."

"So you're saying pass it on to someone else?"

"Precisely," Dagr said. "That is why we have professional judges."

"Difficult to find an impartial judge at this point."

"Unless we find one from the old days," Dagr said.

"They'd probably be friends with him," Kinza said. "Look, let's at least interrogate him a little bit."

A bell at the door then, the Ghazaliya bell, they called it, the knock of rifle butts against splintered wood, the three-second grace time before boots and flashlights, lasers and automatic rifle barrels. Better than the Mahdi Army, who didn't bother to knock, and who had never heard of the three-second rule. Dagr surged toward the front of the house, already sweating, thrusting Kinza back. It was his job to face the American door to doors because he still looked like a professor, soft jawed, harmless, by some chance the exact composite of the innocent Iraqi these farm boys from Minnesota had come to liberate. And Kinza...with his hollow-eyed stare, Kinza would never survive these conversations.

He barely got there in time to save the door. Sweaty, palsied fear, as he jerked his head into the sunlight, facing down two of them, and three more in the Humvee behind. They were like big, idiot children in their heavy armor and helmets, capable of kindness or casual violence as the mood took them, unreadable, random, terrifying.

"Door-to-door, random check, sir," a Captain Fowler said.

"Good morning," Dagr said. Panic made his voice a croak. Door-to-door searches...they would find Kinza, and then Hamid, and it would be a rifle butt to the mouth, burst teeth, no Guantanamo for them, just hands tied behind the waist and a bullet to the head, right here...

"Had some violence down here this morning," Captain Fowler was saying. "Understand the Mahdi Army came down this road, had a tussle with the boys from the SGD. Know anything about that, sir?"

"I was hiding, lying on the floor here," Dagr said. He looked desperately from face to face, sunglasses, helmets, flashlights, all hard edges. Where the hell was Hoffman? Kind, innocent Hoffman, who shared cigarettes and jokes and tipped off Kinza about door-to-door searches...

"You sweating, my man," Fowler casually shifted his weight, his foot blocking the door open, his gun angled just so, changing everything.

"It's hot, we have no water," Dagr said. "No water, nothing in the tank, no flushes working, no electricity either. One fan, and the bastards shot it today..."

"Ok, sir, we're rigging the electricity back. We've had reports of this problem," Fowler stared at him for a little while. "Sir, who else lives in this house? Are you alone in there?"

"Alone," Dagr felt his voice give way. "My house. I live here. Do you want it? Take it, take it, just shoot me, and take it. No water for three days, toilets blocked up for two months, I have to shit in a bucket, bullet holes in every damn wall."

"Calm down, sir," Fowler tapped his gun on the door. "We are looking for one man known to be an arms dealer. We believe he has a safehouse somewhere in this grid."

Dagr sagged against the door, the sweat pouring out of him, his mind a panicky Babel of voices, eyes swiveling from helmet to helmet, trying to find some weakness, some glimmer of the folksy charm they used when they weren't in the killing mood. *Hoffman, where are you for God's sake?*

"You seem to be looking for someone, partner," Fowler said. "Looking for Sergeant Hoffman by any chance?"

"Hoffman? I don't know him. Maybe. He gave me a cigarette once I think. Tall and white? Don't know any Hoffman. There was a nice black man before."

"Hoffman ran patrols here," Fowler said. "He got busted for fooling around with a very bad man. An arms dealer called Kinza. Don't happen to know him?"

"Kinza? Sounds Japanese. I don't know, I hardly go out, Mahdi Army shooting up the streets every day, I've eaten bread and eggs for the last three days, can't even get out to the store, it's three blocks down on 14th, not that they have anything there anyway."

"Alright, sir."

"Please, so rude of me, please come in," Dagr began to step back. "I have a nice couch, no TV though, got robbed last week, I could hear them from my bedroom, but I just stayed in my blanket. I could make you a cup of tea, no milk or sugar, I'm afraid, but, well..."

Fowler stuck his upper body into the room, swiveling his head around. The flashlight on his helmet cut a tight swathe through the gloom, illuminating the pathetic attempts at normalcy: a faded couch, a table loaded with coffee cups, a radio, a pile of textbooks hugging the floor along one wall. The moment hung on a seesaw, Dagr staring at Fowler's foot, willing it to inch back, dreading the one step forward that would signal the end.

"Alright, sir," Fowler stepped back. "You be careful now. Give us a call if this Kinza is spotted anywhere. You can ask for Captain Fowler at the Thresher."

"Yes, captain, yes, I will," Dagr said. "Absolutely. I hope you catch him. He sounds like a bastard Sadr sympathizer. You're doing a good job. Long live America!"

They left and he sagged against the door, aghast at how weak his legs felt. And then he stumbled back inside, remembering that he had left Kinza and Hamid alone for far too long, Kinza drunk and brooding, a man capable of anything. They were in the bathroom, Hamid fetal in the cracked bathtub, hands and legs bound, a filthy handkerchief choking his mouth, two inches of tepid water sloshing a pink tinge. Kinza had a screwdriver and pliers, and his bottle in the crook of his arm, humming.

"Kinza, they're gone," Dagr said, out of breath.

"I think he's ready to tell me all sorts of things," Kinza said. He removed the gag.

"Fuck you," Hamid said. "What the hell is wrong with you?"

"Holding back are you?"

"Fuck you. You haven't asked me anything yet."

"Right," Kinza laughed. "I don't believe you. You're lying." He started again with the screwdriver.

"Kinza, stop it," Dagr said. "The Americans are looking for you. *They know your name.*"

"Hoffman?"

"Caught, reprimanded, I don't know," Dagr said. "Busted. We have to run, Kinza. They know about the guns."

Hamid started laughing, a whistling sound because he had recently lost a tooth. "You two are the stupidest fuckers alive."

"No problem," Kinza put away his tools. "I'll shoot him and then we'll go."

"Where, Kinza?" Dagr asked.

"North, to Shulla," Kinza shrugged. "I have a friend. Or maybe head over to Baqouba. Start again."

"Idiots," Hamid spat out blood. "I know where to go."

"Where?" Dagr asked.

"Shut up," said Kinza.

"Take me to Mosul," Hamid said. "And I will show you the secret bunker of Tareq Aziz."

"Like a sightseeing tour?" Dagr asked, momentarily puzzled.

"It's full of gold, you fool! Bullion bars and coins. I am the only living man who knows its location."

"How?"

"I once served on his personal staff. I'm the only survivor. Everyone else died in peculiar accidents." Hamid seemed particularly proud of that.

"Do you believe this idiot?" Kinza looked at Dagr.

The insectile head of the American soldier haunted him. "Who cares?" Dagr said. "Let's go to Mosul."

2: BARRIERS

"THEY'RE LOOKING FOR YOU, BUDDY." HOFFMAN WAS SMOKING A joint, slumped in the rubble of a destroyed house.

"I know," Kinza took it off him. "You in trouble?"

"Verbal reprimand," Hoffman shrugged. "All them old boys appreciate how much hash I've flowed their way."

"Not for long," Kinza threw a small packet to his friend. "We're off. Make it last."

"Yo, where you all going?"

"North. Anbar. Mosul maybe. Who knows?" Kinza said. "Want to come? There might be a bunker full of gold. We'll cut you in."

"Sure," Hoffman said. "Professor, you gonna teach me some more math along the way?"

"We need some help, Hoffman." Dagr had taught him calculus for the past two weeks, at first as a joke. The Marine looked deceptively stupid, *was* stupid in all likelihood; yet he had picked up integration unerringly. "Get us past the checkpoints into Shulla."

"Sure," Hoffman said. "Hell, I'd go all the way with you boys, but they'd probably nail me for desertion. Call me when you find that bunker. I'll fence it for you."

"Hoffman, you really think there's a bunker in the desert waiting for us?" Kinza laughed. "Who knows, maybe it's filled with 72 virgins as well. Stranger things have happened. We can't stay here anymore. That's for sure."

The Iraqi Army 2nd Cavalry Battalion checkpoint was built into the rubble of no man's land between north and south Ghazaliya, Shi'a and Sunni, the bewildered Iraqi soldiers trying to keep calm and courteous, desperate to still believe the drumming message that there was one Al Qaeda, one insurgency, one enemy. In truth, they kept panicky fingers tight on their triggers, wary of women and children, knowing they were the eternal target, nobody's friend, traitors in every book. Dagr and Hoffman stayed to the front, Hoffman doing the talking. After a desultory search, they were through, parting ways with a slap and a casual smile.

"They should put Hoffman in charge of Baghdad," Dagr said, as they cleared the searchlights into the relieving darkness of evening. "We'd have a lot less tension."

"Forget it," Kinza said. "They should give him Rumsfeld's job."

"Maybe he'll be president one day."

"He could be the joint president of Texas and Iraq."

"Imperialist lapdog," Hamid mumbled.

Hamid was not a happy man these days. His face had puffed up to a misshapen Quasimodo lump, where eyes, nose, and mouth were swimming in irregular proximity to each other. A once vain man, he could no longer bear to look at any reflective surfaces and thus wore dark glasses at all times. He was in constant nagging pain, a condition Kinza was in no hurry to leaven. Too, he had a clearer idea now of the route Kinza planned to take, hopping from bastion to bastion of Shi'a dominance. Not a Saddam sympathizer in sight, his life worth a toothpick in a gunfight in these streets.

In the evening, they walked along a boulevard of garbage and open sewage, traversed by lines of people who looked neither left nor right, hurrying along to their bolt-holes. There were calls for prayer from the mosque nearby, a building wrecked by gunfire and mortar from a desperate battle two weeks ago. They walked in single file, Hamid in the middle, Dagr leading the way because he was Shi'a, and had once lived in the area and people trusted him for some reason.

He recognized a few people but did not hail them as he would have in the old days. It was not certain who was who anymore, which camp, which informant, how many dead in each family, and by whose hand. As night fell, the streets rapidly cleansed themselves of civilians and took on a wholly different breed of walkers. Men with guns circled each block, Insurgents, or civil guards, or JAM militia, or even men who were bewilderingly all three, Iraqi army during the day and everything else at night.

Men with guns lounged in pools of light, unwilling to leave that hazy, pathetic safety, the fear a palpable fog streaming into Dagr's eyes and nose, making him stagger along like a marathon runner. The night belonged to the Ghazaliya dogs, bald and mad, shrapnel marked, barking through garbage. Their shadows capered against the walls, three men on a solitary path, marked by the hopeless stoop of their shoulders.

"We are being watched," Kinza said, as they moved into a wrecked alley. "Be prepared, Dagr."

A short surge, and two men came out of the rubble, guns out, faces wrapped in checkered scarves. At the same time, an old Fiat pulled up behind them.

"Shi'a, Shi'a!" Dagr said, hands raised. "Don't shoot for God's sake."

"Take your hands out of your pockets," the leading gunman said.

Hamid was already on the floor, shielding his face. Kinza stood still, his jacket zipped to his neck, hands jammed into pockets, every line of his body uncompromising.

"Hands out, you."

"You don't want me to do that, friend," Kinza said softly.

"Get your fucking hands out!"

"Kinza, for God's sake," Dagr said, shaking. "Just do as he says."

Kinza shrugged, raised his hands. There was a grenade in his fist. Dagr could see the tension on his thumb, as it pushed down on the pin. Iraqi army standard shrapnel grenade, used to clear rooms in house to house fighting. Somewhere on the checkpoint was a very careless soldier.

"What the hell?" Dagr felt his voice rising sharply.

"You wouldn't." The lead gunman swiveled his pistol from head to head like a metronome, fingers tight and trembling, the gun held lopsided in an amateur grip. Behind him, his partner began to edge back surreptitiously. "You wouldn't."

"Come and find out," Kinza said.

"Let's all relax," Dagr tried to soothe the fever out of his voice. "Look, what do you want?"

"We saw you coming past the checkpost," the gunman said, eyes darting wildly from face to face. "With the American."

"We are just going north, to Shulla," Dagr said. "We don't want this trouble."

"Trouble?" the gunman laughed. "Nobody wants trouble. Trouble comes by itself. Do I want to be like this? We need help. There is no one to help us. You help us, and we'll take you into Shulla."

"Funny way to ask for help," Kinza said. "With guns."

"Is there any other way?"

"Kinza, let me handle this," Dagr slowly lowered his arms. "What makes you think we can help you? We're just ordinary men. I am an economics professor at..."

"You might be normal," the man said. He pointed a stubby finger at Hamid and Kinza. "But those two are jackals. It's them we want. We need beasts to hunt a beast. Plus, you are cozy with Americans."

"Listen, let's talk like reasonable men. What is your name?"

"My name is Amal." The gunman unwound his scarf to reveal an ugly, grizzled face. "There is a man here, called the Lion of Akkad. He is a murderer. We want you to make him go away."

"Go away?"

"The American who helped you cross," Amal said. "Have him deal with it."

"We cannot do that," Dagr said.

"Then have your army friends arrest him," Amal said. "Or you three kill him. We don't care."

"I thought the Jaish Al Mahdi patrol these streets."

"They have been pulling back," Amal said. "And recently they were beaten badly in the south, by the SGD. They're back in Shulla now."

"So, you have guns," Kinza said. "Are you cowards?"

"His brother is in the Mahdi Army, they say," Amal hawked and spat. "If he finds out we did anything, they will kill us all, and our families."

"And we don't have families?"

"You do not look like family men."

"The Lion of Akkad?" Kinza laughed. "What the hell, we'll do it."

––––––––––––––––

"Sit down, Hoffman."

"Sir!"

"Hoffman, we are in a quandary." Captain Fowler's office at the SS Thresher was a textbook military room, no rings on the desk, no overflowing ashtrays, no sticky joysticks, not a file out of place, a room so alien to the rest of the base that even the air seemed crisper, standing to attention, air that was on the constant verge of saluting.

"Sir!"

"It appears, Hoffman, that the investigation into your misconduct has hit a snag."

"Snag, sir!"

"Yes, a snag," Fowler said. "It appears that all of the potential witnesses have disappeared."

"Disappeared, sir!"

"Poof."

"Sir!"

"Hoffman, it is unnecessary to yell at the top of your voice every time I say something," Fowler said.

"Sir!"

"Well, Hoffman, what do you suggest I do with you now?"

"Permission to suggest, sir!"

"At ease, soldier," Fowler said. "Speak your mind."

"Requesting an immediate return to patrol duty, captain!" Hoffman said. "The streets are pretty frisky these days. Something *evil* in the air."

"Hoffman, surely you know that you have been accused of over-fraternizing with the locals," Fowler said, "and specifically, with known criminals. Returning you to regular duty is exactly what I am determined not to do."

"I was gathering intelligence, captain," Hoffman said, offended. "Building bridges with the community. All there in our handbook, captain."

"Hoffman, we've received reports of a certain black-market mastermind brokering heavy weaponry for the local insurgent groups," Fowler said. "A man called Kinza. What do you know about him?"

"A few words here and there, whispered in back alleys," Hoffman said. "He's like a ghost. No one even knows what he looks like. The insurgents think of him as some kind of hero. The JAM find him pretty useful too."

"Is he a ranking member of Al Qaeda in Iraq? Is he Sadr's man in Ghazaliya?"

"No idea, captain."

"Something to investigate further," Fowler said wisely. "We need this man instantly, Hoffman."

"Captain, he's a merchant who plays both sides," Hoffman said. "Sunnis or Shi'as themselves will kill him sooner or later if we sit tight. Even the atheists might get him."

"I have noticed that you understand these A-rab sects," Fowler said. "More than the average soldier. Is that a fair statement?"

"Sir."

"I have noticed that you hang around with these A-rabs during off-duty hours. Is that correct?"

"Yes, sir, gathering vital intelligence, sir."

"Hoffman, are you a homosexual?"

"No, sir!"

Fowler frowned. "Queer? Gay?"

"No, sir!" Hoffman said. "I was married once, sir! She left me for a taxidermist, sir."

"Right," Fowler said. "So what is it you do with these A-rabs, Hoffman?"

"We drink tea and smoke, sir!" Hoffman said. "Good American cigarettes."

"Right," Fowler said.

"And gather intelligence, too," Hoffman said quickly.

"And you can tell the difference between all of them?" Fowler asked, "These Sunnis and Shiites?"

"Mostly, captain," Hoffman said. "Can I ask what this is about?"

"We have an immense opportunity here, Hoffman," Fowler said. "And despite my misgivings about your character, you appear to be the man for the job."

"It is an honor to serve my country! God bless America!"

"Listen closely, Hoffman. We have intel from our informants in Sadr City," Fowler lowered his voice. "It appears that the JAM have been tracking a certain high level member of the A-rab Republican Guard."

"High level?"

"Lunching with Saddam Hussein kind of level," Fowler said. "Now the JAM boys had lost this character, going by the name of Col. Hamid, in a skirmish; they have reliable evidence that he was smuggled into south Ghazaliya by the insurgent Arabs a few days ago. Are you following me, soldier?"

"Yes, sir!"

"The name Kinza has been mentioned. He seems to be harboring this high level A-rab," Fowler said. "It is imperative that we capture these two immediately."

"Right, captain, we need to comb the streets for them," Hoffman jumped up. "I can get a squad together immediately!"

"Hoffman, sit down."

"Sorry, sir," Hoffman said.

"Why am I telling you all this?"

"I don't know, captain."

"Hoffman, I have been directed by HQ to take any steps necessary to apprehend these two deadly insurgents. Gigantic steps! Extrajudicial steps!"

Hoffman, unable to resist, relapsed back to his modus operandi for dealing with high officials. "Extraordinary, sir!"

"I am transferring you to a special command, Hoffman," Fowler said. "You know the streets; you seem to know how these A-rabs think. Capture these two miscreants, and I'll get you a purple heart."

"Right, captain," Hoffman said. "Serve and protect."

"Sign these papers here, soldier," Fowler thrust out a sheaf of high quality paper, wrapped in blue and red military ribbon. "You are now officially part of the Special Forces Unit, Section: Greater Ghazaliya. You report directly to me and my superior, Col. Bradley. I am sure you have heard of Col. Bradley."

"Col. Bradley, sir!"

"The man has single-handedly tamed the wild A-rabs of Baghdad," Fowler said, his eyes glazing over. "You do not want to disappoint Col. Bradley, Hoffman."

"No, sir."

"SFU intelligence indicates that the JAM are desperate to get their hands on Hamid. They think he carries valuable information," Fowler tapped his nose. "And what is valuable to Mr. Sadr is valuable to Col. Bradley. Valuable information, Hoffman. This man Hamid was with all the high ups of the old regime. This could be it, Hoffman. This could be our golden goose."

"The big fish, sir."

"Hoffman, what do you think this Hamid knows?"

"Er, weapons of mass destruction?"

"Precisely, Hoffman," Fowler scowled. "Col. Bradley believes they exist, the president believes they exist, and God himself believes they exist."

"Semper fidelis!"

"Hoffman, get a squad together and get your ass out there," Fowler said. "You find us these two and some WMDs, and I'll personally make sure there's a Nobel Peace Prize in it for you."

3: THE LION OF AKKAD

AMAL OWNED AN AUTOPARTS SHOP IN THE STREET OF NAKAF, IN the very heart of the Lion's territory. He sold tires, rims, and filters, as well as an assortment of used and new batteries. Sometimes, he had engine oil, depending on supply. The Amal empire had not prospered in the war. He had once been a rich man. He had owned two car showrooms, four spare parts dealerships, and stock in an insurance company. One of the showrooms had been obliterated by tank shells during the American liberation. The second had been mistakenly raided as a bomb factory by the Americans and subsequently looted. With profits sliding, his hitherto loyal managers had ransacked three of the four spare parts shops, absconding with the revenue and leaving behind a host of unpaid suppliers.

The insurance company, meanwhile, had not paid. Beset by random acts of destruction, outlandish claims, impossible force majeure, they had done the only sensible thing and filed for bankruptcy. The directors had subsequently fled to their villas in Beirut. And so went the bulk of Amal's stock portfolio. In the end, the man had been reduced to this single shop, which was, incidentally, the one he had first started out with, a piece of circular fate that drove Amal to despair often enough. He lived upstairs in a one bedroom flat with his son. The room at the back of the store had been converted into his office, where he still kept accounts of his many assets, now mainly fictional, a wistful passing of the time, a fiscal fantasy train set providing both employment and misery.

All of this Dagr soaked up as he sat with Amal, cramped in the back room in a haze of stale smoke, plotting and drinking coffee. Kinza sat in the far corner, half asleep, watching football on a tiny set. There was a static tension in the air, the unease of too many strange men in a small place, desultory conversation, the memories of guns and grenades a palpable white elephant, neither side quite believing they are now allies. Hamid was a sullen, oozing wound in the middle of the office, a black hole that swallowed up all normal forms of bonding, the swapping of war stories and misfortunes, sympathies, and secrets.

"You men are young," Amal was saying, after a paltry lunch. "You two can start again, make something of yourselves."

Dagr shrugged. His stomach churned slightly with hunger, and he considered breaking out some chocolate, but he did not want to embarrass his host.

"My life is almost over," Amal continued. "What can I do now, but endure and hope to die in peace? My entire fortune, my whole history, erased. You know the worst thing? I dream about food every night, the scraps I used to throw away from my table. Never did I think I would go hungry again."

"Surely you have savings?"

"Savings, yes," Amal lowered his voice. "But I also have a father with Parkinson's. He used to be in a great nursing home. Fully paid for. Very exclusive. But it went bankrupt after the invasion, and the Americans converted it into a triage. Now I have to keep him in the hospital ward most of the time, not even a private room, and it's still too expensive," Amal grasped Dagr's forearm. "Every day they threaten to throw him out. What can I do? Me and my son live upstairs in one measly room. We eat the rotten stuff that doesn't get sold. Every penny I have, I give for medicine. Now this Lion of Akkad haunts us every day. How can we live?"

"How does anyone live?" Dagr said. "Badly."

"Too right," Amal said. "In days like these, who helps a stranger, eh? Who *asks* help from a stranger?"

"Only the desperate," Dagr said.

"The bastards are all the same," Amal shook his head. "Every bastard with a gun walks the same. We used to have lives before, you know? All that taken away...for what?"

"I used to teach economics, at the university," Dagr said. "My wife taught mathematics. We met there. I had friends, students—hundreds of students. I don't even know what happened to any of them."

"There's no place for people like us," Amal said. "No place safe. This city belongs to them now." He lowered his voice. "Men like your friend."

"He does what he must," Dagr said softly. "Same as you or I."

"Not the same," Amal said. "Not the same. In the alley last night, I believed. I saw his finger on the pin, and I believed, more than in any bastard god, that he would kill us all; that he would rather die than take one step back."

"Kinza is not suicidal," Dagr said. "He just wants to see the world end."

"Then maybe he will be a hero before the end," Amal said. "And rid us of our enemy."

"Who is this Lion of Akkad?"

"No one knows. Six months ago he just appeared in the night," Amal said. "There were random murders, thefts. Some say he works for the Jaish Al Mahdi, here to settle scores and collect debts."

"The Mahdi Army does not collect rent."

"We know," Amal shrugged. "What can we do? Some say that he has a brother in the JAM. Whatever the truth, we asked them for help and received none."

"The police?" Dagr said. Even to him that sounded dubious. No one in Iraq went to the police. That was like asking to be extorted.

Amal snorted. "This man is a killer. He strikes suddenly, in the darkness, knocking on your door, holding a knife to your throat, a gun to your head. No one knows where he eats or sleeps or anything. In the day, poof! He is gone, like a ghost."

"He comes only at night?" Kinza, woken up now, joined them with a faint stir of interest.

"Mostly after the evening patrols," Amal said.

"How often?" Kinza asked. "Once a week?"

"Sometimes more or less," Amal shrugged. "There is no pattern. In the beginning, some of us tried to ambush him. He took a bullet in the chest and kept on walking. Two days later, he cut a little girl's throat. Last week, he threw my neighbor down the stairs. Broke his legs for no reason. We don't even know what he wants. I think he's one of those American serial killers like they have on TV."

"Excellent tactics," Dagr said. "Terror in the night. Random violence. Swift, excessive retribution. Sort of thing the Spartans used to do to the Helots to keep them in line."

"You said you shot him?" Kinza asked. "Did he bleed?"

"It was dark," Amal said. "We couldn't see. He kind of stumbled but then kept on coming. We scattered."

"Kevlar," Kinza said. "Our boy has body armor. Does he use a gun?"

"He carries a revolver," Amal said. "But he prefers to use his knife. It's the size of my arm, almost like a sword. And his fists. He has the strength of ten men."

"Ten Shi'as or ten Americans?" Kinza asked, straight faced.

"What?"

"Just saying," he said. "It might make a difference. Americans are very strong."

"Knives are psychologically more frightening than bullets," Dagr said.

"He wants to stay silent," Kinza said. "He's using the darkness and the fear of these people, the sudden violence, to keep them off balance."

"No one knows what he looks like?" Dagr asked.

"He wears a hood," Amal said. "And he's fast, silent. One minute you're sleeping peacefully in your bed and the next you're on the floor with a knife in your eye."

"Ok, we're getting a picture here," Dagr said. "This Akkadian works alone. He's well armed and wears Kevlar. Probably some kind of military training, too."

"You left out super strength and super speed."

"You mock us," Amal said. "But you have not faced him yet."

"He slinks around at night picking on infants and the elderly," Dagr continued. "He wears a hood. He wants to protect his identity. This suggests that his position with the JAM is not official, at least."

"So, professor, how do we find him?"

"We could always wait," Dagr said. "Camp out here. He's bound to come sooner or later."

"Yeah, maybe in a month," Kinza said. "Not a good option. Plus he will find out about us soon enough. I'm guessing he lives somewhere in this neighborhood."

"Then?" Amal asked.

"He hunts at night," Kinza said. "So must we. We'll take to the streets. Give us a map of the area he covers and all your volunteers. There is an old way to hunt wild game. Let's see if we cross paths with any lions."

The darkness in the streets was a smear of tar, a discombobulating colorant turning harmless daylight noises into the snickering of hyenas. Lights were absent, windows bricked or boarded mostly or shuttered at least against this most deadly hour. The Joint Forces stayed far away in their reinforced boxes; this was not their half of the day, not the time for pretend patrols and breaking down empty fortresses. Nor the time for Mahdi Army men to parade in their black scarves and AK47s, holding aloft their pages of calligraphy. This was the business end of the hour, where the real predators of each side mingled, open season for the ones in the know, springtime for men with guns, when the harmless cowered in their beds and hoped to hear nothing.

It had seemed a fine plan to Dagr, sitting cramped and safe in Amal's fantasy office two days ago. Now the darkness sucked everything out of him, and he was a walking husk, hands jammed into his jacket pocket to stop the shaking. Kinza was ahead, sure-footed, wolfish, snapping into place like the last piece missing from the jigsaw street. Dagr worried at the ancient gun in his pocket, the snub muzzle poking through the silk lining of his coat, fretting that it would go off and cripple him, that he would shoot the wrong person.

They did not belong here, and their convoy of three was disturbing the routine of the regulars. Dagr felt men shuffle close in the darkness, veering off in tangents after a sniff, split second decisions demarking victims and victimizers. Dagr too fell infected with their mindless aggression, heard whimpers and ragged wet tears from far corners, felt with shame some of the exhilaration of walking the night with a gun.

They were following tiny pinpricks of light, a system Dagr himself had designed. Men and women tired of the depredations had risen up in this meager rebellion. Small lamps hung in high, street-facing windows, staggered in a mathematical pattern that Dagr had memorized. The idea was simple. Watchers lined each of these windows. Whoever recognized the Lion of Akkad would put out their light. If he moved away, they would turn their light back on. The blink in the pattern would follow the Akkadian throughout the night, hopefully leading them straight to him.

The first few nights had been unsuccessful. The tracking system had been refined, the watchers reinforced, his probable routes calculated. It worked well on paper, but humans were fallible. Watchers fell asleep or were too scared to act fast. The advantage of the terrain was also with the Lion, as myriad routes became available at night, sudden shortcuts that allowed him to cut the pattern in half.

In the hour just before dawn, luck finally favored them. Weary with nerves, they were resting against a shattered streetlamp when a sliver of light abruptly disappeared from the horizon. Five minutes and another light blinked off, this time closer, barely half a kilometer away. It was unmistakable. Kinza was on his feet, moving swiftly, a quick word behind him, telling his companions to fan out across the street. Dagr felt every neuron firing simultaneously with something akin to terror. The colossal stupidity of this plan smashed the breath out of his ribs. He fought the urge to slink back, making his legs move forward until he was parallel with his friend. Behind him, to the left, he could hear Hamid make similar, reluctant steps, well back. The torturer had little intention of taking part.

The blinking came closer, closer, until he could imagine the entire street lined up and watching, judging. A few hundred meters more and he could almost see the Lion of Akkad, a tall man in a dark coat, an indistinct blur, ensconced no doubt in his Kevlar, a one man tank. In spite of himself, Dagr felt his steps faltering, his stride shortening until he was barely mincing along. Kinza broke ahead, slinking along the walls, two, four, then ten meters away. In some glint of moonlight he actually saw the face, hawk like nose jutting out, a black scarf wound around the rest of his features.

Kinza crouched into the hollow of a doorway winking abruptly out of sight, even as Dagr continued edging forward, his mind frozen into a kind of panicky inertia. A flicker of darkness, a slight bend in the street, and suddenly the Akkadian was gone, disappeared in a breath, leaving Dagr standing paralyzed. He began to edge his gun out, and it caught in the lining; a second later he was face to face with the Lion of Akkad, yellow eyes glinting with feral madness.

A blur of motion and the man was spinning into him, the blade of his knife caught in Dagr's sleeve, buttons popping, slicing a shallow groove along his forearm. Dagr bulled forward, desperately trying to grapple, his knee giving away even as he heard Hamid's pus-ridden voice shouting, "Down, down you fool." Guns barked in close range, blinding and deafening him. A heavy blow knocked him sideways as his hands clawed across the Lion's greatcoat, and Dagr fell away useless. He saw Kinza leaping out of the darkness, a split second of struggle before he was *thrown* back, skittering through the street.

Dagr wrenched himself up on one knee. The street was empty, silent once more. Hamid lay curled nearby, cradling a mangled hand, his fingers blown off by a soft revolver shell. The Lion of Akkad was gone.

———————

A pall hung over their makeshift command center, crowded now with the scents of the triage and the gloom of their co-conspirators.

"Do you believe me now?" Amal was aggrieved.

"You've failed," a nondescript shopkeeper cried. "And now the Lion of Akkad will start killing children again."

"We have to run!" A truck driver said. "To Shulla! I'm getting my truck."

"It did not go as planned," Dagr said. His body was a mass of cuts and bruises.

"You did nothing, you fool," Hamid snapped. "He shot my fingers off."

"The man is strong," Kinza said.

"And fast," Dagr said. "He kind of just appeared in front of me before I could clear my weapon."

"You've made everything worse," Amal said. A dozen men rumbled in agreement. "He will become more brutal now. Our lives are worth shit."

"He's human," Kinza said. "He bleeds. I shot him in the leg. The blood on the street is not ours only."

"So we have some time," Dagr said, thinking again, furiously. "He won't come out wounded. Not when he knows he's being hunted."

"You boys should just leave," Amal said. "I curse the day I stopped you."

"Yes," Hamid hissed into Dagr's face, so close that he could smell the sweet rot of his wounds. "Why the fuck are we wasting time with these yokels? You're supposed to take me to Mo..."

"We're going nowhere," Kinza said. "I said I'd kill this man, and so I will."

"He will become cautious now," Dagr said. He glanced at the watchers. "And I doubt the grid will catch him out again. Even if he doesn't figure out how we tracked him, he'll take steps to counter us. We must devise a new method."

"Oh, what's the use if you *do* catch him?" Amal asked. "He nearly killed the three of you."

Kinza stared him down. "Do you think I can't take a hit? I never walk away from a fight."

"I'm just saying."

"Look," Dagr said. "We won't catch him on the streets again. We have to find out where he hides. We have to attack him in his lair, while he's still wounded."

"There's a reason he works these particular streets," Kinza said. "He moves on foot. He must live within this zone."

"We could send the watchers to canvass the neighborhood," Dagr said. "Look for something suspicious, blood stains perhaps?"

"Get real. You are in Ghazaliya," Amal said. "Which door doesn't have blood on it?" He seemed almost proud of it.

"We need to narrow the area down," Kinza said.

"Two things struck me," Dagr said slowly. "When he was beating the crap out of me, I felt a backpack under his coat. He was carrying something heavy. And he smelled funny. I can't describe it."

"That would be Hoj's candlesticks," Amal said. "Pure silver. He was saving them for his grandsons."

"You said he's a serial killer."

"He does whatever he damn well pleases," Amal said.

"What difference does it make? Often he takes random things," the shopkeeper shrugged. "He has to eat, I guess."

"It might make a big difference, Amal," Dagr sat up straight, weariness disappearing. "A huge difference! Quick, what else has he taken?"

"He took a gilded statue from Ibrahim," the truck driver said. "And he took my iPod."

"Look at the map," Dagr said. "I need exact times and locations for each of his strikes for as far back as possible. And most importantly, I need to know what he took each time."

Amal looked bewildered.

"It's simple mathematics," Dagr began scribbling formulas on the map, cursing how rusty he was. "We know he's on foot, he only hunts in this area, and he works only at night. We calculate his route each night for as far back as we can, data given by his victims. Now we have his average speed. Even if he constantly varies his schedule, we'll find him hitting an average number of victims per night. Given his starting and ending hits, we might be able correlate where he lives. But every time he takes something extra, there will be a deviation. There are a finite amount of candlesticks he can carry, after all. I predict every time he takes something heavy, there will be an unexplained lag. In effect, *he will go home to put away his loot* before moving onto the next house."

Dagr beamed at them. They stared back slack jawed.

"I didn't understand a word of that," Amal said.

4: BLACKBOARD RAGE

DAGR HAD APPROPRIATED THE OFFICE ENTIRELY NOW, RUNNING data, fine tuning his equation. The computer was old, the software almost obsolete. It had taken Dagr half the day to jerry-rig it into doing what he wanted. Amal had fixed a blackboard on the wall, unearthed pieces of orange chalk. It helped him think, the board covered in symbols, calmed him into something like functionality. Men and women were dropping by all day, feeding him bits of data, suspicious until they saw him, his head and arms bandaged, chalk dust on his clothes, something fey in his eyes. They treated him like an idiot savant, talking to him slowly, old women pressing bits of fruit into his hands, taking on faith entirely that he was doing something useful.

The chalk brought him intensely happy memories. The lull of an empty classroom, Dagr perched on his desk, making furious equations all over the board; a grad student walking by, stopping to watch him with gold flecked eyes, a smile crooking her mouth, lighting up a face so achingly earnest. The thin perfume alerted him, and he swiveled, almost falling, falling. She took the chalk and corrected his mistakes, still smiling, at some point getting on the desk, edging him aside, until she arrived at a point she could not reach on tiptoes, and Dagr grabbed her shirt, and they nearly fell over laughing.

That much and no more and he stood bereft, staring, sliding slowly into dismay, awaiting the inevitable reconstruction of reality with its soul-killing loneliness. Blackboard, chair, table, computer, doorframe. Autistic fumbling, as his brain tried to fit them into something palatable and failed repeatedly, and the grayness seeped in. They slipped into his day, these moments, in the most unreasonable of times, pieces from some elusive mirror world, a past that he was unsure had ever existed at all. Surely that classroom stood somewhere, still, chalk dust and laughter.

He saw Kinza approaching, eyes averted, reality tethering him back in.

"Coffee," he said, offering a cup. Neutral.

"I'm alright," Dagr said, "just light-headed."

"Any luck?"

"It's working," Dagr said. "Slowly. I have some patterns. Too many assumptions to be sure." He knew there was an impatient crowd outside, held in check by Kinza's face alone.

"I got word from Shulla," Kinza said. "They are looking for Hamid. We cannot stay here long."

"We can be ready tonight, perhaps," Dagr hesitated. "I have an area narrowed down. An abandoned building, I guess." He pointed to the board, "This equation approximates his speed on foot. The map is plotted with all his stops on any given night. The program catches any big gaps in his schedule and posits where he could have gone during that time. Data from a large period of time narrow these options. Taking into account first and last stops in each night, along with times, and we get a picture."

"Your arm is bleeding," Kinza said. "You don't need to come tonight. Hamid and I will be sufficient."

"No," Dagr said, fighting back a temptation to agree. "No, you can't trust Hamid. We should stick together."

"I am not afraid of Hamid," Kinza said.

"He could shoot you in the back," Dagr said. "There's a look in his eyes, something like religious fervor, except he is certainly not a man of God. Sometimes I think he's completely insane."

"Even madmen know fear."

"Kinza, do you think there really is any gold in Mosul?"

"Probably not."

"What will we do there, then? Provided we get there at all, of course."

"If there's no gold, at least we can sell Hamid," Kinza said.

"I'm sure our good captain has something in mind for us."

"Hamid will betray us somehow," Kinza said, amused. "Then I will dismember him, and you'll probably try to find some reason to keep him alive."

"No happy endings for us I suppose."

"Look around. No happy endings for anyone. Not for a long time. Not ever again, perhaps."

"What makes us go on like this, I wonder?" Dagr said. "Day after day, this whole damned mess."

"Rage. Vengeance."

"God should permit us mass suicide," Dagr said. "Then we could end it once and for all. Leave a clean slate for whoever comes after. No more fathers and brothers to avenge. No more mosques to burn. No more checkpoints. No more rifle butts and blindfolds in the night."

"I doubt God cares either way."

"Kinza, what would you do if we really did find some treasure in that bunker?"

"Die of shock."

"I meant how would you spend your share?"

"I'd get the hell out of here," Kinza said. "Go to Greenland or something. Some place empty and cold. I don't want to see another person for a hundred miles."

"Sounds good. Maybe I'll join you."

———

Into the night once again, and this time they were better armed. In his breast pocket Dagr had his map, with a city block circled in red, which he had finally narrowed down. He was convinced, and they gained something from his confidence, although no one quite understood how he had derived his results.

Physically they were poorer, although the same was undoubtedly true for their quarry. Hamid had lost two fingers from his left hand and was walking hunched over and clumsy, barely able to fumble his gun from his holster. Kinza, too, had taken damage, one entire side glazed black where the Lion of Akkad had thrown him. There was in his face a barely repressed violence, a reckless fire that spoke his intent. Dagr had seen something alike in previous times, when Kinza had placed them in extreme danger, seemingly for the hell of it. There would be a killing tonight.

Their numbers had been bolstered, moreover, by two young men from the streets, armed with old pistols, neighborhood toughs with gelled hair who had dreamed their own grandiose mafia rackets before the Akkadian had shown a most cavalier disregard for their posturing. They came along boastfully, taking oaths and fingering their weapons until Kinza silenced them with a stare.

"We need to check for abandoned buildings," Dagr said. He took out his map.

"There are a couple of Mahdi safehouses there. Old apartment buildings," Yakin said. He was the talkative local. His companion was mostly silent, possibly much more intelligent. It was difficult to tell. "Abandoned mostly now, filled with squatters."

"He could be holed up there somewhere," Dagr said.

"It can't be anywhere else if it's on this street," Yakin said. "We know all the other people. It used to be a pretty good neighborhood. Most of the people still live in their original houses."

"There was a small mosque there last year," the second tough said, "A Sunni imam used to preach for true sons of Islam to rise up against the government. One Friday, he said something about Moqtada Al Sadr's birth. The Jaish Al Mahdi came and set fire to it, with a dozen people locked inside. I saw the whole thing. They barred the doors and windows and threw grenades in."

"How charming," Dagr said.

"No one has gone near it since," Yakin continued. "The Americans came in a Humvee to investigate, but the JAM rigged the street with IEDs and snipers to drive them away. There was a running battle up and down the street. No one ever came back. The bodies are probably still inside."

"It looks about right," Kinza said.

The mosque was a charred shell of partially collapsed concrete. It had once been a mean two-story house, with no dome and no minaret, little of the embellishments of a normal mosque. Blue tile work had once adorned its outside walls, the sole concession to beauty. Grenade shrapnel and bullet holes had taken care of that. Two tenement slums flanked the mosque, buildings slowly gone to ruin over the past few years, windows boarded and doors fortified. The Mahdi Army used many such buildings as rotating hideaways. The families who lived there had adopted a siege mentality; they neither looked out nor asked questions.

They approached the street cautiously, well aware that they were in easy gunshot range. A floor-to-floor search of the first apartment block revealed nothing. A few old women answered their doors, irate in the middle of the night, clutching weapons, professing no knowledge of Mahdi men or Akkadians or beasts of any sort. More than half of the apartments were empty, doors open or kicked in. Not many people wanted to live in a Mahdi safehouse.

"We need to try the mosque," Kinza said finally. "It's the only place left."

They picked their way through rubble into the main hall. The roof had partially collapsed, making the floor impassable. Under the masonry, there were the remnants of bodies: clothing, bones, a pair of glasses. The air was heavy with the overpowering smell of cats. A feline army had taken over the mosque, taking advantage of a grim banquet. They held court now, a large Persian preening on throne-like rubble, his fur plastered back, somehow leonine, no doubt the prized pet of some dead plutocrat. Tabby cats all around, frozen in the act of worship, all glaring accusingly at Dagr so that he almost dropped his gun in shock.

"He's here," Dagr said, clicking. "I said he smelt funny. He smelt of cats. There must be an intact room somewhere."

"The imam's room," Yakin said.

"These cats ate everyone," Dagr said. "Look how fat they are."

"That's what you get for praying in mosques," Kinza said.

They moved in, trying to figure the angles of fire, anticipating a rush out of darkness. They found the imam's room, still intact, door open. There was a bed, chair, table, a radio, an electric stove, a ransacked cabinet.

"He's gone," Dagr was on the floor, looking at dirty bandages. "There is a lot of blood. He was wounded."

The room bore the signs of a hasty exit. The silver candlesticks glittered on the bed, buried under a pile of canned food. A heavy ivory statue lay on the floor, broken in two. A line of books and old newspapers lined one wall, and more lay scattered on the floor, spine up, as if just laid aside by the reader.

"He left in a rush," Kinza said. "He must have figured we were coming."

"Interesting reading material," Dagr said, flipping through the books. "History, philosophy, *math*? Nietzsche's morality. Old religious texts. His or the imam's I wonder?"

"The imam did not read," Yakin said. "He was Al Qaeda, I think."

"These are all about 11th century Islamic history," Dagr sat on the bed, reading absently. "Little-known authors. My friend did a thesis on Islamic alchemists and heretics. I recognize some of these writers."

"A philosopher serial killer? He doesn't sound like your average thug."

"Look, personal papers," Hamid had been rifling through the room with professional thoroughness. "Hidden in these books. He forgot them. It's mostly notes on the history of Syria."

"I'm curious to know his name," Dagr said. "Look for any letters or anything."

"This is garbage," Kinza said, after some time.

"I found something," Hamid said. "It's a watch. A very strange, broken watch. The front is glass. It looks complicated."

"It's probably junk then," Dagr said. "It looks old. Odd, here are some drawings of it in his hand. Diagrams and numbers."

"It has a tourbillion I think," Kinza said, examining the watch. "And what appears to be at least four complications."

"What the hell are you talking about?"

"I like watches. AP, Constantin, Dufour. I used to trade in replicas," Kinza shrugged. "This is a mechanical watch. It *is* very old. Each set of these gears and wheels is a complication. They're supposed to give extra functions to the watch. But I don't see what they do. There is nothing on the dial other than the hour and minute hands. No second hand, no date function, no chronograph either. There is no maker's brand. It is strange. I thought I knew all the watch makers."

"Is it worth anything?" Hamid asked.

"Probably nothing," Kinza said. "It doesn't work. Look for the certificate or a case or something."

"It bears a seal in the back," Dagr said. "And an inscription."

"Saying what?"

"There is a small star. Might be the brand. Five sided, five colors I think, though I can't be sure. Is that the brand mark?"

"I don't know. We'd have to consult an expert. A lot of old watch companies went bankrupt when the Japanese invented the quartz movement."

"There's some writing here. It is one long word I think. Too faded to read. Not any language I have ever seen anyway," Dagr frowned. "Wait, I can read the name."

"What is it?"

"Fouad Jumblatt," Dagr said slowly. "This is Fouad Jumblatt's watch."

"Jumblatt?" Hamid said. "Jumblatt...Jumblatt, I've heard this name before."

"The name's Lebanese," Dagr said. "Wasn't he some kind of politician or something? Look, here's a book on him. He was the governor of the Chouf district in Lebanon."

"I remember now," Hamid said. "Fouad Jumblatt was the grandfather of Walid Jumblatt, the guy who runs some Lebanese political party. He is long dead. He cannot be the Lion of Akkad."

"So why does this guy have Fouad Jumblatt's watch?" Kinza asked.

"Jumblatt was Lebanese," Hamid said. "This is some kind of Lebanese conspiracy."

"That's ludicrous."

"Back in the day, we had some run ins with the Lebanese secret service," Hamid said. "When this was a real country. They must be crawling around here again. The Lebanese are probably thinking about invading us too."

"No, no, I don't think so," Dagr said. He began to flip through one of the books. "Not Lebanese. Druze. *Druze.* Look here. The star is the star of Druze. The writing is gibberish because they have some kind of secret language. Ninety percent of their own tribe don't know their sacred texts. Fouad Jumblatt was one of their luminaries. This watch was either given or worn by Fouad Jumblatt. It would be considered an heirloom. This man is not Mahdi Army. He's not even Shi'a… He's Druze."

"This makes no sense," Hamid said. "Druze? There *are* no Druze in Iraq. Maybe he just stole it from someone."

"He had it hidden away," Dagr said. "He made drawings of it. It must have meant something to him. Otherwise it's just a broken watch. He must have forgotten to take it with him in the rush. Think about it. The Druze are known for keeping hidden. They must have a secret community here."

"There is nothing else here. We need to go back," Kinza said. "Tell the others that he is gone, probably for good. Take whatever you can."

They found Amal waiting up in his store with a small knot of people.

"Did you get him?" The old man asked, shuffling forward. "Is he dead?"

"He fled," Kinza said. He looked around. The shop was full of armed men, cigarettes and nerves. "What the fuck are you all doing here?"

"You brought this trouble on us," Amal pointed his finger accusingly. "This is on your own head. You let the Lion get away, and now the JAM want you."

Kinza drew his gun and pointed it at Amal's forehead. Weapons clicked into place all around them. "JAM? Why bring up those fuckers. You sold us to the Mahdi Army, you fucking traitor? After sharing salt with us? After begging us for help? I will put you down like a dog right now, I swear, I will kill every man in this room."

It stopped them cold. There was a murmur of uncertainty. Some of the men lowered their heads, shamed, but the guns stayed up, circling the three of them, barrels shaking, small circles of pitiless dark hovering like angry wasps. In the street, Dagr heard the rumble of jeeps, the cackle of rifle fire popping in the air. Out of the corner of his eye, he saw Yakin edging toward them, gun out, a gloating look in his eye.

Kinza swiveled his gun smoothly, the barrel locking onto Yakin's face. "Step back, and lower your weapon."

Yakin faltered, sweat beading his forehead, transformed suddenly into a panicky shop boy caught with his hand in the till, facing a certain beating.

"They were coming. We had no choice. They would kill us anyway," Amal wailed. "They're coming. They're here. What could we do? You never found the Lion."

"We're leaving, now," Kinza backed toward the door. "I'll take my chances against the Mahdi fuckers. Any of you step out of this shop, you'll get a bullet in the eye. Hamid get the door."

The rumble of gunfire was incessant now. The street was bathed in fire and headlights, Koranic verses rapping out in between, the midnight calling card of the Mahdi. Dagr could hear the chants of soldiers, the roar of engines. Terror made him slow.

"Amal, he's Druze," Dagr said, waving the broken watch, as Kinza pulled him back toward the door. "Do you understand? The Lion of Akkad is Druze. We found his watch! He has Fouad Jumblatt's watch! He can't have a brother in the Mahdi Army. He's not Shi'a at all. There won't be any retribution, Amal! He's not JAM, Amal. He's Druze!"

"Dagr!" Kinza shouted, shoving him aside. "Run."

5: MAROON INVESTIGATIONS

"You know what this is, Tommy?" Hoffman asked.

"No, Hoff."

"This is a list of stuff I need you to get." Hoffman was lounging in the passenger seat of his newly requisitioned Humvee, smoking a garuda clove cigarette that he had caged from his friend Marconas, the only Indonesian resident of Baghdad.

"Ten gallons of detergent?" Tommy was a slow reader. "Fifteen cases of shotgun shells? Two-dozen barbeque skewers? Ten cases of Skittles?"

"Yes, yes, and yes, my dear lieutenant, all of that and more."

"I'm just a private, sir."

"It's a figure of speech, Tommy. I am the president; you are my vice president. I am the captain; you are the first mate. I am the hero; you are the sidekick. I am the NATO Supreme Allied Commander, and you are the, er, Supreme Allied vice commander," Hoffman said. "You get the picture? Now get your ass to the commissary and get our stuff."

"Hoff," Tommy said. "What should I tell him you want this stuff for?"

"Bargaining power, Tommy," Hoffman said. "Bartering. See, I believe in the soft power of mutually beneficial trade over the brute force that has become, all too sadly, our only currency in this cluster-fucked region."

"You want me to say all that?"

"Tell them it's for the secret mission, Tommy. Tell them it's for Col Bradley."

"Are we leaving finally, then, Hoff?"

"Yes we are," Hoffman said. "Were you getting impatient?"

"Not me, Hoff," Tommy said. "It's just that Captain Fowler told me to report everything you do to him. And he's been getting testy."

"I see," Hoffman said. "And have you been reporting away?"

"I write things down in this notebook," Tommy patted his right breast pocket. "He told me to write down stuff so I don't forget."

"And?"

"And I'm supposed to call him from my sat phone every night on the down low."

"I see," Hoffman said. "That's a tough job, Tommy. All this remembering and writing and reporting."

"Right, Hoff," Tommy said, miserable. "And we ain't even left yet. I got nothing so far. The captain's getting kinda testy."

"Writer's block is a terrible thing," Hoffman said. "I'll get you started. Why don't you write down that you found me sitting in the jeep smoking a garuda?"

"Can you spell garuda for me?"

"You want a hit, Tommy?"

"Is it that clove stuff you got from that Chinese guy?"

"Indonesian, underling," Hoffman said.

"I hate that stuff, Hoff."

"You will find, however, that it serves very admirably to mask the smell of pot," Hoffman said. "Allowing me, in fact, to smoke in public in broad daylight without incurring the wrath of, say, any preachy military-type officials."

"Does that Chinese cigarette have pot in it?" Tommy asked.

"Yes, Tommy. Have a hit. Don't slobber all over the filter."

"Thanks, Hoff. You're the man."

"Listen, Tommy, you come around every night, and I'll help you fill in that notebook," Hoffman said. "You were meant for better things, I'm sure."

"Awesome. Thanks, Hoff," Tommy exhaled. "Fuck Fowler. He's a dickhead officer anyway."

"My sentiments exactly."

"Hoff, we gonna be riding in this jeep?"

"Yes."
"It's got a TV in it," Tommy said.
"Does it?"
"Can we requisition an Xbox then?"
"Nice one, lackey, put it on the list."

———————

Later that night, they were released; Hoffman's squad, handpicked, the fantastic five of misfits from the Greater Ghazaliya division, unleashed like hounds from the starting gate, tearing through the narrow streets in their steel demon, breathing garuda fumes and the threat of massive fire, roof-mounted automatic cannon rattling in its cage, Hoffman cackling incessantly from the visions of bad mushrooms, his driving erratic and dangerous, the belly of the beast converted into a gaming den, four-player button-jamming NFL action, while Tommy spat random reports into his sat phone on a deliberately open frequency, apprising all interested parties of their progress, as they swept past bemused checkpoints, leaving stolid Iraqi soldiers debating whether to shoot or salute.

Into North Ghazaliya, past the great mosque, two hundred meters from the checkpoint into Shulla, they ran into a joint forces patrol, led by one Sergeant Tony Perdoso. After some mutual sniffing around, they realized they knew each other and guns were lowered, visors raised, knuckles slapped around in greeting, while the Iraqi army men stood by passively, hoping that so many Americans on a street corner would not invite an impromptu bombing.

"Hoffman, you motherfucker," Sergeant Tony was a barrel-chested Latino with a bar room voice. "I've been looking for you."

"You ran out already?" Hoffman asked, incredulous.

"Not the suppositories!" Tony snapped. "It's the two fucking civs you sent my way, maricon."

"They made it alright into Shulla?" Hoffman leaned forward in a whisper.

"They fucking started a firefight," Tony said. "Right on my doorstep. Three in the morning, two JAM trucks came rolling in, guns blazing. Showing off. They're here to collect *your* boys."

"They were? Did you stop them?"

"Shit, Hoff, I was fast asleep."

"Safe, Tony," Hoffman said. "I asked you to get them *safely* into Shulla. Does letting them get fucked by the JAM sound safe to you?"

"Calm down, pendejo," Tony said. "Who said anything about getting fucked?"

"What?"

"Your boy dropped some bodies," Tony said. "Pop, pop, pop, like a fucking cowboy."

"They're still alive?"

"I hauled a bunch of dead JAM off the street. Ain't none of them your guys," Tony said.

"You're sure?" Hoffman asked.

"Fuck off, Hoffman," Tony said. "I'm from San Diego. All brown guys don't look alike to *me*."

"What was the body count, Tony?"

"Four JAM dead, including Alihassan, not more than a couple hundred feet from my patrol," Tony said.

"Alihassan? The son of Hassan Salemi?"

"Damn right. I gotta jump through hoops now keeping him happy. But Alihassan had it coming. I told that boy a hundred times, carry on like that in the middle of the night, with the guns and the religious chanting and all that and someone's liable to put a bullet through you."

"Lucky it wasn't one of your men then," Hoffman said.

"Hassan Salemi doesn't care who it was," Tony said. "He wants blood."

"So who shot him?"

"Your boy Kinza shot Alihassan in the head. One shot, right between the eyebrows, mafia style. That's what the witnesses say. Your guy's got quite a name on the street. He then fled in the general direction of my patrol in a goddamn running battle with the JAM."

"It was the Wednesday night roster?" Hoffman interrupted.

"Exactly."

"Your patrol was Sunni."

"Too damn right, genius," the sergeant said. "You should have seen it. Hell, you should have *been* in it. It's your fucking fault. Man, when these pendejos see each other, it's like they forget that we even started this war. Goddamn riot in the street like it was the 4th of July, with my fucking handpicked squad officer leading the way. I got three injured, one dead, and at least five more dead JAM, although they took their bodies back, so I can't be sure. Sometimes my guys like to show off and exaggerate the body count. All this blood on *my* fucking street, which is why I'm patrolling out here in this puta sun. Apparently, 'I can't keep the streets clean by sitting on my ass inside the base eating nachos.' Fucking faggot officer. Stop laughing, Hoffman. I swear I'm going to kick your ass right here."

"So what happened to my guys?"

"They fucking waltzed into Shulla while all this was happening," Tony said, indignant. "No signing in, no hellos, nothing."

"Well, I owe your squaddies then, Tony," Hoffman signaled to his hummer. "I got some candy bars for 'em."

"That's real sweet of you, Papa Noel."

"You want some detergent instead?"

"Just gimme the fucking candy."

"You're getting fat. You know that, Tony. Maybe your CO was right."

"Fuck that shit," Tony swallowed a Mars bar whole and then spat out the wrapper with a rasping choke. "Listen, Hoff. You know I don't ask questions about your business and all, but this chingado Kinza is getting to be a real pain. Lotta guys after him. I got orders to bring him in myself for questioning. Hassan Salemi just posted a ten thousand dollar bounty on his head, double that if he's caught alive. My CO's busting a gut trying to catch him before the JAM start dropping pieces of him all over town."

"Hold off on that for a while," Hoffman said. "I'm on special assignment on this guy, straight from Bradley. He has some information we need."

"Col. Bradley? That lunatic motherfucker?" Tony shook his head. "Listen, Hoff. That maricon still sees Saddam's ghost in every street corner. Just last week, he called in an air strike on a fucking model tank. It was made of fucking wood for chrissakes. The local JAM boys nearly died laughing. Now they're putting up papier-mâché T-72 tanks everywhere hoping to get bombed."

"Yeah, it's funny how the army promotes all the psychos," Hoffman said. "You happen to know what my guys were doing here for so long?"

"Sure," Tony said. "They were hanging around a grocery store for three days. Had the whole street riled up about something. Someone there called in the JAM, anyway. Old pendejo called Sheikh Amal runs the store. I was going up there to have a look."

"Leave it to me, Tony. I'll take care of it," Hoffman said. "In the meantime, have some Skittles."

6: TEA PARTY AT THE HOUSE OF FURIES

Deep into the serpentine heart of Shulla, there was an abandoned Jaish Al Mahdi safehouse, sparsely furnished, stocked with old canned food, a remnant of ancient times before all of Shulla became the playground of Sadr, now largely forgotten, the old revolutionaries dead or retired, old guns stilled finally, replaced by the shrill voices of youth shiny and privileged, born with a swagger in their pants, pacing Shulla like hair dried lions, the old caves for old jackals now cast off like so many moth-ridden clothes.

In this one lived three ladies, two of them veiled in old lace, the third a crone of such wrinkled age that the veil was deemed superfluous, almost an insult for such a pedigreed garment. They had washed up here on the mysterious tides that wracked the city, swirling its inhabitants from corner to corner with a cavalier disregard for ownership, leaving them miraculously upright in a foreign house, fully stocked with the detritus of someone else's life, leaving them alone in the quiet, hopeful of being forgotten, letting the shock dissipate, until finally, with a shrug, they picked up the threads and started all over again.

The three ladies had lost a lot. Their men folk lay dead or dying across the city. Some were buried, some rotting in pieces, some thrown into the air in violent red embers. Sons, husbands, and brothers were absent, so much so that there were doubts if they had ever existed to begin with, for the women rarely spoke of such things. One might even consider that it was no great loss, this sacrifice of men to the grand war machine, for the men had constructed the machine in the first place, in dim caveman times, and it was their natural fate to keep feeding it now. Not to say that the ladies adhered to this view, for such things were never vocalized, and indeed, the pattern of life had made conversation largely unnecessary by this time; lacking foreign intrusions, silence was the order of the house, carefully built on a series of rituals.

Alas, Baghdad was a city in flux and even silence was not to last. The safehouse, largely forgotten, existed still in the mind of the little boy Xervish, who had once lived next door to it and, in one vivid night, had seen in full moonlight three men in checkered scarves executing one of their number with a sword, there in the arched doorway, the severed head bouncing down the stairs like a football. This boy, grown now into manhood, recalled every step of the old house, every door, ever window. He dreamed of the house often and in idle moments blamed the direction of his life on that single steel arc of arterial red, on the wet noise of the head bouncing, a moment of explosive violence that had somehow infected him and haunted him remorselessly thereafter.

Twenty years later, sitting in a café, pressed by Kinza for a safehouse, his mind immediately went to the one house he most definitely *did not* consider safe. Yet as he rotated the idea in his head, it took hold that this was precisely the place for his old friend, now come suddenly stalking into his life, an iron shod warhorse showering sparks all over the most tenuous papering of his days.

"There is a place for you to go," Xervish said. "An old place. Forgotten by the new JAM, forgotten perhaps by anyone still living."

"You want me to hide from the JAM in a *JAM* safehouse?" Kinza asked. "The idea is ridiculous. I might even do it."

"Hassan Salemi wants you," Xervish said. "Hassan Salemi." Saying the words made him glassy with fear. "You need to get off the streets fast."

"Did I ask Hassan Salemi to send his stupid son after me?" Kinza shrugged. "Forget Hassan Salemi. Let him come out of his cave if he wants to find me. I'll put a bullet in his head."

Xervish stared at his friend, aghast, his mind unable to reconcile this man with the boy he had once played football with. "Hassan Salemi," he repeated, as if intoning the name enough times would drum the direness of the situation into Kinza. "He has ordered five jars of vinegar. He keeps them on his desk and polishes them every day. He has sworn to take your head, your hands, and your feet for trophies."

"He should take my balls," Kinza said.

Xervish shuddered. "How can you joke about this? Please, Kinza, just go to the house. I'll smuggle you out of town as soon as I can."

"There are three of us," Kinza said.

"What?" Xervish felt the acid snaking in his stomach, a churning anguish prophesying disaster, the certainty that he would soon be tested, and fail, as he had done repeatedly in the past, to make the right choices.

"Kinza, you have to dump them," he wailed. "You have to think of yourself. Salemi is already looking for all of you. He has the descriptions—you, the soft man with glasses, the crippled man. Three of you together will be so easy to find. You must forget about them. If Salemi takes them, then maybe he will be satisfied and call off his dogs."

"I don't give a fuck about Hassan Salemi," Kinza said quietly. "I'm not giving up anybody. You make arrangements for three."

"Kinza, he'll cut your *head off*."

Kinza laughed. "I have a grenade in my left hand that says otherwise. When I die, you'll hear the earth shake."

"Why do you make it so *hard*?" Xervish cried out, his equilibrium gone. "Why can't you for once just…"

"I remember when two Syrians kidnapped your sister, old friend," Kinza said. "They raped her and then killed her. Do you remember?"

"You know I do."

"I found them for you, Xervish," Kinza said. "I hunted them and I tied them down. I cut them for you, friend, when you couldn't hold your knife straight. I held you up so you could see them scream their voices away. And when you looked away, I shot them for you. Do you remember, friend?"

"I wish you hadn't," Xervish said. "I wish to god you had never gone near them. I wish they were still alive somewhere, I wish I couldn't see them anymore. Do you think you fixed anything? I'll do as you say, Kinza. Go to the house. You'll be as safe as anywhere. I'll find a way to get you out of Shulla."

Thus, the three men found their way to the House of Furies. The blue doors were faded, gummed shut with cobwebs. Xervish stirred nervously and left them in the stairwell, his parting words hurried, lost in the thick swirls of wind dusting through the alley.

"Where the hell have you landed us now?" Hamid asked.

"A place to lie low for a while," Kinza said. "Xervish is lining up a way to get us out of here."

"You're making a mistake," Hamid said. "That man is broken. He'll betray us."

"I've known him for a long time."

"I've looked into the eyes of a thousand men like him," Hamid said. "Grown men have wept at the sound of my voice, soiled themselves at the fall of my foot."

"What's your point?"

"My point is, why do you consistently disregard my experience?" Hamid said. "I can read men like a whore reads your wallet. I know when they are lying, when they are holding back. That man Xervish is afraid of you, and he hates you for it. Do you think some childish attachment will count for anything when he is put to the test by the Mahdi dogs? Are you really that much of a fool?"

"Should we part ways then?" Kinza asked.

"No," Hamid said, looking away, his voice dull. "What would be the point of that? None of us would get to Mosul then."

"And all that gold," Kinza snorted.

Dagr meanwhile was standing, entranced, by the door, tracing the lines on the blue, remembering, long ago, another blue door, with handprints smudged three feet from the floor, where his daughter used to push, breathless, wobbling into their apartment, as he chased her, growling hideously, sometimes a bear, sometimes a giant dog. The door was always open because they knew all the other tenants, were like a family, really, the old couple below, adopted grandparents who would babysit at a moment's notice, every day even, and the landlord on the ground floor, a kind-faced engineer drifting into unwilling bachelorhood, who used to make small brass toys by hand, hiding them all over the building so that her holidays were an ongoing, elaborate treasure hunt.

The hallways had been narrow, cluttered with the smell of cooking, the sound of his daughter shrieking, running from door to door, under the impression that the whole building was hers, the other tenants mere extensions of her will. Each of the doors had been painted blue by the engineer landlord, who believed fiercely in the efficacy of paint, and it had worked out for him, in the end, for he had died on the street on his way to work and not home in bed as he had feared.

Dagr leaned forward, oblivious, and the door opened of its own accord, making him stumble into a dark hallway. He fell near a pair of slippered feet, stockinged, rising up through varied clothing to a diminutive, incredibly old head.

"Welcome, dear," the crone said, reaching forth a feathery hand and ruffling his hair. "Are you certain you are at the right door?"

"Door...no," Dagr said. "It looks like a door I once knew. *My* door. It was open. This door, I mean. Xervish brought us here."

"Xervish," the crone said. "A good boy. He is haunted by this house. This door, specifically. It frames the substance of all his dreams. Thus, he consigns to this place all those who disturb him."

"My friends are outside," Dagr said, rising to his feet. "Two of them. May we come in?"

"Are you asking permission?"

"Yes."

"Why?" The crone asked. "Your friends outside have guns. Even now they are moments from drawing them."

"We are not here to turn you from your home," Dagr said. "If you want us to leave, we will go away."

"You might, dear boy," the crone said. "You might go away. But those two outside would not. Do you venture to speak for them?"

"I do."

The crone smiled, revealing a most awkward dental landscape. "What a good boy you are. I am Mother Davala. You may come in. This house has been home to many. Three more will not tip the balance."

"Is there room enough, for us, grandmother?" Dagr asked, letting the others in.

"Oh yes," Mother Davala said. "Plenty of room. Would you like some tea?"

Bizarrely, within minutes, they found themselves in the sitting room, drinking glasses of mint tea from a silver filigreed teapot, a most elegant setting, the room well lit from semi-shuttered windows, a fine, faded Persian carpet on the floor, the furniture old and shabby yet still noticeably better than anything from the shops, the tea things appearing so much a part of the room that they scarcely questioned who had brewed it so fresh, with just the right number of cups, steaming at exactly the right temperature.

In a separate alcove by the window, far from the coffee table, were two striped armchairs most advantageously positioned, commanding the light as well as a fine view of the street. Two ladies sat there, dark eyed, veiled in lace, ages indeterminable but for the thin white hands moving like graceful spiders, warping, wefting.

"Don't mind them, dears, they hardly ever speak," Mother Davala said.

"Why is that?" Dagr asked.

"Tragedies, dear, tragedies," Mother Davala said airily. "Destroyed homes and missing families, lost loves, and soured ambitions, futures catastrophically forked into a directionless mire. What is there to speak of, little boys, when all possibilities are gone and life is reduced to single moments of consciousness, unmoored from either past or future? Great silences stack up on each side, like my sisters here. We suffer impenetrable silences, the absence of those voices stilled forever, and when the sum of these is great enough, there seems no more purpose in speaking. This is life for those of us left behind."

"Left behind?" Dagr asked.

"Left behind when men decide in which peculiar holocaust they will end their world."

"Women do not perpetrate holocausts?" Dagr asked.

"Only in reaction. In the claiming of retribution," the crone said cheerfully. "We do not initiate the madness. But sometimes we must seek redress to approach balance."

"I notice that the 'great silences' have not affected you overmuch," Kinza said.

"I speak for those who are struck literally speechless," Mother Davala said. "Those who continually lose must, at some time, begin to take back. We arrive at this conclusion at different times of our lives but arrive we must, even if at the edge of a knife, in a tub of hot water."

"You babble, woman," Hamid said. "Living in this empty house has robbed your mind of sense."

"I know you, Torturer," Mother Davala said. "You are a man who has found joy in your profession. What frightens you is the vengeance that is owed to you, that has been piling high since the day you first embarked on your career. Do you think you can avoid it forever?"

"What do you know, witch?" Hamid shouted. "Whom have you told? Kinza, we are betrayed! That shit Xervish has sold us out!"

"Do you think to command me now?"

"No," Hamid said in a low voice. "No."

"What game is this, old mother?" Dagr asked. "What secrets do you know of us?"

"No secrets," Davala said. "Not by some nefarious path. I only use my eyes. Your nature, for example, is written on your face plain as the day. Your losses, dear one, mount up higher than you can bear. Soon, you, too, will live in silence. What have you left to wager, after all? You could float away, unfettered, invisible, *valueless*."

"You assign value most carelessly," Kinza said.

"The city changes its currency. One would be blind to miss it," Mother Davala turned to him. "Your friend is mere nostalgia. His day is gone. Will it return again? Who knows? It is *your* time now, the hour of the wolf."

"You mock me."

"No, dear one, I *need* you," Mother Davala said. "Our sons and grandsons are dead and scattered. Nephews, uncles, cousins—all gone. Do you not see here a dearth of men? So our business lies unfinished."

"What business?" Kinza asked.

"The business of debit and credit. Of ledgers unbalanced for too long," she said. "The killers of our families still walk free, unafraid. They must be taught fear. They must be driven mad with suffering. You can do that, surely? It is what you were born for."

"Who do you want killed?" Kinza asked.

"Many, oh many men need killing who walk this earth. Many men for whom death is too good a punishment," Mother Davala said. "Seven months ago, Captain Eric Hollow of the occupation forces thought he saw a man on a truck with an AK47 during a midday patrol through a crowded market. He opened fire with his machine gun, emptying his magazine. He must have been blind. It was my great grand nephew, playing on the truck bed with a piece of wood. He was three years old. A round blew his entire head off. When the boy's father started crying hysterically, the captain arrested him for inciting a riot and took him away. They left the headless boy on the street. Later, I received a note saying compensation was denied for the accidental deaths of both father and son, as the event could not be verified. A condolence payment of $1,500 was enclosed."

"Captain Eric Hollow," Kinza said, with a peculiar emphasis, and it seemed to Dagr as if some giant magnet were trained on his friend, inexorably drawing him in, resonating on frequencies unseen, thrumming the rage out of some reservoir. Kinza's fingers curled unwillingly now around imaginary triggers, the hollows of his eyes darkening with the sight of some invisible enemy, and he seemed adrift in time, loose from the moorings of reality in some hyperplane where he was free to pursue justice in any way he saw fit.

"Thirteen months ago, Commander Ismail Al-Abdur-Rashid of the New Iraqi Army arrested a young woman on the street. She was the fiancé of my grandson, the daughter of an old friend, the deceased Dr. Erban. The commander took her to his holding cell, where he and his squad repeatedly raped her for four days. They let her go afterwards, claiming that they had gotten the wrong person. She lodged a complaint with the court. The judge threw out the case and subsequently alerted his friend, the commander. That night, a squad arrested both my grandson and his fiancé on charges of prostitution. Their bodies were found in a ditch later, apparently victims of suicide. No note or condolence, however. The New Iraqi Army does not deal in such niceties."

"Eighteen months ago, the imam of the Al Sha-"

"Enough," Kinza said. "Enough. These things happen every day in every street of Baghdad. I am not here to seek vengeance for borrowed causes."

"Someone must speak for them," the lady said.

"I am not the person you need, old mother," Kinza said.

"I know, dear, not yet," Mother Davala said. "But one day you will be."

7: HEAVILY DRUGGED
AND DEMENTED

"Klonopin, Zoloft, Ambien, OxyContin," Hoffman read off a list. "Tommy, what the hell is this?"

"Prescriptions, admiral," Tommy said. "For Private Ancelloti."

"Ancelloti? Our main gunner? Is he trying to get high?" Hoffman asked. "Does he think I'm an idiot? Don't answer that."

"No, sir," Tommy said. "He's hurting bad, sir. No joke. Last night I woke up to take a piss. Found him chewing on my leg, sir."

"Gnawing on your leg?" Hoffman puffed on his cigar, incredulous. "Is that some kind of gay slang? Are you gay, Tommy?"

"No way, Hoff," Tommy said. "I like women. You remember that titty bar we went to, and I pulled down that stripper in the black nun's outfit?"

"Ahem," Hoffman said. "That was not a titty bar, Tommy. Not by a long shot. How do I know? No titty bars in all of Baghdad. Fact. And that was no nun's habit either. That was a hijab. And finally, Tommy, that was not a stripper. Not by a long shot, no."

"Right, Hoff." Tommy looked down, abashed.

"About Ancelloti," Hoffman said. "You woke up to find him actually biting your leg, you say?"

"Yeah," Tommy rolled up his pants to show a purpling circular wound denoting a marked overbite. "He was sleep-walking. Bit my leg and then started to make a house out of all our gear. And then he tried to make a bullet soup."

"Tommy, this is a terrible failure in leadership," Hoffman said. "I made you, er, vice admiral of this fleet. I gave you rank, status, actual duties. I put you in charge of the whole squad. Now I see you're messing around making bullet soup. What the hell is bullet soup by the way?"

"Campbell's canned tomato with bullets in it. Everybody knows that," Tommy said. "I'm sorry, Hoff, but Ancelloti does crazy shit when he runs out of Klonopin."

"I see. And you've spoken to his doctor, I suppose?" Hoffman asked. "Or are you hiding a medical degree under that helmet, kid?"

"No, Hoff, honest," Tommy said, worried. "I ain't a doctor."

"Hmm, must be the hash then," Hoffman said. "Even makes me paranoid sometimes."

"The psych told him to take it," Tommy said, relieved. "He's been taking it for a year now. Except they stopped refilling his perspective six months ago."

"His perspective is empty, you say? Sounds serious."

"Right, his perspective is finished, that's what I said, Hoff."

"You mean prescription, Tommy."

"Huh?"

"I think," Hoffman said, "you had better call Ancelloti over."

Private Ancelloti was a jittery, wheezing mess, a tall, olive-skinned man who had once been handsome. He had tomato soup all over his shirt and a bullet in his pocket.

"Ancelloti, what is the problem here?"

"Nothing, Hoff," Ancelloti mumbled. "Can't sleep too good."

"Trouble with your meds?" Hoffman asked.

"Ran out," Ancelloti grinned, revealing bloodstained teeth, where he had ground down his gums. "Two, three months ago."

"Sit down, son," Hoffman sparked a joint and handed it over. "What the hell you on so many meds for anyway?"

"I was gunner on a street patrol in Basra. We didn't have that mine resistant armored crap the reporters ride. Just the normal shit," Ancelloti said. "Got hit by IED. Knocked us flat on our ass. I got thrown clear. Then the bastards came and threw grenades at us. Little kids with guns, coming at us outta windows. Shooting at us, throwing shit at us. Like a goddamn party for the whole neighborhood…it was raining legs, Hoff. Captain's boot hit me in the face, knocked me out for a few seconds. They put two bullets in me and fucked off."

"How many you lose?" Hoffman asked.

"The whole damn squad," Ancelloti said. "Whole damn squad. I was wearing half of them."

"Bad luck."

"Can't sleep at night anymore," Ancelloti said. "Can't shut my eyes—swear, Hoff. My hands shake when I get up on that turret. Takes me half an hour to feed the damn bullets into the machine. I lost half my peripheral vision. Can't see more than 45 degrees either side."

"What the hell did they send you back here for?" Hoffman asked.

"Hospital discharged me," Ancelloti shrugged. "I told them about the shaking and the vision problem. They said it was psychological. Spent one hour with a grief counselor. He sent me to the psych ward. Thought I was faking it. Psych gave me Klonopin and buncha other stuff. Worked for a while. Knocked me out every night."

"But now you're out of Klonopin," Hoffman said. "Why the hell didn't you get refills?"

"I tried, Hoff," Ancelloti said. "Pharmacy told me the army stopped issuing Klonopin months ago. Drug companies changed. They got a new supplier, new drug. Something called Icopin. Took Icopin for a week. It just made me puke and pass out. Couldn't even get outta bed. New psych gave me Zoloft and Ambien to counter the Icopin. I took all of 'em. Now they're saying I'm a god damn drug addict."

"Well, you are."

"Yeah, but," Ancelloti said, "what the hell, Hoff, they made me take this shit in the first place. They shoulda sent me home."

"Got any family at home?"

"Got a two-year-old daughter. Beautiful," Ancelloti said. "And my wife. They go to church every Sunday, pray for me, take a picture outside. I get a picture every Sunday. That's why I ain't blown up yet."

"Lucky," Hoffman smiled. "Nice."

"Yeah," Ancelloti looked miserable. "Except now I'm stumbling around at night chewing on Tommy's leg. What if I go home and start making bullet soup in the middle of the night, Hoff? Scare the shit outta that little girl? What if they see me acting weird and leave me? Send me to some psych ward or something?"

"Hmm," Hoffman said. "We need a gunner. Can't run a patrol without a gunner. Top secret mission. Can't send you home. You know too much already. Means we're going to fix you up. That, or kill you."

"Haw haw. You're joking, right, Hoff? Joking? Please, Hoff."

"Er, right," Hoffman removed his hand from his sidearm surreptitiously. "Way I see it, private, is that the army's diagnosis is correct."

"Correct?"

"Precisely," Hoffman let out a professorial plume of smoke. "They correctly identified you as a drug addict. The hitch, to me, is obvious."

"Sir?"

"The problem," Hoffman continued, "is the kind of drugs you have been prescribed. What you need, private, is a new prescription. I have just the man to help you."

Back again, Hoffman at the wheel, racing through narrow Shulla streets with scant regard for pedestrians, barely avoiding disaster at every turn, the blind gunner Ancelloti lolling in his turret puking out tomato paste. Someone had, bizarrely, painted their hummer in the guise of a Holstein cow. The sight of the black and white vehicle barreling around tight corners on the wrong side of the road was enough to set a gaggle of laughing children after them, much to the consternation of Ancelloti, who tracked his gun around now in real fear. He was about to let loose when Hoffman pulled into a weed-grown courtyard, stopping abruptly to the horrible gnashing death knell of his transmission.

They stepped out into a small paved space, surrounded by running balconies eight stories high, an old building broken up into apartments, all of them using the yard as a rubbish dump. A garbage-fed dog sunbathed under a defunct fountain, too lazy to even growl at the marines.

"Hoffman!" A guttural cry, far above, from an immensely fat man. "You bastard, rot in hell!"

"Behruse, my friend. I want to come up."

"Get lost!"

"My friend, I can explain. It was not me with your wife. I swear!"

"What's the use," Behruse shouted down. "She's left me anyways."

Taking this as assent, Hoffman hoofed up the steps, dragging Ancelloti with him. On the sixth floor balcony, they found Behruse blocking their way, holding an archaic looking shotgun. He was well over six feet, running to mountainous fat, wearing a red cape and a makeshift superman T-shirt, which had ridden up to reveal a well-carpeted stomach.

"Costume party," Behruse said, holding up one sweaty palm. "Every time, I get stupid superman. They think it's funny that I have to wear my underwear over my pants. Stupid, useless kids."

Behruse was retired Iraqi secret service: an old friend, drinking partner, supplier and gossip monger, a great tentacled octopus spreading corruption throughout the city with good natured cheer.

"My friend," Hoffman approached to give him a hug, sidling around the shotgun. "I have missed you dearly."

"I want to crush you like a bug," Behruse rumbled. "Many nights I have dreamed of doing just that."

"Vicious lies," Hoffman said. "I swear, upon the life of your mother, I never..."

"Forget it," Behruse slumped against his door, making it tremble. "She left last week. Took off with a Syrian dentist."

"Forget her, Behruse, she was a troll. You're better off without her. I feel sorry for the Syrians," Hoffman said. "Besides, I have the perfect chick for you. She's a marine, could tear the neck off a giraffe, looks a bit like you, come to think of it."

"Come inside, my friends," Behruse ushered them into a surprisingly elegant living room. "Tea? Hoffman, your friend looks a little bit ill."

"No thanks," Hoffman said. "He's the reason why I'm here. Well, partially."

"So?"

"He's having trouble sleeping," Hoffman said. "Nightmares, the shakes, sleepwalking, strange visions..."

"Bombed-in-the-street-syndrome?" Behruse asked.

"Yeah," Hoffman said. "His whole squad got paid."

"What the hell am I supposed to do?"

"You can counsel him, Behruse," Hoffman said. "You know exactly what it feels like. How many people you lost over here?"

"Pfft," Behruse said. "Thirteen direct bloodline. Twenty-five slanted bloodline. IEDs, hand grenades, land mines, falling buildings, tank shells, mortar shells, air strikes, crossfire, sniper fire, friendly fire, electric fire; and my uncle—he died when Saddam's statue fell on him. First casualty of the civil war. Fact."

"That's a lotta people Behruse," Ancelloti said. "Could be, we did some of that shit to you."

"So what?" Behruse said. "It's a war. We kill you. You kill us. Who cares? The important thing is to have a sense of humor about it. When we were bombing the Kurds, do you think they were crying like babies?"

"I keep seeing those flying legs though, you know?" Ancelloti said.

"That's nothing," Behruse said. "I once saw... hmft well, never mind. What you need, my friend, is something to calm the spirit."

"That's exactly what I said," Hoffman said. "Fuck that chemical shit. We need something natural."

"Plum wine," Behruse began to bring out numerous packets, including a dusky bottle. "To ease the digestion and give you pleasant dreams. And this high quality Afghan hashish, dried on the thighs of beautiful Pashtun virgins."

"That's a joke right?" Hoffman guffawed. "Cause there ain't any Pashtun virgins."

"Not among the women, anyways," Behruse winked. "You interrupt. Dried on the thighs of beautiful Pashtun virgins, rolled in the down above their lips. You take this, my friend, to steady your hands and slow down time. And finally, this bottle, containing tear drops of the finest opium, save it for those sleepless nights, guaranteed to give you the finest visions. Not too much of the opium, mind. Here, I'll put it in a bag for you."

Ancelloti stared at the packet for a moment and then crushed it tightly against his chest. He appeared pathetically grateful.

"Now, Hoffman."

"I have here, Behruse, ten packets of America's finest detergent," Hoffman pulled out a catalogue. "Just pick your color."

"What the hell am I going to do with detergent?"

"Huh?" Hoffman said. "Wash stuff. I'll throw in a washing machine."

"You got a washing machine in there?" Behruse looked down at the parked hummer in admiration.

"Well, it's for the second part of the favor," Hoffman said.

"What else you need?"

"I had a chat a couple of days ago with an old guy called Sheikh Amal," Hoffman said. "Runs a dry goods store in Ghazaliya. Know him?"

"No," Behruse scowled. "What the hell? Am I supposed to know every old fuck in town?"

"He's an interesting man," Hoffman said, "in that he, and his neighborhood, were recently victimized by a very weird criminal. Someone called the Lion of Akkad."

"Never heard of that fucker either."

"Heard of something called the Druze watch?"

"What?" Behruse flicked his eyes around.

"Just learned about the Druze. Easy name to remember. It's so close to booze. They're like a super secret bunch of heretics. Kinda like Mormons, I think. Arab Mormons. Except they're like a thousand years old, and they don't let anyone join their secret society. They probably know a lot of secret shit, like where the weapons of mass destruction are hiding."

"What?" Behruse asked.

"I googled them. All true."

"There aren't any Druze in Iraq," Behruse shook his head, looking wary.

"Actually, sounds like they are back in Baghdad," Hoffman said. "And they've lost a watch a lot of people would like to have."

"Even if they were here, it's not safe to talk about them," Behruse said.

I'll tell you something for free, Behruse," Hoffman said. "Said artifact apparently exists, and I know exactly who has it."

"I don't care!" Behruse snapped. "Who?"

"Man called Kinza. Heard of him?" Hoffman asked.

"No," Behruse said.

"He's the one who killed Hassan Salemi's son," Hoffman said. "Know him now?"

Behruse whistled.

"Kinza's a friend of mine. He's hiding somewhere now and probably needs my help. I need you to find him."

"Hassan Salemi will kill anyone who interferes in this," Behruse said.

"Hassan Salemi doesn't have any detergent," Hoffman said. "What, are you afraid of him?"

"I didn't say that."

"Tell me, friend, what is the Druze watch all about?"

"It's a stupid fairytale," Behruse shrugged. "And I've heard it before. Every few years some thief comes up with a piece of junk and hawks it around as the Druze watch. Supposed to belong to one of the lost tribes of Druze. It's a watch but not a watch, meaning it's not supposed to tell time but something else. Religious crap. Some people take it seriously."

"People who pay?"

"Maybe," Behruse said.

"The right people might find Kinza in return for the watch," Hoffman said. "Might get him out of Baghdad safely. Him and his friends."

"It is possible."

"I can't interfere directly in this, you understand."

"Something can be worked out, perhaps," Behruse said.

"I would be very grateful."

"Detergent grateful or something actually useful?"

"Ha ha," Hoffman got up to leave. "What exactly are we thinking about here?"

"An Apache," Behruse said. "I want a gunship."

8: HOUSE OF MANY DOORS

THIS PLACE IS A MAD HOUSE," HAMID SAID FINALLY. "WE NEED TO get out of here."

They were lost, stranded in corridors. Doors hung in abundance, leading nowhere, sometimes into impossibly shaped rooms or closets or into dark air; painted doors and fine polished teak ones, plain and carved, crazily hinged, sometimes boarded shut from the outside, or the inside, keeping back unimaginable prey within and without. The corridors extended far beyond the outward bounds of the building, inclining and declining at will, at places smartly dressed, and then cobwebbed and musty, sections pocked with shrapnel, until it seemed to Dagr that they were roaming the entire block with impunity, passing unseen through neighboring buildings, catching snatches of their day to day lives, the smell of couscous, a tea kettle wailing against Al Jazeera, some stifled murmurs of illicit sex.

"We should have gone left from the Jar Room," Dagr said. "I thought I heard the old ladies. I'm sure the living room was just below."

"Damn your Jar Room," Hamid said. "What the hell were in those jars, eh? Those women are damned witches. This is a damn witch house."

The Jar Room was a fixed point of reference, a large ornate door with a tasseled key in the lock, a room that they had found twice in the same place during their wandering, a phenomenon not to be taken for granted in this labyrinth of a house. They had gone inside. The room had been cold, the air heavy and muffled, pressured peculiarly like the graveled bed of some ancient, dank sea. The blue tiled floor was covered in amphorae of different heights, each sealed carefully with red wax and ornate signet, the seal of some magnificent king, the outer clay skins sweating with a ghostly condensate, each jar vibrating minutely, a susurration of wasp wings growing louder, ever louder. The decision to retreat had been unanimous. In their power-walking haste, they had lost what few bearings they retained.

"I'm telling you," Hamid said, "I have a peerless sense of direction. I am a trained scout. These corridors have taken us far away from the house. We are going through parallel buildings. And still there are doors. What the hell is behind this locked door? It should be a solid boundary wall. But look below—there is light."

"It's a safehouse," Kinza said. "They are supposed to have ways in and out. The whole neighborhood was rebel. They probably built all these damn passages and then forgot about them."

"Shh," Dagr held out his hand. "I can hear footsteps. Do you hear that?"

"Damn footsteps. We're being followed," Hamid said. "I've been telling you it smells of cats. Does it smell of cats? It's that damned Druze. He's come to finish us off."

"But how can he follow us here? Is he invisible now?" Dagr asked, his voice breaking, for in this dim light, such a thing seemed entirely possible.

"How did he convince those cats do to his bidding, eh?" Hamid asked. "Those were man eating cats, don't forget."

"Back to the Jar Room, boys!" Dagr turned tail again, leading the route, back again in the direction they had initially retreated from in the first place.

A few more wrong turns and they were somehow on a different level, a floor below the Jar Room, which could be still easily identified, however, by the angry wasping sound rapping out in syncopated volume. Hamid, his gums bleeding from the rhythmic assault, drew his gun, imagining, in his fevered state, a coordinated attack of cats and jars, anticipating how many of each he would shoot down before, inevitably, turning the last bullet on himself.

"Put that away, idiot," Dagr shouted, taking cover all the same.

The first shot took the ceiling, punching a hole through rotten cement, straight into the Jar Room, the bullet lodging into a great fat clay vessel that instantly went still, a baritone drone disappearing noticeably from the susurration. The three of them froze.

The section of wall Dagr was leaning on gave way suddenly. Multiple layers of wallpaper tore open, as an ancient, forgotten door caved in on rotted hinges, depositing the hapless professor into an island of calm. He looked around, stunned. He was sprawled over a huge pile of rotting books. On either side of him were haphazard stacks, tottering toward the ceiling like crooked fingers. More stacks behind them, onward for several rows. Through the irregular gaps in the books, Dagr could see that the library had originally been shelved floor to ceiling and stocked in a civilized manner, but the obvious influx of books had long outstripped any attempt to maintain aesthetics. The smell of damp paper was overpowering.

He got up quickly to make room for the others, afraid their entry would set off an avalanche. He glanced behind, saw that Hamid had put his gun away finally. The central isle had shrunk to barely two feet, room enough for them to sidle on, single file, sucking their stomachs in. Dagr studied the books as they shuffled forward. Myriad languages and subjects, jumbled together, old and new. Here and there, he spied attempts at order, some small hand trying to sort by topic or alphabet or author. Futile, of course, for no order was possible in this literary deluge. Forty-watt bulbs guttered from the ceiling every few meters, adding their rotten yellow to the general fug of dust, mildew, and neglect.

The room appeared to be long and careless, winding slightly, as if the architect had not bothered to draw a straight line. Or it might have been the books themselves enforcing this curvature, for the walls were barely visible and it was impossible to tell.

"What the hell is this place?" Hamid asked. "No one's been here for years."

"Shhh," Dagr said. "I can hear something ahead."

They arrived a few seconds later at a makeshift alcove, where the books had been shoveled around to make room for an antique rocking chair. A stable pile of hardbacks served as a side table. Upon the broad back of a 1957 Encyclopedia Atlas, there rested a faded porcelain cup and saucer.

"Tea," Hamid said, his gun out again. "Still warm." He drank it all. "Not bad. Peppermint."

"Keep going," Kinza motioned. "Hamid, get your finger off the trigger. We don't need to shoot up a tea party."

A few meters on and the path narrowed into a barricade, about five feet high and at least eight books wide. Peering over in the dim light, Dagr saw varied signs of domesticity. A rolled up tatami rested neatly against the inner wall of the barricade, topped by a small pillow, and a woolen camouflage army blanket. In the other corner, there was a small electric stove, a Swiss army knife, a tin pot, a tin cup, assorted tin cutlery, and a stack of ceramic plates inlaid with gold floral designs.

Beyond this line, the blockade faded into near darkness, although Dagr could make out some vague emanations of light some distance away, which made him think the interior of this cave was larger than he had supposed. Close by, too, were other signs of life: an indistinct hard cover turned spine up, a cushion with the posterior indentation slowly fading, the faint smell of some kind of canned stew, the burn of kerosene, or lighter fluid, and almost subliminally, a faint tweet tweet of bird chatter.

Hamid, identifying some obscure threat, began to push forward, his gun out in his mangled fist, face swinging side to side in the twilight like a hammerhead shark. He got two steps forward before Kinza clamped a steely hand on his shoulder, yanking him away.

"Professor, if you please."

Dagr leaned over the barricade, resting his weight on a pile of hardcover Sandman graphic novels.

"Excuse me...Anyone home?"

"Stand ba-ba-back. Away from the wall please." A hollow male voice, followed by the unmistakable click of a large bore firearm, and Dagr felt the familiar rush of sweat and fear, realizing that no matter how many times he had bullets trained on him, he would never ever get accustomed to that first rush of chemical terror.

Dagr raised his hands and then retreated a foot slowly, fighting down the knowledge that even now, Kinza and Hamid were slinking back into shadows behind him, their own guns out and about, ready to answer in kind, with only Dagr's flesh standing hesitant between this metallic conversation.

"Sorry for intruding," he said quickly. "Sorry. We came here accidentally. Saw the tea. We can leave if you like."

"No one knows this place," the voice in the barricade said. "You are the police. How did you find me? After all this time. Are you the Mukhabarat?"

"Mukhabarat? You mean the Ba'athist secret police?" Dagr peered into the gloom uncertainly. "No, no, the Intelligence Service is disbanded I think. Or working for the Americans these days."

"You are lying," the voice said. "Who has the power to disband the Mukhabarat? The president would never allow it."

"My friend, Saddam is dead."

"What?"

"Saddam is dead. The whole country saw it on the Internet. We are ruled by American sheikhs now."

"Impossible. You're lying. You're with them."

The voice was wild, fevered. Another click, the sound of a bullet being chambered or the hammer being cocked, although the room echoed strangely, and Dagr was not sure whether the sound was in front or behind him, only that the situation was not getting any better.

"I'm not Mukhabarat. I'm not," Dagr said, sweat on his forehead, more afraid of the men behind him than the one in front. "I'm a professor, I teach at the...I taught at the Abu Bakr university, I taught higher mathematics, in room 208, there were two windows next to my desk, and a lemon tree outside, I could smell it everyday, that smell and coffee, and sometimes students would play the guitar outside, and I loved that room, I met my wife in that room..."

"You were a teacher?" the voice was hesitant, the pressure releasing a bit.

"Yes, yes, I taught basic stuff at first, economics and entry level differential calculus, but then some spaces opened up and I got graduate students and we started working on some molecular mathematics."

A figure abruptly stepped forward from the dark. He was wild haired and bearded, a sinewy man, skin drawn tight over bones, naked save for a tattered blanket draped like a sarong, a walnut-stocked crossbow cradled in thin fingers, like a child's toy, and it was a boy's face beneath the mane, eyes light and loony. Dagr saw him and felt a shaft of sudden sympathy. He stepped forward deliberately, spreading his arms, blocking the lines of sight behind him.

"My father was a librarian," the man said, as if that explained everything. He came forward, laying down the crossbow on the barricade. "I am Mikhail Alwari. You can come inside now if you wish."

Dagr climbed over clumsily, his feet cracking spines, sending volumes A–F of Encyclopedia Britannica 1964 clattering. He followed the strange man in, past the interior of the barricade, which he realized was merely an antechamber of sorts, serving as a terrace to the main body of this habitat, which stretched inward further than he could have imagined. As his eyes grew accustomed to the dark, he found himself in a storage room, stacked high with crates and crates of supplies, pilfered stores from regiments and hospitals, a stockpile of almost epic proportions, the forgotten sustenance of a rebel army. Festooned amid these crates were more irregular pieces of luggage, bags, and cases of all sorts, some of them burst open, revealing a pathetic banality of innards, the dregs of a seemingly countless wave of refugees, now faded away.

Spaces had been carved out here, functional niches for sleeping and eating presumably. Somewhere off to the side, there was the sound of water pouring in fits and starts.

"Mikhail, my friends are outside. Two of them," Dagr said carefully. "We are sorry to disturb you. We stumbled into this area. Could I invite them in here? They will not harm you. I assure you."

"Are they teachers, too?" Mikhail asked, a strange wistfulness in his eyes. "I saw your friends, in the shadow. They frightened me."

"They…are not here to harm you. You have my word."

Mikhail looked around his room uncertainly and then stared at Dagr's face. A long moment later, he said, "Ok, bring them here. Would you like some tea?"

In a moment, the three of them were seated in various nooks, watching, bemused, as their host started making hot water in a small Japanese kettle on his electric heat pad. His movements were neat, sparing, and he hummed softly under his breath, as if forgetting completely his unwanted guests. In a few minutes, he came with three porcelain cups of hot water, flavored tea bags soaking in each, and a clutch of saccharine sachets in his hand. They sat there in bewildered silence, sipping tea awkwardly, as Mikhail's eyes darted from face to face as if he were some small animal caught in onrushing traffic.

"Mikhail, how did you come to be here?" Dagr asked, finally.

"My father was the librarian," Mikhail said.

"Yes, you said."

Mikhail hesitated. "I remember…steel shelves, and small plastic tools to stand on."

"Those books outside," Dagr said, flashing a connection. "Are they your father's?"

"Yes," Mikhail said. "We brought them here. I was small. I remember at night, my father made trips here, all night, bringing books in a truck. Then we came here, and it was nice, like his library, only smaller."

"What happened to your father, Mikhail?" Dagr asked gently.

"My father was the librarian," Mikhail replied, his face creasing into a frown.

"Where did your father go?" Dagr asked. "Why did he leave you here?"

"He was a librarian," Mikhail said. He began to rock back and forth on his stool, humming, the distress roiling off him in waves.

"Why did you bring the books here, Mikhail?" Dagr asked, finally understanding that this man's mind worked only in certain directions.

"The Mukhabarat!" Mikhail bolted upright. "The Mukhabarat were after us. I remember that. They were going to burn the library, I think. We had to protect the books. It was our duty. My father told me that. I remember him clearly saying that. He said 'Mikhail, my son, we must save the books!'"

"Is that why you came here?"

"Yes," Mikhail said eagerly. "Yes, that must be right."

"Do you know where you are, Mikhail?"

"I...no...this house is safe," Mikhail said. "I know that. The old ladies said so. I remember the Old Lady. She gives me treasures to keep, sometimes. I know her. We are safe here because the Mukhabarat have forgotten about this place. This is the new library. I must preserve the library. If I keep still, I'll be ok."

He stared up at them with his big eyes, and Dagr could see the emotions flitting across his face, bemusement, worry, gnawing dread, and it occurred to him that this creature possessed no mental defenses, had never learned, perhaps, those mechanisms with which men could hide their thoughts.

"You don't have to worry about them anymore, Mikhail," Dagr said softly.

"This place is safe," Mikhail said. "Do you want...you can stay, here if you want." He glanced uncertainly at Hamid and Kinza.

"No, we have another place to stay," Dagr said. "But maybe I could come to visit you sometimes. If you're not busy?"

"Visit?" Mikhail looked at him doubtfully. "I have to read every day. And dust the books, you know. They get really dusty sometimes. And I have to take care of the scrolls and the papyrus, and the really old things written on skins. Do you want to see?"

"Well, maybe I'll come during tea time when you're taking a break," Dagr said. "Just to visit."

"And I set the mousetrap, just like father said, because mice are the enemy! And I make sure the water doesn't get to the shelves."

"You take good care of the books," Dagr said. "I saw that coming in. They are in excellent condition. You are the librarian now."

"I am the librarian," Mikhail beamed. "Yes! I am the librarian."

"Tell me, how old were you when you first came here?" Hamid asked finally.

"I don't know," Mikhail Alwari said doubtfully. "On my last birthday, I think I was ten. But that was a long, long time ago."

9: INSIDE THE WATCHMAKER

"IED! IED! DUCK!"

The men inside the hummer cringed into fetal positions, screaming instinctively, as the vehicle careened around the street, the wheel freely spinning in Hoffman's hands. IEDs were mostly homemade bombs, the weapon of choice for insurgents in many parts of the country. Up above, his ears plugged with opium and Ravel, Ancelloti lolled in the gun turret, oblivious.

"I! E! D!" Behruse punctuated with a lit cigar and split his sides laughing.

"What the fuck, Behruse?" Hoffman said, righting the vehicle. "What the hell is wrong with you? That shit isn't funny."

"False alarm," Behruse said. "Oops. You should have seen your faces."

"Where the hell are we now? I'm fucking lost."

"Next two right turns, then hundred yards, then left, then third right, then ask me again after two hundred yards," Behruse said.

"You're getting us lost deliberately," Hoffman said. "But I got GPS, so fuck you, Behruse."

"Fuck your GPS," Behruse said good-naturedly. "And where we're going, you have to follow certain routes. They tell the neighborhood that you're safe. You want the watchers to start taking shots at us?"

"More of your secret service shit?" Hoffman puffed on a clove. "I thought you guys were all hiding under your grannies' mattresses."

"Hey, don't disrespect the Mukhabarat," Behruse said. "We were good. Damned *good*. We fought *wars*, man. And we kept this place running, and we would have kept it running too if you fools had had the sense to use us."

"Hey, I'm just a foot soldier," Hoffman said.

"And you think we're just *gone* now?" Behruse scoffed. "What, we just forgot how to do shit? Sold our guns? Let me tell you, my friend, your governors have already started making enquires...taking resumes...*hiring*, you understand?"

"You going back legit, Behruse?" Hoffman asked. "Or just reminiscing?"

"All I'm saying...those faggots growing beards and waving Kalashnikovs had better start remembering how to shave again," Behruse said, serious all of a sudden, the crinkles in his eyes fading, making Hoffman remember with a shiver what the man had once been and might become again. "Pull over. We walk from here. Sidearms only, just you and me."

Into a rabbit warren of buildings now, Behruse taking deliberately obtuse routes, which narrowed to a single file of rough, lichen-scrawled bricks, wet to the touch, the sharp ammonia of gutter water making Hoffman's eyes tear up. He lost all sense of direction after a while, retaining only the feeling of being pressed by ancient masonry and people alike, unfriendly eyes watching from above, blue slatted windows blinking in and out of existence in the darkness.

Many minutes of this mind-numbing disorientation, Hoffman barely restraining himself from clutching at Behruse's broad coat tail, like a child seeking reassurance. Some corner of his mind reflected that the Mukhabarat craft was basic and effective, as good as anything they taught in Abu Gharib or Langley. These secret policemen had their own successful techniques in this old, old city. At last, they stopped in a nondescript archway, shielded from sight in front of an unlatched door. Behruse stopped him here.

"Hoffman, listen," the big man seemed curiously hesitant. "The man we are visiting he is not like us. He is a very learned man. He was unwilling to see you. I had to call in a personal favor. You have to treat him with respect. I don't know what agency you're with or what agendas you have, and to be frank, I don't want to know. I need your guarantee that this man will be off limits and off any official transcripts."

"You have my word," Hoffman said promptly. "And for your information, I am following a brief to locate the bunker of Tarek Aziz at all costs, where I fully expect to find weapons of mass destruction. Now, who is this guy? Some kind of old spook? Will he be of any use?"

"You'll see," Behruse pushed open the door. "Just remember, after tonight, he doesn't exist for you."

They entered into a dingy hallway cluttered with canes, umbrellas, shoes, and hats in varying stages of disrepair, as well as other paraphernalia required for negotiating the different climates of Baghdad. Clambering over this junk, they reached a door almost grimed shut.

"He doesn't get out much," Behruse said apologetically.

It took the full momentum of his weight to effect an opening. Inside was a rectangular room slashed with irregular lighting, permeated with the tang of machine oil strong enough to send Hoffman reeling. He saw a vast jumble of mechanical devices, electric arc welders, precision lathes, milling machines, transistors, dismantled radios, racks of soldering irons and hand borers, and an aged IBM mainframe the size of a sofa, among the things that he could actually recognize. In the far corner in an island of well lit calm, an old man in a dirty smock stood at a long work table covered in green felt, moving his hands lightly over a set of minute tools, seeming, from far away, like an ancient croupier presiding over some insane casino.

As they approached, he looked up and greeted them, showing a thin, aristocratic face, somewhat marred by the jeweler's monocle attached to his left eye, which made his pupil appear horrendously large. On the baize in front of him were six minute gears the size of match heads and a set of jewelers' tongs and calipers.

"Ehm. Welcome, Behruse. Welcome, unknown guest."

"Thank you, sir." Behruse did a creditable half bow, the courtliness of the gesture momentarily leaving Hoffman bereft of speech.

"Hoffman, this is, um, you may refer to him as Mr. Avicenna." Behruse grinned.

"What, is that like some kind of disguise?"

"Forgive our slightly obese friend," the old man straightened, and put down his tools. "He is merely giving you the Latin version of my name. I imagine he thinks it's funny. For a fat man, his sense of humor is curiously flat."

Hoffman pulled up into a full parade salute. From the corner of his eye, he saw Behruse hanging his head, strangely crushed. "Sergeant Hoffman at your service, sir!"

"Hoffman, why on earth are you saluting?" Avicenna fixed his enlarged left eye on him.

"Recognizing a superior officer, sir!"

"Don't be ridiculous Hoffman," Avicenna said. "You appear to be a man of sense. Stop this posturing."

"Merely noting that you appear to be a gentleman of rank," Hoffman said. "Old Guard? Mukhabarat?"

"Rank?" Avicenna smiled. "Very sly, soldier. No Hoffman, I hold no command nor any title to lands. Any respect I garner is merely... symbolic."

"Well then, sir, consider my salute entirely symbolic." Hoffman smiled, still quivering with rigid parade intensity.

"At ease you ridiculous boy," Avicenna said. "Now I presume you have found me for a reason?"

"I have some friends," Hoffman said.

"How fortunate for you," Avicenna said politely.

"They're in trouble," Hoffman continued. "You may have heard of the killing of Hassan Salemi's son."

"Heard about it? I am surrounded by oafs who speak of nothing else. I am heartily sick of Hassan Salemi and his dead son."

"Yes, well, my friend might have been...*was*...responsible for that," Hoffman said. "Unknowingly, I'm sure."

"That is most unfortunate," Avicenna said. "Your friend shot Hassan Salemi's son. Even now, that man is tearing apart the neighborhoods searching for the culprit. Your friends are most likely dead."

"Not yet but they will be unless someone helps them," Hoffman said.

"Do you imagine I can help them?" Avicenna smiled sadly. "Save them from Hassan Salemi? He has an army of gunmen and half of Baghdad's police force on his payroll. I merely have this workshop full of old trinkets."

"Yes, about the workshop, I understand you're a watchmaker," Hoffman said.

"I am, among other things," Avicenna inclined his head. "Hassan Salemi, however, is not very interested in mechanical watches."

"Hmm, it's just that my friend Dagr, who's a professor of higher mathematics, by the way, has in his possession a kind of artifact. The Druze watch is what they are calling it."

"The Druze watch?" Avicenna smiled. "Behruse, do you have any reason to believe this drivel?"

"I interviewed ten witnesses who saw it with their own eyes," Hoffman said. "It is an old mechanical watch with a large rotating rim and just two equal-sized hands. The man who saw it close up described it as 'Fouad Jumblatt's watch, inscribed with a colored Druze star'."

"Mr. Hoffman, as I am surprised Behruse has neglected to tell you, the Druze watch is an irritatingly recurring meme in the backstreets of Baghdad. Every dozen or so years, thieves and char-latans entertain each other with tall tales of a watch that tells no time, lumbering guardians with superhuman powers, and a secret gathering of evil Druze," Avicenna said. "I think you have fallen into a tourist trap."

"Well, this watch actually came with an evil guardian," Hoffman said. "Someone called the Lion of Akkad, the King of Cats, who pos-sessed inhuman strength, superman speed, and imperviousness to bullets. They ran him off and found the watch in his hiding place, with other papers and books, all of which I have in my hot little hands."

"I saw it all," Behruse said. "There are drawings of a watch, dia-grams and such."

"Witnesses, you say?" Avicenna asked. "Hysterical old women and gullible boys?"

"More like gnarly old shopkeepers and street thugs," Hoffman said. "They hadn't heard about any mythical watch, and they didn't care about any Druze either. They were more than happy to hand over everything from the sorry mess and forget the thing ever happened."

"Tell me, Hoffman, are you a treasure hunter?"

"No, sir."

"Do you dream of some vast Druze conspiracy?"

"No, sir. I dream only in American."

"What then, do you want?"

"I want you to help my friends. In return for the watch," Hoffman said. "Behruse said you were *somebody*."

"And who do *you* represent, Mr. Hoffman?"

"Me? No one at all," Hoffman shrugged. "I'm just a cog."

"Alright, we'll leave it at that for now," Avicenna said. "When we are further along in our partnership, we might revisit your identity. Now come with me."

10: FURTHER INSIDE
THE WATCHMAKER

THEY FOLLOWED AVICENNA OUT OF THE WORKSHOP INTO A NAR-
row archway, which opened abruptly into a small courtyard garden
ripe with the smell of olives. Hoffman, long accustomed to finding
strange hidden places in this city, was nonetheless stunned by the
geometric perfection of this space. An empty bird cage hung from a
stunted tree, the small door unlatched. Beneath the cage, there were
two weathered benches, shaded no doubt in the morning heat, now
deliciously cool and speckled by moonlight. Avicenna motioned them
to sit and then rang a small bell. A manservant came from the interior,
bearing a silver tray of refreshments and glasses of black coffee. After
the service, the old man turned to them.

"Now, gentlemen, what do you know about the Druze in Iraq?"

"There aren't supposed to be any," Hoffman said. "It's right there
in the CIA country report. I checked."

Behruse sniggered.

"Hush, Behruse," Avicenna said. "You're quite right, Hoffman,
there are no civilian Druze in Iraq. What do you know about the
religion?"

"Nothing," Hoffman said. "A cult?"

"Close enough," Avicenna said. "What faith are you, Hoffman?"

"Protestant agnostic."

"Clever," Avicenna smiled. "Would you agree that every religion
has an esoteric core underneath the orthodox *literal* meaning?"

"Man, I don't even understand what that means," Hoffman fid-
dled with a vest pocket and produced a joint. "Do you mind if I light
this up?"

"Feel free," Avicenna said. "The smoking of hashish was a common practice for the founders of this city. I was speaking of hidden metaphoric meaning, beneath the literal words and rituals of our religions."

"I guess," Hoffman coughed and waived away smoke.

"It is certainly one of the dividing lines of Islam," Avicenna said. "Among our philosophers, the esoteric core is almost universally accepted. The Sunni orthodoxy maintain that the inner meaning is truly fathomable only by the divine will. It is out of reach of mankind, in other words, and we must be content with following the literal will of God."

"Makes sense to me," Hoffman said. "Most people don't bother with all this shit. Just give us clear easy rules to follow."

"Other sects have different approaches, the gist of it being certain men can access the deeper meanings found in the religion, either through intellectual power or inspiration or through direct divine revelation," Avicenna said. "I'm not boring you, am I?"

Hoffman, whose eyes had indeed begun to glaze over, now attempted to prop himself upright. "No, no, it's all fascinating," he protested. "The fact book doesn't have any of this shit in it."

"The Druze started as something close to the Ismaili faith, but its radical divergence was very fast," Avicenna continued. "The Druze believe in layers and layers of arcane knowledge, each accessible to fewer and fewer people. A most secretive sect. Are you familiar with the concept of 'Taqiyya'?"

"Erm, no," Hoffman said.

"It is the art of dissimulation. A verse in the Koran allows us to hide ourselves, should we be threatened by unbelievers," Avicenna said. "It is a practice the Druze have emphasized from the very beginning. They might spend generations pretending to be Sunni or Shi'a or Christian or Jew. They have been persecuted almost from the beginning of their founding. It has made them most adept at hiding."

"Like the Mukhabarat," Hoffman said.

"Precisely. Hidden in plain sight," Avicenna said. "The modern day intelligence cells, or terrorist cells, are nothing compared to these people, who have hidden the core of their faith for over one thousand years. Their religion, too, is organized along ranks of knowledge. The laymen—the Jukkul—are exposed only to esoteric knowledge and make up the visible part of their population. They are mostly harmless, living in picturesque Syrian villages, campaigning for minority rights, etc.

Their leadership is veiled in layers of secrecy; the higher one ascends, the greater the knowledge and resources revealed. The true beliefs and aims of the Druze are known to only this upper echelon, the Uqqul. Indeed, there are higher levels that are not spoken of, the true power of the Druze on this earth, who would never reveal their face and who keep with them the most abstruse of the esoteric knowledge, the very highest truths they have discovered in their ages of study."

"So you guys think these secret Druze are in Iraq?" Hoffman asked.

"Assuredly they are," Avicenna said. "Behruse himself knows something of this. Speak, Behruse."

"There were persistent rumors in the service some years ago," Behruse said. "The Mukhabarat were compromised...*infiltrated*. Barzan Ibrahim the Tikriti, half brother to Saddam himself, ordered at least four known purges of the secret service. The word Druze was never mentioned explicitly. The official line was Syrian Ba'athists."

"And did you find anything?" Hoffman asked.

"No Druze," Behruse said. "No one confessed to being Druze. Over twenty low level agents confessed to being Syrian Ba'athists."

"That is not surprising," Avicenna said. "To understand fully, you must know certain other things about the Druze. First, the circumstances of their founding: their founding imam was the Caliph Al-Hakim Amr Allah, of the Fatimid Caliphate in Cairo. Caliph and messiah, two roles in one, a most powerful conjunction. His divinity was proclaimed by his people, among whom certain followers would come to be known as the Druze. This was in 1010 AD. For a period of eleven years, the *entire* Fatimid Caliphate, one of the most powerful Islamic empires *ever* in existence, was run by the Druze. They became so powerful, in fact, that the Abbasid Caliph of Baghdad grew alarmed. He gathered his Sunni and Shi'a scholars and created a doctrine that he had proclaimed from mosque to mosque."

"Denouncing the Druze, I take it?"

"At that time, it was aimed largely at Al-Hakim, who was imam and caliph of all of Ismailidom," Avicenna said. "Only later would the majority of the Ismailis abandon him. You see, Al-Hakim could not be defeated by force. He was far too powerful, and he enjoyed the full fervor of his people—*messianic* support. He was repeatedly proclaimed the Mahdi, the final prophet of the Ismailis. The Baghdad proclamation was aimed at defaming Al-Hakim. The Abbasids were afraid of him. Afraid that he was, in fact, the Mahdi, that he was the final caliph and imam on earth. They said that he was no true descendent of Mohammed and Fatima but, rather, the son of Christian and Jewish forefathers. The treatise on his lineage was shouted from minaret to minaret, all throughout the Abbasid demesne."

"Let me guess. It didn't work?" Hoffman said.

"Indeed, Al-Hakim's philosophies were shaking the entire edifice of Shi'a. But then, in 1021, poof."

"Poof?"

"He disappeared," Avicenna said. "His practice was to go out of the city to meditate. His donkey was found, with bloody remnants of his clothes. No body, however."

"So you Iraqis killed him," Hoffman said. "No wonder the Druze are pissed."

"Not so," Avicenna said. "Well, perhaps. It is disputed what happened to Al-Hakim. His elder sister might have killed him. The Abbasids might have. There is a third alternative."

"He went into hiding?"

"There is a Druze—and Shi'a—concept called occultation. Perhaps you are familiar with it, Mr. Hoffman?"

"Avi, dude, now you're just jerking me around," Hoffman said. "This is worse than high school."

"Necessary, nonetheless," Avicenna said. "For you to understand what you are dealing with, certain background information is critical. Occultation is the disappearance of the prophet—the removal of his person from the earthly realm, in fact. The Druze claim that Al-Hakim removed himself from imminent danger and will reappear when the time of his kingdom is ordained."

"Judgment day?"

"Not so much," Avicenna said. "As I understand it, when his time comes, he will return to earthly rule and bring justice to the world. I have heard some versions where his return will reveal some power to his true followers—the faithful Druze—allowing them to rise up."

"Like literally?" Hoffman frowned.

"There is such a train of thought," Avicenna shrugged slightly. "But others say that his return is symbolic, that indeed, the concept of the last prophet, *the Mahdi*, is symbolic. Anyway, after Al-Hakim's disappearance, things went downhill very fast. His son, under the regency of his elder sister, started persecuting his followers. The movement centered on Al-Hakim's divinity: the Druze—was persecuted. The new caliph declared in no uncertain terms that his father was *not* the Mahdi. They were driven underground, the tenets of their faith derided and subverted. They were deemed heretical by both Sunni and Shi'a, accused of Gnosticism, devil worshipping, plurality, subversion of the Koran—the usual litany of heresies."

"So they closed up shop. Went into hiding, started speaking in code, started creating cells of information, started chains of command to protect their top people." Hoffman, stoned, happily imagined it all.

"Like the Mukhabarat," Behruse cut in. "Like Al Qaeda."

"Like the other famous society, the Hashisheen of Alamut of Hassan ibn Sabah," Avicenna said. "The principles of covert action, my friend, are ever the same. The Druze went one further. In 1043, they closed their ranks completely. Proselytizing was forbidden. No more new members since then. For almost a thousand years now, you have to be born to full blood Druze parents to be considered Druze."

"But are these Druze dangerous?" Hoffman asked. "What do they want?"

"They want the return of their Mahdi, of course," Avicenna said. "A return to pre-eminence, perhaps. Certainly, they want their vengeance against Sunni and Shi'a alike. The rest is conjecture, really. Who knows what their mandate is after so many years."

"And the watch?" Hoffman sniffed at the air. A lot of time seemed to pass before he could shake himself awake: "What the hell is up with this watch?"

"Ah the watch," Avicenna leaned forward. "The watch, I believe is a kind of map. It is a cipher to help the Druze preserve their knowledge."

"What knowledge?" Hoffman asked. "Do they have any weapons of mass destruction?"

"Conjecture, again."

"Well your guess is certainly better than mine," Hoffman drawled tiredly.

"I firmly believe the watch hides the knowledge of finding the one thing the Druze have yearned for all these years."

"And what's that?"

"Nothing less than the old dream of the alchemists, the secret to—"

But Hoffman was slumping, losing the thread.

"Cool, man," he muttered, "You think you could alchemize a sandwich or something for me? I'm starving."

11: LOST IN SPACE

On Sunday, Dagr was invited for tea to the visiting room of Mother Davala, where she regularly held court with a surprising number of visitors. Having spent the past two days in relative boredom, enduring the paranoid ravings of Hamid and the dark chafing impatience of Kinza, he was glad for the respite. Sweet mint tea was on offer this time, and as Mother Davala had dispensed with her silent, veiled companions, they were able to occupy the two wing back chairs in the alcove by the window, and thus bathed in the filtered light of the late afternoon sun, enjoy a repast complete with sweet fig cake and some aged baklava.

Over the past three days, Dagr had been the victim of highly irregular meal times. The kitchen was ruled by a mute tyrant, an emaciated man with a drooping mustache, who, far from taking requests, declined to even speak to any of his fellows. His helper was a pasty-faced sneak, a half urchin caught in some mysterious warp of growth, who appeared twelve one day and sixteen the next. In return for certain deposits to the kitchen fund, these two miscreants bought and prepared the barely edible fare of hummus and lamb, which was served to the rooms at almost any peculiar hour *except* for mealtimes. Neither bribes nor threats had so far had any impact on these men.

Dagr brought this issue up delicately with his hostess and was promptly rebuffed. She declared that the chef had been in her family for generations, that he had cooked for fallen princes and deposed kings in his time, had catered to heads of state on the run, and was the possessor of 71 bona fide secret recipes, including the all famous ageless baklava they were eating at the very moment. Thus, taking the risk of offending him was out of the question.

Dagr, who had been about to eat this brick-like dessert, now held it up to the sunlight to appreciate it further. The corners of the pastry were translucent, where the honey had hardened into a fine knife's edge. In this pale yellow sap, he could discern the thousand layers of dough, finer than tracing paper, folded and refolded in secret almond paste. He was about to eat it, when his hostess informed him that this very batch had been prepared at her last wedding feast, over four decades ago.

"We have had little reason to celebrate since then," Mother Davala said. "Besides, sugar from middle age onwards is deadly."

"You say last wedding feast," Dagr said, astonished.

"Oh I've put more than one husband into the grave," the crone grinned. "You do, you know, when you get to live as long as I have."

"Well," Dagr said, "women seem to live much longer than men."

"Particularly Iraqi men," Mother Davala said. "It's the temper of the blood. Leads to apoplexy. Like your friend Kinza. He won't be dying in bed, I'd say."

"He doesn't even want to, the fool," Dagr said glumly.

"I received a message from that boy Xervish," Mother Davala said. "He wants to speak with you privately."

"With me?"

"Certainly."

"I don't know him."

"I imagine he felt you were the most reasonable man in your little party," Mother Davala said.

"The most cowardly, you mean," Dagr said.

"The world is upside down, professor," Mother Davala said. "You, who had a family, a respected profession, a bright future, are now worthless dross. Men like Kinza, petty criminals destined for imprisonment, are now the only ones with the skill to survive."

"What do you know of my family?" He put down his cup with a rattle, spilling tea over his pants.

"Nothing," Mother Davala said. "Merely that you once had one and now evidently do not."

"I once had one," Dagr said mechanically. *I still have them. Do you think they just go away?*

He stared down blindly, loaded down by the weight of ancient baklava in his hand. Its faint perfume of honey and butter wafted out, settling a miasma over him, letting his mind drift back unmoored, back to his old kitchen. He remembered his wife's dark curls spilling out of her scarf as she bent over the wooden counter, kneading dough with butter. The little blue ashtray in which she always deposited her two rings, one from him, a dull gold one from her father; his own ineffectual motion around the small, heated space, dancing around with his daughter, taking turns trying to crush nuts in the stone mortar, spilling things, and getting scolded.

It had been her fifth birthday, her last birthday. They were making baklava from scratch, an ambitious project, for neither of them cooked very well. Dagr tended to burn everything, and Zenere tried to follow recipes with mathematical exactitude, causing her to take hours over the simplest task. They had failed in the undertaking of course, and she finally stopped folding the dough when Dagr pretended to faint with hunger, his body twitching comically on the kitchen floor, while their daughter giggled hysterically. In the end, he had gotten out the store-bought cake he had stashed away, chocolate with orange peel inside and dark icing, and five candles, and Zenere had scowled at him, muttering threats of never ever baking for them again.

Threats that came oddly true, for they *had* never baked again, and bit by bit the pastry sheets, the rolling pins, the cookie cutters had faded away, until they existed now only in his mind. It had been a good birthday. The power went off but they ate cake in the candlelight, and Zenere had played the guitar, and they had all danced together.

The physical sweetness of this memory swept everything away so that he sat lost in his armchair until his tea was cold, and even Mother Davala's conversation had run dry. His reverie was broken by the entrance of Xervish. The past few days had not been kind to him, Dagr immediately saw. Circles shaded his eyes, his hair hung down in greasy locks, melding into a heavy four-day beard. He dragged a chair over to them at the behest of Davala and sank into it heavily.

"Xervish, dear, you look awful." Mother Davala handed him the tea things.

"You don't know what it's like out there," Xervish said. Exhaustion framed every line of his body, from his shaking knees to the ticking muscle in the side of his neck.

"You wanted to speak most particularly to the professor," Mother Davala said. "I suggest you take this opportunity for I do not know how long Kinza will stay distracted."

"The Americans are looking for you. They know your names. They know about *Hamid*," Xervish said. "Hassan Salemi is looking for you. His people are everywhere. Now there are whispers in the alleys that some old Mukhabarat is asking for information too. Every informant rat walking the streets is looking for you."

"Mukhabarat? Why?" Dagr asked, confused, his brain still scrambled by the smell of half-baked baklava, in a kitchen which no longer existed.

"I don't know," Xervish grabbed his arm feverishly. "But they're bad news. You think they're finished? They're not. They'll kill everybody. Or Hassan Salemi will." He laughed. "You guys are fucked. We're all fucked. They'll find this house. They'll burn it to the ground."

"What did you want to say to me, then?" Dagr asked, suddenly irritated. "I never wanted Kinza to call you. We should have just stayed on our own."

"On your own?" Xervish said. "You wouldn't get ten yards down the street on your own. I can help you. I can help Kinza. I *have* to help him. I have a way."

"So?"

"There's too many of you!" Xervish cried. "I told Kinza this, but he never listens. I *told* him, but he just never does the easy thing. I came to you because you seemed reasonable. Please, just listen to me. I have a setup with some Blackwater truck drivers. They're taking a convoy out to Mosul in a few days. That's where you want to go, right? The trucks are going to be empty. They'll smuggle you out."

"Empty?"

"Yeah, they get hazard pay for every mile they drive," Xervish said. "So they make extra runs every month, just drive out and back, whether anyone needs anything or not. They got armed escorts, man. They got helicopter support. It's *safe*."

"And they'll take us?"

"The driver is a friend of a friend," Xervish said. "He doesn't care about politics. He just wants to get paid. I set it up already. But he won't take all three of you. There's no room in his rig. There's a little hollow space under the seats. It fits one person, maybe two. No way three will fit."

"So that's the problem."

"I know Kinza," Xervish said bitterly. "He won't go. He's a stubborn fool. He always was, even as a child."

"And you want me to tell him what?" Dagr asked, knowing already why Xervish was staring at him with those pleading eyes.

"I would think that was obvious, professor," Mother Davala said mockingly. "One of you is surplus."

"Hassan Salemi only wants Kinza, really. And the Americans want Hamid and Kinza, mostly," Xervish said. "They don't really want you. No one really wants you...I mean no one wants to specifically kill you. If they got out of town, you could just lay low for awhile."

"I understand," Dagr said, feeling cold. And he did understand, of course. Xervish was sticking his neck out, had already risked everything to set this up. He owed Kinza from before, was still clearly terrified of him, but how far could that bond stretch? In these times, who did favors for strangers? But Kinza had made his wishes plain, had stated in cold fact that he wouldn't go alone, and perhaps on some level he did not want to go at all. He was manic about words once uttered and would never, *could* never, back down from a declaration like that.

No, Kinza would send Xervish away and, after brooding for days, would quite possibly decide to take the fight to Salemi himself. He was not a man who accepted higher authority, or *force* for that matter; it had been Dagr who had kept them going before, Dagr backing down, negotiating, finding ways, staying low. And now those dynamics had changed. Now they had Hamid, stuck to Kinza like a piece of lint, whispering poison in his ear every day, encouraging that brutal side of him, trying to use him like a weapon, perhaps, and Dagr wondered what would happen to his friend, eventually.

"He'll listen to you!" Xervish said. "You have to convince him. It's the only way. They have to leave now!"

"He might listen." Dagr hesitated. Kinza might, if Dagr convinced him he *wanted* to stay back, that it was time to part ways. But Kinza was not stupid, was eerily smart at reading people and assessing situations, and he would possibly see through the charade. And if it came to a contest of wills, there was no doubt in Dagr's mind who would win.

"You will try?"

"And what happens to me?" Dagr asked. He saw Xervish's head droop, the eyes swiveling furtively, and knew that there *was* no plan for him, that he would be left behind, cast away like the rubbish of so many other lives. Oddly, this did not upset him too much. It was a sort of relief, almost. He wanted to put his hands up and say, it's ok, you tried. I tried. It's over now. Whatever happens now can just happen.

"I'll hide you somewhere else," Xervish babbled. "I'll move you around until they make the next run to Mosul. One month wait, maybe, the heat should die way down by then."

"Or maybe Hassan Salemi will be satisfied with just me," Dagr said. "Whatever. I don't care. I'll try to get to Mosul somehow on my own." He couldn't resist that last jibe, couldn't trust Xervish at all, this man who so blithely demanded his sacrifice.

"You think I'll sell you to them," Xervish stared darkly at him and then shuddered. "Trust me. No one deals with Hassan Salemi and wins. There's death, and there's painful death. That's all he knows. Do you think a man like me could stand in front of him and *negotiate*?

They know about me. They'll know I helped Kinza escape." He looked at Dagr with big bruised eyes, an appeal full of weakness. A man who would try to do the right thing and invariably fail, yet he was believable all the same, at least in the terror folded into every crease of his eyelids, the cable-taut muscle that pulled compulsively in his jaw. Dagr believed that much, that it wasn't a deliberate trap, and it gave him some relief, some hope that he might be able to slip through the cracks.

"They'll *come* for me sooner or later. Don't you understand that?" Xervish said, "You think Imam Salemi's just going to let it go? I'm finished, like you, like Kinza...my whole life here...gone. Kinza doesn't know what he asked for. You don't mess with these people. They don't let things go..."

"I know that," Dagr said. "But Kinza doesn't accept consequences like normal men. He won't bend, you see. People like us get crushed in his wake."*Sympathy for you? Yes, because we're probably both dead, unless one of us shops the other first, and even then, you're absolutely right. There is no winning with people like Salemi.*

"I'll come to Mosul with you!" Xervish said, grabbing his arm. "I swear, you and I will take the next empty run to Mosul. I told you, they do it every month. We'll go together, get out of this damn city."

Dagr looked at him with pity. "Sure we will."

12: REPRISALS

THE STREET TOUGH CALLED YAKIN, WHO HAD ONCE ESCORTED Kinza to the home of the Lion, was now an important man in his small patch of Shulla. In the chaos following the death of Ali Salemi, there had been a power vacuum of sorts, which he had been able to adroitly fill, given his proximity to all the action.

The neighborhood did not know the details of the fatal occurrences of that night, and his quick thinking had given birth to a new truth. He, Yakin, had chased away the Lion of Akkad, that Druze criminal who had been plaguing them with impunity. *His* gun had ensured the safety of the people. After the midday prayers, he had taken everyone to see the Lion's hideout, pointing out the various places where they had fought. The people had seen the blood stains, the remnants of that pitiful hoard of loot, and taken note of Yakin as a man to watch.

In the following days, as it became apparent to Yakin that neither the Lion of Akkad, nor Kinza, nor Ali Salemi's lieutenants were going to return, he began to remember additional truths. He, Yakin, had sensed that Kinza was a criminal. *He* had alerted Ali Salemi of this fact. When Kinza had ruthlessly shot the poor imam's son in the street, *he, Yakin,* had shot at him and chased him off, probably killed him outright, because he certainly remembered winging him. Oh yes. The other two men who had been with Kinza were also dangerous criminals. The man called the professor had been a bomb maker, some kind of technical wizard. And the other man, that Hamid, had been one of the high ups of Saddam's regime, a most dangerous secret service type, who had murdered hundreds of Shi'a in the night.

In his feral youth, Yakin had learned that power was ethereal; in a vacuum, if the skin of power was donned quickly enough, if those first few rivals were put down fast, if those first adherents did not falter, then it all became *real*.

Already, people in the street were greeting him differently, offering the *salaam* first, with the bowed head, and lately, he had stopped paying for all food and drink in return for making his rounds. Important for the first time in his life, his one anxiety was Amal. Day after day, he waited for the hammer to drop, for that grizzled shopkeeper to show up his lies.

He took to visiting Amal day and night, giving him the eye, making sure he had at least two or three thugs with him at all times. Amal, however, had trouble meeting his gaze. At first, with a gratifying flush of power, Yakin thought it was out of genuine fear. Later, upon reflection, he decided that this was unlikely. Amal had guns, after all. He had lived through loss and heartache and the worst of the war. Moreover, Amal knew exactly what had occurred that night, who had shot at whom. Drawn by fear, he took to hanging on Amal's doorstep, trying to elicit a reaction, to figure out how far Amal would let this play.

In the end, he learned another valuable lesson about the weakness of man. Amal, he realized, was actually *ashamed*. He had some kind of antiquated moral code. He believed in useless things like honor and debt—frivolous, intangible things—that possibly mattered once but no longer. The truth of the New Baghdad was far different. Freedom had a price, as the Americans loved saying. In the balance book of Yakin's mental list, it was evident that it was this fallibility of other men that was his primary asset, for other men couldn't commit to the primacy of self, to damn the world for a dollar in his pocket, to fuck all the tomorrows for one hour today. He was, he knew, a hyena on two legs, but no part of him regretted this.

Thus, it was near dusk on the seventh day of his reign that found Yakin sitting in his favorite chair outside the stylish Dervishes Café, smoking shisha and drinking coffee, the bulge of his revolver very evident in his waistband, although he had prudently taken out the chambered bullet, for he had heard countless tales of men shooting themselves in the balls. His tobacco was first rate, the best blend of the Swirling Dervish, gratis, which was a good thing since he had never been able to afford it before. The coffee, too, was delectable, the best in Shulla, maybe the best in Baghdad, which was, in truth, the best in the world, for Baghdad was undoubtedly the birthplace of coffee, regardless of what those men in Seattle said.

Yakin was reasonably happy. He had money in his pocket. He had two companions sitting across him laughing at his jokes. Just this afternoon, he had met Saira in the room above the café, had kissed her and felt her up beneath her skirt, had extracted promises of more. So when he saw three men in Salemi clan scarves ambling up the road, he wasn't really surprised. In his experience, God waited for moments such as these to fuck him over.

Only seven days, for God's sake, he thought. I haven't even gotten laid yet. His friends were melting away. The other café patrons hastened inside. He wanted to move, but he couldn't. Some deeply honed instinct, critical for bullies, told him he was outgunned and that it was better to sit tight and preserve some dignity. The revolver barrel felt hot against his crotch. He wanted to pull out the gun, but his muscles felt loose, disjointed. Too late. *Seven days…*He could see the black fabric bunched up around Saira's thighs, the thin shading of down going up, and the smell of her, still on his fingers…*it's not fair.*

All too soon, the three beards reached his table. They sat down without a by-your-leave—a studied rudeness that left no doubt in all the patrons of the Dervishes which way this conversation was going to be conducted. Saira was watching from the cash register. He could see the side of her face. The others, his neighbors, so respectful just this morning, were watching avidly, weighing him, no doubt mentally cancelling him out. It was intolerable. It was the story of his life.

"Salaam," Yakin said, trying for that black stare, but his eyes faltered when he looked at the man in front of his face.

"Salaam, peacock," the man replied. He was tall, in a spotless long coat, his beard neat and gray, his eyes also gray, but lighter and filled with dreadful intelligence. His scarf was tied around his neck with all the care of a cravat and he sat easily at Yakin's table, as if he owned the café and was welcome to sit at any table. There were no weapons on him, and this, too was a palpable fact.

"I am Hassan Salemi," he said.

"I know," Yakin croaked. "Sir."

"I have been waiting," Hassan Salemi said, "for six days, for a visit from you. Hearing that you are a busy man, I have finally decided to come see you myself. Are you a busy man, peacock?"

"No, not so busy," Yakin said, suppressing a shiver. "Sorry, sir. And please accept my condolences. I was on the verge of seeking an audience, imam, but I expected you were busy with the funeral."

"Ah yes, my poor son," Hassan Salemi smiled. "I told him not to play with guns. He was a fool. Don't you think so, peacock?"

"No, imam," Yakin floundered. "It is a great loss to the..."

"Community, yes, a very great loss. The community will hardly survive without his posturing," Hassan Salemi said. "He was decidedly a fool. But he was my son, nonetheless. No doubt he deserved what happened to him. But to be called out in the night and then ambushed and slaughtered like a dog in the street, that is somewhat insulting to me."

"It was a tragedy, imam," Yakin said. He's mad, he thought numbly. He doesn't care at all about his son, and so he's going to kill me too, without any remorse. Yakin's fingers trembled on his lap, and he thought wildly about going for his gun, about shooting this cold monstrosity in front of him. But his courage was gone, his body flaccid, and all he managed was to slump deeper in his chair.

"I need to know some facts, peacock. Just plain speaking, as if we were honest men," Hassan Salemi said calmly. "First, who called my son that night?"

"Old Amal," Yakin said, thinking frantically how much blame he could shift. "He spoke to your son on the phone."

"Who else was there with him?"

"About ten or so others from the neighborhood," Yakin said.

"Including yourself?"

"Yes," Yakin said, afraid, reliving those fatal moments, remembering now that it had been his own idea, him and his friends', that Amal had disagreed at first. Madness. How much would Amal refute? Was it possible to silence him? No, even in the heyday of his power, gone scarcely ten minutes ago, Amal had treated him with only grudging acceptance—more as another burden, he realized now, rather than as an overlord. He had been blind, *blind*. Why hadn't he foreseen this day? Why hadn't he tidied up behind him?

"Now, what exactly was your collective intention here?" Hassan Salemi, who had been studying him, now broke through his panicked thoughts.

"Nothing," Yakin stammered. "We wanted to hand over the fugitives. We thought we would get a reward."

"A reward?" Hassan Salemi smiled. "You may yet get a reward."

I don't doubt what sort of reward you have planned for us, Yakin thought.

"Now, dear peacock," the Imam continued. "How did you come to meet these men, these killers?"

"Amal, it was Amal!" Yakin almost wept, cursing the old man. "He wanted them to kill the Lion of Akkad, but they failed, and instead they killed your son!"

"Ah yes, this elusive lion," Hassan Salemi leaned forward. "Do you think I believe in fairy stories, peacock?"

There was the unmistakable sound of a pistol cocking, somewhere behind him, and Yakin knew they would not hesitate to blow him away in this very café, in broad daylight.

"Ask anyone," he said, deadly still. "I would not lie to you, imam."

"That remains to be seen," Hassan Salemi said. "Now, where did these men come from? There were three of them, I believe."

"They walked over from Ghazaliya. That's all I know."

"Walked over from Ghazaliya," Hassan Salemi said slowly. "Funny, I remember an American checkpoint across that ditch. I myself would have trouble walking into Shulla from South Ghazaliya. Yet these three men magically appear. Was one of them white by any chance?"

"No, of course not," Yakin said sullenly. "They were like us, ordinary. One of them was a professor. It was his stupid idea to find the Lion. And the other two were thugs, regular gun men, I think, criminals probably."

"Street thugs, you say?" Hassan Salemi frowned. "Men like that don't get past American checkpoints. Men like that don't shoot bullets at my son *in Shulla*. Are you merely stupid, peacock, or are you hiding something?"

"I don't know. I told you Amal found them," Yakin said. "Ask him."

"Yes, I think it is time to do exactly that." The imam got up. His men pulled at Yakin's shirt, hauling him to his feet, deliberately shaming him. "Come, peacock. You live for a while longer."

They shoved him down the street, making a show of it. The imam strolled behind them, unconcerned, letting his men have their fun. They wanted him cowed and beaten. Yakin was glad enough for the abuse; it meant they weren't going to shove him into an alley and blow his head off—not right away at least.

The old man was in his shop, as always, counting his rotten fruit. He looked up morosely at their noisy entrance, eyes drooping, resigned to the visit, it seemed. Yakin cast his mind back, remembering Amal's curious apathy throughout the week, and realized that the man had been expecting this visit, possibly anticipating his own death.

"Imam," Amal salaamed deeply, the respect genuine. "I have been expecting you."

"Then let us get to the point," Hassan Salemi said brusquely. "You, shopkeeper, tell me the story. Leave nothing out."

"We stopped three men who crossed into Shulla," Amal said. "There was a man preying on us whom we called the Lion of Akkad. It was said he was working for you."

"That is incorrect," Hassan Salemi said. "I do not rob people in that fashion."

"Not by explicit command, perhaps, imam," Amal said carefully. "But your men—your captains—it is not possible to refuse them, sir, nor to seek clarifications on their demands."

"I see."

"Lord, also it is not always money they desire," Amal said. "I say this to you to show anyways what life is like for us. We are at the mercy of passing wolves."

"How you live is of no interest to me. Continue,"said Hassan Salemi.

"We asked these men for help," Amal said bitterly. "These strangers. We asked them for help when our own couldn't help us. And they were honorable men for what it's worth. They tried their best and maybe even succeeded. We made the mistake of calling your son, of betraying them."

"Now you interest me," Hassan Salemi said. "What were the terms of this betrayal?"

"There was rumor," Amal said, "of a renegade Ba'athist; one of the old guard, a vicious man, who had tortured and murdered many Shi'a. We thought one of these men…we thought one was he. We called your son. He was excited. He wanted them right away. He gave no time for planning," Amal spread his hands. "I warned him. I tried to tell him these men would not go quietly."

"He was a fool, in fact, my son," Hassan Salemi said quietly.

Amal paused, startled. "Yes, yes he was a fool," he said finally. "He came loudly, with trucks full of men, firing in the air. They shot back. It was a fair fight, imam, I swear."

"Fair fight or ambush, I have yet to decide," Hassan Salemi said. "Now where are these men hiding?"

"I don't know," Amal said. "They escaped. The police came. There was a gunfight in the streets."

"So strangers come to help you, you betray them, and then they kill my son," the imam said. "They evade my son's men, and our fine national police help them escape. One of them, you say, is an escaped Ba'athist, a wanted man who crosses American checkpoints with impunity. Tell me, Amal, that it is so simple."

"I swear I know nothing else."

"Perhaps," Salemi said.

He signaled, and one of his men left Yakin to go upstairs. Amal stared after him, aghast, and then bulled forward with a cry when he understood. The second gunman intercepted, throwing him to the floor, his gun out. There was a scuffle, and then Amal was flat on the ground, his head pushed to one side, a boot on his neck. The gun swiveled once from the prostrate shopkeeper to Yakin, a lazy circuit, its meaning clear. He was now almost superfluous. He sat absolutely still, willing Amal to desist.

"Hush, hush." Hassan Salemi crouched in front of the old man.

"Please, lord, we didn't know. Imam, in the name of God have mercy."

"You have no more answers, you say," Hassan Salemi said softly. "Be at peace then, old man. I too have lost a son. The pain...passes."

"No, no!" Amal cried, his face contorted against the floor. "Please, imam, mercy. He is the only one I have left!"

There were sounds of scuffling upstairs, dull, ugly noises, and the sharp screams of an adolescent, painfully high.

"Come, you know nothing else?" Hassan Salemi asked. "These men were not friends of yours? You weren't helping them escape? To ambush my son?"

"No, no, I'm Shi'a! Shi'a! I swear, I don't know them. I don't know any Sunni scum."

"You truly do not know where they hide?"

"I don't know them!" Amal shouted. "Yakin knows them better than me. For God's sake, he spent days with them!"

"Be at peace then." The imam walked to the door.

Yakin started to rise, to protest, but two great noises shuddered through the house one after the other, and he sat back down stupidly, stunned. Fat drops of red hit his face, and he thought it was his own. But it was Amal's blood, and the old man thrashed incoherently, his spine ruined. The gunman came down the stairs, pistol slack in his hand, and Yakin understood that the boy, too, was dead.

"Come, peacock," Hassan Salemi said. "This is your lucky day."

13: ROOTS OF THE LION

HOFFMAN WOKE UP IN DISARRAY, HIS EYEBALLS TURNED INSIDE out, his throat raw from smoke, and a midget triphammer gunning in his cortex. His first instinct was to reach for his cigarettes, which were gone from their usual place beneath his pillow. Half awake now, he fumbled for his 9 mm, which also was not under the pillow. His Navy MK III knife, won at cards from a disgraced admiral, was not in his boot, where it normally spent nights. For that matter, his boots were not there on the floor beside his bed either.

A slow reconnaissance was in order, and he performed this with due stealth. The room was unfamiliar and elegant. The sun streamed in from an open window, and it was this brutal light that had woken him. He got to his feet, found his way into a dressing room. Propped up on a stool was the full complement of his gear, his clothes pressed and folded, the knife sheathed to the boot, his holster and gun placed thoughtfully on top.

He dressed, lit a cigarette, winced at the drumming in his head, and started to wander out. Avicenna's house, he vaguely recalled from last night, was a series of deliberately confusing passages. He caught the smell of black coffee and followed it blindly, reaching the court-yard eventually, where a small table had been laid in the shade.

A dark-haired lady sat under the stunted olive, sporting over-sized dark glasses and a floral patterned Hermes scarf tied loosely around her neck. She was drinking coffee from a glass and smoking a thin, elongated cigarette, flipping through some glossy maga-zine, one slim Chanel enclosed foot tapping impatiently against the flagstones.

This sight was so incongruous that Hoffman stood slack jawed for several moments, the cigarette hanging from his lip like a hook from some kind of giant idiot fish. She deigned to notice him after a minute, looked up, and scowled at him.

"Don't stand there like a damned fool," she said. "What's the matter with you? Are you autistic?"Her voice was gravelly, attractive. Not least because, Hoffman had to admit, she didn't look at all like a mustachioed elephant draped in black, the standard of Iraqi ladies he'd normally met during his rounds on the streets of Ghazaliya.

"What? No." Hoffman shuffled forward, trying to avoid the sun.

"I heard many Americans are autistic," she said. "Some kind of genetic defect, I think."

"I'm just hung over," Hoffman said. He paused at the edge of the table and offered a snap salute, marred somewhat by his misshapen posture. "Sergeant Hoffman at your service... er, ma'am."

"We were introduced last night, idiot," she said. "You were drunk."

"Ah well, Avicenna offered me a whole bunch of bottles," Hoffman said. "You must be his...girlfriend? Nurse? Fourth wife?"

"My name is Sabeen. Granddaughter," she said. She pointed at the coffee pot with one manicured finger. "Help yourself. You look like something unpleasant died in your throat."

"Thanks," Hoffman said, pouring some into a chipped white mug. "I don't remember anything from last night. Did I do anything embarrassing?"

"Well, you ate and drank like an ill-bred buffoon. And then near the end, you puked and passed out," Sabeen said. "So, no, you simply reinforced my view of uncouth Americans. I'd say you behaved perfectly."

Hoffman tried for a winning smile and failed. "I hope I didn't offend you in any way."

"Not specifically, no," Sabeen said. She went back to flipping the pages of her magazine.

Hoffman said after some time. "Could I speak to Avi, maybe?"

"No," Sabeen said.

"Er, ok," Hoffman said. "Behruse then?"

"I sent that oaf out to work," Sabeen said, not looking up.

"Doing what?"

"None of your business," Sabeen said.

"Listen, I really don't remember about last night. I'm sorry if I pissed you off," Hoffman said, extending his hand. "Can we start over?"

"You probably think that's charming," Sabeen said, not moving an inch.

"Your English is really good," Hoffman persevered.

"I was at Oxford," Sabeen said.

"What did you do there?"

"Studied English."

"What do you do now?"

"My grandfather controls numerous assets," Sabeen said. "I am his chief of security. I make sure no one bothers him."

"Hey, Behruse brought me here," Hoffman raised his hands in the air. "I'm not a hostile."

"I know. Grandfather sent me to protect you," Sabeen said. "He finds you interesting for some reason. He's finally gone senile I think."

"Protect me? Ma'am, I'm a United States Marine."

"Marine?" Sabeen smiled genuinely for the first time. "Your uniform is infantry, and your sergeant's stripes look pretty new, so either they're fake, or some other moron saw fit to actually promote you."

"There is a Humvee full of extremely dangerous men at my beck and call," Hoffman said. "I am a death dealing machine, armed to the tooth."

"Have you actually looked at your gun?" Sabeen asked.

Hoffman pulled his prized desert eagle out with a flourish and cocked it theatrically. The sound was hollow, decidedly wrong. A closer inspection revealed that the clip was empty, as was his ammunition pouch. His face fell.

"I'm pretty sure I didn't shoot anyone," he said.

"No. But you passed out with your gun aimed at your crotch and the safety off," Sabeen said. "Anyone that moronic doesn't deserve to play with bullets."

"Heh, you'd love the other guys in my squad."

"Thank God I won't have to meet them." Sabeen stood up. Hoffman tried to rise and leer at her at the same time; blood rushed to his head, and he fell backwards, sending his chair sprawling.

"Sorry," Hoffman said, climbing to his knees. "I feel like I've been run over by a truck."

"No need to apologize," Sabeen said, helping him up. Her hand was surprisingly strong. "You've been poisoned. The head spinning is a common side effect."

"Eh? Poisoned?" Hoffman said.

"My grandfather is somewhat of a savant when it comes to chemistry," Sabeen seemed amused. "Or alchemy, if you prefer."

"Ohmigod my throat is seizing," Hoffman said. He clutched at his face convulsively. "I can feel my eyeballs popping. Are my eyeballs popping? Help me!"

"Relax, that's probably the alcohol," Sabeen said. "The poison *is* real, of course. It's slow acting, however."

"What kind of lunatics are you?"

"Stop whining," Sabeen said. "You don't think I'd just let you loose around my grandfather without any insurance, do you?"

"I just wanted to know about the Druze watch," Hoffman said. "I'm going to kill Behruse when I see him."

"Don't cry," Sabeen said. "I'll give you an antidote. It binds with the chemical compound currently in your blood. It should neutralize it in a week or so."

"A week or so? Should? Don't you know?"

"Well, it's not an exact science, is it?" Sabeen said. "Just tell me when you start feeling ill, and I'll give you a pastille."

"I'm feeling ill *now*," Hoffman moaned. "This isn't fair. What kind of person poisons an innocent stranger?"

"Really?" Sabeen said. "What kind of person makes up ridiculous lies about a random country, invades it, destroys all its civil institutions, brands all its citizens as terrorists, causes a civil war, and then pretends everything is alright?"

Hoffman glowered with righteous indignation but said nothing.

"Right. We have to go now," Sabeen said, adjusting her scarf around her head in one practiced motion. "Behruse is waiting. I'll drive."

There was a nondescript Toyota up front, which had the unnaturally scrubbed appearance of a car straight from the lot. En route, Sabeen informed him it was part of a fleet of "dead cars" they maintained. With the huge, unrecorded number of civilian deaths and migrations in the city, perfectly clean, registered cars were floating around with no legal owners. A cadre of bureaucrats from the General Directorate of Traffic with ties to the Mukhabarat had started a quiet side business of selling these "safe" cars. For a premium, one could borrow the identity of the deceased owner too: doctored licenses, registration papers, fitness records, even parking fines. Then too, there were many people who had to commute through Sunni and Shi'a strongholds and thus needed two separate identities. Anbar license plates, in particular, were anathema in Shi'a areas, where death squads, often the police themselves, hunted and shot motorists from that locality.

Sabeen drove with the exacting precision of a German car mechanic maneuvering a prototype. Iraqi police, she explained, loved pulling over women drivers, especially ones who did not wear the full hijab. While she carried a revolver in her purse and a shotgun under the passenger seat for exactly these kinds of emergencies, it was just common sense to follow traffic rules. She had been, she said, obliged to shoot two would-be rapists so far. Silly men, they had come at her with knives. Hoffman could only marvel at her blunt pronouncements and spent the entire ride staring with idiotic rapture at her profile.

The café they pulled into promised Lebanese food in big green lettering and was just short of swanky. She was evidently known here. As she set foot inside, the entire staff, including the cashier and the owner, converged on her, each one trying to outdo the next in salaaming deeper. Hoffman noted genuine respect, lust, and even downright terror in the menagerie; she must have shot some of *them* in the past too.

Behruse sat in a corner table facing the door, eating and drinking, his neck and shoulders creating an obscene shadow on the tablecloth. An array of half-finished dishes, Lebanese and otherwise, said that far from working, Behruse had, in fact, been sitting here for most of the day.

"God, how can you eat like that, Behruse?" Hoffman flopped down across from him.

"Eh? You want some lamb?" Behruse waved his hand unenthusiastically at him. "No? More for me. Have coffee instead. Americans love coffee."

"You're a sick man. I need some beer."

"This is lunch for me," Behruse said. "I already had breakfast."

"What the hell did you guys do to me last night?" Hoffman asked.

"You told him about the mushrooms?" Behruse looked at Sabeen, who shrugged.

"Mushrooms?"

"Sure," Behruse said. "Very rare stuff. It acts like a kind of retrovirus. Nestles in your spine in a dormant state for days. Then it starts releasing chemicals into your bloodstream. You start seeing shit. Grade A hallucinations, believe me."

"That doesn't sound so bad," Hoffman said.

"And then you start bleeding from all your orifices," Sabeen said.

"Oh."

"Don't worry. Sabeen has the stuff to keep it in check," Behruse said. "So long you don't piss her off, of course."

"After all our scams, all the money we've made together, this is what it comes down to?" Hoffman asked, with feeling. "We were brothers, man—and you go and poison me? What would your mom think?"

"Hell, the boss poisoned me too, first time he met me," Behruse said. "It's standard operating procedure with him. It messed up my metabolism. That's why I'm fat. You should have seen me before. I was like Mr. Baghdad. Eventually it goes away. By that time, he either trusts you or kills you."

Hoffman could only whimper.

"Stop your whining," Sabeen said. "Last night you couldn't wait to eat the mushrooms. Behruse, you have anything on the watch?"

"I checked all the drop boxes," Behruse said. "Mostly crap. Oh, Maliki is a fag apparently."

"Drop boxes?" Hoffman asked.

"Old school stuff," Behruse said. "You guys monitor cell phones and air waves. Heh, like pros use phones anymore. We got mailboxes rigged up all across town. Paper and pencil, baby, that's the way to go."

"I gotta remember this," Hoffman muttered.

"Don't worry. You work for Sab now," Behruse said. "I once saw her kill a man just by touching some nerves on his neck. Dim Mak, you know, the death strike."

Sabeen ignored the comment, asking: "Did you do anything at all useful today, Behruse? I'm not paying for this lunch by the way."

"It's on Hoffy's tab," Behruse said with a belch. "While I was sitting here resting after breakfast, I started thinking about the Druze stuff. I remembered an old report. Underneath the basement of the Al-Rashid Mental Hospital, there is a hidden ward for violent mental patients. About nine months ago, some Blackwater guys accidentally bombed it. Word was, they thought the crazy fucker Uday had stashed some of daddy's gold in there. Couple of his friends had suites there. Come to think of it, he even visited them sometimes. Anyways, I digress. After the Blackwater guys killed the guards and searched the place, they found no gold bars, so they pulled out. The place was wide open for like ten days before government officers came to lock it back up. A lot of patients simply wandered out."

"Behruse, is there a point to this?" Sabeen asked.

"One of our old Mukhabarat boys was put in charge of covering it up," Behruse said. "And he told me about a very interesting inmate. Their most dangerous inmate, in fact. They kept him sedated and shackled at all times. Apparently, he had the strength of ten men and could take 200 volts and keep walking. They used to trank him up and run bets on how many tazer hits he could take. His file name was Afzal Taha. Some of his ramblings included crazy religious stuff about reincarnation. As I always say, after breakfast my brain reaches genius levels. Superhuman strength, nutty attitude, religious crazy—something clicked. So right before lunch, I went over and got the file from my friend. Do you want to see it?"

"You haven't even looked at it yet? Give it here." Hoffman snatched it from Behruse's pudgy fist. It was a yellowed file discolored from water damage, tied with red string, bristling with papers of different sizes. The latest noting was done in a close, formal English handwriting in red ink, affixed with numerous seals. Hoffman read the script with his finger, his lips moving laboriously.

"Behruse, you're a genius!" Hoffman announced, forgetting momentarily that he had been effectively kidnapped and poisoned. "This man is the Lion of Akkad."

Then the smell of the lamb hit him, and he promptly threw up over the file, Behruse, and a tiny part of Sabeen's shoe.

14: WARDS OF THE STATE

THE FILE ON AFZAL TAHA WAS A CONUNDRUM. THE INDEX PROM-
ised an immense farrago of paperwork from over ten different public
institutions; sealed dossiers, letters of transfer, contradictory treatments and diagnoses, rosters of crimes committed, punishments
meted out, varied medications, experimental procedures carried out
on him, amid a sea of bureaucratic waffle and blame shifting. The body,
however, contained only a single volume in close handwriting, the
English extremely precise and formal, language typical of someone
whose fluency in a second language had been hard won. Small notes
had been penciled in cryptic Arabic in the margins, which Sabeen
said were mostly clarifications or references to other files, none of
which were included in the dossier.

This single report was the work of Dr. Sawad, who had been chief
administrator of the restricted wing of the Al-Rashid. His credentials identified him as a specialist in schizophrenia in violent offend-
ers. Stumped, Sabeen and Hoffman took turns trying to decipher the
pages, and Hoffman's attempts were desultory at best. Behruse, near
somnolent with the weight of three mid-day meals, lay basking in the
glory of his original good idea, flicking ash on the table, scattering
flies with his deep rumble, offering advice from afar.

"Here's Sawad's CV," Sabeen said. "Big credentials."

"Mukhabarat," Behruse said, looking over the picture. "I can tell."

"What, he has a secret haircut or something?" Hoffman asked.
"Seriously, Behruse, sometimes I think you just make shit up."

"You think the chief of the 'restricted' mental ward of a place like
Al-Rashid is not going to be Mukhabarat?" Behruse said. "What do
you think 'restricted' means? I'll tell you. Experimental procedures

equals: interrogation techniques, biological warfare, chemical warfare. Standard practice for Mukhabarat."

"You tested interrogation torture methods on mentally ill patients?" Sabeen asked. "That was standard procedure?"

"Hey, it's better than monkeys," Behruse said. "From a data gathering point of view, I mean."

"Listen to this," Hoffman cut in self-importantly. "I quote: 'Patient 99% certainty suffers from auditory command hallucination. These episodes are extremely powerful. Patient believes he is communicating with some unidentifiable religious icon. He is extremely secretive regarding these communications and refuses to divulge any details as to the nature of the hallucinations, despite intense questioning. Acute paranoia is present even in periods of lucidity."

"Hah!" Behruse said. "Intense questioning. What you think that means, habibi? Mukhabarat all the way."

"Anything about treatment there?" Sabeen asked.

"Some heavy drugs," Hoffman said. "Speaking of treatment, you wanna give me some more antidote? I'm feeling faint. Also, I think I'm seeing two of Behruse. I could swear he's gained weight since morning."

"I gave you a pill just two hours ago, for God's sake."

"I'm delicate," Hoffman moaned. "My insides are burning. I'm not a fat bastard like Behruse."

"Your insides burn because you're constantly high or drunk or eating weird shit," Sabeen said. "Now what were the treatments for this patient?"

"Mostly tranks," Hoffman said with a martyred air. "Sawad writes that the patient was extremely dangerous and responsible for injuring medical staff on three different occasions. He was kept in isolation and heavily drugged except for specific 'interview' days. These interviews were conducted by Sawad himself."

"And?"

"I can't find any details on these interviews anywhere. All references and annexure have been removed," Hoffman said. "Behruse is right. This guy seems to be hiding the good stuff."

"Wait," Sabeen said. "He wrote a long note in Arabic here. He's talking about enough interesting details to make a stand-alone paper. I think he wanted to submit something to the medical journals. He might have pulled all the annexure files for that reason."

"So we go and find this guy," Behruse said. "If he's Mukhabarat, he'll probably help us. If he isn't, we'll have to try out some interviewing techniques of our own. I'll call my friend."

An hour later, after a series of conversations, Behruse's mood had considerably darkened.

"This Sawad prick lived alone and worked alone," Behruse said. "Typical Mukhabarat. No friends, not much family, and they all appeared to hate him anyways. So no one missed him, really, when he *fell off his roof two weeks ago.*"

"He reminds me of you," Hoffman said. "Was it an accident?"

"His apartment was robbed two days prior to that," Behruse said. "What do you think?"

"The police didn't investigate?" Hoffman asked.

"Police? In this city?" Behruse said. "Robberies are pretty common, and falling off your roof is pretty common too. Two separate reports were filed with the police station, only because he was a government employee. No follow ups afterwards. I had an old friend pull up the police file. Guess what? The file got 'left behind' by accident when they shifted stations."

"You think it's the Druze silencing him?" Sabeen asked.

"Someone pretty well connected, anyway."

"So where'd his stuff go?" Hoffman asked. "Any kin? I thought you guys all had fifteen kids each."

"One daughter," Behruse said. "She might know something about his work. She's also a doctor, but she lives in the green zone. Can you get us in?"

"Hmmm," Hoffman said. "I might actually be in some trouble over there."

"For what?" Sabeen asked. "Deserting? Isn't that a shooting offence? Can we get invitations to the gallery?"

"No, they reprimand you strongly," Hoffman said, injured. "And you don't have to sound so excited about it."

"I'd like to watch if they shoot you," Sabeen said.

"I'm on a top secret mission, FYI," Hoffman said. "Full authority from high up. I just haven't checked in lately. Actually, you guys might be able to help me. You don't have any WMDs stashed away anywhere? Just a few would do."

"Are you high?" Sabeen asked.

"Well, I just had that one joint in the car, plus that last dose of the antidote, which, I gotta' say makes for a sweet head rush."

"For God's sake, Hoffman, you're not supposed to use the antidote to get stoned," she said, exasperated.

"Maybe Avi could arrange for one?"

Sabeen stared icily, "One what?"

"A WMD."

"No," Sabeen said. "And don't bandy his name about. Not if you want to keep your head."

"Just something small?"

"For God's sake, you idiot."

"I guess we'll have to improvise," Hoffman said. "Come on. Let's go. I might get stopped and questioned at some point. Just play along like a dumb foreigner."

The path across the Tigris was a continuous snake of traffic, slowed to an inching worm by the check-posts on the bridge. The 14th of July Bridge, originally called after the date of Ba'athist rise to power, had retained its name despite efforts by the Americans to change it to the Fourth of July Bridge, and, bizarrely, by the Georgian contingent to the "Tbilisi Bridge." The Georgians claimed that they, in fact, had captured the bridge originally and should have the conquerors' right of renaming it. For some reason, the Georgian name had stuck for some time, and a Tbilisi café had even sprung up nearby. Suspecting a conspiracy, the American high command had rotated the Georgian contingent away from bridge duty to some other part of the green zone; the Tbilisi lobby had faded away, and the bridge had reverted back to the old 14th of July.

The checkpoints here were staggered, manned by Iraqi security forces, and frequently peppered by incendiaries. While killing white skins were always a priority for militants, the new Iraqi army was also a popular target in a junior terrorist training exercise kind of way. Largely derided as imperialist lapdogs by militants, treated with contempt by the white soldiers, sneered at by former republican dogs, and with no esprit de corps or history to fall back on, these men were beset on all sides, on the verge of deserting at all times. Hoffman's stripes and easy banter got them across the bridge and several hundred meters into the green zone.

Approaching the hospital compound, however, they were stopped by a second checkpoint of American soldiers. The conversation here proved much tougher. Hoffman's papers were scrutinized, his "mandate" discarded with suspicion, Behruse questioned intensively. Somewhat discomfited by Sabeen's glare, they left her alone for the large part. Finally, it was decided that they should be escorted to the colonel's office for verification. The colonel, unfortunately, was detained elsewhere. Hoffman's status in the office was somewhat of a gray area. While his papers were signed and sealed by the colonel, any further records were consigned into the secret bowels of the vast black ops machinery the colonel purportedly controlled. The colonel, being widely known as secretive to the point of paranoia, did not like his various assets mixing.

Thus, they were largely ignored for several hours, until the arrival of Captain Fowler brought the office to life.

"Hoffman!" Fowler ushered them into a debriefing chamber. This was where the friendlier conversations took place. "Where the hell is your squad?"

"Searching out leads, captain!" Hoffman yelled at parade ground volume. The glass vibrated.

"At ease, soldier," Fowler glared at his companions. "What are you doing with these two I-raqis? This fat one looks like a criminal."

"They can speak English, sir!" Hoffman shouted.

"Sit down, all of you," Fowler said. "Explain yourself now, Hoffman. Colonel Bradley is most displeased with your lack of progress—and reports. Just the other day, we were discussing your court martial over a grilled squid brunch."

"Captain, these I-raqi citizens have helped me track down what we are looking for!" Hoffman said. "We are on the verge of a breakthrough."

"You mean it?" Captain Fowler leaned forward.

"The real thing, sir!" Hoffman brought forth a small carton of laundry detergent. "I have brought a small sample for you and the colonel!"

"What is this?" Captain Fowler took the box. "It smells like detergent."

"It's a partial weapons grade anthrax, sir!" Hoffman said. "Please be careful, sir! You have some on your cuff there."

"What?" Captain Fowler thrust the box back. "Anthrax? In laundry detergent? They have weaponized laundry detergent?"

"Precisely, sir!" Hoffman said. "Weaponized laundry detergent. Imagine our barracks flooded with this stuff, no shirts safe, no pants safe, not even skivvies."

"A devious plan," Captain Fowler stroked his cleft chin and then abruptly began to shake his infected cuff. "Precisely what we were looking for. You're onto something here, Hoffman. What are their production capabilities? Where are their processing plants? We'll bomb them to hell!"

"Sir, we are on the verge of finding this out," Hoffman said. "We need more time. And, er…, more cash funds, sir, for intelligence gathering. Also, a gunship on call in case I, er, need to call an airstrike."

"Right, that sounds reasonable," Captain Fowler said. "Weaponized detergent. I'd never have believed it. The devious cock suckers. The colonel will be apoplectic."

"Right, sir," Hoffman said. "I myself was extremely excited by the discovery. There are large caches of this stuff hidden away. Al Qaeda could get to it any second. We're on the right track. It's an amazingly delicate time. Any stray action can wreck our chances. In fact, we were on the way to interrogating someone in the hospital compound when we were violently stopped. By Sergeant Evans. You might want to investigate him. He looked a little uppity to me…probably a traitor…might even be CIA?"

"Hmm, yes, well don't worry about that. We know how to deal with other agencies trying to muscle in and take credit. Evans, you said? I'll post him to Kandahar. He won't be spying on us anytime soon. You get back to work. I'm giving you full clearance in the green zone," Captain Fowler said. "I need a written report, Hoffman."

"Reports, right, captain, Private Tommy has been making reports nonstop," Hoffman said. "I'm surprised you haven't gotten them yet."

"And give that sample to our hazmat team," Captain Fowler said, gingerly poking the detergent with a pencil. "We need to analyze it."

"Right, sir," Hoffman said, rising to leave. "I'll be sure to remember that."

Outside, a very young West Point graduate handed Hoffman a wad of unmarked bills, both Iraqi and US currency. In earnest tones, he quoted to Hoffman relevant passages from the CIA guidebook to bribery: Technical Assessment of Alternative Reward Based Systems (TAARBSTM), and made him sign and fingerprint various forms in triplicate. He then provided Hoffman with a hefty sat phone, capable of connecting directly with the pilot of Col. Bradley's personal AH64-A Apache, which apparently had gilded machine gun barrels and a bourbon bar in the rear cabin. A sealed file carried protocols and firing codes.

"See this?" Hoffman waved the phone at Behruse. "This is your gunship right here." He looked at the wads of cash in his hands and grinned "Get your dancing shoes on, boys and girls, we're gonna party green zone style."

15: OLD MEN

Dr. Nur Sawad was unmarried and no surprise since she was extremely unpleasant. Supercilious, suspicious, and scowling, her brusqueness was the product of a defensive shell that had hardened over time. She lived in a modern apartment block so far unscarred by bombing that had previously housed prominent Ba'athist families. With the advent of the new order, the Americans had moved their own critical staff into the green zone.

Dr. Nur had risen far under the aegis of her father, who had always wished for a son and cheated by fate had raised his only offspring in a pressure cooker of gender mixing confusion. A single parent, Dr. Sawad had forced on her both the need to succeed in the medical field and to fulfill the traditional duties of home and family.

Their long simmering resentment for each other had finally come to a head over her refusal to marry or have children. The physical split was further reinforced by Dr. Nur's relocation to the green zone to work for the Americans, a hideous defection in the eyes of her father. In the end, Dr. Nur had changed her surname and fully cut herself off from her only living relative.

They got past apartment security flashing Hoffman's varied credentials and caught Dr. Nur just as she was leaving for work.

"What do you want?" She cracked the door open an inch. There were various chains and other security measures. She appeared to be holding a weapon of some sort as well.

"Military intelligence," Hoffman said. "Just a few questions, ma'am."

"You have no jurisdiction here," Dr. Nur said. "Iraqi civilians are under the authority of Iraqi police. And your uniform is wrong. You look like a common infantryman to me."

"Er, yes, ah that is…"

"Excuse me, ma'am," Behruse shouldered himself into the narrow crack. "I am Lieutenant Behruse of the IPS, plainclothes detective. We are investigating your father's death, and its possible connection to the Al-Rashid Mental Hospital incident."

"I've already spoken to policemen," she said.

"We think he was murdered."

"Go away."

"Lady, let me in or I'm kicking the door." Behruse flashed a badge with his pudgy fist.

Apparently, this kind of behavior was more in line with standard police ops since Dr. Nur abruptly shut the door. There was the rattle of numerous chains being pulled, the snap of a padlock, and the door finally reopened wide enough for them to squeeze through.

"Who are you?" Dr. Nur asked, moving to block Sabeen.

"I am an executive partner of the law firm of Ibn Sina and Associates," Sabeen looked down her nose at the doctor. "We have an interest in the investigation of your father during his tenure at the Al-Rashid."

"I don't speak to lawyers," Dr. Nur said. "Please leave me a—"

"Specifically, of the restricted wing of the Al-Rashid, of which we know your father was the chief administrator," Sabeen continued.

"Get out of my house."

"Even more specifically, of the *experimental methods* your father used," Sabeen said. "For treatment of his patients, if you could call it treatment. What is your opinion now, doctor?"

Dr. Nur visibly deflated. "I told him not to take that job."

"Really?" Sabeen moved inside, like some kind of panther on the prowl. "Good advice. I wonder why he didn't follow it."

"He was too ambitious," Dr. Nur said. "He had full government backing at the time. More power than he knew what to do with. It went to his head."

"Full government backing, yes," Behruse said. "A government now extinct, unfortunately. The new regime is not so happy with him.

He experimented on human lives. What of his medical ethics, doctor? What of the Hippocratic oath?"

"Hippocratic oath?" Dr. Nur laughed, an ugly sound. "He didn't even know what that was."

"We want to know more about the time your father was killed," Sabeen said.

"What?" Dr. Nur said. "Your colleagues told me it was suicide. They refused to investigate anything. And they took money from me to leave me alone. Haven't you spoken to them?"

"They said it was suicide?" Sabeen asked. "What do you think?"

"It couldn't be. I told the police that," Dr. Nur said.

"He wasn't depressed?" Hoffman asked.

Dr. Nur shot him a withering look. "Of course not! He loved torturing those poor mental patients."

"Doctor, we have this file from your father's papers," Sabeen said. "It seems as if he was working on a special project, a scientific paper for publication perhaps or even a book. It would have been very important to him."

"He had a lot of secrets," Dr. Nur said. "And I didn't want anything to do with any of his work. It was one of the reasons we fell out."

"She's covering her own ass," Behruse whispered to Hoffman. "She knows something."

"How do you know?" Hoffman whispered back.

"I have a gut feeling."

"Behruse, you do know you aren't actually a cop, right?"

"Doctor," Sabeen said, glaring at them. "Your father was a Mukhabarat agent. Are you familiar with that term? That was the secret police apparatus of Saddam Hussein."

"I know nothing about this," Dr. Nur said.

"This paper he was working on, it was on a man named Afzal Taha," Sabeen said. "Are you familiar with that name?"

"No."

"Doctor, your father was killed because of this paper. We have a verbal statement from the coroner; he found burn marks on the body, like you would get if you put a lit cigar into someone's skin. He was tortured and then thrown off the roof."

"That's horrible."

"The police file is missing," Sabeen said. "The coroner's report is missing. Dr. Sawad's own papers are missing. Dr. Nur, I am quite certain your father talked before he was killed. His murderers are looking for his work, and I am sure they will find you sooner or later. You think you are safe in the green zone, but these are very resourceful people."

"Just go away. I told you I don't know anything."

"Fine," Sabeen said. "You know what we're going to do? We'll put a watch on your door, and then we'll spread the word that you have Dr. Sawad's personal effects. It'll be very interesting to see what kind of men come after you then."

"What!? You can't do that."

"Of course I can. I'm a lawyer. We don't have any morals."

"You're the police," Dr. Nur turned to Behruse. "You're supposed to protect me."

"Well, see, actually I'm going to turn a blind eye on this one."

Sabeen brought out the index file. "Do you have any of the documents mentioned here, doctor? Yes or no."

"Yes, fine," Dr. Nur said. "Father sent me some things to look over. He wanted my medical opinion. He was very excited."

"Bring us everything you have."

"What are you going to do with the papers?"

"Confiscate them of course," Sabeen said. "They are part of our investigation."

"You can't have them," Dr. Nur said. "I need them for my work."

"I don't understand."

"I am going to publish the case study," Dr. Nur said. "A joint work, with both our names."

"What? You'd rather we didn't find your father's killers?"

"Look, my father was a genius, and this case study was the culmination of his best work," Dr. Nur said. "It's my inheritance. I intend to cash in on it. It will make me famous. I might even get some sort of prize."

"You do understand, that people killed him to keep him silent?" Sabeen asked. "We need to remove these things from you for your own safety."

"Yes, well, I doubt these thugs read medical journals," Dr. Nur said. "Ours is a rarified world of academics, dear. You all wouldn't even understand half of the language being used. I'll just make some cosmetic changes to protect names and identities; it's done all the time in psychiatric case studies."

"All the same, we need the papers," Sabeen said. "Look, I'll write out a full receipt on my legal pad. You can reclaim them after the investigation is over."

Dr. Nur said. "Yes, fine, I'll show you what I have. But I want it in writing that you will return everything undamaged. No one knows I have them, and they won't know until I'm ready to publish. And if you find the remainder of his papers, I need your word in writing that I will have access to them first and that eventually they will be returned to me as part of his estate."

"Yes, fine," Sabeen said. She wrote out a contract on her legal pad.

"Wait here then," Dr. Nur said. "And don't touch anything."

She returned moments later struggling under the weight of a black Samsonite briefcase. She cracked it open and stroked the papers lovingly, like a miser polishing her horde. Grudgingly, she turned the case around. The briefcase was stuffed with a cacophony of papers, sealed, yellowed, typed, handwritten, some documents heavily scored with notes, many bound loosely together with yarn, and a few ancient-looking texts laminated in plastic to hold them together. Each document had been lovingly tagged with markers, numbered, and there were letters interspersed with them, handwritten in Sawad's script, presumably the silent conversation he had been having with his daughter in the days preceding his death.

"Like I said, dear, you probably won't understand half of it."

"Yeah, we're stupid, doctor," Hoffman leapt to his feet, pushed up by a poisoned anxiety. "Can you kinda give us the gist of it?"

"Gist of it?"

"Like give us the cliff notes version. The summary," Hoffman said. "What's this all about?"

Hoffman's presence, like a pointlessly cute kitten, seemed to soothe the woman somehow. Her gaze softened and she addressed him directly: "The patient Afzal Taha was one of the special cases of the restricted ward. He had been placed in absolute isolation by my father's predecessor. That itself was—is—unusual in a mental institute."

"OK," he said gently. He glanced at Sabeen and Behruse, motioning them to be still.

"He had attacked the security guards several times. Two of the men assaulted had actually died, although that was not common knowledge in the ward. The old administrator had been using isolation and electric shock treatments on Taha. The man had just been a stupid thug, not a scientist like my father. He didn't study the results on Taha nor did he notice anything unusual. Because he was in isolation for almost five years, none of the staff knew much about him either."

"So what did your father find out?"

"Well, first of all, that Taha had already been partially lobotomized earlier," Dr. Nur said. "Although there was no record of it at the Al-Rashid. The scars were there, and the kind of incision made indicated a method that is now out of date." She tittered. "I mean, dear, out of date in circles where lobotomy is still practiced, of course."

"Carry on."

"My father was the first one who had actually bothered doing a physical examination of all the patients, including the violent ones," Dr. Nur said. "Like I said, he was a real scientist. The lobotomy greatly intrigued him. He had been doing research along those lines earlier, I know, before I had been born. Anyway, he found some other anomalies too. For example, Taha's physical strength. He could—and had—torn through the normal shackles on several occasions. These were the times he had killed his guards, of course. The old administrator kept Taha sedated, and even then, the sedations were far too strong for a man: enough to knock out a horse, in fact. His was normally tied to a bed with heavy iron chains around arms and legs, as well as the straight jacket."

"A scary guy," Hoffman said.

"Many mental patients are prone to violence," Dr. Nur said. "But Taha actually seemed to want to escape, to retain a sense of purpose, if you will, despite the long period of institutionalization and the drugs. This was unusual."

"What else?"

"Taha's resistance to electric shock was the highest my father had ever seen in any human. I remember the day that he did his final tests. He was so excited, giddy like a school boy. It apparently took a hippo-sized dose to finally put Taha down. My father thought he must have built resistance to shock therapy over time, perhaps. It was very unusual."

"Go on, please, doctor, this is really helpful," Hoffman said gently, brushing at a bead of sweat he had not noticed before, dangling from his nose.

"My father took Taha off the tranquilizers. He started interviewing Taha. He was astonished. The man was extremely lucid and intelligent at some points and then completely hallucinating later. My father thought it was auditory command hallucinations: where the patient believes some external force is commanding him to act in a certain way. These are people who see angels or demons or whatever and are compelled by these visions to act out."

"What did Taha see, doctor?"

"That's the thing I don't know. My father did not share everything with me," Dr. Nur said. "Taha was paranoid. He never spoke about his visions, even under stress. It is unusual. Normally in these cases it is fairly simple to get an idea of what the patient is seeing. My father thought at one point that these visions must be the key to Taha's mystery. He started looking at old files, talking to old patients, anything to find out about the man's past."

"And what did he find then?" The bead of sweat was back, and he swiped again.

"The most unusual thing of all," Dr. Nur said. "He found records of Taha going back, and back, before the restricted ward had even been set up. He found police records years ago of violent crimes committed by Taha, prison records, different doctors testing him, treating him."

"So, he's a psycho with a long history."

"You don't understand," Dr. Nur said. "According to the oldest credible record, Afzal Taha is over a hundred years old."

Hoffman blinked at her and then at Sabeen and Behruse who had sat there listening to what had become an intimate exchange. "This poison is really something else," he said finally. "You got anything to make my nose stop sweating, doctor?"

16: THE BELLY OF THE BEAST

DAGR TURNED THE WATCH OVER AND OVER IN HIS HAND, AS HE had a hundred times before. His fingers had become attuned to the nuances of its surface, its peculiar weightiness. It was heavier than other watches, although Dagr assumed that was because all of his previous watches had been cheap and strictly functional. Kinza had once told him that mechanical watches were heavier, as they relied on actual moving parts, a technology wholly removed from the quartz movements of the cheap Japanese products he had been used to.

Kinza paced in front, with a seething impatience that had been wearing their nerves thin for days. The man had gone silent, but Dagr knew enough to sense the rage boiling close to the surface, and to fear it. Days had passed in discussion of Xervish's offer, slim hopes at first, burgeoning later into something desperate, when the actual contractor had come for a midnight meeting.

Xervish had indeed delivered. The meeting had been brief but convincing, even for Hamid's paranoia. The contractor was middle American, nothing more than a glorified truck driver, earning hazard pay by a peculiar permutation of fortune, hailing from a small town in some state called Idaho, a man so far removed from war that he seemed to carry about him a bubble of disbelief.

He had with him papers, permits, contracts, documentation beyond dispute, and an open friendliness, a desire to repay a debt to Xervish, a clearing of some unknown slate, and with their own assurances of harmlessness, a willingness to bend the rules of war. Dagr had been convinced that the offer was genuine. Hamid, who suspected traps, had run his own interrogation and then grasped at this escape route.

He now whispered in Kinza's ear like some dark crow, day and night stalking him, urging haste, extolling the virtues of moving fast, of arriving at a place that Sunnis considered a fort, where old guard influence still held sway, of connecting once again with men Hamid considered allies, far from Shi'a madness, of Mosul, Mosul, Mosul. Where he had once urged caution, he now urged immediate action.

Still Kinza refused to give him a date. Hamid grew desperate, thinking that perhaps Kinza considered leaving him behind and redoubled his efforts. Dagr knew, however, that it was not so much which two would escape that vexed Kinza. It was the act of running that hurt him, almost physically rooting him down. Hassan Salemi had called him out, put a price on his head, hunted him now like a dog, and Kinza's instinct was to strike back at his enemy, to leave the cover of this house and hit out on the street, into the heart of Shi'a power, and die perhaps.

Either way, Dagr reflected, his own chances were not good. This fact did not disturb him much. Kinza would decide sooner or later, and then the matter would be over. He rose finally, put the watch in his pocket. The feel of it was alluring, a heavy gold nugget in his hand and the slight whirring vibrations it made sometimes, as if the broken mechanism was on the verge of working.

"Where are you going?" Kinza asked.

"Library," Dagr said. *Anything is better than watching you grind your teeth.*

"How goes the mystery of the watch?" Kinza asked. "Found anything yet?"

"I took the casing off yesterday," Dagr said. "The insides are not normal. We're going to really take it apart today." He paused at the door. "You want to come? Might take your mind off…"

"Down there?" Kinza seemed to consider the rabbit warren of the library as some part of the underworld.

"Mikhail is very interested in mechanical objects."

"I don't think he likes me," Kinza said.

"He's afraid of you perhaps," Dagr said. "It took me a few meetings to befriend him. He loves the watch, though, so I don't think he'll mind."

"Alright then, but only for a little while."

"No pacing around though. Don't make him any more nervous with your jumpiness."

"I'm not jumpy."

"Sure."

"Really, I'm calm."

"You've decided then?" Dagr asked.

"I didn't say that."

The librarian awaited them eagerly behind a mountain of books he had gathered: old watch catalogues, extracts on gears and screws, mechanical principles, tomes on the history of watchcraft, trade books, and encyclopedias on mechanical engineering, among many others of dubious use. Some of these were ancient, literally disintegrating at first touch.

Mikhail had raided the volumes of discarded luggage to good effect. There were tweezers, clippers, a magnifying glass, and nail files from some beauty's valise. A physician's case had yielded small hammers, scalpels, needles, clamps, and other surgical tools. A pocket geometry set carried protractors, measuring rulers, and a compass. Then there were toolkits of various provenance, where minute screwdrivers, vises, calipers, tongs, and more had been unearthed.

Mikhail was thrown off by Kinza and hesitated for long moments, unsure of what to do, but the latter was on his best behavior and offered a smile between sips of tea and sat quite still with his hands visible. For all that, he still looked like a wolf that had wandered into the parlor. Refreshments dealt with, they got to the matter at hand.

Dagr fitted the watch face down on the tabletop clamp. He made small jabs at the metal case, at strategic places, small measured blows that in the right sequence caused the back of the case to spring loose. This they had learned by accident.

Inside was the same nightmare of unfamiliarity, bizarre despite hours spent pouring over watch diagrams. There was a spring, attached to the winding mechanism. That much was clear. The purpose of everything else was opaque.

"See the spring," Dagr peered through his handheld micro-scope. They each had one, different colors and sizes. His one was horn rimmed and with the best resolution since he was doing the actual work. "I don't understand what it's connected to. The gears are all wrong. Maybe they used to do it differently back then?"

"Not really," Kinza said. "The basic watch mechanism has been more or less unchanged from the first Breguets."

"There should be a gear like this," Dagr pointed at a glossy dia-gram, their principal source for identifying parts. "The main gear, which should connect to the catchment. And this spring basically retains the tension, which makes the watch go round until it's time for a winding."

"Did you try winding it up?"

"We did that yesterday. The hands don't move."

"But look at the spring. There's tension there. And this gear seems to be moving."

"So it's working?" Dagr looked again.

"It's doing something."

"The hands haven't moved even a single micrometer," Dagr said. He turned the watch over and put a piece of gridlined tracing paper on top to show them. "See, I took the measurements before."

"You're having fun with this, aren't you?"

"It's like a science project," Dagr shrugged. "We have nothing else to do."

"No, I mean, it's good," Kinza said. He smiled reassuringly at Mikhail. Dagr noted Mikhail's immediate alarm and reminded him-self to advise Kinza to avoid reassuring people in the future.

"Back to the spring. It obviously works."

"Are the gears really moving? I can't tell."

"Try to hear it. You might get a sound."

A few minutes of concerted silence, with all three of them bending their ears to the job, their heads comically placed, almost touching, the sound of breathing at first discordant, and then, in fine rhythm, as all three of them adjusted. Five minutes like that, straining—

"I heard that," Dagr said. "Did you hear that?"

"I heard that," Kinza confirmed.

"Yes," Mikhail said, as they both turned their eyes to him.

"Ok so it's a slow tick," Dagr said.

"Wait, be still!"

"What?"

"I heard it again."

"Shhh."

"Hear that?"

"I missed it."

"Dagr stop breathing for God's sake."

"I heard it. I heard it!" Mikhail, excited, clapped his hands.

"It's irregular then," Dagr said. "The beats are irregular."

"It can't be if it's a watch."

"Something might be jammed," Dagr said. "It could be a broken part somewhere inside, and this is just two gear heads rubbing against each other."

"I can't see anything broken."

"Nor can I, but we'd have to take it apart a bit more."

"Can you put it back together again?"

"Maybe. Probably not. I'm going to count the vibrations." Dagr put his finger on the round flat gear and closed his eyes. They sat still for ten minutes. "Ok, there are definite tremors. And it's completely without pattern. It doesn't feel broken. Should I take it apart?"

"I'd hold off," Kinza said.

"Why?"

"Well, either it's broken, or it's not. What if it's not broken?"

"Someone made a watch that tells irregular time?" Dagr looked at him strangely. "And the hands don't move. Not an iota. Either it's broken, or it's not a watch at all."

"That could be it, couldn't it?"

"It's not a watch?" Dagr stared at it, his left eye grown hideously distended through the microscope. "Not a watch. Superficially it looks like one, but it isn't. But someone went to great trouble to disguise it as one."

"The Druze?"

"Hmm, yes, since it's their watch," Dagr said.

"That's an odd thing to do."

"Well, they're Druze, aren't they?"

"True."

"Not that I'm anti-Druze or anything."

"The imam at our mosque always preached that they weren't really Muslim. The Druze, and Ahmadiyas. And on a good day, even Agha Khanis were out."

"You went to a mosque?"

"I used to walk past it sometimes."

"Never went in, did you?"

"To a mosque? Are you mad?"

"I haven't either, in a long time," Dagr said. "Perhaps I should have."

"How would that have helped?"

"Might have learned something about these Druze."

"Don't think an imam would be of much use there."

"I see." Dagr tapped the gear with his tweezers, a little bit disappointed. The urge to take apart the machine was almost unbearable. "Let's assume, for conjecture, that these Druze made a fake watch. What could be some reasons? A practical joke?"

"No one would bother preserving a joke watch," Kinza said. "It was given to Fouad Jumblatt. He's a bigshot, right?"

"Chief of all Druze in Syria at that time, I think."

"Plus, it's made of gold. The case, I mean," Kinza said. "It would be an expensive practical joke."

"Not a joke then," Dagr said. "What else?"

"Really useful if we could get hold of a Druze."

"Yes, even better if we had old Fouad with us."

"Joking aside, there must be a Druze somewhere around here. How did this watch get to Baghdad in the first place?"

"Maybe it's actually junk."

"It's a gold watch with Fouad Jumblatt's name on it. So, not junk."

"Why did the Lion have it?"

"Perhaps he stole it?"

"Perhaps it was his to begin with. Perhaps he *is* the Druze."

"Maybe we should ask him."

"Maybe we should."

17: GUN DAY

Monday was gun day. Or gun delivery day rather. Like a man worrying at a sore tooth, Xervish seemed to be unable to stop himself from returning to them much more often than was safe for him. Today was to fulfill a longstanding request from Kinza. Guns and ammunition and the last of their cash, extracted from a safehouse stash they had previously maintained.

It was a sign of the times that nothing retained stability, not even a hitherto thriving black market business. Without Hoffman's access and Kinza's ferocity to back it up, there remained virtually nothing of their criminal enterprise. Contacts switched off, customers moved on, suppliers dried up, safehouses were overrun: In effect, it was as if someone had taken a gigantic brush of whitewash to their past.

Guns and cash, however, were enough for Dagr, who had not been overly fond of their previous line of work to begin with. In the city, guns and cash opened up vistas of possibility. Yet when he saw Kinza stripping down the Makarov pistols, hands moving in a blur like some kind of violent pianist, he felt a moment of disquiet. There was in his stance a subconscious intent. Dagr wondered if, in the end, he would leave this city so quietly.

Xervish for once was in high spirits, regaling them with wild adventures from his childhood, in which Kinza figured as a chief tor-mentor and instigator. The haggard lines from his face faded and he appeared youthful again when he described how, at age five, they had attempted to rob the neighboring carpet store of its chief window dis-play, had staggered down a side street with a twenty foot long roll at a snail's pace, been caught and soundly thrashed.

They heard about the girls Kinza had stolen from him, the bro-ken Chevrolet they had inherited from an uncle, which Kinza had gradually fixed, the nights they had cruised happily in this vehicle, the bathtub brewery Kinza had persuaded him to make, with a view to augmenting their beer supply, and the acute poisoning Xervish had suffered as a result.

In all of these, Xervish cut a comical or desperate figure and Kinza as some kind of devil. Later, too, there were oblique references to the sister Xervish had lost, and Dagr guessed that she must have been one more thread tying them together, a big one, for Kinza's fingers tightened, and the rage flared in his eyes at any mention of her. Dagr could see the furnace at his core bellowing, could guess that the violence Kinza offered the world was in part still recompense for that previous episode of his life.

Guns. Kinza's choice was the Soviet made Makarov, a snub-nosed semiautomatic, reassuringly heavy. It had been the official Red Army sidearm for forty years, from 1951 to 1991. True to Soviet scorched earth logic, the gun used a 9×18 mm cartridge, where the bullets were 0.2 mm larger in diameter than the standard NATO-issue cartridges used by all other "western" handguns. In case of a full blown NATO attack, the pesky capitalist invaders would not be able to use any Russian ammunition in their fancy designer weapons, and the soldiers of the motherland would be spared the indignity of getting shot with their own bullets.

The Iraqi army had used the Makarov for a long time because it had relatively few moveable parts, rarely malfunctioned, and could be repaired in the field by a one-armed halfwit; also, the Spetsnaz used these guns, and those nightmarish Russian commandoes were held in awe by all the Arab militaries.

For the same reasons, it was a weapon in high demand among the insurgency. It was easily concealable and could be pulled up in a flash to assassinate an unsuspecting collaborator.

Kinza had two of them, but his were actually the much rarer East German model, manufactured in Suhl. The grip bore a stamp of the name Ernst Thaelmann that, for all anyone knew, was either a very popular East German or, bizarrely, the name of the factory. The

East German pistol had always been considered the finest of all the Makarovs, as any fool knew that German engineering, even the lunatic East German sort, was a thousand times better than Russian or Chinese or Bulgarian or any other communist-inspired state. Then too, the aficionados were well aware that the original designer of the Makarov, one Nikolai Federovich Makarov, had basically copied his design from the inestimable Walther PP sidearm, used by the *Luftwaffe* in WWII, so it was only fitting really that the best Makarov be manufactured in German soil. And if anyone thought they knew better than the Luftwaffe, well…

With the nonexistence of that country and the discontinuation of the original line, this gun had earned a cult following. Kinza, who had a healthy interest in concealable semiautomatic handguns, had acquired these from some retired (dead) Republican Guard army buddy, and now had a gaggle of gun enthusiasts following his every move. Many times, on the way to some rendezvous, they had been stopped in dark corners by furtive, bearded men wanting to get a look at the Makarovs. Kinza had turned down offers of hard cash, bricks of opium, titles to bombed out houses, and even gratuitous bearded male sex.

Dagr, who could not be trusted with such serious weapons, was given an old .45 caliber US army issue gun, a sort of hand cannon for amateurs of the point and pray mentality. It had originally been won in a game of cards from Hoffman, himself a terrible shot, who normally called in air cover for anything more serious than a bazaar pickpocket.

Today they were in a celebratory mood, were in fact passing around a bottle of single malt, and using Mother Davala's best crystal glasses. Xervish had fixed up back-to-back trips, an entire convoy heading to Mosul on staggered days with empty trucks, following their own arcane schedule of profit and loss. Xervish, plugged into this system somehow, had put an end to their concerns. Kinza and Hamid would go next Friday, a week from now, and Xervish and Dagr would follow the very next day. They would rendezvous in a safehouse in Mosul, also arranged.

That left a week of upcoming idleness, a period in which Kinza planned to find the Lion of Akkad and wrest from him, if possible, the secret of the watch. Their curiosity had grown; Dagr had kept his finger on the watch doggedly for the past three days and marked down the intervals of the errant fluctuations. Held against a time chart of minutes and seconds, this faint mechanical thrumming took on a different look, a numeric pattern of some sort.

At first, it had been random but finally, on the third day, Dagr had discerned a repetitive sequence. In effect, he had reached the end of a cycle, which indicated to him that either the machine was malfunctioning repetitively, or there was a code of vibrations embedded in it, which was more or less three days long.

This discovery had fired them all up, but after hours of conjecture and feverish speculation, they had been forced to come back to reality. Very possibly, Dagr had glumly concluded, just a mechanical aberration. In fact, given the difficulty of making a watch behave deliberately in this way, it very likely *was* a natural aberration. Still, the alternative was so exciting that it was impossible to dismiss.

Dagr had transposed a 72-hour clock against the vibrations and assigned a numerical value against each one. His grid was essentially a breakdown of 72 hours into seconds: 72(hours) × 60(mins) × 60(secs) = 259,200 seconds. Against each of these points, there was either a 0 (for no vibration) or a 1 (for a vibration). Thus,

S1, S2, S3, S4, S5, S6, S7...
1, 0, 0, 0, 0, 1, 0, ...

The first and obvious assumption, of course, was that this was a binary code, and Dagr had spent some moments of joy at having solved the puzzle so easily. The binary code, used in machine language, was essentially one of the oldest forms of transcribing letters to numbers by simply using a sequence of 0s and 1s. The permutation of a string of 0s and 1s could be used to represent each letter of the alphabet in question, and the string could be as short as or as long as necessary, depending on the size of the alphabet. In computer language, for example, the binary code for each letter was a sequence of seven 0s and 1s, i.e., the letter A might equal 01000001.

The first few binary code analyses, however, had not been fruitful, possible messages being gibberish. Dagr also had to consider that binary code in itself was not so much useful for hiding information, as it was for transcribing letters into numbers so machines could deal with them.

A second kind of relationship had occurred to him, namely, the correspondence of seconds (S) against vibrations (V) on a numeric scale, where say, $S(1) = V(1)$, $S(6) = V(2)$, $S(136) = V(3)$, $S(144) = V(4)...S(259,198) = V(XXX)$. From $S(259,200)$, the entire thing started repeating. Dagr, following this path, was left with a bunch of numbers or fractions or number associations, which he had to sift through. He had put these results through various mathematical algorithms, trying, without much success to come to a scheme where the numbers coalesced into letters. It was difficult enough, but without knowing even which language the code might be in or a hint of what kind of math had been used or some inkling of what kind of words were in the message, it was almost impossible.

Or, as Dagr concluded to Xervish, if he had the use of a US supercomputer, perhaps the one that played chess against Kasparov, he might run through all possible permutations and get some idea of what they had. This was the "brute force" approach to breaking systems, and it was accepted that any code could be broken given enough time and computational power, but where both of these were lacking, it was necessary to obtain extraneous information. For example, if Dagr could guess a set of words that was *likely* to appear in the message, he could devise tests for the frequency of those vowel combinations; he would have, in essence, moved from random to somewhat informed.

Kinza, loath to give up, sent Xervish forth with this new mission. It was apparent to him that the Lion, injured, disoriented perhaps, must be in the city somewhere. Baghdad was now dissected by bunkers and checkpoints into zones with flows of traffic, and it was possible, given a starting area, to narrow down where exactly someone might flee to. Poring over Google earth maps, Dagr had drawn up a grid. The idea was for Xervish to make discreet enquiries to initiate contact, if possible. After all, they had something that belonged to the Lion, some kind of negotiation should be welcome to both sides. Since they couldn't leave the house, it was necessary to bring the Lion to them, voluntarily. In the few days they had left, Kinza hoped to learn something.

The very next day Xervish returned again, like a homing pigeon drawn to his keeper. His first report was not good. No one in the criminal fraternity had heard of the Lion. Hassan Salemi had upped the price on their heads. Hoffman was missing, probably court-martialled. Kinza grimaced but kept his cool.

They had taken to spending the afternoon tea hour at the library, discussing the code with Mikhail. It was not an unpleasant way to kill time. Even the librarian, somewhat convinced by Kinza's teatime manners, could face these sessions with a semblance of equanimity. Dagr could almost believe he was in his old room, surrounded by his texts, working on some obscure equation. Much of the time was spent with Kinza and Mikhail offering outlandish suggestions, which Dagr had to shoot down with tedious explanations in mathematics.

In this time, surrounded by books, he even captured some of his previous donnish nature, the forgotten art of steepling his fingers just so, the constant struggle to enunciate, using mathematical notation on small scraps of looted paper to demonstrate quite obvious points that his audience nonetheless failed to appreciate. He had asked for a blackboard and chalk since he did his best thinking that way, but this turned out to be against the Code of Behavior compiled by Mikhail for proper library etiquette. Ever since Dagr had broken the spine of a 1917 atlas, tearing Greenland asunder forever, the librarian had put him down as one of those individuals who was Inadvertently Dangerous to Books and now kept him under close observation.

It had taken considerable persuasion to allow freehand ink-work in the library, Dagr having had to vociferously express his resolve not to write his name in any books or draw in the margins or tear out pages or any of the other infractions that Mikhail imagined Dagr to be on the constant verge of committing.

Mikhail, who had read up on the Druze, had a number of ideas. His powers of expression, however, were so underdeveloped that he could barely get two words out without stammering and becoming rapidly incoherent. His favored mode of communication was to blurt out a single word and then shy away in a fit of mumbling, the deciphering of which required a form of cryptanalysis in itself.

"We're in a tough spot," Dagr was saying, "The Druze used an alphanumeric code."

"Which means?"

"Numbers equal letters," Dagr said. "For example, the simplest alphanumeric is A=1, B=2, C=3, etc... Computers, for example, commonly use ASCII alphanumerics, which is a seven-number sequence of 0s and 1s, essentially binary code. Another simple code, also used in programming, is Hex, which converts all the characters on a keyboard to a double digit number."

"And the Druze code isn't one of these simple ones?" Kinza asked.

"No, I tried all the obvious stuff already," Dagr said. "In most cases, an alphanumeric code is not really a method of hiding information so much as converting letters into numbers so computers and their programmers can deal with them."

"This Druze thing is a computer code?"

"Probably not," Dagr hesitated. "I mean, why put it into a watch? If it was recent, you could use a disk or pen drive or any other kind of electronic media. This code is put into a *mechanical* object. And it's actually set against time. I think it must be to hide something, something quite long perhaps."

"So how would you break this, professor?"

"Well, this is really more of a job for a cryptanalyst."

"You're just being modest."

"Computers. We need really big computers!" Mikhail blurted out. He spoke low and fast. Oftentimes, only Dagr understood him.

"Right, or computers. Lots of them. Or one really big one."

"Yes, yes, like the one that played chess with Kasparov," Kinza gave a shout of laughter that startled everyone. "You've got some kind of fetish for that thing."

"Well, it's a lot of computing power to waste on something useless like chess," Dagr said, exasperated. "I mean here we've got hundreds of itinerant mathematicians begging for processing space, and the imperialistic white devils are just mocking us by using mainframes to beat third-rate chess players."

"Third rate?"

"Well, he didn't beat the computer, did he?"

"He's the best player who ever lived," Kinza said. "According to FIDE."

"Incorrect. He's the best *professional* player who ever lived," Dagr said. "Chess is just a bunch of permutations of a single scenario. It only looks like a game. In reality, it's just a math puzzle. It's even easier than a completely random puzzle because the same few situations keep repeating themselves. Logically, any first-rate mathematician would be unbeatable in chess. Of course, they'd never play it in the first place because they'd have better things to do."

"So Kasparov would be no good at deciphering the Druze code."

"Precisely."

"Whereas you would be excellent at chess."

"Precisely," Dagr said. "If I bothered playing of course, which I wouldn't because I have better uses of my time."

Except of course, Dagr *had* played chess once, and these days, he dreamed of it often. Sitting in the balcony with his grandfather an hour before kindergarten, the sun just beginning to warm things up, the old man back from his morning walk, natty in his ivory cane and hat. He smelled of soap and tobacco and faint aftershave. They had a ritual, both of them early risers while the rest of the family slept. First, they would open a little packet of pastry, freshly bought, smacking of honey and butter, and then the wooden chess board, with the beautiful grainy pieces, felt lined in the bottom, solid and heavy with its little knights and bishops. The morning game, a secret for no discernible reason; Dagr couldn't imagine anyone objecting to it, but no one else played, and somehow the conspiracy was cherished.

The grandson would always set the board, laboriously putting each piece dead center, and then the old man would take a pawn in each closed fist and offer the choice, and no matter which he picked, some legerdemain always gave him the black. The white pieces started and therefore had the advantage, and his grandfather took a fiendish delight in trouncing him. The black had to defend, and Dagr always lost until he learned to play to a standstill, and then finally to counterattack and win.

Beautiful mornings for two years, until his grandfather had a stroke, and the board was lost, and...

"Alkindus...etaionshrdlu." Mikhail interjected, brandishing a tattered hardcover edition.

It took Dagr a moment to focus; it was difficult to wrench his mind back, the world in the past was too strong, too richly colored compared to what was now left over. "Hmm, Al Kindi?" he finally said. "You're on the right track, but I've tried that already."

"Polyalphabetic—like ENIGMA."

"Rotor like the World War Two stuff, you think? Could be. I've done the obvious frequency analyses for Arabic. Hmm, might be a different language altogether, you think? Sneaky Druze."

"Excuse me, what the hell are you guys talking about?" Kinza asked.

"You know, cryptanalysis," Dagr said.

"Two...two or more languages," Mikhail said.

"Words from two languages? Hmm, that might throw off the frequency counts of course."

"No vowels..." he whispered.

"No vowels? To throw us off? Sneaky Druze."

The unmistakable snicker of an East German Makarov cocking cut him off. "Really, I'm serious. What the hell are you guys talking about?"

18: EMPTY NEST

Tommy didn't know what was happening with Hoffman, but he had his orders to stay put, and he was pretty sure the Army would fall apart if people stopped following orders. The apartment they had appropriated was a bare shell with mattresses, table fans, and little else. The Humvee was parked outside. They had stripped out the electronics, TV, and Xbox so that the men at least had something to do in the sweltering heat. They were bored, uncomfortable, and getting fractious.

Tommy was on a strict budget, and as this was black ops, he was pretty sure resupply was out of the question. Ancelloti, recently reborn as some kind of Rastafarian, was his second in command and quartermaster, occupying the storeroom and guarding it against night time pilferage. The men were afraid of his nocturnal episodes, were loath to disturb his rest. The gunner was saner now if somewhat dazed, and Tommy had promoted him because he needed someone to pow wow with. It was lonely at the top.

"We're clear out of stuff," Ancelloti said during inventory. They were holed up in the supply room, which was an airless hole further polluted by Ancelloti's "medication." "Three days of booze on half rations and maybe a week of food if they can keep down the dry stuff. They're getting antsy. Someone tried to jimmy the lock last night. I made a lot of rattling noises with my bullets and they ran off."

"Good job," Tommy said. It was important to encourage initiative.

"So we need resupply fast."

"I always ask myself, what would Hoffy do?" Tommy said. "And he'd say we have to forge the land."

"Forage, like?"

"Right, right, like live off the land," Tommy said. "And, you're the quartermaster. It's on you, man."

"You want me to forage for stuff?" Ancelloti asked. "You know we're in a city, right? Everything here belongs to someone else?"

"What are ya, some kinda lawyer?"

"Ok, so I guess I'll go and steal some stuff then."

Three days on and no sign of Ancelloti, and Tommy had to reflect on the wisdom of sending out a known drug addict PTSD victim to forage. Now he had no booze, no quartermaster, and most crucially, no gunner. It was tough because a squad without a gunner was hardly ever taken seriously, no matter how big their Humvee was. The men were openly talking mutiny, and he was getting such black looks that he had taken to locking himself inside the armored vehicle for large swathes of time.

It was during one of these episodes that he noticed a knot of local police hanging out by the corner kibbeh stall, which had a shady spot of pavement. The kibbeh was a kind of delicious kebab that Tommy heartily approved of. The police seemed paunchy and content, rather similar to police back home, so much so that he instantly felt a shiver of guilty dread until he remembered that he was a marine and black ops specialist and in fact *outranked* all cops. Watching them closely, he realized that they were doing some kind of brisk business. Of course, it was his duty to investigate.

"Hi guys."

"What?"

"What?"

"Who the fuck are you?"

"Guys, I just wanna buy some stuff. My name's Tommy."

The paunchiest cop spoke perfect English and had a superb waxed moustache that curled up at the edges. He looked Tommy up and down and gave him a patently false grin.

"My friend," he said, "how can I help you? We are just humble police enjoying a break. My name is ah... Abu-Abu."

"You got any of those Indonesian cigarettes?" Tommy asked.

"You want an Indonesian cigarette? My friend, this is Baghdad. We have everything. But I'm not sure."

"You know, the ones with pot in them?" Tommy clarified.

"Ah, yes, pot, hahaha," Abu-Abu said. "We have hashish, my friend, but that is for old ladies and pimply boys. For the military, we have something so much better." He pulled out a packet of pills, red ones, white ones, blue ones with squiggly lines. "Uppers, downers, Iranian 'bloody' Valium, Lebanani, and these Abu Hajib, enough to stone a donkey. You want to party, we'll hook you up no problem."

"Ya, a party'd be great," Tommy said. "See, my squad up there is getting real antsy. We're out of booze and stuff, and they keep wanting to shoot shit up."

"You have a squad of Marines up there?" Abu-Abu squinted at the building.

"Yup, plus our gunner Ancelloti is out here somewhere foraging."

"And that's your Humvee?"

"Yup. Black ops, Abu. I don't mind telling you, but keep it hush hush," Tommy said. "We've got orders from Col. Bradley himself. Airstrikes and everything."

"My friend, no need for colonels and airstrikes," Abu-Abu said. "Why don't we have a party? Free, on us. After all, you are guests in our country."

"Free? That's cool, man, cus' we're out of money."

"Money? Bah what is money between good friends like us? I will give you money, my friend," Abu-Abu pulled him into a conspiratorial huddle. "For a little favor. See my men are toiling on the streets, selling these pills in the heat."

"It is *so* hot here man."

"What if we kept the pills in your apartment?"

"I do have a quartermaster," Tommy said proudly.

"Right, right, let's say we keep them there, and then we can sell from your front step there, and maybe your guys can walk around a bit with us sometime, just to show that we're all friends."

"Yeah man, we're always ready to help the local police, you know?" Tommy said. "Got to serve the people, right?"

"Of course, a joint mission, cross cultural cooperation," Abu-Abu said. "And don't worry about your problems, Commander Tommy, we're gonna take care of all that. Booze, you said? We got arak, vodka, cough syrup, whatever you want."

"Yeah and the guys are getting tired of dry rations too. That shit makes you blocked up if you know what I mean."

"Dry rations? Pfft…" Abu-Abu snapped his finger at the kibbeh chef. "This stall happens to be mine. Or close enough. Kibbeh for everyone! All you can eat, whenever you like, for you and your mates, and a cut from the pill business, of course. Now let's go upstairs and get out of the sun, eh?"

Tommy linked arms with his new friend and beamed. This diplomacy stuff was easy. Hoffy would be so proud when he got back.

19: AL KINDI

"DO YOU KNOW THAT WE INVENTED CRYPTOGRAPHY?" DAGR ASKED.

"No, nor do I particularly care."

"Al Kindi. One of the most brilliant minds ever lived. A mathematician of immense power."

"Do I have to pay for this lecture or is it gratis?"

"Very funny," Dagr pounded on the table. "The intellectual leaps made during our golden age are unparalleled in the history of mankind, comparable only to the Enlightenment period in Europe, when Newton, Hooke, Leibniz, etc. were at work."

"Really, Dagr, you're deliberately boring us now."

"You wanted to know."

"About the watch, professor, the watch."

"Ok, here are my conclusions. First, this watch contains a code. Second, it is a mechanical code. By this, I mean that the code is controlled by a machine inside the watch. There are modern equivalents of this, such as the enigma rotor machine used in WWII, to encrypt data."

"So this thing is at least 60 years old," Kinza said.

"It should be pre-computer age, certainly," Dagr said. "Now, it actually might be very much older. I can narrow the range. We'll touch on that later. The oldest it can possibly be is from Al Kindi's time, which is around 850 AD."

"This ancient mathematician?"

"The father of cryptanalysis, among other things," Dagr said. "He noticed that languages all use different letters and letter combinations in greater or lesser frequency. For example, in English, the letter 'E' is used most often, whereas the letter 'X' is hardly ever used. Ciphers were primitive at that time. People simply replaced one letter with another or with a number. For example, say in my cipher, the letter 'E' is replaced with the number '9'. Now Al Kindi realized that by counting the frequency of the number '9' in a message, he could reasonably guess which letter it represented. This is called frequency analysis and is still one of greatest tools in cryptanalysis. Incidentally, he also invented the study of probability and statistics, although he never gets credit for it."

"So have you figured out the code yet?"

"It's not that simple," Dagr said. "Al Kindi himself started making polyalphabetic ciphers to get away from frequency analysis. Essentially, this uses a key or algorithm in the middle, to encrypt the letters. Thus, in this kind of cipher, '9' is not always equal to 'E'. 'E', in fact, will be represented by different alphanumerics in different parts of the message, depending on the key being used."

"So the only way to decipher this is to know the key."

"Not quite," Dagr said. "The person receiving the message has to know the key as well. Normally, a key has to be something easily transferable. Say I'm using a key that is repeating. If I figured out the length of the key, I'd be able to break down the message into intervals. For example, the first 'E' and the tenth 'E' might use the same encryption if my key is nine alphanumerics long. Once I know this, I can start using brute force frequency analysis by simply trying different combinations until I start getting some words out of the gibberish."

"So what did Al Kindi do?"

"He created algorithms, mathematical functions, so that the key was nonrepeating and as close to random as possible. Essentially, the other person had to know the algorithm. In order to decipher it, he would apply his part of the algorithm to the code and reduce it back to some kind of plain text. The Druze code is probably something along those lines."

"So can you break it?"

"Maybe, maybe not," Dagr said. "I wouldn't count on it. It could be a one-time pad type of thing too."

"Do you enjoy annoying us?"

ESCAPE FROM BAGHDAD! 153

"Er?"

"Talking at length about stuff we have no interest in or idea of."

"Well if you don't want to know, then fine…" Dagr began to pack up his things, which, as it amounted to a pen and several sheets of paper, did not take much time, whereafter he sat back with an injured air. Then, glancing at his companions, he saw that they were laughing at him, which embarrassed him further.

"Alright, alright, don't sulk." Kinza held his hands up.

"One-time pad—what is it?" Mikhail asked.

"It's a completely random key for one-time use. The sender and the receiver have it, and that's it. They were used mostly during WWII. Since it's meant to be just used once, it can't really be cracked. If the key is truly random, we won't get anywhere. It's useless. Of course, what I know about cryptanalysis can be fit onto a single piece of paper."

"You're approaching this wrong," Kinza said. "Put yourself in *their* shoes. Imagine you're the Grand Druze, or whatever, and you wanted to encrypt a message for your descendents. How would you do it?"

"What the hell is a Grand Druze?" Dagr asked, irritably.

"The Chief. El Presidente. The Grand Turk. The Prince of Persia. Whatever."

"Who is the message for?"

"Your successors let's say."

"Hmm. Well obviously I have something to hide. Some kind of advantage I imagine, some secret knowledge or treasure or whatever."

"Don't forget, Druze are cunning and secretive."

"You really *are* a bigot."

"No, I'm just anti religion. All religions. Which includes fucked up ones."

"Nice. Very PC."

"PC is the invention of the Great White Satan."

"Anyways, I'm the Grand Druze. Let's say I've amassed a great treasure, and it's hidden."

"Persecute. Druze always persecuted," Mikhail said.

154 SAAD Z. HOSSAIN

"Right, Mikhail," Dagr said, "Say the Druze are being persecuted and cannot avail themselves of this treasure. Now, logically, we can narrow down these time periods by looking at their history."

"Library. We have books."

"Extremely fortuitous, then, that we are in this *excellent* library," Dagr said, about to clap Mikhail on the back and staying his hand at the last minute as he realized that poor Mikhail would in no way cherish this physical contact. "Guided by a *most excellent* librarian. As such, perhaps we might find a book on the Druze detailing the vagaries of their fortune. Insofar as I recall, Druze history is rather turbulent in that they enjoyed periods of extravagant power, such as the time of the Fatimid Caliphate, and then the more recent episodes in Syria, when they occupied Damascus."

"These digressions, while charming..."

"Right, I, the Grand Druze, have some vital information I must pass on. I need to hide it from my persecutors, however, so I have devised a tool that uses both steganography as well as crypotology."

"What?"

"Steganography is the art of physically hiding the information such as using invisible ink to write a message. In our case, hiding the message in a mechanical watch, which vibrates in a seemingly random sequence over a period of 72 *hours*; Even if the watch is lost, it is unlikely a random person will even realize that there is data hidden here."

"Unless it falls into the hand of a blood-minded mathematician who has a lot of free time."

"Precisely. Now having hidden the data using steganography, I have further used cryptology to make the data illegible to all third parties, even were they to accidentally stumble onto it."

"So this information is really valuable then."

"Well it is valuable to me, as the Grand Druze. It could be something totally useless: like some kind of alchemical rubbish, or some pseudoreligious nonsense," Dagr said. "Now, I have used this method to pass on the information to my successors. I know that it gets as far as Fouad Jumblatt, but after that, things are murky."

"But how are your successors supposed to unlock this code?" Kinza objected. "Where is the key?"

"Someone might have it," Dagr said, running his hands through his hair. "Or it could be lost. We do not know the state of the Druze in Baghdad. Or even if they are here, which is in doubt."

"Well, since they've lost the watch, it would follow that the Druze have also lost the key," Kinza said. "And maybe even knowledge of what the secret is to begin with."

"We need to know more about the story of this watch. If I can guess what this is about, what kinds of words might be encoded in this message, even what era the encryption is from, I will have a much better chance of breaking it," Dagr said. "We are almost blind now. I hope that Xervish will be able to improve our vision."

"Well how old is the watch? You said you had an idea."

"Look at the thing. What is it exactly?"

"It's a wristwatch, right?" Kinza said. "Earliest wristwatches are around 1920s I'd say. So it's between 1920 and the computer age, then."

"And that is around when Fouad Jumblatt lived. Or died, rather. He was assassinated in 1920," Dagr said. "But your hypothesis is wrong. Take a look at the case with the magnifying glass."

"What am I looking at?"

"Some notches on the surface." Dagr said. "And look also at the joints where the wrist bands attach to the case."

"Seems like some kind of wear and tear. Hardly surprising...."

"You're not looking at it right," Dagr said, irritable. "As I spent the last three days holding this bloody thing in my hand counting vibrations, I came to some hypotheses."

"Can you just spit it out?"

"It's a hypothesis because I am not sure, which is why I am telling you my reasons. First, this thing is kind of heavy. Too heavy for a wristwatch, almost. Second, it's a little bit bulky. Too bulky for a wristwatch? Then I started peering at it with the magnifying glasses. What I really needed was a microscope, so I built a makeshift one."

"You built your own microscope?"

"Well it's not that hard. I've got it in my room," Dagr cast a significant look toward Mikhail, who had just slipped away to make some tea. "*It's hidden.*"

"Why are we whispering?"

"I had to break things to make it. A lot of *his* things actually."

"Ok, so you what did you see in your microscope?"

"I saw notches on the casing and signs of soldering on the side handles. The handles themselves are a little bit crude, compared to the rest of the thing. My belief is that this used to be a pocketwatch. Well, that's wrong because it's not actually a watch—what I mean is, it used to be disguised as a pocket watch. Then, when wristwatches came into use, it was made into a wristwatch."

"That's a lot to tell from a few notches."

"Look at the inscription. Compare the writing of that to the flag imprint. See anything?"

"It's messy," Kinza said finally, after a long moment.

"It's amateur," Dagr said. "It was almost certainly done later. And if you look really carefully, using a microscope—which I happened to have done—you can see that the Fouad Jumblatt inscription is actually *on top* of an earlier inscription. And there might be another one *under that one.*"

"So it's really old."

"It's really old."

20: TELOMERES

THE ROADS SEEMED TO EMPTY AND FILL WITH A PECULIAR MAGIC, at times eerily empty and war torn, other times bustling with normalcy, reverberating with snatches of conversation, people hailing each other from across the street, loud voices that sounded aggressive but were in reality gregarious, good natured. Hoffman figured that people were just tired of staying home scared. Suddenly in front of them was a lablabi stall, a food cart selling boiled chickpeas, redolent with lime and chili, people jostling in an irregular line, and beside it another crowded stall selling wood-grilled burgers, and as they paused beside it, the smell drove him wild. He stuck his head out of the window like a dog and took three large lungfuls. Strangers waved at him, and one fashionably scarved middle-aged woman gave him a little newspaper cone of lablabi with a big smile.

Sabeen had changed her spots in the course of the drive, like some kind of leopard shaman, able to transverse identities at will. Stopped by a bored policeman, Hoffman had been about to strut his documentation augmented bluster when he was blindsided by her sudden outstretched arm swathed in medical white, proffering a plastic laminated card that he clearly saw carried the name of Dr. Sabeen Ibn Sina, followed by unintelligible Arabic squiggles. His eyes, following up the arm, took in a head coiffed demurely in a scarf, not the riot of silk he normally associated with her glorious skull, but a blue cotton number that he instantly knew was a doctor kind of thing.

Some moments later, they were waved through into a crowded parking lot and then a crowded hallway filled with the normal chaos of Iraqi hospitals.

"You're a doctor now?" He managed finally.

"It's real," Sabeen said.

Behruse had shouldered his way through the press of sick people, of which there were many, and gunshot victims, of which there were fewer, an expressive ratio, one of many, which could well be used to gauge things in the city for the day. Here they arrived at a different checkpoint where armed military men in gauze facemasks blocked the hallway. Their job was to protect the doctors and equipment, which were both housed securely beyond this point, along with the occasional VIP patients, all of whom were nice targets for insurgent types.

At last, Hoffman had the opportunity to practice his art, consisting of rapid fire, clipped, nonsensical statements he had gleaned largely from his interactions with Col. Bradley accompanied by belligerent thrustings of his writ, which was for once legitimate. Several arguments and some rapid body searches later, they were ushered through into a slightly calmer segment of the building.

They were here because of a name in a file. Dr. Sawad had been eagerly awaiting test results from a colleague. His excitement had been evident even through the dry language of his notes. In his paranoia, he only ever referred to him as Dr. J. This Dr. J was apparently a cunning man well capable of stealing all his research and hogging the credit.

"There are four Dr. Js here: radiologist, urologist, GP, and neurologist," Behruse read from a board. "Could be any of them. Unless J stands for the first name. Sawad really was a miserable bastard."

The GP was a woman who took one look at Behruse and shut the door in his face. The radiologist was in the linen closet with a nurse and therefore unavailable for comment. The urologist had fled abroad. The neurologist, it turned out, was an old man who didn't really see any patients but through cunning hospital politics had managed to occupy a very nice fiefdom consisting of a large office, a waiting room complete with nurse cum receptionist, and even a small lab.

"Good evening, doctor," Sabeen said, barging in over the faffing nurse. "We are friends of Dr. Sawad."

"Dr. Sawad the prick?" Dr. J asked helpfully. "Or Dr. Sawad the heart specialist?"

"The former, I imagine."

"I don't know him."

"He gave you something to research," Sabeen said.

"Who are these guys?" Dr. J looked around. "They don't look like doctors."

"They are Mukhabarat and CIA," Sabeen said.

"Oh my. Recruitment standards have fallen since the old boy left, eh?"

"You don't want to get mixed up in this, really."

"I can see that."

"Going back to Dr. Sawad."

"He was a prick."

"So you did know him?"

"Briefly."

"What did he give you to research?"

"Don't drink that you oaf! It's *not* coffee!"

Behruse, sniffed, made a face and put down the beaker.

"Dr. J, allow me to inform you that we have the authority to take everything in your office," Sabeen said, sitting down forcefully. "Including you."

"Close the door, please, Mr. CIA, be a dear."

"Should I start smashing things up?" Behruse, having found nothing edible in the room, was now growing irritable.

"Dr. J?"

"Two weeks ago Dr. Sawad the prick popped in and asked me to look into some DNA samples."

"And?"

"And nothing. I didn't bother doing it."

"Really?" Sabeen unbuttoned her coat and withdrew a sleek looking gun.

"Oh alright, I had a peek."

"And?"

"Most peculiar stuff."

"Explain."

"Very technical, you lot probably wouldn't understand."

"So everyone keeps telling us," Sabeen sighed. "I happen to be a physician and I *do* understand some fairly big words. The other two, well you might be right there."

"I also know lots of big words," Hoffman said, offended.

"It's about telomerase," Dr. J said, peering at them under bushy white eyebrows. "And senescence."

"I also know calculus," Hoffman said. "The difference-type calculus thing. Ask anyone."

"You see, I study diseases caused by old age," Dr. J said. "And regeneration at a cellular level. Why, for example, cells will repair themselves when you are young yet stop doing so when you're old. Senescence."

"I imagine that's a matter close to your heart."

"At this age, it's the only thing worth studying, really," Dr. J said. "How to cheat death."

"I also know all the countries in the UN, and most of their capitals," Hoffman said.

"What did Dr. Sawad want to know?"

"He gave me some DNA samples from a patient he had," Dr. J said. "A most curious case. If I didn't know Sawad better, I would have thought he was trying to hoax me."

"Was it Afzal Taha?"

"I don't know the patient name. Sawad wouldn't tell me."

"What was so curious about it?"

"Most people, doctors included, think DNA is the be-all and end-all of genetics," Dr. J said. "It's not the case, of course. DNA is like a very large, very redundant instruction manual: in several different languages, with a bunch of gibberish thrown in for good measure. What gets translated, what gets activated, is a matter of complex interactions between proteins."

"Was the sample DNA special?"

"The DNA? No. At the time, I found it perfectly normal," Dr. J said. "What struck me was the peculiarity of the telomeres."

"The excess stuff at the end of chromosomes?"

"Precisely, dear! You *are* a doctor," Dr. J looked faintly disappointed. "Telomeres are excess DNA attached to the ends of chromosomes. They are repetitive chains. Do you know precisely what happens during cellular replication?"

"The chromosomes uncoil, and enzymes bind to each strand, replicating it."

"I know about biology too," Hoffman chimed in. "And the reproductive cycle for humans. I know all the body parts."

"The high-school biology version, yes," Dr. J said with a saucy wink. "Actually, when a chromosome is copied, it is not possible for the replicating mechanism to get all the way to the end: which means the bit at the end of each chromosome doesn't get copied. Now that would mean that each time the chromosome gets copied, a little bit gets left out, a little bit of vital biological programming, possibly. After a certain number of copies, one would imagine there is nothing meaningful left."

"There is obviously something that stops this loss of genetic material."

"The telomeres. The telomere is a RNA-protein complex 'cap' or 'knot' at the ends of each chromosome placed there precisely to prevent vital genetic loss. Each time the chromosome replicates, a segment of telomere gets shortened. These telomere segments are synthesized by an enzyme, the telomerase reverse transcriptase. But due to various factors, including a shortage of these enzymes, the telomere chain gets shorter each time. After a large number of replications, the telomere gets all used up, and the cell stops being able to replicate properly. Hence, the telomere has been theoretically linked to a time bomb heralding old age and death."

"Cellular death programmed into us."

"Right," Dr. J said. "It's actually quite unfair. It's as if someone designed a perfect, self-healing, self-correcting organism, and then went and programmed death into it."

"God?"

"Don't believe in him," Dr. J said. "Although if he did it, it's a very poor sort of joke."

"So if telomeres didn't shorten, our cells would continue to repair themselves, and we would not face old age deterioration?"

"Theoretically, that's one way of looking at it," Dr. J said. "The flip side is cancer, of course. The kinds of cells that achieve immortality by circumventing the telomere death are normally cancer cells. So in an evolutionary sense, programmed cell death might have developed to prevent runaway cancer. Detractors say that tampering with the telomeres will cause massive cancer. Those of us interested in achieving cellular immortality believe this is the key to regaining our natural heritage."

"Natural heritage?"

"A biblical joke of sorts. The Garden of Eden, as it were," Dr. J wagged his finger. "Live forever, heal forever. Our heritage before we crossed God. We could be immortal."

"Until someone with a gun comes along," Behruse said, amused.

"What?"

"Your Dr. Sawad was murdered recently," Sabeen said. "Pushed off a roof."

"I hadn't heard," Dr. J slumped in his chair. "That's terrible."

"My sympathies…"

"Oh, he was a prick. Destined to be murdered," Dr. J said. "I don't mean that. It's terrible that he died without telling me whose blood work I've got."

"We know whose blood you've got."

"Well you need to bring the young man to me immediately."

"He ain't young," Behruse said.

"You're wrong," Dr. J said. "He's very young. His telomeres are pristine. In fact, he looks like he just stepped out of the Garden."

21: HAND IN THE JAR

THE JAR WAS THICK PEBBLED GLASS, UNLABELLED, HOLDING about two liters of formaldehyde. A hand floated inside, ragged at the edges where the bones had been severed untidily, possibly using a cleaver. The chipped edges showed that at least two attempts had been made to effect the separation. Tinges of blood blushed the formaldehyde into a faint pink, a fairly pleasant color, notwithstanding the provenance.

Mother Davala cradled the jar in her arms, as if it were an infant. Tears salted her cheeks in twin tracks, following the crevices of her ancient skin. It was an incongruous sight in that elegant living room, the jar and the crone. The other two ladies knitted silently, and even the click of their needles sounded mournful. Dagr felt a leaden sickness in his stomach, nausea rising. He could smell the blood suffocating him, although he knew it was no such thing. The hand, floating in its artificial womb, looked peculiarly feminine, reduced to a gentleness as if, detached from its host, it had reverted back to a prepubescent level of innocence.

When he saw it, Dagr staggered in his step, for the lay of the hand, the angle of the fingers brought back something else in his mind, a black obscenity he had nearly blotted out. The day he had finally quit his home, had left the keys and all his possessions behind, walked out without even a change of clothes like a dervish in the storm.

He remembered his wife's hand, laying like that on their blue cotton coverlet, severed from life, unnaturally pale and elegant, the tidiness of her limbs on the bed, that grace following her to the afterlife, giving her dignity for a most undignified retreat. He had seen her hand first, the lovely tapered fingers, seen it faintly blue, the wedding band still on, and known the truth. The message was there in the

163

arrangement of her intimate things, her chain, her watch, the wallet with their pictures, the rattle she carried of their baby girl, the little quirks; all wistful tokens of love for a lover who after all, in the very final reckoning, had not been enough.

Dagr had left it all, but carried them still.

"See what they've done," Mother Davala said. "The poor boy."

"Whose hand is that?" Kinza asked quietly. Dagr could see the cold rage pouring out of him, waves and waves of it. It sobered him, gathered again the amorphous mush of his thoughts into the hard kernel of his core. It was *not that* hand. That one was buried.

"Xervish," Mother Davala said, "only poor Xervish."

"Are you sure?" Dagr forced himself to look. "I...I can't remember what his hands look like." *I can only remember one kind of hand.*

"Put the phone down!" Hamid's voice cracked out in parade ground volume, an authority to it Dagr had not heard in a long time.

Kinza froze, his cell phone half way to his ear, eyes swiveling around, mildly surprised, yet Dagr was certain even without looking that his other hand was perilously close to his gun, indeed that he was moments away from blowing a hole in Hamid's head. Hamid too sensed this perhaps, for his next words were low, and stark.

"They have him. They have his cell phone. Your call can be traced back to here."

Kinza put down the phone slowly. "Is he dead?"

"The cutting of limbs is a quirk of Salemi," Mother Davala said. "He burns the ends to keep the body alive. He gives IV blood transfusions if necessary. If Xervish survived the initial shock, he might be alive."

"What next?"

"Two, maybe three days later, another hand. Or foot."

"What does he want?" Dagr cried. "Is he mad? What possible use is this?"

"He wants us," Kinza said. "He wants me. We have two days, then. Where was this found?"

"Outside the mosque," Mother Davala said. "The cook brought it."

"Kinza?" Dagr asked. "Two days for what?"

"To get him back," Kinza said. "Or bury him if he's dead."

"You're mad," Hamid cried. "Let it go, man. We have safe passage to Mosul! We can leave tomorrow. Xervish is dead. You think I haven't cut off hands before? You don't survive that, not without first class treatment."

"You can go," Kinza said quietly. "I free you. Leave now. But you can't use the American truck driver. I will need him."

"You'll leave?"

"No," Kinza said. "He will get me close enough to Salemi."

"Why won't you *leave*?" Hamid asked. There was something like anguish in his voice. "Xervish set it up. He *wanted* us to escape. We can be in Mosul in two days…among friends, among protectors. The gold is real. I swear to you."

"I said you were free."

"What about him?" Hamid stabbed a finger toward Dagr, who sat mute, as he did in most times of crisis. "What about *his* life? You condemn him to death as surely as you do yourself."

"He will stay here," Kinza smiled. "To avenge me if I fail."

"You'll die alone then," Hamid said.

"Yes. One day. Not tomorrow."

"And he will never avenge anything. He is broken. He will die too. This house will burn."

"You misunderstand him."

"You're a stubborn fool," Hamid said.

"I said you were free."

"You will die alone. Without witness."

"Not alone." A ghastly smile.

"Fuck you then," Hamid said. "I'm not dying for that fool."

Kinza looked away, toward Mother Davala. It was as if Hamid no longer existed. "I'll need more guns. Armor. Grenades."

"We need maps," Dagr said. Reluctantly the shock faded from him, replaced with the tired, mundane necessities at hand. "And numbers of men, pictures of the building, and those around it."

"You had best stay behind," Kinza said.

"It seems like a two-man job." *More like ten men. Who cares?*
"Twenty men would be enough," Hamid said bitterly.

"Hassan Salemi does not hide in his own neighborhood," Mother Davala showed her cracked gums. "He does not imagine anyone will have the affront to attack his house. The things you need will be provided."

"By whom, witch?" Kinza asked sharply. "What bargain do we make here?"

"Do you think this is the first hand we've found in a jar?" Mother Davala said. "You will get what you need. The condition I have is for you alone." She put her ruined mouth to his ear, whispered.

"I agree," Kinza laughed uproariously, with genuine amusement, a sound Dagr had not heard for a long time. "Get the stuff quickly. Pictures and information first."

"What does she want?" Dagr asked.

"Later."

Later in the evening, Dagr, bewildered by the blistering speed of events, found himself once again in that faded drawing room, as a procession of nephews arrived, producing with miraculous regularity everything they had wanted. Chief among that was information. Hassan Salemi used a three-story compound as his office, which doubled as both arsenal and the legitimate face of his fledgling political party.

Party members who were retired gunmen lounged there in varying numbers all day, providing a de facto security cordon. Salemi had been forced by the Iraqi police to remove his personal road block, but a number of old cars were regularly parked in haphazard fashion at the head of the street, cutting off ingress.

These descriptions and more were forthcoming from a variety of brats up to age fifteen, all of whom claimed kinship to the old woman and were ruthlessly fed and watered in the house after their report, a few of them even forcibly bathed. No boys over fifteen, all dead or gone, Mother Davala cackled, and Dagr wondered how many of her kin she herself had spent on insanity like this.

Within a few hours, Dagr's head was swimming with crazy details. The man on the roof listened to radio all day and ate falafel. He had a big stick and binoculars. He had an air gun that he used to hit little kids monkeying around. *Sniper? Sentry?* Hassan's doyen was a mute who had had his tongue removed by the Ba'athists. *Your work, Hamid?* He was fat and wore a black sweater, even in summer. *Kevlar?* The front door opened outward but was normally ajar all day. *Can't be kicked in.* The party members sit on the street and smoke shisha all day and drink coffee. *No day jobs. War veterans, probably deserted army personnel. Expect a quick recovery.* In the back of the building, there is a window near the ground, with bars. *Basement. Dungeon.*

"I have made a list," Kinza said. "We need automatic weapons. A dozen grenades. Fragment, not smoke. Flares."

"Get a damn mortar, why not," Hamid said.

"The American takes us past the road block. They won't like it, but they'll have to let him through," Kinza said. "We go in daylight. At night they don't let anything through."

"There are men at the gate and on the roof," Dagr said.

"Grenades for the door," Hamid said. "But the men on the roof will shoot you down. Abandon this idiocy for God's sake."

"The roof," Kinza said, "is a problem."

"You need to hit the roof simultaneously," Hamid said, dragged in. "A sniper on the top, opposite, if you can get up there. Or something heavy, like a bomb or mortar. Get them looking in another direction."

"Very good if we had more men," Kinza said. "We wear Kevlar. We'll probably get hit, but if it's not a headshot, it won't matter."

"Even if you get in the door," Hamid said, "the building will be crawling with men."

"We take our chances."

"And how do we get out?"

Dagr looked at Kinza, saw the momentary blankness on his face, and laughed. "We don't worry about that, Hamid."

"What?"

"We don't worry," Dagr said, "because we won't come out. You think he's ever worried about something trivial like getting out? We kill them all, or not. And then it's over."

"You're insane."

Dagr shrugged. "It's *his* plan. I'm just along for the ride."

"You're both crazy," Hamid moved toward Kinza, grabbed his shoulder. "You don't care? You'd die for this piece of shit Xervish? I don't understand. Why? What sense does it make? You want to die? You want to kill all of us? Fuck you."

"This Salemi," Kinza said. "He thinks he's safe. *Not from me.* Xervish. I saw his sister die in front of me. Someone *put his hand in a jar.* I've had enough. I won't let it go. You run away if you like."

"Oh why the hell not?" Hamid slumped in his chair, "Fuck Mosul then. How far will I make it alone? Let's kill the Shi'a bastards. I hate them all. Not you, Dagr."

"You coming then?" Kinza asked.

"Yes."

"Good. Bring your toolkit," Kinza said. "How are you at working on the run? We might have to ask some questions."

"I was known as Two-Minute Hamid at the academy," Hamid said. "And they weren't talking about my cock either."

"At last, you'll be useful."

"Kinza, what did Mother whisper to you?" Dagr asked.

"That witch?" Kinza smiled. "After I die, she wants my soul—to keep in a jar, apparently."

22: MEETING OF THE MINDS

Life for Yakin had not generally improved after his con-
version from independent street thug to devout Shi'a. The first few
days, he had been merely happy to be alive and thus found profundity
in the simple pleasures of eating, sleeping, and watching sunsets. This
affliction had passed, however, as it became apparent that the imam
had adopted him as a sort of pet dog.

It was now borne on him that he would not be shot for sport, but
rather, only if he transgressed in anyway. This had first engendered a
spineless relief in him, pushing him into a deep lethargy. Now, however, even that had gone away, and he was merely bored and vaguely
dissatisfied.

Contrary to his previous beliefs, members of the imam's gang did
not get a lot of pussy. In fact, sex of any sort except with your wife was
strictly forbidden. The imam was big on the *forms* of religion. Prayers
had to be said on time, cleanliness had to be maintained, proper attire
had to be worn, foul language, drinking, gambling, womanizing were
all prohibited. Yakin had been tempted to point out that shooting
people and cutting off limbs would probably also be frowned upon
by the Prophet.

As he was propelled into the vortex of the imam's compulsions, it
became apparent, too, that his master was insane. It was not the sort
of insanity that impinged on competency but, rather, the scouring,
scourging hot breath of madness that purified the world into a single terrifying image, like the barbed tongue of a lion scraping off the
ghostly remnants of fur, skin, and meat from bleached-white bone. His
problem was that he *believed*. Not in the lapsed, socially compressed
half-assed way of Yakin, not in the going through the motions just-in-
case hypocrisy of bankers and accountants, not in the passive dumb

acceptance of the elderly, but rather in some mad, specific vision that he alone saw, some coruscating alternate truth that allowed him to deliver judgments from immense height with impunity.

This frightened Yakin greatly because, of course, he could find no rational basis for anticipating the whims of the imam. The rest of the crew, he knew, was in a similar dilemma, divided roughly in two. There were the opportunist pretenders, similar to himself, and then there were the other nutcase believers, those touched with a sort of associated, lesser madness, a convergence of visions, perhaps, overlapping slightly or entirely with the engine that drove Salemi. In either case, these days, attrition at the house Salemi was high.

As a favored pet, Yakin followed in the imam's wake, particularly in the current pursuit, where the obsession for vengeance had overtaken his mind, leading him into foxholes deep within the city. One such day, it brought them to an ancient neighborhood of arching masonry, close-set walls, and unfriendly faces. They were admitted into one such house, although the pruned caretaker, through a toothless ruin of a mouth, made it known that only two would be permitted.

To his surprise, then, Yakin was prodded forward by Salemi, causing his heart to flutter like a defective alarm clock. It was a strange place for an execution, but he was now so inured to the irrational turns of Salemi's mind that he could only stumble forward with a litany of half-remembered prayers. The inside of this house, however, proved to be largely inoffensive. A narrow corridor, and then an antechamber, bare with polished marble, and then another turn into a little courtyard, beautifully paved, with the air of antiquity about it, a pocket time capsule a thousand years old, reminiscent of the glory days of Baghdad, when the city sported innumerous pleasure gardens and a generally decadent air.

There was a stunted olive tree, and underneath it sat an old man smoking a cigarette. It wasn't a regular filter tip cigarette but rather, one of those long, hand-rolled ones in fancy brown paper, with a holder made of horn or ivory or something, a bit of detail that absolutely oozed wealth and class. Yakin hated him already, and as he got closer, something naked in the man's face shivered a thrill of ice down his spine, reverting him to instant caution mode, which was pretty much a semicomatose state of inaction and bubbling panic. With the unerring instinct of a lifetime bully, he registered instantly that this old man was neither paternal nor kindly. He felt caught between two starving wolves and understood that he himself was just a piece of disguised meat.

There were two chairs only under the tree, so he was forced to stand like a servant behind Salemi's back, off to one side of course, so as not to spook him. Normally he would have resented this, but prescience told him that in this meeting it was possibly best to stay unobtrusive. And still. Moving prey was caught first, after all.

"Welcome, imam," the old man said with faint irony. "Please, be seated."

The imam, who had already availed himself and who did not follow the niceties of fashion or irony in any case, merely stared him down through his steel-gray eyes.

"Thank you for attending to me," the old man said. "You may call me Avicenna. Would you care for some tea?"

"I know who you are, old man," Hassan Salemi said. Yakin moved to serve his master, but Salemi stopped him with an outstretched hand. "We eat or drink nothing here."

"Oh?" Avicenna raised a withered eyebrow.

"Your reputation is well earned, alchemist," Hassan Salemi said. "I have no desire to be poisoned."

"It was not my intention," Avicenna said. "But I respect your concerns."

"You are a man reputed to be very...*civilized*," Salemi almost spat the word. "Such things are wasted on me. Get to the point quickly."

"You abhor civilization? How interesting," Avicenna said. "And by interesting I mean barbaric."

"Let me rephrase then," Hassan Salemi said. "You no doubt take me as a gun-wielding brute with the banner of Ali nailed to my back; A killer of men, a fanatic, a destroyer."

"Yes, I do."

"I am all of those things."

"It is always nice to have one's observations supported by confession."

"When civilization has let you down, barbarism is the obvious answer."

"Let you down?" Avicenna sat forward, obviously intrigued.

"I have spent my whole life in revolution," Hassan Salemi said. "Against Saddam, against Americans, against the men who rule us now. Early on in life, I understood one thing. It was a singular lesson. Everything afterward has confirmed this."

"A religious epiphany? Extraterrestrials? Djinns?"

"Someday, old man, I may kill you," Hassan Salemi said. It was casual, as if he were speaking of the weather. Yakin remembered Amal's blood cooling on the floor, the reek of it. "I answer to no man. Remember that when you mock me next."

"I am merely curious," Avicenna said, unperturbed. "The lesson you learned."

"Is that no one man is the enemy," Hassan Salemi said. "Nor any one army or company or country. These are all facades of the same thing."

"How profound."

"The system is the enemy," Salemi said, ignoring him. "The system of everything, the system of the world. The system supports tyranny, the control of wealth and power by a handful. It requires the vast majority to live in ignorance and weakness, to work unceasingly toward some dream of prosperity just beyond their grasp. The faces change, but their habits do not."

"This is an abstraction. You are a soldier."

"I am a soldier of God," Hassan Salemi said. "And I answer to no man, although many may claim to be my master. The only way to win is to tear it all down. When I was a foot soldier, I was treated with contempt. When I commanded a brigade, they offered me guns and dinars to fight Saddam. Now they offer me US dollars in Switzerland to fix elections. In five years, they will offer me barrels of oil per day and villas in Spain to run the city. What changes? Nothing."

"And what do you want, then, imam?"

"This game cannot be won. We must change the game. I am doing God's work."

"God's work. He told you so, did He?"

"You have lived a long time Avicenna," Hassan Salemi said. "Yet till now you have found nothing of God? He turns his face from you. You are an abomination."

"Nonetheless, you are here, imam. We are at the same table, working toward the same goal. Do you know what that tells me? It is not God who moves men: It is earthly motivation," Avicenna leaned back. "Imam, I want you to kill some men for me."

"I am not a hired gun."

"In return, I will give you some information," Avicenna said. "It is the only currency I deal in these days."

"What information is worth the life of men?"

"The information you have been searching for so fervently. I will give you the murderers of your son—and the Americans who helped them," Avicenna said. "Is that not sufficient?"

"That is sufficient," Salemi said.

"Very well. Parked beside an abandoned building in an alley off Abu Nuwas Street is an American military vehicle. There are four soldiers stationed with it. You are to kill them. There will be no repercussions from the military. Those four men and the vehicle they are in do not exist in official military logs."

"These Americans killed my son?"

"Yes, they were partially involved," Avicenna said. "Do not mistake me. These men are drug addicts and mass murderers. They are human scum. No god on earth would tolerate their existence for long."

"Do not speak of God, blasphemer. What next?"

"In a certain safehouse, hiding, are the three men who actually pulled the trigger," Avicenna said. "After you have eliminated the Americans, I will give you that location. You may find three women living there, and other...human dross. You may kill them all. And burn the house down."

"You appear very well informed on the murderers of my son."

"As I said, information is my currency. And I am not a hoarder," Avicenna said. "These men are petty criminals, whom no one on earth shall miss. They are insignificant in the greater scheme."

"And the others in this house?"

"War sometimes has a purifying effect. It shakes loose all the human garbage that exists on the fringes of society. This house is full of this ilk: the useless, the discarded, the forgotten dregs. Killing them will be doing a favor to the rest of us."

"If it is so simple, why have you not done it yourself?"

"I am no longer in the business of killing," Avicenna said. "There are three women living in that house, women who bear me some grudge. It would be a favor to me if you destroyed them."

"It is distasteful to me, this killing of rabble."

"This rabble has all had a hand in the death of your son, directly or indirectly."

"I have heard it whispered that you were chasing these men for a reason of your own."

"The three petty thieves, whose description I am sure you have already obtained, carry with them a small object. A watch, stolen from me. It is critical that this object is returned to me. That is all the payment I require for my information."

"Very well."

"After that, I would advise you to erase all proof that these men ever walked the earth. Kill their families, their friends, anyone who knew them in any way," Avicenna said.

"Do you fear retaliation?"

"These men are nothing. They are not capable of retalia-tion. What I seek is to remove all links between us and this busi-ness," Avicenna said. "Trust me it is better for both of us to keep our—association—private."

"This watch," Hassan Salemi said casually. "What is it? Why kill so many men for it?"

"An heirloom," Avicenna said. "I merely object to being stolen from. It's the principle of it. I'm sure you understand."

"I understand that there are some men quite frantic to get this watch," Hassan Salemi said. "Do you think I have no one in the Mukhabarat?"

"Mukhabarat?" Avicenna let out a slow, private smile. "Let me tell you a little secret. The Mukhabarat of Saddam was the great-great-grandchild of a far older organization. Something that I helped to build, in fact. I would not trust the Mukhabarat if I were you."

"I have heard that 'the Old Man is looking for an ancient treasure'," Hassan Salemi said. "And now you ask me to murder a handful of men for a watch."

"Do you seek great treasure, imam? If I knew it were that easy, I would not have bothered meeting you. Write your price on a piece of paper. I will send the amount to whatever bank you trust."

"I am not a dog to do your bidding for a bone," Hassan Salemi said. "There is word of a Druze watch and the mystical secrets it contains. Tell me the truth of this matter."

"The truth? The Druze watch is a myth. There is no great secret; only the remnants of a handful of Druze riffraff, cowering in the shadows somewhere."

"Then why do you pursue them?'

"Because they are my enemy and have been for centuries," Avicenna said. "Because I would destroy them once and for all and close this chapter. When you age, you will realize that one by one every lofty ideal falls away and all we are left with are old grudges."

"You are a man who has stayed hidden in shadow through countless regimes," Hassan Salemi said. "And now you stick your neck out for an old grudge? I am a simple man, but this is too simple even for me."

"I sense that you are destined for great things, imam," Avicenna said. "Be content that after this episode, you will never see or hear from me again."

Outside, Yakin felt the sunlight on his face and shuddered a release of long held tension. The very presence of the old man had been oppressive, an insidious oppression, sneaking up on him and causing subconscious panic. He was used to a low level state of panic in any case; hanging around Hassan Salemi did that to him. He now realized that his mistake had been to assume that Salemi was a unique creature. That other leviathan terrors existed in the world broke upon him now, and he railed for a moment at the unfairness of it. How many of these monsters *were* there, prowling in silence? How was a regular street bully supposed to compete?

"What did you think of our benefactor?" Hassan Salemi asked, in the car.

"He is old," Yakin said, "and evil."

"Yes," Hassan Salemi said. "A very old evil man. I think we will kill him after this little game is finished. God will appreciate that."

23: INTO THE ABATTOIR

Dagr stood on the roof and breathed. The smell of burning trash disturbed the moment, but there was a cool breeze off the river, and he could imagine the Tigris flowing serenely not far away, a silvery reflection of the dawn, unmindful of all this temporary agitation, going back centuries through the Ottomans, the Abbasids, the Persians, back to Babylon and even beyond, to the first men settling on its shores. The river had tasted plenty of blood and ashes. The river didn't care. He saw across the city from this height, and it all looked peaceful. He could tell no difference from now and before, and it surprised him that everything would endure, that soon the bitter little points of his life would be forgotten. He couldn't recall ever standing on the roof and watching the sun rise. He missed the rush of stumbling out of bed, bickering over the sink with his wife, trying to make breakfast and coffee at the same time while she fussed over the girl, combing hair and brushing crumbs, the routine check for errant pencils and books. It seemed far away now, as far as the river.

"This shit burns. Fuck. Don't take it." Kinza joined him, and as usual the world jarred back to the inescapable present.

"I wasn't planning on it," Dagr said. "Where the hell did you get it?"

"The witch's nephew. He's brilliant. Can get you anything. Fucking cut my coke with paracetamol, though, the little bastard," Kinza took another tentative snort. "Not so bad the second time around. Hmm. My nasal passage is perhaps already lacerated."

"He's ten, Kinza."

"So?"

"Just saying."

"Different days, eh, professor? He could have been in a classroom."

"That little shit is a monster," Hamid said absently. He was hunched over in a corner of the roof, working on his mobile kit, thumbscrews and fish hook tools. Dagr didn't want to know.

"What are we doing here, Kinza?"

"Waiting for Mikhail."

"What the hell for?"

"Now, professor, you're not going to like this, but we don't have a choice," Kinza said.

"Like what?"

"I'm thinking we need Mikhail to man the sniper station up top. We're bringing him up here to practice with the gun."

"What? Mikhail? He's a fucking librarian."

"He can shoot, can't he?"

"A crossbow," Dagr said. "He can shoot a crossbow."

"Same principle, really," Kinza said. "Look, it's the safest job. We set him up on the roof with the rifle and let him take pops at the door when we get down. He can take out the armored guy first."

"He won't hit anything, Kinza."

"Even if he hits nothing, sometimes it's worth it just filling the air with bullets. They'll be so worried about a sniper that they'll be hopping around."

"He's going to get killed."

"Five minutes, and he runs," Kinza said. "Look, do you think I'd throw away his life for nothing? Hell, I'd put the Satan nephew up there if I thought he'd be able to lift the damn gun. There is no one else, professor."

"You want me to convince him, is that it?"

"No," Kinza said. "He's already agreed."

"What?"

"Let it go, professor," Hamid laughed from his corner. "Kinza told him that they're coming to burn the library down. He's putting on war paint as we speak. You couldn't hold him back even if you wanted to."

Later on, in the living room cum command center, Dagr stood in a heroic pose, like Hector, as the three women of the house decked him with martial accoutrements.

"You are the tank," Kinza said, apologetically.

"That's not a good thing, I take it?" Dagr asked. The women were attaching vests, shin-guards, arm guards to him, all Kevlar, but weighing a ton, evidence of some nefarious doctoring.

"You can't shoot," Hamid said bluntly. "Not straight, anyway. So you got to be the human shield."

"Not exactly," Kinza said. "Basically, the tank soaks up pressure. You get down first and look the most threatening. We give you the biggest gun, make you the most dangerous looking dude there."

"Er, I'm not fully understanding the plan here," Dagr said weakly. He was already faint from the enormous weight of the things the women were attaching to him.

"There's good news and bad news," Kinza said. "The good news is that you've got nearly impenetrable armor: the very best we could get: Marine issue Kevlar, which has been reinforced by steel plates for your chest, with outsized double stitching along the hems for a stylish finish. Then forearm guards of Kevlar, and shin-guards too, also of Kevlar. Your thighs are also Kevlar with steel plates to protect the major arteries. Your helmet is the Marine-issue K-pot, picked out in the latest desert camouflage pattern."

"Stop being an ass. What is the bad news?"

"You're most probably going to get shot a bunch of times," Kinza said. "Just don't get shot in the face. Otherwise you should be fine."

"Shot a bunch of times?"

"The tank has to draw fire," Kinza said. "You get out first and start blasting around your machine gun. The assholes think you're Rambo and all concentrate on bringing you down. Meanwhile, Hamid and I start dropping them and Mikhail takes the big guy down with a headshot."

"That's the plan?"

"Yes."

"Me getting shot up, that's your plan? Seriously?"

"Look, it's a good plan," Kinza said. "You'll get hit maximum once or twice. Trust me. We only got one suit of Kevlar. You'll be the safest guy there."

"Think you can handle it, professor?" Hamid asked. "Don't piss in the Kevlar. We have to give it back after the job is done."

"It's on loan? What if it gets shot up?" Dagr asked, aghast.

"Well we'd lose our deposits," Kinza said. "We can't afford this shit outright. It's very expensive. Mother Davala had to call in a lot of favors for this one."

"I'm going to drop dead in it. I know it. Dead in borrowed Kevlar."

"You'll be fine," Kinza said. "You always moan, but you pull through when it counts."

Rumbling in the container of the Blackwater truck, Dagr felt the acute discomfort of the ride and realized with faint chagrin that while he was facing certain death, all he could think about was the stifling heat. He updated his mental inventory of various hells to include this; held immobile in a steel box in sweltering Baghdad noon, strapped down with heavy armor and helmet, forbidden to make a noise or fan himself, or even have a drink.

He tried to fix his mind on trivial matters, his varied aches and pains, the itch on the inside of his calf, the pommel of the pistol jabbing his hip, to reduce mounting apprehension of certain death. It seemed almost comical that anyone could expect this of him, to jump down from a moving truck into a mass of armed men. Yet Kinza had a way of making these things seem common place, and Dagr supposed it was because he had a singular lack of imagination.

They lounged beside him almost gracefully in the truck, lithe as panthers, sleek and dark, their guns out, looking fit, relaxed. He felt like the sacrificial cattle of Eid, clumsy in panic, herded left and right by the butcher's men.

The truck swayed through the streets, and native Iraqi police did not stop them, such was the power of the emblem on its side. If they were afraid of the US Army, they were terrified of Blackwater. The driver was plodding dull, a man who didn't want to know anything beyond the rotation of his tires and the steady accumulation of hazard pay in his account.

Dagr counted the minutes, and then reflexively ran over probable speeds and distances, pinpointing on his mental map where they were. Such were the tools of the mathematician, but the numbers comforted him little. Too soon, they stopped on the street, as Hassan Salemi's men voiced their objections. The dull man in the cab shrugged, face closed, ignoring the jabbering of monkeys, his hands repeatedly making the same motion: open the gate, open the gate. Eventually, the color of his skin and the latent power of Blackwater dented even the Shi'a confidence in their own barricade.

The truck rolled slowly and the driver honked twice, as previously agreed. Hamid and Kinza were at the doors, jacking them open, and Dagr found himself stumbling forward, out of some sick compulsion. It was like the one time he had gone bungee jumping in Dubai. The sunlight hit him and he staggered down like a drunk, the M4 carbine semiautomatic cradled in his arms. His knee banged against the lip of the fender, and he howled in excruciating pain. The truck eased away and he collapsed to one knee, off balance, his helmet slick with sweat. His peripheral vision was shit. He heard the other two landing several meters behind him, exposed.

Salemi's men were staring at them, aghast, momentarily frozen around their two round café tables, spending those precious miniseconds trying to register. Dagr saw one putting out his cigarette into a full mug of tea and felt an odd pang for ruining his morning. He remembered abruptly what he was supposed to be doing; his finger automatically tightened on the trigger, and the M4 started roaring in his hand. Bullets sprayed into the ground, hitting nothing, and then the vicious recoil lifted the muzzle up, and he saw the tables being hit, upturned, wood and glass flying. Perhaps he hit something, he wasn't sure, but from behind he could hear the whine of single shot pistols, as Kinza and Hamid, kneeling, did their business with more efficacy. Men ducked away. Guns roared.

There was return fire from somewhere in the doorway. Aghast, Dagr remembered suddenly that the bear-man in armor was nowhere in sight. He must have ducked inside for some reason. This plan was shit, he thought, even as something hit him with the force of a mule-kick, punching him back on his ass, the M4 spinning away. The air whooshed out of his trunk. He lay on the ground, paralyzed, eyes circling around floor level to see the tarmac littered with cigarette butts and slow pools of blood leaking from other unfortunates.

The bear man stood in the doorway, shotgun in hand, calmly reloading. Dagr stared at him, willing someone to kill him, but perhaps they were already dead. The plan seemed sadly awry. He tried to make some effort to move, but his arms and legs were not responding and it seemed pointless in any case.

The bear man stepped forward, shotgun draped over his arm and pointing down, close enough that Dagr could see the twin barrels. In this last instant, Dagr felt an intense desire to live a few minutes longer, for some miracle reprieve, and the still rational parts of his mind marveled at this pure animal instinct for had he not settled his accounts with life many months ago? Where then, did this yearning to breathe come from, this terrible fear, even as the bear fingers tightened on the trigger.

There was a loud crack surprisingly far away, and Dagr, who was a mass of pain, could not tell what further damage there was, until he saw the bear man pitching backwards, a mass of smoke coming from his chest.

Abruptly, a surge of adrenalin cleared away some of the fog, and feeling returned to his extremities. *Mikhail.* He couldn't help mapping the trajectory of the bullet and knew that the librarian had somehow saved him. Then it occurred to him that the bear man was still alive, himself wearing Kevlar, and it was now a slow contest of who could rise first. Dagr crawled to his belly and then half slithered away toward the edge of the building then remembered that he was supposed to *tank*, that Kinza and Hamid were fighting without the benefit of armor or second chances. Indecision gripped him and he ended up sprawled on the ground against a half-wrecked table, behind which one enemy was noisily dying.

He wanted to take his helmet off but his fingers were stiff and the strap too tight. His chest throbbed. *The bruise must be something to see. My ribs are cracked for sure.* He laughed weakly, tried to vomit, ended up spitting ineffectually into the dust.

To his alarm, the bear man showed signs of fight. He had already recovered to a semistanding position when Kinza finally reached him. Dagr saw the shot gun pump, and then his right paw disappeared into a fine mist of blood and bone as Kinza shot him at almost point blank range.

"Get him in the doorway," Kinza said, cool. He was talking to Hamid, who skulked over to Dagr.

"There's men on the roof, you fool," Hamid spat. "Do you want to get shot?"

Dragged unceremoniously into the hallway, Dagr saw Kinza bent over the bear man, his pistol burning a tattoo into his forehead. The bear man was moaning incoherently, holding up the ruin of one massive arm.

"Hamid get to work," Kinza said, waving him over.

"What you want to know?"

"Where is Salemi? How many men inside the building, and where," Kinza said, reloading his Makarovs. "And Xervish."

"Easy."

Dagr craned his neck, went dizzy, closed his eyes, and then reopened them. He regretted doing so, because Hamid had the bear man's head in some kind of vise and was probing with two long bent sticks.

"Pressure points inside the face," Hamid said, as he worked.

"Are you alright?" Kinza extended a hand to Dagr, picking him up to a slightly wobbly crouch.

"Shot in the chest." Dagr poked stiff fingers into the mangled plates in his vest, and then hissed in pain as they got scorched.

"You took it well," Kinza said, poking his head around the corridor. There were muffled sounds over there, and the bolt actions of AK47s being cocked. "Hmm, what we don't want is a kind of siege here."

There was a loud shriek from the vicinity of Hamid. The right arm of the bear man shot up, fingers grasping, and then was still after some muffled swings of a gun butt.

"Shit, sorry," Hamid called up. "He's dead. All he said was Salemi is out with the peacock."

"What the fuck, Hamid?" Kinza said. "You've crossed the line to absolutely fucking useless now."

"Weak heart," Hamid said, irritated. "The fat fuck had a weak heart. Just spasmed on me."

"I thought you were some kind of pro," Kinza said, poking his head out again. This time there was shouting at the other end of the corridor, and a gun barrel stuck out cautiously.

"AK47s," Dagr said. "They've got us pinned. Their reinforcements will be coming up the front soon too. Is it too soon to get the fuck out of here?"

"It's more art than science," Hamid said. "There isn't a fucking textbook for this, you know."

"Actually, I thought Cheney might have made one," Dagr said. "I remember reading something about water-boarding manuals."

"You ladies better take cover," Kinza said.

He had a grenade out and was holding it rather casually.

"Cover? Where the fuck do you see cover?"

"Use the bear guy, quick."

"What fucking bear guy?" Hamid howled.

Dagr got the mountainous corpse up just in time, as Kinza's grenade went skittering down the floor. His throw had a bit of side spin on it that made it bounce against the wall and roll a few feet into the open doorway presumably jammed with enemy combatants. Said combatants, upon seeing this, tried to kick it back as evidenced by a sandaled foot swinging out. Unfortunately this proto footballer's technique was amateur at best, and he ended up bouncing it directly off the wall back into his own shin, whereupon it exploded.

Concussive waves flattened Dagr beneath the bear man. Something hard hit him on the forehead, making his head rattle inside the helmet. He looked down to see the sandaled foot in his lap, blown off neatly at the ankle.

"He'll never play again," Kinza said. He rushed in, Makarovs out.

"The fat fuck had a pre-existing condition," Hamid said, following. "Anyone could see that."

"Am I supposed to tank still?" Dagr asked, worried.

The room was a small office, four desks, computers, and a lot of filing but was now a charnel house of grenade shrapnel and blood. The footballer had been blown to pieces. Three others were in various stages of disrepair. As they entered, Kinza delivered the coup de grace to two of them.

"You want another shot?" He motioned Hamid toward a bearded Fanatic type office worker cringing in a fetal position.

"Look, I didn't have a stable work environment," Hamid said, crouching down.

"You ok, professor?" Kinza seemed unruffled.

"This helmet is killing me," Dagr said. "We should be heading downward. The probable response time for reinforcement is about fifteen minutes."

"It was my first go," Hamid said. "I've been out of practice. You can't judge me on my first go."

"Find out how many soldiers in the building," Kinza said.

Hamid, muttering, had his ear to the office Fanatic, and his hands in various places. There were needles in his fingers. He looked like a mad acupuncturist. The conversation between the two was terse and seemingly one sided.

"He's an accounts clerk," Hamid said finally. "Takes care of ration cards and shit for Salemi. Thinks there are six or seven soldiers in the top floors. Although sometimes there are two dozen or so if the local cadre is reporting."

186 SAAD Z. HOSSAIN

"So what is it, six men or 24?"

More hushed conversation, accompanied by squelching sounds, and sharp grunts of what could be high-pitched agony, thankfully muffled by the woolen gag Hamid had thoughtfully included in his field kit.

"He's saying he doesn't know. The armed men meet on the higher floors and don't really come down here," Hamid said.

"You're not impressing me," Kinza said. He moved over to the whimpering accountant. "Where is the prisoner?"

"What?" The man spat out blood.

"The prisoner. Xervish. Where is he?"

Hamid applied some pressure.

"Basement...still alive."

"Good," Kinza said. "How did you find him?"

"I don't know...informant."

"Who?"

"I don't know."

"You must have paid him."

"No payment!" The man screamed, as Hamid did something clever. "No payment! I'd know. It was free. I remember that. No payment. Some old man."

"Old man? Give me more."

"A gift," the clerk said. "Imam said it was a gift, from the Old Man. I...arrgh...I know nothing else. I just keep the numbers."

"Er, I think I hear people coming." Dagr was craning his head around like an alien because the helmet was too big, and his ears were ringing from the explosion in any case.

"Ok let's move," Kinza said.

Hamid shot the clerk. "Well I don't want him moaning on like that."

Another room, a disheveled office in which a single man was cowering under his desk, mumbling prayers. This irritated Kinza because he broke stride to shoot the man point blank in the back of the head, covering himself with gore in the process, and coating Dagr with a fair bit too.

"You'll have to wash the Kevlar before giving it back," Hamid said. "Getting blood out is a bitch."

"What the fuck was he praying for?" Kinza asked, mystified, as they broke into another little corridor. "I had a fucking gun."

A narrow stairway down and they ran into two men sprinting up, both armed with revolvers. Literally ran into, for it was a blind corner. Dagr bowled into them and in his panicked state tripped over the steps, sending everyone tumbling back. He landed heavily on top of a beard.

"You got one, finally," Hamid said.

"What?"

"You broke his neck." Hamid kicked the beard twitching beneath him.

Kinza was pistol whipping the second man in calm, economic one-two movements.

"Stop it. Stop it," Hamid said. "He's dead. You're ruining the Ernst Thaelmann."

Dagr scrambled away from the dead beard. He had pissed his Djalleba, causing an awful stink. He blundered forward into a thick wooden door reinforced with iron bars.

"Guys," he said. "I've found the dungeon."

24: DUNGEONS AND DRAGONS

"SEVENTEEN PIECES." DAGR DID THE COUNT, AND THEN THREW UP in the corner.

Seventeen pieces and a body still alive, hooked into a fairly newish Japanese life support unit. A head lolled on the cot, earless, tongueless, noseless, something barely human, a lone eye. An inventory of parts, lined up neatly in jars, five fingers of the left hand, the square palm, the left forearm; the left foot, the left shin, up to the knee; the right foot; a single eye; a nose; a shriveled tongue. Ears floating like petals in the brine. A scattering of teeth. A mind long fled.

"It is incredible that he is still alive," Hamid said. He was being careful. "The man is expert."

Kinza was white faced, drawn tight. He seemed incapable of speech.

"Shall I shut it down?" Hamid asked.

"He's still alive." Dagr looked at the wretch and doubted the veracity of his words. Yet the chest rose and fell in shallow breaths. The animal still struggled feebly in the rib cage.

"The mind cannot survive this kind of thing," Hamid said quietly. "He will die from the trauma soon, perhaps two or three days. The pain is constant. It is cruel to revive him."

They stood for several moments, looking to Kinza for direction. He stood hunched over the body, shaking. Tears coursed down his cheeks, fell on the misshapen half face beneath him; the single roving eye stirred beneath the lid, a restless sentinel. Dagr stared at his friend and felt an absurd urge to shoot him in the back of the head now, while he was vulnerable. It seemed to him they would perhaps never get another chance, that Kinza was minutes from becoming enraged, not the irrational simmering anger he had for humanity in general, but a far worse, specific rage, which would unleash some kind of holocaust. He marveled that if he had the courage, he could end this stupidity right now, sink them all into oblivion.

Where do these thoughts come from? Am I prescient now? Near death, were these unhallowed gifts coming from God? *I should have died long ago. I could have taken my own life. Was it cowardice that stayed me? Is there a difference between suicide and murder?*

Dagr, coward at heart, could only stare dumbly, stutter stop the old numb hesitation that dogged his life. The bed swam before him, the slow drip poisoning Xervish with life. *They're keeping this boy alive. Would it be a sin to end him?* One of them would, soon. And they would take the body and the parts and bury him perhaps if they fought loose. The huddled body on the white sheets, the travesty of medical care, he looked so small, like a child. Dark memories froze him in time, his daughter in her school uniform, skipping ahead of him, curls flying, her book bag in his hand, unreasonably heavy, the cramp in his shoulder, a twinge in his knee, the signs of age, and he remarked the peculiar contentment he had felt then, that almost-wisdom of becoming old in his mind.

One-two-three-four
Get that finger off the floor
Five-six-seven-eight
Get that thumb off the gate

Fire and heat and blinding light. It was darkness that brought peace. There was nothing good about fire, heat, and blinding light. Whose bomb was it, who knew, who cared? Something inside him gibbered *I wasn't there I wasn't there I wasn't there.*

The car lifted like a matchbox in a whoosh of sound. Books flew from his hand, the strap torn, charred, his hand miraculously unmarked. He saw her head snap back, the body arcing up, hair flailing, pastel blue sky. He felt the sound of blood drumming in his ears, and too much light in his eyes.

And then the hospital, the sheets red and then brown and then white again. Of course they took her to the hospital, and the doctor spoke to him like a human because he was a professor, an educated man, and his wife staring into space was pretty, with her wild eyes and knotted fingers. They changed the sheets to take away the blood, and there was the acrid cut of disinfectant and the pan with some parts of her gathered, the shoe, the leg—no point attaching it back, although the doctor murmured in his ear that he could do something to tidy up, so he could take the body back with dignity. Family, they said, call your family. *This is my family. This is it. It's over.*

White sheets and disinfectant, it lingered in the cesspit of his mind, crowding his nights. The sibilant breath of Xervish drew him back. He saw the stark lines of Kinza's face, the desolation contained within. *Cut off. Unmoored. We are all the same now. Unconnected links, adrift in time. Ghosts, lurking. God has taken back whatever grace he gave us. We have been removed from the tribes of humanity and now flounder purposeless.*

He thought that he knew why Hamid followed now, why he himself continued to march. Kinza drew them with the strength of his purpose, with that loose promise that there was a cause hidden somewhere, some reason for their existence. And now Dagr thought with sinking heart that perhaps it was all a myth, that Kinza perhaps was as lost as the rest of them, his fury empty, a dashing of tides against the sand.

Heavy footfalls drummed above, the rough shouts of warriors trying to impose order.

"They come," Hamid said, finally. "We're trapped."

"We are where we need to be," Kinza said after a moment. He pulled out grenades from his bag, two, three of them.

"What are you going to do?" Hamid asked. "Kill us all?"

"Tell me, Hamid, what kind of questioning occasions the removal of seventeen body parts?"

"None," Hamid said. "This is...something else."

"How long did it take?" Kinza asked. "In your professional opinion?"

"Two to three days," Hamid said. "Kinza, I was an interrogator. We extracted information using threats and pain. Most of the time fear was enough. This is far beyond anything I have ever seen or heard of."

"He had to send a message I suppose," Kinza said. "Why do people always want to send me a message?"

Dagr was wondering the very same thing, and the rising nausea told him there was a reason they were stuck in this perpetual cycle of escalation. "Can we get out of here now?"

"We will." Kinza was calm now.

"You want to send a message back, I suppose?"

"Hamid, how are you at scalping?"

"What?"

"Peeling heads."

"Not bad. We practiced a bit during med school."

"You went to med school?" Dagr looked skeptical.

"Of sorts," Hamid said. "Not the kind you're thinking of, not really."

"Good doctor," Kinza said. He was dry eyed now. "Turn off the life support. It's time."

25: HUNTERS

A WARM BREEZE WAFTED OVER HOFFMAN, RUFFLING HIS HAIR, filling his dream with the scent of lemon trees. The bite of the Arak dominated his thoughts, making all things cloudy. His joint, rolled cunningly into a regular cigarette, had fallen from his fingers and burnt a neat hole into the polyethylene deck chair. Around him were the remnants of the vast quantities of Mezze he had consumed in a hashish inspired lunch. In one hand, he greedily clutched the vial of little antidote pills, appropriated from Sabeen's purse, which transferred him to such gentle reveries. Moreover, he had stripped to complete nudity and now lay covered only by a large dinner napkin.

The waiters of the hotel, instructed to leave the crazed American alone, had done nothing to prevent his excesses. Sabeen, or more likely her grandfather, had some connection to the owners of the hotel, and an entire corner of the rooftop pool was devoted to them. This was no mean feat, as the infinity pool was not that large, and there were several other parties of guests wading around the other end, trying to ignore the Marine-issue eyesore.

Behruse was in a similar comatose state, except he slumped in the shade to protect his complexion, and unlike Hoffman, he had had enough decorum to maintain his clothing. Despite this being a nonsmoking zone, there were several lit cigars around his person. Their appointment with Sabeen had been at 2 pm for lunch, but she had been late, and Hoffman had unwisely chosen the hair of the dog as a means of combating his initial hangover from the excesses of last night.

All of which was most unfortunate, he thought, as a cool, slim hand slapped him awake. Hoffman, caught in psychedelic dreams where he was a snaky river fish, spluttered awake and gasped for air through imaginary gills. He saw Sabeen staring down at him, a halo of light framing her head, an eyebrow raised in a perfect expression of inquiry, admonishment, and derision.

Hoffman tried to get up, flex his various muscles, and suck in his stomach at the same time. The dreadful Arak stymied all of this, and he just slumped hard into the chair. The napkin, thankfully, had not moved, but the sudden proximity of Sabeen was about to have a disastrous consequence for his modesty.

"Could you, babe, step back a bit and hand me my Marine-issue pants?" Hoffman mustered with great dignity. "And then wake up Behruse. That pig has made a shitsty of himself."

"I'm awake, Hoffy." Behruse loomed in front of him. Fully clothed.

"Yeah well, some punk has taken my clothes," Hoffman said. "Give 'em to me."

"Actually, Hoffman, the waiter tells me that you threw everything off, 'capered like a monkey'—his words incidentally, not mine, and then tried to sing some 'West Virginia' song, before passing out," Sabeen said.

"Well, yeah," Hoffman said. "That would be *his* version."

"What did the Big Man say?" Behruse, asked, retreating back into the shade.

Sabeen flicked away Hoffman's pants, and took a seat.

"He wants us to pick up Afzal," she said. "He said that time is running out."

"So easy, right?" Hoffman asked. "Just pick him up."

"From the medical evidence, it appears that Afzal Taha has been lobotomized at least twice and subsequently recovered."

"Something that is impossible," Behruse said. "Imagine everyone growing back all the bits and pieces we've cut off over the years—the whole industry would just fall apart."

"He has some special DNA that allows physical recovery. Partial regeneration, even," Sabeen said. "The key is in trying to track his mental state from his medical history. Profiling him, basically, and then setting a trap."

"Well, you doctors have been messing him around a bit," Hoffman said. "Lobsterizing him and giving him shock therapy and shit. I wouldn't be too happy with you guys if I was him."

"So he's going around looking for revenge?" Behruse asked. "You think he pushed that doc off the roof?"

"Probably." Sabeen said.

"You guys think his brain grew back?" Hoffman said.

"It seems to have recovered some functionality, anyway."

"But what about his memories?" Hoffman asked. "That shit doesn't grow back. He's been messed up, he's confused and shit, he's probably just blundering around trying to figure shit out."

"What's your point?"

"Well, he ain't some kind of evil mastermind, is he? Sure he's got some fancy DNA, but what's he done so far with it? He ain't driving a Ferrari, is he? He ain't in the Caribbean drinking Mai Tais, is he? He's just blundered around in the same old hoods looking for some stupid shit and killing a bunch of random people."

"So he's stupid," Behruse said. His world was often black and white. "He's a big stupid fucker who doesn't remember what he's supposed to do."

"To find him we have to think like him," Hoffman crouched down into what he considered his "predator mode." "We have to study his every move, like hyenas hunting gazelle."

"Think like a guy with half his brain off," Behruse laughed. "That's a good one for you, Hoffman."

"Ha fucking *ha*," Hoffman said. "You are so predictable, fat head."

"We hit the streets," Behruse said. "Give me the word, Sab," the man cracked his knuckles. "Drum this guy out. We can get the old police commissioner up."

"We have to be quiet," Sabeen said.

"Quiet?"

"Other people might be interested," Sabeen said. "We don't want a manhunt."

"Hoffy can't you get the CIA to stick a drone up his ass?" Behruse asked.

"The CIA does not and never has operated any contraband drone-type objects in any orifice of any noncombatant," Hoffman said. "Section 32 Subsection D: furthermore…"

"So you *are* CIA."

"Not at all," Hoffman looked aggrieved. "That psycho Bradley made me memorize the entire handbook. Then he made me take standardized tests, too!"

"How'd you do?"

"I don't know. I marked down all the c's," Hoffman said. "Multiple choice. Everyone knows you gotta go for the c's."

"Nobody," Sabeen said icily, "can be as stupid as you pretend to be, Hoffman. It just isn't physically possible."

"Well la-di-da."

Sabeen threw down a sheaf of the medical documents they had gathered over the past few days.

"Look at Dr. J's bloodwork," she said.

"I don't understand this medical crap," Hoffman said, trying to shield his eyes from the sun.

"Look at the dates," Sabeen seemed pissed off. "I can't believe we missed it. Grandfather had a field day laughing at me."

"I don't see it," Hoffman said.

"The date Dr. J's secretary accepted the blood is here. July 8th. Dr. Sawad dated the vial when he took the blood sample; July 7th. There is a gap of about a day," Sabeen said. "Fine, that is normal. He took the blood from Taha, ran over to the clinic, twisted his old friend's arm, and got some sophisticated bloodwork done."

"So what?" Behruse, too, was puzzled.

"Yeah, so what?" Hoffman hiccupped. "Hey, you guys want some sambuca?"

"Sawad *took* Taha's blood on Saturday the 7th," Sabeen said. "*Fresh blood*. But Taha escaped from the basement of Al-Rashid almost six months *before* that."

"Woah," Hoffman said. "Where the hell was he all this time?"

"Not in that prick's apartment," Behruse said. "He'd need a strongroom to hold Taha. Shackles and chains at the least. Plus medical equipment I'd guess."

"Not the apartment, no," Sabeen said.

"His daughter?" Hoffman asked. "She seemed snooty."

"Yeah, let's go bust up her house," Behruse said.

"Hmm, I'm not sure she knew anything," Sabeen said. "Sawad wasn't sharing Taha like that. No, he has a safehouse somewhere we don't know about. He kept Taha immobilized for six months. Probably worked on him too. And Taha got free, maybe. Now he's on the run, killing people. How long till he returns to the place he was held captive? We have to find this safehouse."

"So Sawad had a place in the city," Hoffman said. "Something close to where he lived maybe or on the way to his work, areas of the city he had access to anyways."

"We check bank accounts, leases, apartment registers," Behruse ticked off on sausage fingers. "Relatives, friends, any connections to the recently deceased."

"Nurses," Sabeen said. "He'd need subordinates to help him, especially if he was housing Taha off campus for six months. But he wouldn't trust another doctor. He didn't even trust his own daughter fully."

"We need old hospital personnel files," Behruse said.

"Back to the Al-Rashid then."

"They aren't there precisely," Behruse said. "When the hospital got sacked, old papers were moved to the ministry. The hospital was re-opened on emergency basis by presidential order, but the ministry still retains all of the old files. Personnel, patients, financial…"

"Ministry?" Hoffman blinked.

"Can your piece of paper get us in?" Sabeen asked mockingly.

"Ministry of Health?"

"Yes," Behruse said. "It's Shi'a run. Sadr has a lot of men in there. Not long ago their militiamen were dragging Sunnis out of hospital beds and sticking knives in them."

"I can get in anywhere," Hoffman boasted. Then quietly to Sabeen: "And if you were to go out with me sometime, you'd realize that I actually have the keys to this city. I'm like frigging royalty over here."

Sabeen stared at him disbelievingly. Hoffman had a crush on his poisoner.

26: DEATH BY KIBBEH

TOMMY HAD JUST WON A BIG HAND AT POKER. KING HIGH SPADE flush on the turn, beating a guy with trips and another guy with pocket aces. They had chased him all the way, calling and raising, taking him for a mook. His first win yet, and it had been a princely hand. Those Iraqi police boys had been taking him for a ride all week; they were sharp players too, knew their odds, knew how to count cards. He couldn't quite figure out how they knew so much about Texas hold'em. Apparently it was globalization.

Now, waiting in line for the postgame winners' dinner treat, he replayed each bet, savoring his fellows' reactions. The flushed face on the crop bearded Abu-Abu, his beady eyes flashing disbelief. The aces spilling from his hand…priceless.

They had been forced to congratulate him of course, to own up at last that *he*, in fact, was the main man, the alpha dog, the captain of the ship. He didn't quite know where this new tradition had come up from, of treating everyone to dinner, but they all insisted it was the rule, even his own squad mates. They brought up numerous vague instances that he did not recall, all the while chivvying him toward the kibbeh stand.

In the end, flush with victory, he didn't really care. Everything was perfect, other than Ancelloti, who was inexplicably still out foraging. The kibbeh vendor was excellent, the best food he had found on the streets. It wasn't that spicy like some of the kebabs, didn't make him sick with the runs. Waiting with his mates in line, acknowledging the respectful nods of the locals, a few called-out greetings from known regulars, he felt a wash of contentment come over him. This was the life, yessir, nothing like cold Michigan winters, freezing-ass lake winds hitting you at 100 miles per hour.

This weather was balmy. Yes it was. Hellish hot sometimes, to be sure, but hot was a lot better than cold, wasn't it? And this assignment was the best of all time. He had Hoffy to thank for that. Nothing but playing games and loafing all day. And once he'd made friends with the Iraqi police boys, well, the card games had started, and that was just fine with him.

There were plenty of things he didn't understand about this city, like why it had a goddamn huge river running through it or why they had those big ass swords crossed over the big highway. Didn't they know that swords didn't mean shit in a gunfight? He'd have torn down the swords and put up M64s up there. Giant crossed semiautos, that would scare the shit out of the camels. Still, it beat the shit out of running a junkyard in a dead beat town packed in snow, watching old people shuffling around drinking cheap whiskey and moaning about the car industry. Hell yeah, the car industry had moved. They'd moved all the way to fucken China, probably cos it wasn't so fricking cold all the time over there.

Tommy neared the kibbeh stand, just as the vendor started a new batch. He always watched him closely. This guy was an artist. Tommy almost knew the recipe by heart, it was so easy. He wanted to take this guy to Chicago and set him up in front of the Sears Tower. No way anyone would eat hot dogs if they had this guy out there.

The vendor was getting into his groove now, and more than one regular stood around, watching appreciatively. He started on the stuffing by cooking finely chopped onions in oil until they were soft and filmy. Then some ground beef, until it browned, and then draining it out, he mixed it together and mashed it into a fine paste, with a little bit of salt and pepper. With deft twitches he portioned out little balls of the stuff, pushing an almond, a couple of raisins, and a little bit of herb mix into the middle. This was the stuffing, good enough to eat on its own. It took him a few seconds to make each one, and within a minute, he had filled a bowl full.

The actual kibbeh came next. He had ground rice, premixed with ground beef. Many vendors used a wheat mixture for the shell, but Tommy knew the inside scoop; rice was the best. Rice was the secret. The vendor made bulk quantities of this at home and brought ice cream boxes of the stuff to his cart every morning, gently thawing throughout the day. This, he had once explained, was also a secret. The one day old mash of rice and ground beef was a lot better than fresh.

Now, he mixed in salt, pepper, and a bit of lime juice into the mash, remixing the stuff with a fine wooden spoon. He took out egg-shaped scoops and used his thumb to hollow out the center into a kind of meat donut. The stuffing balls went in there, and two quick pinches on either side completed the kibbeh, beautiful ovals with a single pointy end.

Into the fire, the whole three dozen of them, and they hopped in the oil, developing that beautiful crunchy outer shell. The vendor had his pita breads lined up; the kibbeh went in there, nestled in some lettuce and tomatoes and other irrelevant stuff, and the dash of tahini and lime juice, and harissa if you wanted it. It was like an edible plate. You had to give it to these guys. They were smart. No point wasting time on crockery.

Tommy liked the blood red harissa, even though it burned through his mouth every time. It was just something so alien. It attracted him with an almost superstitious dread. The vendor recognized him and waved. Tommy beamed. He liked being recognized.

Ahh the first bite. The heat of the kibbeh, the coolness of the garlic yogurt. He slapped down the money on the counter and saw for the first time the light red glow beneath the cart. Something cringed inside him. *IED IED IED*. He began to gibber in fright, dropping the food, turning, leaping, all in his mind, unfortunately. Kibbeh lodged in his gullet, choking.

He began to claw at his throat. Something slammed into his stomach—a big hairy Iraqi police fist, some kind of frontal Heimlich maneuver, and bits of kibbeh flew out; "IED! IED," he shouted at the top of his lungs and saw the panic on his friends around him. And then, with *unfair* finality, the horizon expanded with concussive fire.

———————

Ancelloti heard that familiar dull thump of improvised ordinance. It woke him up from his drug-addled nap. It was a common enough noise that he did not immediately react. In fact, his first concern was the splitting headache and the rapidly growing bump on his skull.

A bump caused by sudden impact between his forehead and the hummer axle. Recovering from moments of confusion, he realized that he had somehow fallen asleep under the parked vehicle. He remembered. Tommy had sent him to forage, and he'd just started aimlessly wandering around, living rough. He was about to roll out, when he heard another thump of explosion, this time much closer.

The tinkle of glass hitting the pavement told him that it was almost certainly the apartment building directly overhead. Curious, since that was their temporary bivouac, arranged by the fat rascal Behruse to be precise. His suspicions were further roused as he heard sandaled feet slapping up the pavement and then several pairs of hairy ankles appeared. He lay silent, as a group of men appeared to be jimmying open his car.

There was a lot of back slapping and general jubilation. The hairy ankles exchanged rapid fire Arabic, some of which Ancelloti understood, primarily the phrases"death to Americans" and "to hell with infidels and Jews."The words filled him with dread. His hashish-clogged brain struggled to process. The exhaust roared all of a sudden, and he barely missed cracking his head again on the chassis. The hummer lurched forward with a clash of mangled gears, coating him with a mist of motor oil and dust. The hairy ankles all piled in, and the hummer roared off down the street. No one looked back.

Ancelloti got to his feet. Around him, the neighborhood had suddenly realized they had been bombed and were going through the usual reactions: disbelief, anger, exhibitionist wailing. Ancelloti staggered a few steps toward the scene, enough to verify the remnants of Tommy and his squaddies. He found a dog tag, absently pocketed it. Down the street, the stolen hummer accelerated and then took a corner, whooping. Wearily, Ancelloti began to follow.

27: MINISTRY

THE MINISTRY TURNED OUT TO BE EASY. HOFFMAN PRETENDED TO be a visiting colonel on tour. He wore the stripes he had stolen from Colonel Bradley. Sabeen pretended to be a doctor liaising with the UN and his interpreter. Behruse had to stay in the car because he couldn't pretend to be anything other than a stone thug.

Harder than access was actually finding anything coherent. The bureaucrats were on strike because their salaries were late. The building was having problems with electricity, and the phone lines had been cut last night by vandals. Inside the vaults, hundreds of thousands of paper files were being protected by two rival armies of clerks. Two-thirds of them were the "New Nationalists." One-third was Ba'athist loyalists. The New Nationalists had the political might, but the Ba'athists knew where everything was. It was a stalemate.

This was, in fact, Hoffman's comfort zone. He smoked, gossiped, and bribed his way into the Ba'athist headquarter, where a quick deal with the chief clerk netted him a jar of Vaseline and two hours alone with the Al-Rashid Hospital files. The chief clerk, did, in fact, charge by the hour for alone time with files, and moreover, he had his rates printed out on a piece of cardboard. Hoffman was able to avail himself of the "American Liberator" discount but could not swindle the ultra-low "Secret Ba'athist Sympathizer" rate.

The files themselves were in chaos, but Sabeen was quick, and she knew how hospital bureaucracy worked. It turned out that Dr. Sawad, being a suspicious man, tended to rotate his staff with extreme efficiency. Interns, junior techs, even nurses were changed with regularity, and all of them left him with highly negative recommendations. It was as if once having used them up, his earnest desire was to bury them somewhere far from sight.

"This is useless," Hoffman sneezed. "This guy was paranoid."

"Not a single medical staff stuck," Sabeen said. "He had no team. Could he do his work single handed?"

"No way a single man could handle Taha. Not even sedated."

"He trusted no doctor or nurse," Sabeen said. "He lived alone. He was mostly estranged from his daughter. No friends to speak of. No colleagues. The man was a hermit. How on earth could he have a partner?"

Hoffman laughed. "Look for the invisible people; cleaners, guards, cooks. They wouldn't be able to steal his work. And he would be able to control them easily."

Sabeen shrugged and grudgingly dug into further packets of mildewed files. Hoffman, whose Arabic was not up to scratch, basked in the light of his great idea.

"None of these files track the lower staff," she complained. "Ah, payrolls. Interesting."

"What is it?"

"Shit, you were right," Sabeen said. "Janitor. Was at the Al-Rashid with him the entire time. Got full marks from Sawad, regular raises. Quit five months ago, no reasons given. Sawad recommended him for redundancy and full pension."

"Address?"

"Yes, but four years old," Sabeen said. "Full name. Ali Mazra. Kurdish. Phone number crossed out. We'll have to tease him out."

"Behruse has been wanting to hound somebody for ages," Hoffman said. "Best let him do it."

Behruse, it turned out, was surprisingly good at hounding random people down. Having numerous old friends at police stations, post offices, and municipal authorities, he had access to the dry bureaucratic bones of the city. Apartment records, cell phone registrations, marriage certificates, voter records, income tax returns—Ali Mazra had them all. Sawad, if he had been trying to hide himself, had been woefully amateurish.

It took Behruse only a day to track down Mazra's current address, two apartments in a half-abandoned tenement building. One year's worth of rent had been paid in advance in cash.

"Now where does he get that kind of money? Hmm?" Sabeen said, on the way over. She held a pistol in her slim fingers, a 22 caliber Beretta. There was a small grin on her face, the instinctive excitement of a predator catching a scent. Hoffman couldn't stop leering.

"You think Taha's come back here?" Hoffman asked.

"If we're lucky," Sabeen said. "Or we'll get a better idea, at least."

"Mazra will talk," Behruse said. "Leave it to me."

The building was in a bad neighborhood and had lately suffered both bombing and looting. Several plots were burnt husks. The people on the streets were rough, many of them openly armed. The apartments themselves had no elevator, only a narrow stairway smelling of urine. The lights were gone, and they had to climb in near darkness, the false light of dusk filtering in through broken windows in the landings.

"Camera," Hoffman said, pointing.

"It moved," Sabeen drew her gun. "Someone knows we're here."

Behruse knocked on one of three doors, a heavy BAM-BAM-BAM, reminiscent of police everywhere. There was no answer. He moved to the next one, tried again. Shrugging, he lifted his foot and started kicking methodically, using the sole of his boot.

"Stop, stop," a muffled voice said from within.

"Ali Mazra?" Behruse asked, in his cop voice.

"Yes, yes."

"Open the door. Police," Behruse said. "Be very slow."

"What do you want?" Ali Mazra cracked the door open as far as the security chain would allow. "I have paid the monthly gift to Sergeant Ali Kharimi already."

"Kharimi is out, and I'm in," Behruse said. "Transferred last month. He conned you. Now let me in."

"What? Transferred?"

"Your boss Sawad made arrangements with me. Said you'd settle up," Behruse said. "Now open the door."

Ali Mazra opened grudgingly. He was a huge man, well over six feet, of cavernous height and build. Large, raw hands gripped a cleaver. He was ill at ease, his face sunken and blemished with lack of sleep, his body stinking of unwashed clothes and various chemicals.

Behruse barged in, into a small antechamber, cluttered with garbage and cardboard boxes. The door in the back was heavy wood, fortified with bands of iron. It was partially ajar, but the interior was cloaked in darkness.

"You aren't police," Ali Mazra said, staring at Sabeen and Hoffman. His hands gripped convulsively on the knife. The hilt of a tranquilizer gun peeped from his waistband. The hallway seemed ridiculously over crowded. Hoffman didn't mind the smell, but the Kurd looked crazed, capable of anything. Surreptitiously, he tried to maneuver Behruse's bulk between himself and the janitor.

"Relax," Sabeen said. "Not police. Mukhabarat."

"What?" Ali Mazra said.

"We are friends of Dr. Sawad," Sabeen said. "He told us where to find you."

"Where is he?" Ali Mazra asked. "We don't have any friends."

"Relax, Ali Mazra," Sabeen said. There was some hypnotic cadence to her voice, which, Hoffman couldn't help but notice, seemed to soothe even the most savage humans. "You have been alone too long. We have come to help you."

"Get out of here," Mazra said, gesturing to the door. "Leave. It's not safe."

"You think the Lion will come to get you," Hoffman said. "The Lion is loose, and he might want revenge. How long can you stand guard? How long can you even stay awake?"

"Sawad will come back." Mazra stared at Hoffman, as if daring him to disagree. The cleaver wavered between Behruse and Hoffman. The Kurd had his back to the wall and, even in his debilitated state, could probably take both of them. There was in him a sense of pure animal strength and desperation.

"Dr. Sawad is dead," Sabeen said flatly. "I have his autopsy and death certificate. He was murdered not long ago."

"No," Ali Mazra seemed to collapse into himself. "No."

"In my bag," Sabeen indicated her slim leather case. "You must know that Sawad was working for us. We are Mukhabarat. I am the doctor who was monitoring him. I will take over his work."

"Murdered how?"

"Thrown off the roof," Sabeen said. "By Afzal Taha, his patient, who even now might be looking for you. You are in danger, Ali Mazra, out on your own. We are your only aid."

"Taha killed the doctor?" Ali Mazra laughed hysterically. "Or maybe the Old Man killed him, Mukhabarat bitch. He was running from *you*."

"A misunderstanding," Sabeen said, smooth. "There are factions in the service. Some elements—like the Old Man—wanted to take over the doctor's research for selfish gain. We are the other side of the Mukhabarat, the reasonable side. We have the government mandate. We are legal."

"And him?" Ali Mazra pointed the cleaver at Hoffman. "Who is this rat?"

"CIA," Sabeen said. "Dr. Sawad was an important man. This project is of international importance. We can take care of everything if you let us."

"The doctor..."

"He's really dead," Sabeen said. She removed the autopsy picture gently from her case. "There is nothing else."

Ali Mazra stared at the picture and as acceptance finally clouded his eyes, the weariness of the past weeks caught up with him, and he sat abruptly against the cardboard boxes. This was a man who had survived purely on adrenaline and hope, and now it crashed away, leaving him broken.

"We are going to airlift you and the patient both to America," Hoffman chimed in. "Straight to Washington DC. Get you into the program."

"Patients," Ali Mazra said. He waved to the dark interior. "You think Taha was the only one?"

28: THE STRANGE ISLAND OF DR. SAWAD

THE STENCH OF ROTTING FLESH AND MORGUE CHEMICALS HIT Hoffman, an olfactory assault coiled around the room like a serpent. There was, cutting through it all, the sharp edge of chlorine, strong enough to make his eyes water and his nose tingle. Behruse, of a frail constitution, went so far as to gag discreetly in the corner. For a fat man, he had a surprisingly weak stomach.

Mazra was limping through in the dark, his torch light wavering. "They don't like the light," he said in passing. Hoffman dreaded to think whom he was referring to. The chamber ran through the breadth of the apartment and was furnished with four large laboratory tables, each one scarred with beakers, Petri dishes, varieties of chemical stocks, and reams and reams of papers.

This, the inner sanctum of Doctor Sawad and Mazra, revealed an unruly side to the great man. Everything was in chaos. No thought had been given to tidiness. Books, journals, references lay haphazardly wherever they had been last used. Blackboards along the wall were covered in scientific shorthand, some of it chemistry, some of it Arabic, some of it unique to Sawad.

There was an abandoned fish tank in one place, with the fish and water out, replaced by stacks and stacks of dirty Petri dishes and test tubes. Another bin was full of used syringes, like a graveyard for heroin addicts.

As his eyes got accustomed to the dark fugue, Hoffman saw that one-third of the room was closed off by a curtain, a great green dirty thing, half dragged on the floor, and splotched with dull red stains.

Beyond this, lay three cots, hospital issue, no doubt stolen from the Al-Rashid, with makeshift shackles welded on.

Two of these were side by side, occupied by a man and woman. They were hooked up to life support machines. In the vague green light, Hoffman could see tumors on their faces. They were skeletally thin and ill cared for. Their diapers stank, and they were covered in bed sores. Multiple drips fed into their veins. He could judge that they were not far from death. The shackles were undone, for in truth they were no threat to anyone. The third cot, ominously, was empty, the sheets covered in dried blood and feces. Behind was a padlocked door with a small barred cutout. Hands extended out from here, raw with wounds, and an unintelligible moaning ensued.

"Dog Boy," Mazra said, "too dangerous to let out without tranks."

Mazra led them on into a corner of this section, where his own bed lay, a more comfortable version of the hospital cot, minus the shackles. He slumped into it, with unfeigned weariness.

"You poor man," Sabeen said.

The Kurd glared at her. "Three weeks, all alone. Every day I thought the doctor would come. We are out of food, tranquilizers, almost everything. And the constant moaning. I haven't slept in days."

"You'll be alright now," Sabeen said. "We'll make a list of everything you need here and get it to you. You'll have help too, trusted men. Plus security."

Dog Boy saw them through bars somehow or just saw the wavering light of Mazra's torch, because he started howling right then, shouting obscenities and pleas, begging for water, begging to be let out or put to sleep or killed.

"He's gone mad," Mazra said. "Patient 3. I'm supposed to keep him under, but he uses up the tranks too fast."

"These patients, are they from the Al-Rashid too?" Sabeen asked.

"No. At the Al-Rashid we only had Taha," Mazra said. "We got these after."

"What exactly happened with Taha?"

"The doctor was close to success with Taha," Mazra said. "And then he became afraid of the Old Man. He had to hide all his research. Said there was someone after him to steal the research and kill all of us. He told me to find a safe place. I set up this apartment, and we moved all the equipment here bit by bit. We had a schedule, but the Al-Rashid got broken into, and we decided to move Taha then."

"What happened after that?"

"It was stupid," Mazra said. "Taha is almost immune to tranquilizers. We both knew that. The cell was a temporary structure. It wasn't strong enough. Taha broke out one day."

Mazra lifted his sleeve. "He gave me this scar, nearly killed me. The doctor was enraged when he got back."

"Where did you get these other patients from?"

"I got those two in the beginning. They used to live in this building. Quiet couple, no family. I drugged them and brought them here," Mazra said. "We got Dog Boy later, after Taha left. But things weren't good without Taha. The doctor said we needed him to finish the work."

"We will find Taha, don't worry," Sabeen said. "The work will be finished. How far along exactly was the doctor?"

"He thought that with Taha's blood and the Old Man's papers, he could make these two work," Mazra motioned at the hapless couple. "But they kept getting worse. It was my job to monitor them for improvement. I kept charts of everything, even the Dog Boy." He motioned at a neat stack by the foot of his bed.

"Very good charts too," Sabeen said. "You are as good as any nurse or lab tech, Ali Mazra."

"The doctor taught me," Mazra said. He sounded very pleased to be compared to a nurse.

"Where are his papers, Mazra?" Sabeen leaned forward. "Where is the research of the brilliant Dr. Sawad?"

"He told me to destroy his formulas," Mazra said, "if he ever went missing for more than a week."

"You destroyed all his work??"

"He memorized everything," Mazra said. "He didn't need the papers."

"But he's dead!"

"That's not something he anticipated."

"Well what are we supposed to do now?"

"He didn't leave any orders for after this death."

"What papers are left?"

"I didn't destroy his personal journals," Mazra shrugged. "You can have those."

29: THE JOURNALS
OF DR. SAWAD

LOG 1, DAY 13. AL-RASHID, BASEMENT WING. STUDIES ON SUBJECT 0, Afzal Taha, continuing at fast pace after initial breakthrough. OM help invaluable. Telomere mutation expected to be main cause of Taha rapid cellular healing and age. OM suggests to study telomerase levels present in Taha cells. This is the enzyme that extends telomeres in cells. High levels are most often found in cancer cells, which is one of the reasons cancer cells don't die. Performed tests by replacing cancer patient's blood sample with Taha's. Lab returned positive result. Must be careful to erase tracks. Might be necessary to bring in geneticist into study at some point. Dr. J, perhaps. I shall definitely get promoted for this work.

Log 3, Day 21, Al-Rashid, Basement Wing. Telomerase present in large quantities but no cancer. Very unusual to find high levels of telomerase in healthy cells. Have written to the American genetics company Geron to gain preliminary technical information. OM seems to know a lot more than he is telling. It's just like him to obstruct medical progress.

Log 8, Day 23, Al-Rashid, Basement Wing. Research at a complete halt. No working theories as to why S0 (Subject Zero) has high levels of telomerase in cells but no cancers. Consulting OM again. Threefold situation likely: (a) Telomerase increased initially in host body by some unknown means, (b) hyper immune system developed to suppress cancers and prevent late onset mutations, and (c) telomerase levels kept stable to prevent cell death without continued input of telomerase-making enzymes.

Log 10, Day 28, Al-Rashid, Basement Wing. Taha is highly resistant to disease, highly resistant to tissue damage, with faster than normal regeneration powers. Also confirmed reduction of senescence. Discussions with Dr. J. Might have to bring him in soon. Need blood. work confirmed 100% for research papers. Taha's immune system alone is remarkable. Nobel Prize possible. Could he just be a genetic freak of nature?

Log 11, Day 29, Al-Rashid, Basement Wing. OM quashed research paper emphatically. Refuses to understand what a marvel Taha is. Has become unreasonably autocratic. OM having me watched, I think. Forbade me to speak to anyone, even consulting specialists. I cannot work in a vacuum anymore. This is high level genetics. I have demanded more explanations. Am certain OM knows everything. Asked my Mukhabarat supervisor discreetly. That bastard told me to follow OM's directions explicitly. What the hell are they interested in genetics for? Biological weapons perhaps?

"Guys, we should really try to find this OM cat," Hoffman said. "I can't believe I've actually found some weapons of mass destruction."

"You'll probably get a promotion for this," Behruse said. "They'll make you general or something. I'll have to salute you probably."

The Dog Boy moaned in the background, promising sexual favors to anyone who would let him out of the cell.

Log 15, Day 34, Al-Rashid, Parking Lot. Office bugged. New male nurse and security guard surely Mukhabarat spies. Must warn Mazra. We must prepare to remove Taha from here. I can continue research on my own, perhaps with Dr. J's help. Will contact Nur, if necessary. This is too big for one person. Nobel Prizes for everyone! Except Mazra of course. I need some other human subjects to experiment on.

Log 19, Day 38, Al-Rashid, Parking Lot. Long discussion with OM. Pretending to be his lackey. Need to make a move soon. Taha growing increasingly resistant to heavy tranks. He is recovering somewhat from earlier partial lobotomies. Incredible. OM offers key insights into telomerase creation enzymes. He has given me many notebooks. Appears to be translations. Medical notations are strange, even archaic. Annotations from some third person Geber. Also sections written entirely by Geber. A collaborative effort, clearly. OM is almost certainly a biomedical professional of no small power. He is finally taking me into his confidence, I think. Today he told me that he thinks of me like a son.

Log 21, Day 41, Al-Rashid, Bathroom. Geber might be THE GEBER. Jabir Ibn Hayyan of Egypt, the ALCHEMIST. How old is this formula?? The notation matches alchemy notation of eighth century Cairo. How old is OM then?? This is incredible. Might be a hoax. But OM vouched for by the service. And Taha is living proof? PS librarian was very helpful. Must remember to thank him for references.

"Did you dudes know anything about this Geber guy?" Hoffman asked.

Behruse, who had stopped reading and was trying to make some coffee, did not answer.

"Geber lived in the eighth century AD, in Kufa," Sabeen said absently. "He was reputedly the first and foremost alchemist, the Father of Alchemy. He also invented almost all of the alchemical instruments used throughout."

"You think this is the same guy?"

"One of Geber's root interests was '*Tawkin*': the creation of artificial life. He was particularly renowned for trying to prolong a scorpion's life or to recreate one artificially. He probably succeeded," Sabeen said. "Incidentally, there is another scientist called Pseudo-Geber, who anonymously published a lot of alchemical papers in Latin some 500 years after Geber's purported death. So perhaps he *did* manage to live for so long."

"That's incredible!" Hoffman said. "How can you be so calm?"

"Hush, dear, I'm trying to read."

Log 23, Day 44, Al-Rashid, Bathroom. Geber notes are amazing. The man is a genius. I wonder if he still lives. He might have succeeded. This is the initial work done on this project, nearly 13 centuries ago. How old is Taha then? Who exactly is OM? Desperate to get OM blood sample, but no chance of that I fear. Do not want to tip him off about this line of speculation. Taha and OM both likely 13 centuries old. Could OM be original collaborator of Geber in development of telomerase project? OM also very interested in something called the Druze watch. Keeps wanting me to interrogate Taha on this subject. He has grown increasingly unhinged for results. Am certain OM plans to kill me after he gets what he wants.

———————

"Woah, guys, this dude knows about the watch," Hoffman said, "He's like the mastermind of the whole thing. We got to show this shit to Avi. Speaking of which, did Avi say anything about helping my boys?"

"Yes, I forgot to tell you," Sabeen said. "He's gotten in touch with Salemi. Things should be taken care of soon."

———————

Log 29, Day 53, Al-Rashid, Public Ward 2. Recovering from superficial injuries during break in. Remarkable luck! We were not ready to move, Mazra in particular was very reluctant. But what great luck! So many patients escaped! We smuggled Taha out, sedated, and then destroyed all his papers. I am the only man alive now who knows the full extent of this experiment. It is the greatest single scientific endeavor of human history, stretching over 14 centuries!

———————

Log 29, Day 53, Safe House 1, Office. Ahhh, finally I can write in peace. Met OM, explained breakout by Taha. Told him about the resistance to tranks and other drugs (which is true!). OM was very agitated. He almost smashed the little olive tree. I am on pain of death now. Have to be very careful. Am sending notes to Nur so that some aspect of my research survives. But not the deep end of it, of course. Dr. J knows now. Need his help for the more complex genetic work. How did Geber perform these tests without modern technology?? What a mind! I am no longer sure about Nobel Prizes. This work should not be revealed to the public, maybe. Is it possible to live forever? Geber, at least, added a few hundred years to his life, if not more. Same for Taha. OM, I am sure, is old as sin. I can feel it. The truth is at my fingertips. If Geber and the OM discovered this through alchemy, surely modern science can reverse engineer it. Imagine the work I could achieve with 200 years more?

"Olive tree? Old Man?" Hoffman had his jaw open. "Sab, is it Avi?"

"Hush, dear, keep reading, we're just at the interesting bit."

"It's Avi, isn't it? Your grandfather." A cool finger rested on his lips. She was too close. Hoffman breathed in deeply, the light citrus of her skin filling his head. He leaned back, disoriented.

"I'll explain everything. Let's just finish, ok?"

Log 35, Day 68, Safe House 1, Office. Subject 1, male, 34 years. Subject 2, female, 29 years. Mazra has finally found some suitable candidates for our clinical trial. So far, the analysis of Taha's blood and DNA reveals many clues as to the methods Geber/OM must have used. Yet some part is missing, some critical portion. Something that OM himself does not know, presumably. He is pressing me to go over old notes and look for mentions of the Druze watch. I have fobbed him off for now. I am growing convinced that the Druze watch has the missing link of this alchemical immortality. Mazra and I have taken turns questioning Taha, but he is growing very difficult to control. Mazra has him locked in the cell full time now. Taha refuses to answer questions about the watch. I wish I had a professional interrogator to work on him. I have discussed the situation hypothetically with Dr. J. He suspects, of course but can never know the true extent of the situation.

Log 39, Day 72, Safe House 1, Lab. Disaster! Taha has escaped! He overpowered Mazra during feeding time. The tranks must be like water to him now. He's gone! God knows where. Luckily Subjects 1 and 2 are ok. Mazra has brought in Subject 3, male, 25 years. I must continue the work without Taha. Cancer is a big problem. Subject 2 already showing tumors. The delivery method is another issue. It must be like a disease, like a virus, which can affect almost every cell in the human body. Only a very potent virus would be able to effect wholesale changes in the host human body. Something like herpes simplex, perhaps, which has different latency stages and does not cause immediate cell death. The virus could have a long lysogenic cycle, where it would copy itself into the host DNA and lie dormant, allowing the host cell to multiply normally. I must try to graft the telomerase-making protein code or some similar device to a viral DNA that can successfully penetrate the human body, spread to most of the key cells—perhaps mainly stem cells—and then not cause cancers or other ill effects, but rather, simply prevent senescence. Is this even possible? It boggles the mind to think someone 1,300 years ago might have thought of this.

The problem would be easier to fix if it just caused a genetic mutation in the sperm or egg cells. The beneficiary, of course, would be the offspring. Yet this is not the case. OM, Geber, even Taha most likely were not born but transmuted, as the alchemist would say. I cannot help but wonder: if these alchemists discovered immortality so long ago, then are these terrible old men floating around now, ruling the world in secret?

———————

"Ah, Sawad, the prick knew too much, really." The vulgarity sounded ill on Sabeen's lips, made her face somehow cruel.

Hoffman made to withdraw, uneasy suddenly that Behruse was behind him. BANG! He jumped in the air, half expecting to be shot. The shockwave of the bullet reverberated around the closed space and set Dog Boy off moaning again. Hoffman rolled to a crouching position, his nose bleeding, to see the tree trunk body of the Kurd toppling slowly, a red ruin in the center of his face, a gaping hole that Hoffman could almost see through. Too late, he scrambled for his gun.

"Sorry, Hoffy." Behruse had the pistol on him, so close, that he could feel the heat from the discharge.

Sabeen lit a cigarette and pulled deeply. Her eyes were cold. "It could have played out differently."

Hoffman sprawled on the ground, hands out. "Sawad worked for you."

"Yes, from the start," Sabeen said. "He betrayed us, of course."

"Who pushed him off the roof?"

"That would be me," Behruse laughed. He did not appear so kindly anymore. "I was supposed to capture him, but he made a run for it—*to the roof.* I swear, what the fuck did he expect to find there? A stairway to heaven? The idiot practically jumped rather than get caught."

"You fucked me, Behruse."

"Hey, Hoffy, it was just pure bad luck," Behruse smiled and then his boot came down, smashing into Hoffman's knee. "You shouldn't have fucked my bitch wife."

"Enough!" Sabeen's voice was a whiplash; it left in no doubt who was master here.

"Sab, what the hell was this?" Hoffman asked from the ground. "Why play me for so long?"

"We needed you, sweet one," Sabeen said. "We needed you to take us places where we could not go. We needed to find out the full extent of Sawad's betrayals. Grandfather saw the potential in you, and he was right."

"Dr. Nur?"

"Dead, strangled by you," Sabeen said.

"Dr. J?"

"Soon to be shot using your gun. You also pushed Dr. Sawad off the roof, in case you were wondering."

"My friends?"

"Salemi knows where they are hiding. He'll take care of them," Sabeen said. "And return the watch if they have it."

"He'll kill them."

"Lucky, if they die quick," Behruse said. "Hassan Salemi likes to toy with his food before eating it, I hear."

"So you win everything," Hoffman said. He let his head fall back flat on the ground. Ali Mazra's blood pooled nearby, steaming.

"Taha is still loose," Sabeen shrugged. "He will return here, one day soon. It is the only refuge he knows. We'll take him then."

"Oh yeah, and your men," Behruse said. "They're dead. Salemi got them two days ago. IED. Islamic Jihadi Grand Council of Shulla took responsibility on the radio for it."

"You *didn't have to do that*," Hoffman cried. "They didn't know anything."

Sabeen shook her head. "You think grandfather takes chances anymore?"

"I shoot myself now, I guess?" Hoffman asked. "You want me to write a note?"

"I'm not going to kill you, dear," Sabeen said. "You're far too precious. Grandfather wants to know who you really work for. And again, you might have to stand trial for all those murders."

"At least give me some more pills," he said, panicked at the sudden thought of all that poison eating up his insides.

"Oh, Hoffman, you're addicted to them," Sabeen said. "You've taken so many that I think you're impervious to *all* poison now."

"That won't help if I put a bullet in your gut though. Get up. No bullshit now." Behruse kicked Hoffman in the back, not in anger, more with a sort of professional force, enough to hurt, not enough for permanent damage.

Hoffman curled up, whimpering. He felt no compulsion to hold up under torture of any kind. He knew very clearly that he would blurt out any and all truths at the first opportunity. Behruse swore disgustedly, grabbed him under the armpits, and started to drag him away. The sound of the Dog Boy's incoherence got louder.

"Wait, wait!" Hoffman shouted. "Do not put me in with that freak! Behruse! Behruse! Aarrrggghh."

30: BURNING BOOKS

YAKIN GRIPPED HIS AK47 WITH TRUCULENCE. IT WAS JUST HIS LUCK to get a bum weapon. He had asked for the Bulgarian gun with the beechwood stock because that was the best, but of course, he had been overruled. They hadn't even given him a Chinese one. No. Instead, he was holding some mangled reject made in Bangladesh, which didn't even have a gun manufactory. It was probably made on some boat by a fisherman. The gun had a 75% misfire rate! 75%! It was actually safer to give the gun to the enemy and let it blow *his* hand off.

Even though he was shadowing the imam, and therefore probably going to be the first one to die, he still did not garner the respect he deserved. The others called him names behind his back and were trying to kill him. They hated him and wanted him out of the way.

That was the only answer. How was he supposed to get on in life if his own side was trying to kill him? He had asked for a bulletproof vest and a helmet, but the imam had laughed him away, and their de facto quartermaster had given him a red scarf. A red scarf? How the hell was that supposed to stop bullets? In fact, it would probably attract bullets. The enemy would single him out as a champion warrior because he was the only idiot wearing a red scarf. Of course, Yakin reflected bitterly, if he now refused to wear the red scarf, they would all gang up on him and call him disloyal, and a traitor, and unwilling to die for God.

This was the one epithet to be avoided at all costs in this crew. To be eager to die for God was the one credo the imam consistently loved, no matter what kind of madness was the current flavor of the month. To be fairly lukewarm about the idea of dying for God was a surefire way of getting pressed into the front lines.

The imam was on a roll. Things had been going very well for him after the initial disappointment of having his house blown up. This was bad news for Yakin, who had realized some time ago that whenever things went well for people around him, it meant inevitably that he was somehow going to land in the shit. This, he reflected bitterly, was the story of his life.

The partnership with the Old Man had borne fruit. The imam's bomb squad had just taken out a group of American soldiers, without any reprisal from the Americans. At the current market rate of 1 white body equaling 78.3 olive-skinned bodies, this was a massive coup in the streets, and his name was being touted for the state legislature.

The bomb squad had even brought back a Humvee, that most prized possession of American soldiers and rap stars alike. And now, they were on the way to the abandoned safehouse to correct the one blot on the imam's record, the final and just punishment of the murderer of his son. Yakin, by this point, was heartily sick of the imam's dead son, who in life had been a fickle dilettante of lost causes, not much good to anybody, and most likely impotent to boot. In life the imam, too, had hated him. In death, however, he had developed some kind of inconceivable status, an unlikely martyrdom imbuing him with all sorts of virtues.

Fanatics on the street now claimed that he was 6'6", when he had in fact been 5'8". They said he had had a full beard of unusual lustrousity, when he had in fact worn a womanish pencil thin goatee. They said that he had been a devout Shi'a, when in fact he had on many occasions declared his disbelief in any deity higher than the US dollar.

Now they were bouncing along on a half-sprung truck, going to avenge this good for nothing. Yakin had his Bangladeshi gun, his pistol, and an old knife. He sat in the back of the covered van with half of their force. The imam was an egalitarian. He rode in front with the driver, wearing a vest, but no helmet. It was unusual for him to go murdering in person, but this was an issue of family honor, and he had lost a lot of face over the continued defiance of these petty criminals.

Yakin wanted to pee, but there was no way they were going to stop the truck for him. People in the neighborhood had gotten wind of this upcoming disaster and were making themselves scarce. Like rats. Fleeing, craven rats. How he wished he was with them.

All too soon, the truck ride was over. It was a dead-end street, and among some abandoned buildings there was an old blue door. Yakin loitered behind, pretending to tie his laces until the others had leapt out. He was sure Kinza would recognize him and shoot him first. Having seen them fight, he had no doubt that this would come to a bloody end. The imam couldn't imagine how a single man could bring his house down and so believed erroneously that this was actually a splinter insurgency band, probably foreigner Sunnis trying to muscle in. Yakin had explained that this was nothing more than the black malign will of Kinza, which had a gravity of its own and could pull innocent bystanders into its bizarre, violent vortex.

The chaos started right away, as the first Fanatic kicked in the door, while the imam chanted obscure suras Yakin had never heard before. Two rifle butts and the blue door slammed back, splintered. Two of the men leapt in, directly into the flaming muzzle of an M60, a swiveling, racketing nightmare of a gun, manned by a cackling ten year old. Splinters and bullets sprayed outside, and Yakin rolled on the floor. Salemi's soldiers were Gulf War veterans. They returned fire, and soon the boy was thrown back from his perch in mangled pieces.

Yakin had no sympathy to waste for the kid. His enemies were already propelling him forward, and all too soon he was clambering over the carcass of the smoking M60. The second he entered, he felt the hair on his neck rise. This was a cursed house. There was an eeriness not entirely produced by the ringing in ears. Yakin tried to position himself into the middle of the convoy following Salemi, whose calm authority had quelled the panic of the Fanatics for a space.

The policy was simple: knock down empty doors and keep firing. The first door was an abandoned room and the second and the third, until Yakin himself was confused whether they were coming or going.

The wall suddenly opened up behind a tapestry, and an ancient cook leapt out. He had his apron and a cleaver and smelled of onion soup. The man was deranged. Within seconds he had chopped off someone's hand and disappeared back into the wall, taking the appendage with him. No doubt he intended to cook it later.

"Get in there after him!" Salemi said over the thunder of gunfire.

"Just a minute, I've got a stitch," Yakin said. He slumped unconvincingly against a wall well away from that gaping tapestry tunnel.

One of the braver Fanatics rushed in. There were gunshots and terrible splattering noises reminiscent of cleavers hitting raw meat. The noises grew fainter. The tapestry slowly twitched back into place like an awful sphincter closing.

"Imam, perhaps we should retreat," Yakin said.

"What?"

"It's just that we've lost two Fanatics and one True Believer already," Yakin said. "Soon we'll be down to a handful of Pious. It doesn't look like Kinza is even here…" He trailed off and started fiddling with his gun, not least because Salemi looked like he wanted to shoot someone.

They were forced to move on. They soon came to a dining room that was filled up with an immense table, seating ten to each side, although there was barely enough room for the chairs. Candles and place settings of tarnished silver gleamed in the darkness. Everything was covered in cobwebs.

"This place is scaring the shit out of me," Yakin said to one of the Pious.

The next room over was a sitting room, full of mint tea and nice floral chairs. Two ladies in full hijab sat knitting by the window. Yakin was halfway toward them with the intention of yanking off their robes before he remembered that this sort of thing was severely frowned upon by the imam. *It was alright to dismember people and put them in jars, oh yes, but try a little rape and pillage, and it's down the ranks with you.* He wanted to stop for some tea, but the Fanatics were smashing things up, and the mood just didn't seem right.

"Tie them up and take them," said the imam, putting the matter to rest.

They moved into the next room, swaggering a little bit now, even though they had yet to apprehend any of the prime targets. Yakin figured it was something primal about taking women captives. He tried to get a glimpse of the two prisoners, but they were so thoroughly shielded in black that it was impossible to guess anything; although one pair of eyes looked middle aged and the other seemed nice and young. He contrived to bump against the younger one several times, until one of the Fanatics swore at him and pushed him away.

The younger eyes glared at him, and he could see her lips moving beneath the veil. He felt something shrivel in his crotch and panic flooded his brain.

"Sorry, sorry," he said, pushing his way to Salemi. "They're witches!"

"So?"

"She made my—ah, that is, she. Shouldn't we just shoot them? Isn't that what the old guy wanted?"

"We are not the Old Man's errand boys," Salemi said. "If he wants them dead, he can do the job himself. I don't murder women. I only execute those who have transgressed against the laws of God."

Yakin, who could not much see the difference between the two, lacked the courage to say so and simply ducked into line behind a veteran Fanatic. They entered another interminable hallway the walls warped and cracked, lathered in crazy shades of white paint. The floors vibrated with a peculiar buzzing sound. It got into Yakin's head like a bee inside his skull, a manly baritone bee droning some kind of Coptic chant just below the frequency of registered speech.

"Can you hear that? What the hell is that?"

"Shut up, peacock."

Fanatics didn't get nervous, fueled by the same insanity that drove Salemi, but the True Believers had their hands on their triggers and the Opportunistic Faithful class was looking distinctly jittery. It was clear to Yakin that there was something very wrong with this house, aside from the unnatural width and breadth of its rooms and the impossible number of twisting corridors and staircases. Men were getting lost in here, coming out from distant rooms harried by the lunatic cook who leapt from space to space like a quantum particle with a knife-wielding disdain for things like time and distance.

There was a commotion ahead, and suddenly one wall caved in completely, burying them in moth-eaten books, scrolls, and scabs of gray paint. An Opportunist Faithful, trapped under there, started yelling that the words were sharp. Gunfire riddled into the mound from panicked fingers, and too late they realized that they had simply shot their own man down. Black ink oozed out with blood. There was the dull thud of metal hitting bone, and the man beside Yakin went down, a steel crossbow bored three inches into his head. They all froze. Except for Yakin, who turned to run.

He even got a few steps, until the cold barrel of Salemi's gun brought him up short.

"Turn around, peacock," Hassan Salemi said. He picked up an errant book, thumbed through it nonchalantly. "These books are very old. This is, I think, what remains of the lost library. These words are all heresies. Burn the place down."

Later, chased by smoke, Yakin followed shadowy figures through the labyrinth, not sure who was on his side, half terrified of flying cooks and six-inch steel bolts. The buzzing was getting worse. They had taken more prisoners and had lost some men. Salemi was somewhere up ahead; Yakin could hear snatches of commands, translated down with contradictory shouts. Left! Right! Forward! Burn!

It was clear by now that Kinza was not here, although Salemi was unwilling to accept this. The house was on fire, and it was reacting badly to it. They had lost men in the darkness, when corridors looped unaccountably back into each other, causing nervous bursts of friendly fire. The archer was still at large, some kind of expert sniper with his crossbow, and those dull thuds brought terror to Yakin's brain. They were down to only two Fanatics, the brothers Al-Hama and Borsha, grievous losses considering the paucity of results.

It occurred to Yakin that the Old Man might have sold them down the river, sent them to this mad library house to tie up loose ends. Al-Hama shouldered aside a door and the clammy breath of a rotting seaside hit them in the face. It was a cavernous dark room, sloped like the hull of a ship, and *cold*, at least several degrees below ambient temperature.

Ancient earthenware jars lined the sides of the room, amphorae with red wax seals, slimy with underwater sediment, sweating ooze, and that horrible sawing, vibrating sound was clawing through Yakin making him puke abruptly by Al-Hama's sandaled feet. The Fanatic bulled in, unafraid, his gun out ready to scythe down jars of bellicose mud.

Something terrible happened to Yakin's ears. The pressure changed abruptly, and he found himself on his knees, blood spurting from his nose. Al-Hama was shouting, his figure convulsing on the trigger, making bullets spray. The noise was deafening, even worse, jars were shattering, and gray fog filled the room with the nauseating smell of rotten sea, dead things floating up, and it seemed to Yakin as if terrible demons were lurching out of the amphorae. A change in pressure made his eardrums stretch to bursting.

Al-Hama was reciting verses, shouted words of defiance, while his bullets tore up the fog with little effect until something strangled in his throat, and blood mist rose in fine droplets around him. Yakin staggered away from the Fanatic, trying desperately to get out, out of the cavern, out of the doorway, anywhere but here. The floor was shaking now. It was an earthquake, wood and wall paper and cement all tumbling down around him. Water lapped at his feet, and then his ankles, rising rapidly, a terrible hot kind of water that burned his skin.

Their party was lost, stumbling around, Hassan Salemi trying to rally somewhere far away but his voice was a distant siren, a drowned radio.

"Run!" Yakin savagely pushed Borsha away, who was stupidly blocking the door looking for his dead brother. "Run, you fools!"

He dodged between slices of fog, from demonic grasping hands, from tumbling masonry, and somehow made it to the hallway and then into some other bizarre room that had been overturned by some giant's footfall. He saw bodies floating in the air without gravity and a terrible burning light behind him, dark willowy things his eyes refused to register. *Run, run.* It was the only chord he understood; that he still lived and he had to run. Behind him the house started to burn in earnest.

31: UNEXPECTED HELP

DAGR WAS COLD, HUNGRY, AND MISERABLE. HE HAD NOT expected to survive this episode and had therefore not bothered to plan for an aftermath. Just his luck. Now, homeless, they squatted in a gutted building with a caved in roof. There was an unexploded shell in the corner, which was why the neighbors left the place alone. It was a dud CBU-105 cluster bomb, a fat torpedo-shaped case with fins, designed to open midair to release its submunitions. This particular bomb, having selfishly kept its bomblets to itself, now nestled peacefully in the corner of the room, lightly peppered in rat droppings, dented, scratched, and rusty, but still smirking. Dagr knew that the little bombs inside were potent and indeed, the cluster bomb was designed with the thought in mind that in case it failed to explode right away, it could function as a very effective land mine and explode at a later date with hardly any reduction in enemy casualties.

"We could have sold this, eh?" Kinza said. His face was drawn, seemingly aged overnight. The berserker fury had left him when enough of Salemi's men had died and the entire building had wept blood. Now he seemed numb, an exhausted shell of a man. They were wounded, perhaps seriously, but in the dark their clothes were soaked black anyways with whose blood indistinguishable.

The terror remained in Dagr's eyes though, cutting through all the shrapnel cuts and aches, the adrenaline dump that left his body floating on lassitude. He had seen everything from behind and now could never get the cries of screaming men out of his mind. *We both stayed behind him. If we had been in front of him, he would have killed us. I've never seen anything like this. He would have killed us. He's not human.*

"We need food," Dagr said finally. "Water, blankets, medicine. Anyone bring any money?"

Hamid pulled out a stack of wallets from his vest.

"You looted them?"

"Spoils of war." Hamid shrugged, lopsided. There was something wrong with his arm.

"It was good thinking," Kinza said.

"These men had families," Dagr pawed his way through the wallets, horrified at the way his hands adjusted to this life with such ease. "You never think these Fanatics have wives, children." There were pictures in the wallets of women, children.

"Xervish had a family too," Kinza said. His voice was weary. It was a half-hearted attempt. Kinza was no longer concerned about right or wrong. Dagr could read it in his face. In the vastness of the enemy facing them, he simply wanted to *do some damage* before the end.

"I'll get the supplies," Dagr said finally.

Outside, he walked with a checkered scarf muffling his features, hoping the fugue of dusk disguised him from chance informants. They had crippled Salemi's organizations here, at the heart of his power, but he had other houses, other men. Demons like him did not die easily. Already, Dagr knew, US dollars were changing hands through anonymous text messages offering new bounties on three men who were considered very much walking dead. Whatever favors they had accumulated were spent now. They were on their own.

He entered a sorry-looking corner store, deliberately picking the one with a guttering light and half empty shelves. Some of the commodities were tight, like cough medicine, or even simple bottled water. Many of the familiar local brands were gone, the factories shut. He had a commandeered wallet stuffed with cash, but not enough. Salemi's men had carried little money. They would have to eke it out, and it still would not be enough, not to get them anywhere near Mosul. *Who are we kidding? We're never leaving this city alive.*

In the end, he took bandages, antiseptic cream, water, dry Chinese biscuits, and as many bananas as they had, the best he could

232 SAAD Z. HOSSAIN

do. In the counter, he grabbed cigarettes and matches. They needed hot food but the cafes were out of the question, and most were closed in anticipation of trouble. The shopkeeper stared at him, one hand beneath the counter, holding a weapon no doubt.

"Is there any hot food out there? Any stalls open?"

"No," said the shopkeeper. "What street are you from, *friend*?"

Dagr looked down, saw to his horror that the wallet in his hand had flipped open, the plastic flap clearly showing a driver's license with the picture of a bearded man with flowing white hair. His gun nestled in his pocket. He quenched the urge to go for it.

"Here's your money." Exaggerated care to move slowly, keeping his hands visible. He left the cash on the counter and backed out, not waiting for the change.

Back home, he dropped the packages on the floor. Kinza and Hamid were drowsing, each huddled in a different corner, as far away from the cluster bomb as possible.

"Sorry, we have a problem."

"What? No food in the stores?"

"I used this wallet." Dagr threw it on the floor.

"You carried a stolen wallet?" Kinza asked. "Without emptying it?"

"I was tired. I didn't think," Dagr sat down. "It flipped open. The shopkeeper saw the license. He was suspicious."

"You showed it to a shopkeeper?" Hamid looked disgusted. "Are you insane?"

"Were you followed?" Kinza asked.

"No…maybe…no, definitely not," Dagr said. "I walked around the block, took a long route."

"We have to move out of here," Kinza said.

"Some advice: we're exhausted," Hamid said. "We need to eat, sleep. We can't get through this without rest. Too many mistakes are made by fools who think they're supermen. I've seen that first hand in the army."

"Ok," Kinza said. He slumped down, and the depth of his exhaustion was evident. "You're right. This place can be hardly more dangerous than the streets. But we keep watch. You, professor, get the middle watch, because you fucked up."

When Dagr spilled out the meager stash of medicine and food, they gathered in the petering light of the single naked bulb, and he realized that his companions were injured far more than he had thought. Kinza with a huge hole in his side and a laceration down his neck needing stitches; Hamid had a useless right arm, tucked in with a crude sling he had fashioned, the bone perhaps fractured, the bullet still inside. It was impossible to tell. They bore their pain with a dull stoicism, too tired to think, and finishing the cold food, fell into deep exhausted sleep.

Dagr, the least hurt of the three, drowsed alone through the night, sleeping in fits, the gun constantly slipping from his hands. Then close to dawn, at the hour of the first prayer, he heard footfalls near their door. He struggled to his feet and lurched outside, thinking to buy some time, sketching together some pathetic bluff, too tired in truth to even panic properly.

It was an elderly man carrying a bag and the grocery clerk with a bulge in his jacket.

"You're those men," the elder said, "the ones who hit Salemi."

"No, no for God's sake, I'm just a professor. I was travelling. We got robbed."

"You had Ibn Waleed's purse," said the elder.

Dagr glanced back, half hoping to see the backup muzzle of Kinza's guns, but the men were sleeping each in their corner, oblivious.

"Yes, you are them," the elder said. "They said there were ten of you. I see only three here. Your friends are injured?"

"Half dead," Dagr said. "They'll fight back all the same. We've got a cluster bomb in there. I've rigged it to explode on a trigger."

"Oh, keep your bomb." The grizzled man smiled suddenly.

Dagr stared at him, his brain barely functioning. "What exactly do you want?"

"We've brought you food," the elder said. He motioned at the shopkeeper. "Faiz said you needed food and medicine." He brought out an ancient black leather medical bag from inside his jacket. "I am a doctor."

"What?"

"I'm with him."

The two moved aside, and a great hulking figure loomed in the doorway, wide faced, wild hair, and beard drizzled with gray.

"Who?" Dagr stepped back in alarm, confused. Then the faint smell of cats wafted up, with half-dredged memories of flashing silver hair in the moonlight and an immense, inhuman strength. He slumped down in resignation. "I thought he'd find us sooner or later."

Dog Boy was insane. This was clear when he tried to mount Hoffman while simultaneously trying to eat him at the same time. Biting and buggery. Not something to take lying down. Although Hoffman's body was wasted from withdrawal, abuse, and lack of exercise, its underlying structure was still some kind of Marine-issue specimen, albeit of a very inferior kind. Long-suppressed memories of unarmed combat classes came back to him, causing him to flail around trying to effect some sort of judo throw.

Finally, as the choke hold of Dog Boy caused his face to purple and blackout seemed eminent, he reached even further back into his past to barely registered backyard fights and bar room brawls. Teeth and elbows. Some dimly remembered precept that this was unsporting occurred to him. But then so was the tumescent penis jammed into his hip. He found some bit of Dog Boy's forearm and sank in his teeth. His elbow swung back in short, sharp jabs, MMA fashion, scoring along Dog Boy's baying face.

A sickening crunch, broken nose, claret flying, and the pressure eased somewhat. Hoffman pursued this line relentlessly, elbows to the face and then managed to turn somewhat in Dog Boy's grasp and bring his knees to bear. And finally, he ended with a Hoffman special, which was ramming the top of his skull into whatever delicate apparatus adorned Dog Boy's open neck and jaw, a sufficiently hard blow that sent the lunatic spinning back gasping for air.

The man flopped in place and started blubbering. It crossed Hoffman's mind that he ought to take this opportunity to strangle Dog Boy. Somehow, the idea of choking the life from that mangled, mournful face made him want to cry. It made him realize that despite being a veteran Marine war machine and decorated combat hero, he had never actually killed anyone. He remembered Sabeen's cool finger on his lips and railed at the general unfairness of it all. Things had been going so well with her. Cursing Behruse, he began to tear up sheets to shackle his cell mate.

32: INTERVIEW WITH A LION

DAGR WAS HAVING TEA WITH THE LION. IT WASN'T A PLEASANT experience. The man was frightening. His face was seamed with old scars, the ragged edged ones from fighting, but also scalpel straight ones from countless operations. They formed a cross-hatched seam across his head and neck, a chess board of pain and humiliation. And his eyes—his eyes were *old*. Weary. Clouded with despair. There was something otherworldly in them but not of the cute fairy variety. This kind of elfin spoke of madness, of eerie darkness and the depths to which the world was deeply fucked up beyond the small patina of normality that coated most lives and the very long way a man could fall once he plunged through this meager safety net. Dagr thought back on the fantastic tale of the watch and shuddered.

"Your friends, they are well?" Afzal Taha's voice was damaged, a bare whisper of force.

"They will recover," Dagr said. *They're half dead. Kinza is halfway in a coma. They gave me all the armor, and then paid the price.* "Thanks for the doctor." The Lion had moved them to a different place, a house with actual beds and some form of hygiene. The doctor brought them hot food and looked after their injuries with a dedication that went beyond payment.

"He owes me," the Lion said.

"Well, you've probably saved Kinza's life," Dagr said. "Sorry, by the way, about shooting you. That episode didn't turn out so well for us. The neighborhood people told us you were a murderer."

"I am."

"Oh well," Dagr tried to keep his grin fixed in place, "who isn't, these days. They turned on us though, sold us to Hassan Salemi."

"They tend to do that."

236

"So it's very kind of you, really, to come back like this. I thought you would be more interested in shooting us, to be honest."

"The thought had crossed my mind," Afzal Taha said. "But the situation is fluid."

"I see."

"There is a way for us to live," Taha said. "All of us."

"I am a bit confused."

"The watch."

"I have it," Dagr almost tripped himself in his eagerness to get it out. "See, safe. I knew you'd want it back."

"Keep it." Taha waved his hand.

Dagr had expected a bullet by this time, the doctor notwithstanding, and his subsequent observations on this man's stability had done nothing to bolster any hopes to the contrary. Thus, with exaggerated care, he put the watch down on the tea table between them in a place he hoped sufficed as middle ground where he wouldn't be accused of disobeying a direct order to 'keep it' while at the same time making it abundantly clear that the object, in fact, did not belong to him and he was most willing to return it. This bit of mental weaselly left him feeling slightly soiled. With nothing left to do, he sat back and drank his tea.

"You have been fighting Salemi. What do you know of him?"

"Fanatic?" Dagr asked. "Not a man to be crossed? We killed his son by accident. I have never expected to come out of this alive after that night. In a way, it's a relief that you have found us."

"I am not proposing to kill you right now."

"Thanks."

"Provided you help me."

"Yesterday we attacked Salemi's fortress, just the three of us. We killed all his men. It was the most horrific thing I have ever seen in my life. My partners are injured grievously. We have no money, no more bullets, no more friends or connections. And I freely admit that I am the most useless of our trinity. Right now, I'll do whatever you say."

238 SAAD Z. HOSSAIN

"You are wrong," the Lion said.

"What?"

"You have one friend."

"Eh?"

"An American named Hoffman," Afzal Taha said. "He has been trying to help you."

"He's still alive?"

"Yes, most likely," Taha said. "Americans do not die so easily in Baghdad."

"And helping us? How? I swear, we have neither heard nor seen him since we left our house."

"Nevertheless, he has been trying to help you," Taha said. "Tell me, is he mentally deficient in any way?"

"What?"

"Is he retarded?"

"No. Well, not really. He's very clever in his own way."

"I ask because in trying to help you, he has brought down upon you the enmity of a most dangerous man," Taha said.

"I have no idea about this."

"It all comes down to the watch," Taha said. "When you took the watch, you changed the trajectory of your life in a radical way."

"I have some ideas about the watch."

"It is a bauble," Taha said. "Sought by some very powerful men. When you took it from me and escaped, you started a chain of events. Hoffman followed you and learned some things about the watch. He understood—perhaps in his cunning way—that it was valuable beyond the sum of its parts. He made enquiries, particularly among members of the retired Mukhabarat. A very foolish thing to do, for The Enemy knows everything of the Mukhabarat, indeed, that organization was first founded by him."

"Then what happened?"

"The Enemy met Hoffman, and recruited him. The Enemy effects the disguise of a harmless old man. He probably promised to help

Hoffman, help all of you, in return for the watch, or some such nonsense."

"He was not helping us or Hoffman then?" Dagr tried to follow.

"No. For the past few weeks, agents of The Enemy have been scouring the streets looking for you. And he found you. He found Hassan Salemi. He found your poor dead friend Xervish, who lies in pieces."

"I see. He wants the watch?"

"Yes. He has been working on a project, which has two missing pieces: the watch and myself. I will get back to the bigger story. For your part, The Enemy approached Salemi and recruited him. With what promises and threats I do not know, but rest assured that The Enemy is much more resourceful than a hundred Salemis. Salemi was to kill you, that was his reward, vengeance for the slaughter of his son. The Enemy would get the watch. Accordingly, Salemi received the location of the safehouse. Everything was in place."

"Except we left," Dagr said slowly.

"Yes, you did something crazy. You attacked Salemi, threw his organization into disarray," the Lion said. "And then you did not return to the safehouse. Had you done so, you would be dead now. Because as of this morning, that house no longer exists. It has been blown to bits, with no survivors. There were priceless things in there. The destruction of the Great Library is finally complete."

Dagr slumped back in his chair. Tears sprung up unbidden to his eyes. He felt his face redden. There was no dignified way for a grown man to cry that he knew of, so he just wiped his face with his sleeves a number of times and sniffed loudly.

"Meanwhile, The Enemy was using your friend Hoffman for a different task: to find *me*."

"I see."

"And now his time is up. If he is still alive, he will not be for long."

"You see, The Enemy knows I am here, somewhere in this part of the city, and his net is closing in. Time is his friend, and he will win sooner or later. He will find both of us, singly or together, and then it will be over."

"So there is no hope for any of us?"

"Well, you see, I have been running from this man my entire life," the Lion said. "And it has never done me much good. But now I have a better idea."

"What?"

"When your friend decided to attack Salemi, the depth of his madness gave me hope."

"I don't understand."

"He showed me a way. When running avails nothing, the only option is to attack."

"Attack what? I don't understand."

"Attack The Enemy. He is a thousand times better protected than Salemi. His security has been built layer by layer, neighborhood by neighborhood over hundreds of years, literally. Yet in all this accretion of power, he has never been tested. We will surprise him. To tell the truth, I'm tired. I have nothing left. This might be my last attempt. I wish to make a decent effort."

"You want to attack this man who orders Salemi around?" Dagr was aghast. "This man who set up the Mukhabarat?"

"Yes," the Lion said. "Your real enemy is not Salemi, it is the Old Man of the Mukhabarat, known as Avicenna, Ibn Sina, the Alchemist, and by a hundred other names. He wants you dead and me captured. I am not here to kill you. I want to join you."

Dagr stifled an urge to laugh. *You should have been speaking to Kinza. He's going to love this.*

"What do you say?" the Lion asked.

Dagr spread his hands out. "Well, of course I agree."

"Listen, then, to my tale," the Lion said. "It is incredible, but true."

33: LION'S STORY

"THE STORY STARTS OVER A THOUSAND YEARS AGO, SOMETIME IN the eighth century of the Gregorian calendar. It is really the story of alchemy. Well, it starts even earlier than that, with the Greeks and the Egyptians, but then everything for us starts there. My story is the story of Jabber Ibn Hayyan, known to the Latin world as Geber. I have heard much of the story directly from him. Some other details were given to me by his contemporaries, and some secrets were entrusted to me by my master, of whom I will speak later.

"Young Geber was born into an affluent family in Persia. His father was an alchemist of some renown, not in the Egyptian or Greek schools, which were based on mystical rites but rather, something new, following the principles of experimentation and logic. Geber himself told me that he received his schooling in his father's shop from the age of 3, at first simply learning the names of each ingredient, but later actively mixing and measuring them.

"Geber was a polymath. He could read and write at 4. His family moved around a lot. I am not sure, but I get the feeling that his father was a member of some hermetic brotherhood. They were by nature a profession rife with secret societies.

"At the age of 13, Geber was sent to Kufa to study with his uncle. Not a blood relative, but a friend of his father's I imagine. Geber was a modest man but I understand that by this time he had outstripped his father in knowledge and application, and moreover his grasp of mathematics was already beyond most of the Persian masters in Khorsaon. In Kufa, he received further esoteric knowledge in alchemy. He was inducted into the brotherhood of the golden ram, a lineage of mystics stretching all the way back to ancient Egypt. He travelled for a time with an unknown master, whose name he did not reveal even to me. I suspect he toured the old worlds of Egypt, Greece, and India. He kept this part of his life secret, even from his closest friends, with good reason perhaps.

"I have heard that when he returned he was a changed man, harder, colder, struggling under some burden. His master did not return with him. There was rumor of murder. He would struggle under this stigma for many years, although I think that he was probably incapable of such an act. Life to him was sacrosanct, above all else, even service to God. Whatever happened to him in those years is a mystery, and it transformed his character greatly.

"Thereafter, he became obsessed with *Tawkin:* the creation of life. It is commonly believed that all we care about is turning lead into gold. This is a misconception, perhaps deliberately fostered by the Orders. The obsession of alchemy has always been life: to create it, to mold it, to prolong it indefinitely. Ultimately, it is the practical usurpation of that which is solely the provenance of God.

"This may sound blasphemous to you. It was at that time, anathema. Geber, like many of the savants of his day, led a dual life. In the public sphere, he was the foremost alchemist of the Great Caliph's court, Harun Ur Rashid, ruler of Baghdad. He invented practically every scientific apparatus for chemistry. He worked with gold, he invented acids, and improved a hundred industrial processes. In today's legal world, he would have been the richest man on earth from patents alone.

"His real work, however, was with *Tawkin.* He succeeded at first in prolonging his own life, through application of elixirs. They say that these chemical cures were tortuous and left him hideously disfigured. The savants of the day began to compete with him and then to persecute him as a Satanist. Geber began encoding all of his works so that they said one thing to laymen and something else to his disciples. Near the end of what would have been his natural life, he went into hiding, faking his own death. He had cheated death for some time and escaped his persecutors by the same chance. It bought him some years to perfect his craft: for he was not after a charlatan's prize, but rather, true immortality itself, pristine in its perfection.

"In the course of time, he met my master, the caliph-imam of the Fatimid world, Al-Hakim. We were the forerunners of the faith now called the Druze. Al-Hakim was the messiah, beloved of an entire people. Yet his enemies were powerful and against him was the entire Sunni Caliphate, as well as members of his own Shi'a world who feared him. Al-Hakim was not merely a religious leader. He was one of the foremost savants of his day, an architect, a linguist, and an expert mathematician.

"Their correspondence and later, their friendship, led to the first accord: the recondite brotherhood of Geber's was married with the messianic cult of Al-Hakim. Geber shared with Al-Hakim the secrets of *Tawkin*, the imperfect art. Together they improved it, and I have heard, cured some of Geber's ailments. My master created the Druze doctrine based on secrecy, to protect Geber, his priceless works, and finally, as the escape hatch he would need to avoid his own enemies.

"He was a brilliant man, my master. Although he was caliph for a time, his power was undermined from within by his sister, who conspired with his enemies to murder him. Geber's arts saved him but not without the sacrifice of 100 Druze companions. I was one of that number, one of only three survivors of that flight. In those nights of terror and mayhem, I earned the sobriquet Lion, or the Lion of Akkad, and thus I met Geber himself. My master had been poisoned and stabbed. When we arrived at the hidden stronghold of Mount Chouff, in Syria, he was nigh dead from exhaustion and bloodloss. I know not what arts Geber used, but I saw the strain on him, and I knew that he sacrificed much of his own health to save my master's.

"In the aftermath, neither man recovered fully, although they both lived. Geber, you must realize, was already over 300 years old at this point, kept alive by his arts and the dedication of his acolytes, yet hideously weakened. I sometimes believed he survived by will alone, such was the power of his mind.

"It was thanks to *Tawkin* that they lived, for my master too had dedicated his life to this pursuit. They created secret underground chambers deep in the mountain, and surrounded by a few loyal men, they started to work. You must understand that their work was neither for God, nor against. It was merely for the glory of man, for their secret creed was that anything conceived in this world by the human mind belonged to man, was his birthright from the Almighty. They believed that the human body was frail and unfit to house the power and beauty of such a thing as the mind.

"They worked some years in secret, these men whom the world thought dead, but always they were beset by enemies who knew better. I was one of their constant companions. Of the 100 Druze, only three of us remained alive, and we three were the favorites of our master, the most trusted cabal and kingdom of the man who had once been caliph of all Fatimid Egypt.

"So you see, in a very small way, I, too was a part of this story. I lived among these giants. Geber offered each of us the gift of longevity, but we saw the hideous price he paid for it, and each of us declined. He was getting desperate. His health was broken, he was already an invalid. He could not leave his cave. It would be his tomb. My master shouldered all of the risk of roaming the world looking for the elements critical to their research.

"Then, I believe, Geber made a fatal error. He had been corresponding with a most brilliant physician and philosopher, a young man by the name of Ibn Sina, known to the world as Avicenna in later years. This man was his protégé in many ways, although he had no idea who Geber really was. Geber often spoke of him to us. His mastery of the human body was unparalleled. Already he had discovered cures that were hailed as miracles.

"In Geber's mind, Avicenna was the missing member of our group. Fatally, single-handedly, he invited Avicenna into the secret. Avicenna was a master of the human body, particularly of disease and the immune system. Even then, by himself, he had fathomed much of the nature of bacteria and viruses. He is a truly brilliant man, his intellect sharper than my master's for it took him only days to ingest the work that my caliph had spent years generating. He was powerful, yes, a fearsome mind. Yet his will was cold. He lacked the empathy of my master, who loved all men. He performed terrible operations on live subjects, caring only for knowledge, ruthless against their suffering. For that reason, my master was wary of him, and advised me to watch him.

"Geber was delighted. He set to work with a demonic will. It was their belief that the human body itself carried the potential to be immortal, that the key merely had to be found to unlock it. Geber had collected many specimen of peculiar nature: trees that lived for thousands of years, animals that could shrug off grievous injuries, insects that regenerated detached limbs. It was all proof that life was remarkable.

"In the end, Geber was right. The three of them succeeded where the two had failed. They needed trusted men to carry out the final tests. My brothers and I were those men. By then, the three had grown slightly distrustful of each other, through the manipulations of Avicenna.

"They took us separately to different chambers. I never saw my brothers again, for which I was most aggrieved for many years. I remember being blindfolded and then drugged. I could hear the voices of Geber and Avicenna. I was afraid of them. Then they left, and I heard the voice of my caliph and felt at peace. He assured me that I, at least, would live. I remember numerous needles all over my body, hot stings from some devilish instrument. I was violently sick. I remember terrible pain and swelling everywhere.

"I believe I fell into a coma, for I have no clear memory of several months. That could be due to my later misfortunes, however. When I recovered my wits, I found out that disaster had struck us.

"My two brothers, also tested, had both died. I had lived, and it seemed as if they believed that I was a successful outcome. The Druze elders said that some weeks after the experiment, there was a terrible fire in the subterranean chambers of Geber. The cabal had betrayed itself. Geber had been burnt alive. Avicenna and Al-Hakim both had fled in different directions, one to Baghdad and one to the village by the Chouff. The great game seemed over.

"Of course, it was not. I had thought their experiment a failure. When I studied the bodies of my brothers, I found them both deliberately burnt with oil. It was one more crime I am certain can be laid at the feet of Avicenna, for Al-Hakim would never burn the bodies of his beloved Druze, even by mistake. My master was now working feverishly, and although I was his most trusted lieutenant, I was so weak that he had no use for me but bade me rest. Still I slept close to him and kept my weapons by me, for we expected Avicenna to strike at us.

"I later learned that we had not failed but succeeded. What was done to me had worked. Incredibly, both Avicenna and Al-Hakim believed I was now virtually immortal. I learned that in the last few years of their collaboration, each of them had grown so mistrustful as to hide their separate research from each other. They had in effect split up the work so that no one man might know the entire process. Avicenna, in seducing and then killing Geber, had the secret of *Tawkin*, and perhaps the lion's share. Yet my master had retained the critical part of it, the technique of the final transformation, which unleashed the body's own power and made the change permanent from mortal to immortal. He alone knew how to turn off the death clock.

"I told him that I remembered the hot needles striking every part of my body and the terrible pain afterward, and he merely smiled. He said that was it. This was the secret. This was what Avicenna lacked, what he must never find because by now we were sure that the man was evil. What a terrible curse on humanity to have such a man become immortal! We grieved sorely for poor burnt Geber, my master particularly, for although they had fallen out near the end, they had worked and lived together for generations.

"Now our lonely work started. My master abandoned his other works and devised a system for hiding the knowledge. He split up our people and sent them across the world, carrying the doctrine of the Druze. Hidden in it was the truth—to be revealed only to a few—of the nature of what we protected. Then he made several artifacts to carry the precious knowledge itself. I helped him in all his endeavors, although I never understood then that he was in fact preparing for his own death. He was creating the apparatus that would fight the enemy from beyond the grave, which would protect us all from his wrath.

"To the people of the Druze, he bequeathed ignorance. Only the elders knew of the true nature of the faith, and so The Enemy found no profit in persecuting the laity and left them alone. To me, he had already given immortality and great physical prowess. He gave me also the master lists of all the Druze Elders of the Chouff, those men and women he had scattered throughout the caliphate. They were to be my succor in his absence. Finally, he showed me the watch. He said that it carried the final secret.

"And then, he and the watch disappeared. For many years, I cherished the hope that he lived, but it came to nothing. Avicenna had won. He came after the Druze, and he came after me. We all went into hiding. I was chased relentlessly, for several lifetimes, until I had covered almost every blade of grass in the world. For years, I hid in peace, but always the old man Avicenna would find me.

"Finally in the outer reaches of Mongolia, his men captured me. I then learned what he had been doing, what he wanted. His experiments on me were gruesome. He had the arts of Geber, and his intellect was such that he had improved on it immeasurably. He was able to prolong his own life, although the foul alchemy he relied on took up much of his time and, I believe, caused him great misery. I remember the efforts that poor, crippled Geber undertook merely to keep his heart beating.

"Avicenna knew that Al-Hakim had the final secret, that I was the living testament. It was his belief that he could get it out of me. The unspeakable things he did to me I will not divulge. I was his captive for over six years before I managed to escape. I believe I went mad during this time. Certainly my memories are bizarre, truncated. I had by this time given up hope that my master was alive. Of the three Old

Men, two were fully dead. It fell to me, then, to carry the fight to the last member of the cabal.

"I marshaled the Druze and struck back in the silent war. This was over four hundred years ago, you understand. We crippled Avicenna's networks, killed his men—it was all things unexpected to him. In fear, he went into hiding, believing that Al-Hakim had returned for vengeance. Still, the spider was not so easily quashed. He had gathered wealth and power for hundreds of years. He held powerful men in thrall with the arts of his alchemy, his powers to cure illness and prolong life.

"Bit by bit, he built the foundations of the Mukhabarat, his own secret apparatus to counter the power of the Druze. In this way, we fought a slow war over the centuries. It became a political game with many players, but always at the heart of it were he and I. He wanted *Tawkin*. I wanted to kill him and end this ungodly ambition. I speak no ill of my master, but I curse the day that Geber started on this path to cheat death, for it has brought no happiness to any of us. What use is unending life when one is forced to run and hide and fight continuously for every breath of air, every scintilla of shade?

"The centuries of life had taught us to stay hidden. We had outlived our enemies, none knew of our existence; our hatred grew into obsession. It was now the era of the Ottomans. We lived in the shadow of that great empire, pulling strings. Our war faded somewhat, as we each became diverted with other things. Avicenna's lust for power and wealth bore dividends. He accumulated a great deal of both. I thought him finally sated and relaxed my guard.

"And then, suddenly, I received word of the watch. It seemed incredible, but it had survived and resurfaced somehow. It gave me hope that my master was still alive. I began to hunt in earnest. It was inevitable that Avicenna, too, would come for it. I found it first, buried in a thief's warren in Smyrna. It was damaged. I had never learned the secret of the watch. I did not crave for eternal life, I had that already. It had brought me nothing but misery. But I still had faith in Al-Hakim. I had to hope that if the watch had survived the centuries then why not my master? I believed, naively perhaps, that in his hands this power would have done some good to mankind.

"It was the beginning of the end for me. The watch invited a convergence. There were others in the shadows, other men and women who had tinkered with immortality, who had approached *Tawkin* from their own unique angles. I had been aware of them, had foolishly ignored them. I did not understand that the watch would draw them like ravens. Too late I learned that Avicenna was not my only enemy.

"I was at a disadvantage, you must understand. I was fighting men and women of rare genius. Yet I was an accidental warrior, a footnote elevated to the principal role. What luck I had was used up. In the summer of 1585 of the Christian era, in the battle of Ayn Sawfar, the Ottoman Empire was induced to send the cream of their Janissary corps against my poor Druze. In truth, it was an attempt to capture or assassinate me, to destroy the flower of the Druze elders who carried the legacy of Al-Hakim.

"It was the witch Mother Davala who got me in the end, her power that turned the tide against us. I can only imagine what blandishments Avicenna offered to ally her. You have seen war, but let me tell you that there is nothing more awesome in this world than the sight of the Janissary corps advancing on you, firing their muskets in clockwork succession. It is like a mechanical scythe: remorseless, meatgrinding fire. They were the finest army in the history of mankind up to that point.

"My Druze were swordsmen. What chance did they have against Janissary bullets? We died in waves. The elders were wiped out, and those who survived and scattered were picked off by Avicenna. He was playing the long game. It was his plan to infiltrate the Druze organization, to kill the head, and replace it with his own sycophants.

"I was once again on the run, unsure now of my own people. In the chaos of battle, the watch was lost; more than one immortal was fighting for it now. The Witch Mother Davala had it for some time, I believe. In the disarray of the Druze, many vultures came to take advantage. I do not know if Avicenna ever got his hands on it. If he did, he never kept it for long.

"Luck favored me for a time. I was able to hide in distant China, with enemies of the Alchemist. Avicenna too fell ill for a time. His struggle to cure himself took precedence, giving me some years of breathing space. It was not for long though. He recovered, and his power grew with the modernization of the world. In the turn of the previous century, he caught wind of me finally. He lured me back here to Baghdad, the center of his web, again with the promise of the watch. It is a lure I can never resist. I curse this watch. I curse Al-Hakim for ever leaving behind this relic. It has brought us nothing but heartbreak."

"The rest of it, I think you know," Afzal Taha said. "I have been in and out of medical facilities for a hundred years, tortured, medicated, experimented on. When I escaped from the last round, I was disoriented, suffering from memory loss. Those months I was hiding in Shulla, I barely knew who I was. I thought I was schizophrenic. When you attacked me, I panicked and ran. I have since recovered, *remembered*."

"You've been brutal," Dagr said. "Punished innocents in the name of your suffering."

"I will make no excuses,"the Lion shrugged. "I am not a saint. I'm just better than the alternative."

"You can have the watch back," Dagr said.

"Thank you."

"It's not broken you know."

"The hands do not move. It has been broken ever since I remember."

"It sends an irregular pulse of vibration if you hold it in a certain way," Dagr said. "I know because I have held it clenched in my palm for three days straight without eating or sleeping."

The Druze immortal looked dumbstruck, which gave Dagr a jolt of satisfaction.

"I was really bored at that time," Dagr said. "Al-Hakim was a mathematician, you said?"

"Yes."

"It makes sense because I think there is a mathematical code in there," Dagr said. "I'm pretty sure I've figured out the watch."

34: THE CIRCUS IS IN TOWN

YAKIN DIDN'T KNOW THE WOMAN WHO STOOD BESIDE THE OLD
Man, but she was clearly a class apart from anything he had ever seen
in his short life. This was, he reflected bitterly, the kind of woman he
deserved. The way she wore her scarf, it was a fashion statement, a sex
bomb, *not* what the clerics had had in mind when they had dreamt
up the hijab. This was the kind of piece he should have been with. But
would he ever get the chance? Would she ever give him a second look?
Fuck no. She was even throwing the imam off balance. He could literally see the smoke coming out of Hassan Salemi's ears. Or actually
that was real smoke, for bits of his clothing were smoldering. Not for
the first time Yakin wondered whether the Imam was actually mentally impaired.

The Old Man had been affable the last time, offering them refreshments. He sat like an emperor now, granting an audience. Hassan
Salemi's stock had diminished somewhat in recent times. Kinza had
burnt down his house and killed his men. His retaliation had netted
him a few hostages and little else. No Kinza, no professor, *no watch.*
What was the world coming to when any random street tough could
come and rough up a Sadr parliamentarian candidate in Shulla? They
were at the denial stage now. No mention was to be made of the name
Kinza ever.

"So, Salemi," he said. "I cannot say this meeting brings me any
great pleasure."

"You sent us into a trap, Old Man."

"A trap? Of what? Women and servants? Mad librarians?"
Avicenna laughed. "Your reputation has been exaggerated indeed."

"There were djinns there, Old Man," Salemi's voice was flat. Yakin
could see a little muscle jumping in the side of his neck. The lunatic

was on the verge of doing something stupid. "The demons made of smokeless fire."

Yakin tried to maneuver himself away from his master, but an enormously brutish looking man with a shotgun glared at him. He looked like a torturer. They said he was Mukhabarat and that the Old Man was Mukhabarat through and through. Just that word alone was enough to make most people piss their pants. Yakin slumped. He was so tired he wanted to lie down on the floor and go to sleep.

"Djinns were there? Floating around? Possessing the furniture perhaps?"

"No," Hassan Salemi said. "They were in jars. Great earthenware jars stoppered with red wax, which were cold to the touch and covered with sediments from the ocean. Do you think me stupid, Old Man? There was a room full of sealed jars!"

"Jars, you say?" Avicenna leant forward. "Now you interest me. Have you brought them?"

"My men shot them," Hassan Salemi said.

"Oh dear."

"Everything exploded then."

"Yes," Avicenna said bitterly. "If one is stupid enough to shoot up a room full of djinns, then anything might happen. I trust that you searched the wreckage of the house?"

"What house?" Salemi laughed bitterly. "The entire block was destroyed. Cluster bombed, more like. I have lost all my men but four."

"So the witch Davala held the djinns of Solomon, it seems," Avicenna said to the lady beside him. "I wonder why she never unleashed them. Is she dead at least?"

"I don't know about the old witch," Hassan Salemi said. "But you spoke of three women there. I have brought you two of them."

"Have you now?" Avicenna said. "Well, that is good. Very good. I warned you that the women were dangerous. Still, you haven't done too badly."

"What now then?"

"Now we must prepare. Imam, I must open your eyes. You have stumbled unfortunately into a war long in the making. It is, I believe, reaching a watershed moment," Avicenna said. "Our enemies have never been weaker. You have broken the witches' power. The cursed Druze is addled and alone. The watch is in the hands of a petty psychotic who lacks the intelligence to even know its value. We are in a position, imam, to sweep the board. You will be in at the death, imam. In the end, I will restore you to your former puissance and fearsome reputation."

Yakin groaned. Big words aside, the Old Man was ready to fuck them all over again.

Hoffman had crafted a diabolical escape plan. It would end with Behruse incapacitated, the Dog Boy out of commission, and Sabeen completely in his power and lovingly grateful to him for saving her life. The plan involved rope, a belt, Scotch tape, nails, a Swiss army knife— a plan of such genius that it could not help but succeed through sheer chutzpah alone.

All he needed to do was kill time now. It occurred to him that Behruse was taking overly long to visit him this time. Normally the fat man came every three days to change the water, food, and slop buckets. It was now the fourth day. Hoffman wasn't hungry or thirsty because he had appropriated Dog Boy's rations. Dog Boy was on hunger strike, refusing any food and only drinking a third of his portion. Hoffman had tried to reason with him, but Dog Boy wasn't having any of it.

He wanted his own cell back and a return to the old administration. In his more lucid moments, he made a list of demands that included immediate reinstatement of Dr. Sawad, single cells for every prisoner, and at least one electro-therapy a week to keep the juices flowing. Hoffman spent his idle time trying to train Dog Boy to use the slop bucket properly and dreaming about taking revenge on Sabeen, which would involve her being wrested from her evil grandfather and somehow converted into his caring, devoted follower, perhaps a second lieutenant to replace Tommy.

Her casual betrayal had in fact enflamed his passion from mere love to something transcendental. He craved physical contact with her, was sure he could turn her! He wrote poetry about her (not rhyming) and recited these verses to Dog Boy, taking care to ensure that Dog Boy understood clearly that the poetry was not meant for him, and he should not take it as any sign of encouragement. By the fifth day, he was getting a bit worried. Behruse still hadn't arrived. It was possible that something had happened to the fat man.

By the sixth day, he was hungry and thirsty and starting to rethink his strategy. He had almost despaired when loud noises at the door woke him from lethargy. There was a small explosion, the wood splintered out, cutting him in some places and setting off Dog Boy into fairly weak paroxysms (he was near dead from the hunger strike).

When Hoffman managed to open his eyes, he saw in front of him a most fearsome old woman holding a gnarled walking stick and an ancient six-chambered revolver, still smoking. Her face was singed: eyebrows gone, the wispy hair on her head burnt off in patches. She had lost her dentures and so spoke with a lisp, a single tooth sticking up visibly like a decrepit building.

"You're welcome, soldier," said Mother Davala.

"What? Er, you're not Behruse."

"No."

Hoffman scratched his head. "Well could you fix up the door again?"

"You want to stay in your cell?"

"It's just that I had this great plan for him."

"He's left you for dead, soldier," Mother Davala said. "You and your men."

"Dead?"

"All of them. Butchered in the street like dogs. The shell of your big car lies in a fronted garage in Shulla."

Hoffman shut his eyes. "I was afraid of that." He looked ready to cry.

"So rise up now, soldier," Mother Davala said. "Throw off this sheep's clothing and show yourself true. Like you, my children lie slaughtered, my sisters taken, my house razed to the ground. Yet we still stand. It is time to strike back at the betra—"

"Wait a minute. You want me to kill Behruse and Sabeen?"

"Of cou—"

"Are you crazy? I don't want to kill them," Hoffman said. "I love Sabeen. I want to marry her."

"Pardon me, boy?" "Yeah, I love that girl," Hoffman said, "There's this little snoring sound she makes when she's napping in the car."

"You are serious?" Mother Davala looked stunned.

"Yeah, it's the cutest thing."

"She left you for dead and killed all your men," Mother Davala said.

"Sure, we're gonna have to talk about that," Hoffman said, "and Behruse is gonna get fixed. Don't get me wrong. Plus he might have to get with Dog Boy here. But—"

"Do you know who these people are?" Mother Davala demanded.

"Sure, this Avi character is like a thousand years old," Hoffman said, "and he's been looking for this Lion dude, some kind of old grudge or something. It's like Battle of the Titans, man. Oh, and they want the watch that the professor's got. It has some kind of immortal life secret thing in it. Yeah, we gotta stop Avi for sure. Can't have him going around living forever and shit. I mean, he'd like take over the world or something. But Sab's not like that. I mean, she's really pretty and even when she was like thinking about killing me, she just couldn't do it. I mean, there's a heart underneath all that."

"I don't believe this."

"Hey, when we get out of here, can you take me to a store? I wanna buy some flowers."

For the first time in almost six hundred years, Mother Davala was literally bereft of speech.

"I'll kill them all," Kinza said. "Salemi and every man living who was in the room when they cut Xervish. Every man who burnt down that house. And then I'm going to start killing old men. I'll kill every old man in Shulla, every old man in Baghdad if I have to. If Hoffman is dead, you can add that to my account too. I'm not running anymore."

And then he sat back, exhausted. His face was a pasty gray, eyes rimmed with fever, the skin taut over his bones, hands trembling as he tried to drink his broth. There was nothing left in this thin, broken man. His words were laughable. Yet whenever he looked at Kinza, Dagr saw the bodies of dead men piled up in grenade-charred rooms, saw the fire from the awful burning of Salemi's house. He smelled the blood and heard the Makarovs barking. And so he said nothing and prayed for God's forgiveness.

"It is not easy to kill the Old Man," Afzal Taha said. "It will not be easy to even *get* to him. The entire neighborhood is designed to hide and protect him. There will be Mukhabarat, mercenaries, random street thugs who don't even know whom they are working for. And Salemi took hostages from the safehouse, more friends of yours, I think."

"Salemi thought he was safe too," Kinza said, in a hoarse whisper. "Everyone thinks they are safe."

"And whom can we count on?" Afzal Taha asked. "You three are half dead, even worse off than me. I'm beginning to have grave doubts."

"You think that will stop him?" Hamid laughed bitterly. "You think logic operates anywhere in this entire fucking circus?"

"You were free to leave a long time ago," Kinza said.

"Leave? Leave? Fuck you, Kinza. I've been shot thirteen times since you fuckers took me in. Thirteen times. I've lost two fingers, four pints of blood, and just recently I've got two cracked ribs, never mind the cuts, bruises, and internal organ damage—"

"What the hell are you complaining about? You're walking around, aren't you?"

"The entire fucking Republican Guard didn't see this much fighting during the war," Hamid said. "The entire fucking fedayeen didn't go so far out of their way to get killed."

"You know, Hamid, for a torturer, you're getting damned squeamish," Kinza said, "plus you weren't exactly stellar back there."

"The guy had a heart condition," Hamid said. "He was two months from dying. You can't expect me to…aw fuck it. We should get some vests."

"What?" Dagr asked, surprised out of his comatose state.

"Vests," Hamid said. "You know, the suicide bomber ones with the detonators."

"You want to wear a bomber vest to a gunfight?"

"It's perfectly safe," Hamid said. "They don't blow up without the detonator."

"Hmm, vests wouldn't be bad," Kinza said, leaning forward, exhaustion apparently forgotten. "We can always bluff with them, and if everything fails, we can just blow it all up."

"Right, half those Mukhabarat fuckers will shit their pants when they see us in vests," Hamid said. "Trust me. I know these fuckers. They act all tough and CIA, but when some peasant in a homemade bomb suit walks up, they all piss themselves and run."

"And we need a sniper. Where's Mikhail?"

"Dead or with Salemi," Dagr said. "And we dragged him into it."

"Ok, we'll get him back," Kinza said. "Dagr you're the tank, again. We'll need a lot more firepower this time, I think."

"Yeah, it's a whole neighborhood this time, not one fucking house," Hamid said. "Mortars and bombs, I think. Maybe a car or two rigged with IEDs."

The Lion, who had been staring at them in bemusement, finally managed to edge into the conversation. "Are you all insane?"

"You've been hiding too long, Druze," Kinza said. "You want to kill this guy, right? We'll go right down his throat and kick in his door."

"Can you get some guns, Druze?" Hamid asked. "I'm making a list here."

"Ye-es," Afzal Taha said, after a long pause. "Yes, I've got all the guns in the world."

―――――――――――

"Behruse, you fat fuck, he's gone!" When Sabeen was truly angry, she resorted to two things: foul language and waving her gun around. It was, Yakin reflected, both terrifying and exciting at the same time. Hassan Salemi would have burst a blood vessel. There was nothing in the imam's lexicon to even describe a woman like Sabeen. If he was thinking by now that he had allied himself with the devil, this display would have easily pushed him over the edge. Hassan Salemi wasn't the big man in town anymore, however. He was off sulking and plotting, and Avicenna felt no need to pander to him.

Yakin, with all the carefully honed instincts of a turncoat, had found it prudent to slowly detach himself from Salemi. Not only was the casualty rate in Salemi's camp prohibitively high, he also knew from experience that the man called Kinza was a murderous bastard who took things very personally. This lunatic, despite everyone's best efforts, was still very much at large and might be inclined to hold a grudge against the barbarisms practiced upon his friend.

According to the new strategy, Yakin simply took to following Behruse around. Behruse was an affable fat man, fairly high in Avicenna's command and therefore unlikely to meet the enemy on the field. By running his menial errands and assiduously plying him with compliments, Yakin was able to squirm into his circle fairly quickly. And now, as was their wont, Avicenna and Sabeen treated him like the furniture, or some sort of barely tolerable pet-type creature.

"Yes," Behruse said, dejected.

"The door was blown open, and he's gone," Sabeen said. "Also that other test case. Both of them are gone. What the fuck were you doing?"

"I had a guard posted outside," Behruse said. "He's gone too."

"You've lost the American," Avicenna said. "Well done. Why did you not kill him, Sabeen?"

"I—" For once, Sabeen seemed at a loss for words.

"Eh? I thought you wanted us to keep him alive?" Behruse asked.

Avicenna was staring at Sabeen. "I must not have been clear. I believe I wanted him alive as long as he was useful. And controlled. Having him roam around at will is neither, is it?"

"He was to be our leverage with the Americans," Sabeen said. "I had him pinned for all the murders."

"Do you know something interesting, Sabeen?" Avicenna said. "I made some queries about this Hoffman. No American agency or service acknowledges him. He appears to be a bumbling idiot criminal deserter. Yet he's traipsing around Baghdad with impunity. He is getting into sensitive information with impunity. He is *getting out of locked rooms* with impunity."

"He's a fool, grandfather, an infatuated buffoon," Sabeen said with a wave of her hand. "You can't spend five minutes with him without realizing that."

"The situation speaks otherwise," Avicenna said coldly. "Perhaps you are the fool, Sabeen, you and Behruse both. Perhaps *you* are infatuated with *him*. Six months ago, I had Taha in my grasp, I was about to find the watch, and no one knew I was alive. Now I don't have Taha, some two-bit criminal has my watch, the old witch is riled up, I have to deal with Salemi, and your fucking *Hoffman* knows my face. Do you think this is under control, hmmm, Sabeen? Do you?"

"No," Sabeen said, defeated by his cold will. "What do you want us to do?"

"We must find and kill the peons who burnt Salemi's house. Kill them, and take the watch. That is the most important thing," Avicenna said. "Hoffman is worrying me. He knows all of us. He can place all of us. *He knows where we live.* He knows about Dr. Sawad and Geber and all that ancient history. We will have to negotiate with him, I think."

"I can handle him, grandfather."

"No," Avicenna said. "No. He's done something to you. Don't go near him."

"I can spread the word if you want," Behruse said. "We want to talk. He might turn up."

"Yes, do that," Avicenna said. "But do not underestimate him again. And call the Mukhabarat. I want protection doubled here. I want absolute calm. I do not wish to leave Baghdad, but if there are any more fireworks, we will have to."

"Leave? Surely you're overreacting," Sabeen said.

"Do you think I have survived for a thousand years by making explosions in the streets and firing guns in the air?" Avicenna was livid. "Do you think no one will notice a massacre in Salemi's house? Do you think this is the time to take part in a pitched battle? I'm telling you, get me my watch, and then we're getting the hell out of here."

The Druze safehouse was under a very old mosque, a relic of the Baghdad of the Caliph Harun ur Rashid. In 1258 A.D., the Mongols had sacked Baghdad, massacring up to a million people and destroying almost the whole city, including its famed libraries and universities. It was the end of the Golden Age of the alchemists, the end of the caliphate, a most emphatic end to Baghdad. That dream city, home to all the knowledge of the world, torch bearer of the new science and philosophy, was gone utterly.

The Mongols had taken the books from the libraries and used them to block the Tigris, creating great soggy bridges of ink and paper. It had amused them for a time, watching the scholars throw themselves into the water in despair. The world up to this point had never known a more terrible race than the Mongols.

The Mosque of the Red Corner was reputedly one of the few buildings that had survived, by some accident surely since Mongols did not spare mosques by rule. Still, after the weeklong raid, things returned somewhat to normal. The new governor, by order of Helugu Khan, brother of the Great Khan in Karakorum, set down to rebuild the city and try and knock it back into some sort of profitable venture. The Mosque of the Red Corner served as a prison for some time, then as a bureaucratic headquarters, and then as a tax office, before finally returning to its primary function.

In the course of all of this, the city had somehow been infiltrated by the Druze. In times of chaos, many secret sects descended upon Baghdad, vultures on the bloated corpse of the caliphate, to steal treasures or books or to cement power in the new city. Thus, the Mosque of the Red Corner was one of the humblest, but oldest, Druze quarters in the city, a most hidden place run by a very old imam still faithful to the precepts of the caliph Hakim.

This saintly old man recognized the signs of the Druze and led them down into the cellar, which was a small room stocked with foodstuff. Under a hidden trapdoor, there was a subbasement, which was a kind of walk-in closet filled with guns: semiautomatics, machine guns, mortars, grenades, and an old RPG, plus rifles with sniper scopes and boxes of ammunition. They were still in their original boxes; American, French, British—a last chance saloon for lost weapons, like forlorn prom dates sitting in corners, waiting, waiting. Kinza saw them, and something in his expression flickered. A calm acceptance came over him, as if some decision had been settled. The fever tremor left his body. He limped into the room.

"I don't understand this," said the Lion. "There is no plan here, no advantage. What am I missing? How many countless men are we facing?"

"Don't ask me. I never wanted any of this," Dagr said, leaning over the steps. The smell of gun oil made him nauseated.

"He can barely walk. He's half dead with fever. Is he mad?"

"It won't make a difference," Dagr said. "When the fight comes out, it makes no difference at all. Just stay behind him."

"What?"

"He's a berserker, see?" Dagr said. "With Kinza, *life* is the enemy, really. He wants the world to be still, and when it doesn't comply, he's willing to force it. Don't worry. After a while, it just becomes normal. I always thought violence wasn't the solution. But then, look where we are. It certainly buys you some space. When the rage comes, just stay behind him, that's all. I used to be scared all the time. But even that gets old."

"You are frightened?" Afzal Taha looked puzzled. "You defied all these men for no reason. You attacked Salemi's house for no reason. You held the watch."

"I used to have a family, Druze," Dagr said. "Three years ago, I had a daughter and a wife and a job. We had enough money, friends. We used to worry about promotions and schools for the little one, and cholesterol. My wife used to worry about getting fat. Do you know that? She used to look in the mirror backwards with her head screwed damn near all the way around and keep asking: Am I fat? Am I fat? Three weeks ago I would have died to get those worries back again. If I could, I would fill my head with those worries. I would breathe them into my lungs. I would smother myself with them and die laughing. But then you have to wake up. Reality isn't there anymore. What do I have left? The world is gray to me, Druze. What would I miss that is so frightening?"

"You have no hope then?"

"Hope? Not that kind. I think I've finally realized that. The clock will never go back again. That life is over," Dagr said. "Whatever happens now, I can never return to that. We've waded through blood, Druze." He glanced down into the darkened cellar where Hamid and Kinza stood in silence, stripping guns, their conversation one of metallic clicks and ratchets, with no disagreements. "Two friends left in all the world. What's the point of running now?"

"And I have none," the Druze said. "After centuries, half my brain scooped out and no friend left alive. You're right, professor. What's the use of running now?"

Dagr sat back. It was the second time he had impressed himself before this half-god. He had, in effect, convinced the Lion to give up. The cost of it was another matter.

35: BORN IN FIRE

BACK IN THE BLACKWATER TRUCK, THE FOUR OF THEM CONTORTED into a miniscule space, crammed in with guns, bullets, bombs, and more. Dagr sweated in the corner, cradling large packets of explosives, literally shivering with fear despite the immense heat. It had taken a lot of persuasion to get the truck driver back on board. As it were, he barely got them past the checkpoints, refusing point blank to go anywhere near their target location.

"You're crazy," he said, as he drove off. "I heard what happened before."

Kinza smiled. "This time will be much worse."

Then, ensconced in a roadside café, replete with shishas and mint tea, they plotted.

The entrance into Avicenna's neighborhood was a narrow street, wide enough for single lanes of traffic. Dagr could see that the flow of cars was being subtly discouraged. A heavy food cart stood at the mouth, and there were a knot of rough-looking men by the stall, pretending to eat dinner and drink tea. Motorcycles had been parked around it, taking up half the street, choking both ways of traffic into a single narrow lane. There was a snarling traffic jam, swearing, threatening, and then stoic indifference. People parked their cars haphazardly and walked.

It was not such a huge inconvenience. Further down the street, the way narrowed even more. Alleys branched off onto either side, all of them dead ends. The street itself took a left turn and continued onward, reducing in width until it was barely four feet across. It was a neat solution, a self-contained neighborhood, the houses acting as enfilading barriers. Near the center of the mass was Avicenna's own house, on subtly high ground, like a citadel. Satellite imagery from

Google earth revealed that, from the air, the whole neighborhood looked, in fact, like a fort, with a curtain wall of houses, narrow avenues for movement, and a number of strategically placed tall buildings that would serve very well as towers.

"See the covered truck on the main road," Hamid said. "That's theirs too. They can block the entrance of their street by just backing it up. Thirty seconds. Probably a machine gun under the tarp."

"Funny, I was hoping we could ram a car right down that street," Dagr said. "What about snipers?"

"Two flanking towers," Hamid said. "Left and right. Plus the men by the cart are all armed, six of them at least."

"Do we have to use this street?"

"This is the only entrance into the neighborhood. The houses on the perimeter all around are like walls," Hamid said. "The people living on the lower floors don't know it. The upper floors and roofs are controlled by Mukhabarat. The roofs are almost continuous—like the battlements of a turret wall. I even saw places where gaps between buildings were bridged with sheet iron."

"How many men does he have patrolling on top?" Dagr asked.

"Must be over 200 men if they take shifts," Hamid said. "He isn't fucking around. This is wartime footing."

"Can we break into one of the perimeter buildings and climb to the roof?" Kinza asked. "If we can get to the roof, they're fucked. Their precious little fort becomes a nice high road for us to walk around on."

"He has every inch scoped by security cameras," Hamid said. "I counted them. Not the cheap Chinese ones either; these move around and everything. He'll know the minute anyone unauthorized enters any of those buildings."

"The perimeter buildings will also be rigged with explosives and alarms," the Lion said. "I have seen this system before in Damascus. Avicenna blew up an entire six-story building there to kill a single enemy. He has no respect for innocent life."

"Don't worry, neither do we," Kinza said.

"It's a fort right?" Dagr said, doodling on a pad. "It's like a medieval fort set inside a neighborhood. As any military historian of note will tell you, the weakest point of any fortification is always the gate."

"The gate being the street," Kinza said.

"If we can get in there somehow, we bypass the perimeter defenses entirely," Dagr said. "They have to regroup, fall back in. Their high ground, their cameras, the boobytraps—everything becomes neutralized."

"Once inside, we slip into the interior buildings, start creating a panic," Hamid said. "Blow shit up."

"They'll fall back to Avicenna's house, try to control the center, maybe," Dagr said. "Any chaos is our friend. But it's a moot point because I don't see how we can get past the gate. Not without casualties."

"Well we don't want casualties," said Kinza. "Not yet anyways."

"We have Kevlar," Hamid said. "We can take a couple of hits."

"So this is the plan," Kinza said. "We hit it at night. Hamid RPGs the towers from a hidden location. At the same time, the Druze hits the truck and takes it over. Best case, he crashes it into the street, blocking the road from further use. We'll want some privacy once we're inside."

"And us?" Dagr asked.

"While this is happening, we are innocently approaching the fake cart for some dinner. You go in front 'cause you look harmless. As soon as the RPG hits, we start knifing those boys on the ground."

"You want me to knife six men?"

"Ok, actually what I meant was that *I* will knife them," Kinza said. "Then we drop the food and run into one of the dead-end alleys. There should be confusion at this point, what with the explosions and crashing trucks."

"Let me guess, I get to be the tank."

"What happens to us?" Hamid asked.

"You two get up to the roof," Kinza said. "Take the high ground. Find cover. Hold them off. Move around. Get seen on camera."

"Get seen?" Afzal Taha was looking puzzled.

"Don't you understand?" Hamid laughed. *We* make the noise. All those Mukhabarat cunts come buzzing after us. The Old Man sees you and starts to get excited. Kinza gets in free. *Maybe*."

Dagr, too, was understanding the implications of the plan. Nausea welled up inside him. He stared at Kinza, saw nothing comforting in his face.

"You might not survive," Kinza said. "Hamid knows."

"You send us to certain death," Afzal Taha said. "For what gain?"

"He'll be loose behind their lines," Hamid said, a desperate yearning on his face. "He'll get *close*."

"Yes," Kinza said. He looked hard at the Lion. "Is it worth it, to kill this man?"

The Lion looked away, troubled. "I don't know. I think so. I used to think so."

Kinza laughed.

"How close will you get, Kinza?" Hamid asked.

"Maybe close enough."

"And if not?"

Kinza pulled out his bag, cracked the zip. Nestled in wax paper were six bricks of putty colored *plastique*. The neatly lettered insignia of the French Foreign Legions were stamped in each corner. A solid black finger press detonator lurked like a fat beetle in the middle, gun oil shining blue off the metal.

"Satisfied?" Kinza asked.

"Yes," said Hamid. He looked at peace.

"What we need, is a helicopter," Hoffman said. He glanced at Mother Davala, saw her frowning, and allowed his grin to widen. "A helicopter, my lovely dove, to whisk us away!"

"Shut up, you moron," Mother Davala said.

"Fly me to the moon." Hoffman sang.

"You imbecile," Mother Davala cried. "You utterly brainless ninny. Dead! All of them are dead! Kinza, Hamid, all your men."

"Not all dead," Hoffman said. His face darkened momentarily. "Not quite. Some little Indians got away."

"How am I going to kill Avicenna?" Mother Davala rested her head on her outsized revolver. "Who will I use now?"

"Hmm, as I was saying, what we need is a helicopter. Do you want to know why?"

"Oh what's the use?" Mother Davala said. "I wish to God I'd never rescued you from that creature."

"We need it, Elderly One, because it's about to go down," Hoffman said.

"What?"

"The shit is about to hit the fan," Hoffman said. "Kinza is not dead, no, not by a long shot. And Kinza is not the man to take this kind of shit lying down. He's not a friendly kinda guy like me, unfortunately—"

"Not dead?"

"Oh no," Hoffman said. "And neither is my former gunner Ancelloti. My new faithful lieutenant! My admiring Robin!"

"So we're not finished?"

"My man reports that Kinza, at this moment, is sitting in a café in the general neighborhood of our friend Avicenna's house," Hoffman said. "And do you know who with? None other than our mysterious Druze dude!"

"What?"

"Well, I wouldn't trust Ancelloti. He's a drug addict after all, but I think it's safe to say that Kinza is not really that interested in coffee," Hoffman said.

"You sly dog," Mother Davala poked him with the revolver. "Here I thought you were a bumbling idiot. We need to get over there. Let them create the cover, we can slip in."

"Not in, Mother, but over," Hoffman said. "Excuse me while I make a call."

"Hello! Hello!" A voice crackled over the static of the outsized sat phone.

"Alfred! Prepare the batmobile!"

"What? Who the fuck is this?"

"Colonel Bradley speaking here," Hoffman said. "I said, prepare the batmobile."

"Sir?!"

"Pilot, I am giving you the authorization code alpha Charlie foxtrot niner niner niner sigma sigma fullstop," Hoffman said.

"Sir!"

"Standby for action! Man the torpedoes."

"Sir, we have no torpedoes."

"I meant the giant lasers!"

"Er, no lasers, sir."

"Then what have you got?"

"Hellfire air-to-surface missiles, sir!"

"Excellent. Now listen carefully. This is a top secret mission. Tell no one. I repeat we have a mole in the team. Tell no one!"

"A mole, sir?"

"A leak! A traitor!" Hoffman shrieked into the phone, spittle flying everywhere. "A commie bastard Benedict Arnold! And it's probably that pedophile Fowler!"

"Sir!"

"In fact, I want you to shoot him in the leg the next time you see him!"

"Sir?"

"The leg, Marine!"

"Sir!"

"Now, load up and bring the chopper to the following location. Fly low, avoid all radar—"

"Sir, the only radar up here is ours."

"Pilot, shut up!" Hoffman said. "Trust no one! The truth is out there! My most trusted secret agent, Agent, er Hoffman, is ready and waiting. You will rendezvous with him at 33 × 21'18" north and 44 ×

23'39" east coordinates. Codename Batman. I repeat. His codename is Batman. For the purposes of this mission, you are to refer to him as such."

"Sir?"

"Obey Batman at all times."

"Sir!"

"And bring the hellfires, boy," Hoffman said. "We gonna blow shit up."

———————

Ancelloti stood shivering against a wall, wearing the nondescript clothes of a down and out day laborer. Luckily, his Latin coloring and the sheer quantity of dirt on his skin was enough to obscure the fact that he was not, in fact, Iraqi. This wasn't the best neighborhood in any case, and these days, pedestrians tended to give anyone shivering against a wall a wide berth.

The shivering was actually real. He was suffering from extreme withdrawal from the vast cocktail of drugs his body was acclimatized to. He had scored a solid cube of hash for the last of his money, and this was tiding him over. Barely. The problem with Hoffman's plans, he reflected, was that they went awry all too often. Every time, in fact. On the other hand, he had never seen anyone else land on their feet with such regular panache.

Fact was, he was either AWOL or believed dead, and either case suited him fine. He could always roll up to camp mumbling about Gulf War syndrome. His condition was well documented. They wouldn't want to make a big deal about him. He supposed he was crazy.

Not as crazy as the four Arabs walking past him. One guy was huge, the other three regular sized, although they moved with the heavy, measured gait of people wearing armor. They had bags of guns. And the half-fingered one had a RPG over his shoulder, wrapped in cloth. It wasn't even a good disguise. They walked like the four horsemen of the apocalypse. Ancelloti remembered his church had a stained glass window of the four horsemen back in Reno. He felt an odd rush of affection for the one with the RPG. He liked the way he carried it, casual; don't mind me, this is just a rocket launcher attached to my shoulder. Crazy.

These were the friends Hoffman had been trying to find. He had seen Hoffman smoking dope with two of them, drinking and laughing. Ancelloti didn't have any friends left, but his drug-addled mind recalled the time when he had been part of a squad. He missed those people vaguely. He supposed these Arabs were the new squad. He wanted to reach out and touch them, to reassure them that he was there, on their side. On the other hand, perhaps that was not so reassuring. After all, every squad he'd been a part of so far had been blown to bits in front of his eyes.

———————

"This is a good spot," Hamid said.

They watched Dagr and Kinza walking casually toward them, two harmless men intent on their cigarettes.

"I can't believe this plan," the Lion said.

"It's all about incentives," Hamid said.

"What?"

"Incentives," Hamid smiled. "When I was an interrogator, that's the lever we would use. Find the right incentive and you can get anyone."

"You used to torture people, I heard."

"It was a job," Hamid said, "which taught me a lot about human nature."

"You're saying Kinza has some hidden incentive?" The Lion said. "I don't get it."

"You wouldn't," Hamid said. "You still think this is all about you."

"I've been fighting this war for a millennium."

"You've done fuck all for a millennium," Hamid said. "Incentives. You want to win. You want to restore whatever dumbfuck Druze order you grew up in. You want to resurrect your old boss. These are not the right incentives."

"So what's your incentive?"

"Me? I have none. Not anymore," Hamid said. "See, Kinza taught me that. When I understood, it all clicked."

"And am I to benefit from this Zen moment?"

"Sure," Hamid said. "We are the perfect zeros. Kinza is the perfect zero. He has no prospects. He has no past. There's nothing he wants. *There is nothing here to tempt him.* How do you stop someone like that from doing whatever the fuck he wants?"

"I'm not sure I understand."

"The normal controls of society are gone," Hamid said. "And then you realize that you don't have to take their shit anymore." He licked his finger and checked the wind. On a tower across the street, a sniper lounged against the wall, his head lolling in the heat. "Never mind. It's time. Go hit the truck. When you start backing up, I'll fire the RPG."

"Whose shit?"

"What?"

"Whose shit don't you have to take anymore?"

"What the fuck are we talking for?"

"I'm trying to understand."

"Everyone's shit. Your teacher, your boss, your banker, the bill collector, the cop, the army. It's all gone now. Don't you understand? No more parents. We're free. No promotions, no retirement plans, no more hamster on the fucking wheel. I'm going to fire an RPG in the middle of the city. It's the fucking end times. You get it now?"

"You're all mad."

Hamid smiled. "You're the fucker with a lobotomy. Hang on. I almost forgot to do something."

He stepped across Dagr, stopping him momentarily. He thrust a folded note into Dagr's fist.

"Here, take it," he said.

"What?" The Professor looked confused.

Hamid smiled. "Copy of the coordinates. In case you survive."

"Mosul? Are you serious?"

"It's full of gold, Dagr. And a whole bunch of other stuff. I don't know how to get in, but you're a smart guy, you'll figure it out."

"You were telling the truth?"

"Doesn't matter much now, does it?" Hamid shrugged.

Dagr and Kinza reached the cart early. There was a slight, hot breeze, perhaps some kind of A/C exhaust. It ruffled their loose cotton shirts, worn over the vest. It was too obvious though, even under the weak street light; any second now, someone would take a closer look at the unnaturally rotund men buying dinner.

Hamid had been right. The Mukhabarat men were relaxed, off duty. They didn't take the job seriously and were content to joke around and smoke shisha. They had moustaches and fat bellies, cheap-looking clothes. There was an unkempt edge about them, in the curl of over long hair at the nape of the neck to frayed cuffs and dirty, scuffed soles. Salaries had been irregular, too many service men had been laid off. Men used to riding government cars were now on foot, reduced to guard dogs, baying for their supper.

There were five of them. They should have been spread out, alert. Instead they had gathered plastic chairs around the cart, feet up, smoking and eating. One of them looked up, took in the bumbling incompetence of Dagr, and sat back down. Dagr stood in line, ordered, and paid, feeling ridiculously let down at having to part with the last of their money. He resisted the urge to look back. The explosions did not come. He took a bite of the kebab roll, felt the bite of the pickled onions in the back of his throat. It was good, the yogurt sauce rich and fresh.

He stopped the urge to gag. Kinza was ethereal beside him, seeming to melt into shadows. He gave him a roll, and ludicrously, they stood by the cart and ate. Dagr couldn't talk. He clenched his bowels. The seconds moved on. Finally, he heard snatches of shouting, the rush of tires and something heavy moving toward them. The truck was backing in, at speed, lurching drunkenly. Dagr scattered aside, ducking into the confusion. He felt Kinza dive across his vision, ending behind the Mukhabarat.

The truck hit the cart and careened sideways with a sick tear of metal, a high-pitched rending noise. The engine smoked as it continued to slew sideways on semibald tires until it smashed into the side of a building. Screams from onlookers and then pure astonishment, as a comet of fire raced across their retinas and slammed into the tall corner building. The explosion of the RPG threw them all flat and rained masonry down on the just and unjust alike.

Even though he had been expecting it, it took Dagr several precious seconds to regain his balance. The Mukhabarat men were faster, already up, guns waving, crucially, mistakenly *looking up*. Dagr saw Kinza float in, a thin stiletto in his right hand and a heavy Marine-issue K-Bar knife in his left. The first two were already down, the K-Bar nearly severing one man's head from his shoulders, leaving an ugly dark red yawning maw of a wound. The second slumped face down, stiletto in the eye, twitching.

Dagr bulled forward, tackling the man closest to him waist high, and getting a heavy knee in the chest in the process. His adversary was fat, too fat to get his hands around. He felt himself sliding down and took another blow to the shoulder. Flailing, Dagr managed to stab the man in one meaty calf and felt his balance waver. The Mukhabarat agent yelled and punched down at an awkward angle, hitting Dagr between the shoulder blades. Doggedly, Dagr hung on, channeling some dimly recalled playground precept about going to the ground and getting kicked in the head.

Somehow the knife turned in his hand and he stabbed again, hitting a hairy thigh through a shiny polyester pant leg. The man screamed louder, and this time blood sprayed out, covering Dagr's hands. The blows slowed as the man tried to extract his gun from his shoulder holster. This time, his belly impeded him; the gun had slid behind one fat armpit, the butt tilted back, hanging awkwardly out of reach. Dagr pushed forward with his legs, driving forward, finally taking him down.

Dagr felt the body jerk abruptly beneath him and then spasm. He looked up, saw a jagged hole in the man's neck. Kinza wiped his K-Bar on the man's suit. The rest of the Mukhabarat were dead. Kinza's head was misted with blood. He looked demonic. Around them was burning chaos. The fires from the RPG were still raging. Only a few minutes had passed. Kinza slipped into an open doorway into the stairwell of an apartment building. The space was deserted. These people knew better than to leave their houses after an explosion.

"Up?" Dagr asked.

"No, through," Kinza said. "Act like a tenant."

They moved by ways into a narrow unlit passage, which disgorged them to a rear entrance. There was a lock on the door, a small combination number Kinza shattered with the butt of his K-Bar. The noise chimed like a bell but no one came to investigate. There were faint shouts coming from outside and sporadic gunfire. Dagr looked back, his heart pounding. There was no one. No one was coming after them.

"Hamid and the Druze must have engaged," Kinza said. "The Mukhabarat don't know we're here."

36: BIRDS OF PEACE

"THERE THEY FUCKING ARE!" AVICENNA SNARLED. THE CAMERA screens painted his face green. "It's the damned Druze. Get him!"

In the bustle of guns, sandaled feet, and a barking hodge-podge of orders, Yakin was able to slink into a corner by the CCTVs, fiddle around with wires until everyone cleared out. It was not his intention to get shot up by some Druze.

His eyes lingered over the bank of TV screens, marveling at the thoroughness of the Old Man. The explosion had knocked out some of the cameras. He rewound the tape. The RPG explosion looked unreal on black and white film. He rewound some of the other cameras, trying to look busy in case anyone came to collect him. He could hear Salemi nearby, marshalling his troops.

The cart caught his eye. He had eaten kebab rolls from there just last night. Men were eating there, strangers. Two of them looked familiar. They were bulky, their clothes puffed up. Yakin froze the image in his mind. There was a partial profile of one. Something clenched in his bowels, he pissed himself in a shock of hot urine. He kept staring, his mouth open, frozen in terror. It was Kinza. No doubt about it. He was inside the cordon.

Dagr blundered around the corner of an ancient sagging gray tenement, the walls stained with flaking paint and water damage, reeking of old urine. It gave him a strong sense of déjà vu, this nightmare haze of violence that seemed to persist around him. It painted everything in garish smells, of cordite and barely suppressed vomit, of the iron mist of sprayed blood, the bare lucidity of moving forward

277

278   SAAD Z. HOSSAIN

through smoke and chaos. Men came the other way, ill-fitted suits of Mukhabarat sweating in the heat, dark patches around their armpits, guns, and moustaches, inspiring an ingrained fear in him.

It was, he reflected, why he was so useful—that instinctive flinching that marked him out as sheep, the perfect civilian cowering that could never be feigned, his pant-wetting terror made the Mukhabarat smile inside. They shoved him aside, they glowered and cursed at the cloud of maladroit bumbling that permeated him, but they let him pass. And in his wake came the dark wolf, almost invisible in his gliding edge, the other half of the coin skating along the most unlikely shadows.

Three times, they ran into soldiers after that, distracted men with hard faces. They noticed Dagr, tried to stop, went down in fans of dark blood. Kinza with a knife was deadly. It was quiet work, and if they left bodies in their wake, it was too chaotic to tell.

"Close," Kinza said, when they were within sight of the house where the Old Man lived. His smile was genuine, the simple pleasure of a man contemplating his heart's desire.

"They're too close," the Lion said. Never in the unending years of his existence had he been this desperate. "We're pinned down."

They were on a rooftop behind a water tank, a solid iron one with a full skin of rust, an old school tank of the kind unavailable now, so heavy that it must have been carried up piecemeal at the time of construction and assembled on site. Mukhabarat came from two sides, pinning them with rifle fire. There was a way to the next building, a sprint across open space and a two foot jump, a corridor now covered by gunfire.

"I will make it," Hamid said.

"It's stupid," the Lion felt a sudden loss of courage. "It's mad."

"We will be dead in minutes," Hamid said. "If I must die, I should take some of them with me."

"You speak with bravado for a torturer."

"Before that, I was a soldier in the Republican Guard," Hamid said. "It is true, I am assassin and torturer both, I killed in the night, and I cared nothing for innocence or guilt. I make no excuses, violence has been my life. Let it be said, however, that I died under the open sky, fighting with my comrades."

"I have struggled so long against the Old Man," the Lion said. "To die thus…"

"Down there is a man who will finish what you should have done years ago," Hamid said. "Stay here if you like. You have lived long, but you've not understood that sometimes, it is important to show good form."

He spun around the tank, hands unfurling like petals, two grenades arcing up, catching the light, like two black rooks falling from the sky. Bullets riddled into him and then he was clear, skipping ahead as explosions rocked all around him and his enemies took cover. The Lion looked, astonished, as Hamid barely slowed, leaking blood across the roof, making the jump easily, scattering scarlet droplets behind. He followed.

———

The Apache gunship hovered, its Gatling cannon pounding the earth, making a two-story building fold in on itself, its ancient timber and brick frame just disintegrating. The witch Mother Davala smiled around her Cuban and let cigar smoke fill the cockpit. Hoffman tried to see whom he was shooting, but it was too difficult to make out the figures through the smoke. He aimed mostly for people in suits.

———

The gunner Ancelloti tried to signal the helicopter and took a bullet in the leg for his trouble. The man he recognized as Hassan Salemi shot him. He crawled away in the dirt into an alley way by the side

of an old building. There was a way up and he took it. He wanted
to be up on the roof, where the fighting seemed hottest. Plus, the
ground was never safe with an Apache gunship in the air, no matter
whose side it was on. In reality, the cannons were so addictive that
most of the time the gunship ended up killing everyone. He tried to
staunch the bleeding with a tourniquet. He was woozy by the time
he got to the top of the stairs. He poked his head around the corner
and saw Behruse on an opposite roof. The fat man was gesticulat-
ing wildly, an AK47 in his hands. They seemed to be at an impasse.
Larger weapons were being called for. Eventually, he supposed they
would simply blow up the building. Ancelloti decided to take a break
and lit up a cigarette.

Yakin wanted to run away. He also wanted to warn somebody. These
conflicting emotions created a deep existential crisis within him,
causing him to remain rooted to one spot. Naturally, during a crisis, he watched TV. The cameras showed him insane footage. Hamid
on a roof, causing havoc. Some large man beside him, both of them
bleeding, armed to the teeth. There was a convergence of Mukhabarat
around them.

Sabeen was leading commandos on another roof, trying to bring
down a chopper. The wind was molding her clothes against her body.
Her scarf had flown off, her hair was streaming back; she looked fero-
cious. He felt something like an erection. It stiffened his resolve.

Halfway out of the door, he thought of the prisoners held captive
in the back of the house. The two silent witches, in particular, excited
him. He tried to recall whether they were guarded and remembered
Avicenna waving all the men out. He did not think the retard from the
library would put up much resistance.

"In a time of madness, God forgives small crimes," he said to
himself.

He decided to go back up for some sport.

"We have to go down!" Hoffman screamed. He had stopped firing.

"Are you stupid?" The pilot shouted back. "Sir?"

"What?"

"It is against protocol to land in a combat zone during a fire fight," the pilot said.

"See that woman?" Hoffman pointed at Sabeen, who was all too visibly trying to shoot them down. "She carries vital information. Nuclear information, if you get my drift."

"What?" The pilot was decidedly unconvinced. "That's sounds like a load of crap, sir!"

Hoffman pointed a gun at the pilot's head. "Take the ship down now, or I'm shooting you under the Official Secrets Act."

"Dude, are you crazy?"

"Don't argue with me, I'm Batman!"

Dagr cowered against the side of a building, surrounded by debris. He was stunned, bleeding from nose and mouth, choking on masonry dust. He was in this state because the 30mm bullets from the M230 Boeing chaingun affixed to the bottom of the Apache gunship fuselage had ripped indiscriminately through the buildings and populace of the alley. Dagr was unsure if he was hit; the sheer earth shaking power of the bullets and the terrible damage to the street had paralyzed his body to such an extent that he could barely take cover.

It was, he reflected, no real surprise that he could see Hoffman's awkward-shaped head through the rapidly dropping helicopter and the crazed grin of Mother Davala, although why she was billowing smoke was a mystery. Perhaps he was delirious from loss of blood.

It occurred to him to look for Kinza, but he couldn't spot him anywhere in the wreckage. Eventually the dust from the rotor was sufficiently irritating to make him crawl further into a recess in the side of a building. He found himself in someone's living room, half the wall and window ripped away by gunfire. There was a television that flickered with static. He sat down in an old chintz armchair and tried to catch his breath.

Several minutes later, Kinza staggered in through the same hole, face slick with blood.

"What the hell are you doing?" he asked.

"Resting," Dagr said. "You?"

"Cleaning up a bit," Kinza said. He gestured slightly with his knife. "Mukhabarat guys. Never liked them. Couple of beards too."

"Salemi's or random people?"

"Does it really matter at this point?"

"Guess not."

"Is that fucking Hoffman?"

"Yeah, I think so," Dagr said. "I thought I was hallucinating."

"Should have fucking known he'd come and fuck things up," Kinza said. He looked profoundly disgusted. "What's he doing?"

"He appears to be trying to give that woman some flowers."

"She's hot."

"She's shooting at him," Dagr said.

"Fucking Hoffman," Kinza said.

"It must be the wrong kind of flowers."

"Are you just about rested up?"

"I guess," Dagr looked around the living room. "You want some tea or something?"

"I had a Coke earlier."

"That Apache is blocking the way,"

"We'll just have to go around," Kinza said. "Fucking Hoffman."

———

Avicenna, ensconced in the safe room of his command center, was not having a particularly happy time. First of all, the fuckwit Yakin had deserted his post, which meant the cameras were unmanned.

Second, he had pissed on the floor. The room was not very large and poorly ventilated; Avicenna now had to spend the duration of the fight breathing in the shithead's urine.

His main concern, however, was the absence of Red Hawk 1 and 2 on radio. The likelihood of both teams manning the eastern quadrant going incommunicado appeared slim. The actual fighting should have been confined to the southern quadrant, where Hassan Salemi had already reported that the enemy was pinned down behind cover and soon to be annihilated.

He spent fifteen minutes repeatedly flashing them; it was possible that the equipment was faulty, particularly in a crisis. And then he called Red Hawk 3, which was a two-man sniper team on the roof. They were stationary, as much eyes and ears in the sky as anything offensive. Red Hawk 3 also did not answer. He began to feel the first moments of disquiet. It was the Lion, after all, the old enemy who just wouldn't go away. It was a bit of a relief when Red Hawk 4 answered. He sent them to go investigate.

———————————

Red Hawk 4 consisted of two retired desk workers who had spent most of their careers pushing papers and interrogating mild criminals of dubious intelligence. They wore ill-fitting suits and cheap rubber-soled shoes. The only gunplay they had experienced had been in the firing range during the mandatory practices. They looked more like pigeons than hawks.

It was not surprising, therefore, that when they saw Dagr sauntering around the vicinity of the eastern quadrant, they did not, at first, find it suspicious. He did, in fact, appear to be the quintessential civilian: clumsy, furtive, ridiculous. Then Kinza slipped in behind them from a patch of shadow, knives in each hand, stabbing up beneath the ribs, lifting the first man damn near two feet off the ground.

He let the knives go and caromed into secret agent number two, tripping him and ending up mounted on his chest, raining down

284   SAAD Z. HOSSAIN

hammer fists. The nose pulped, the teeth caved in, and then the flailing stopped as the man went limp. Behind him, Dagr was turning over the knife victim, planting his feet against the gurgling chest to try and retrieve the K-Bar. The suction of the chest cavity held the blade firm. In the end, it took both men to pull it out.

"The worst thing about knife fighting is when it gets stuck," Kinza said.

"No," Dagr said. "The worst thing is being the guy who gets stabbed."

Behruse was rather annoyed. The enemy Taha was pinned behind a parapet on a roof but refusing to give. He had slightly higher ground and was thus able to prevent saturation fire from all sides. Salemi's men were behind him but unable to make the jump due to there being *two* of the fuckers, both wielding automatic weapons. He had called for the grenade launcher, but the dumbfucks of Blue Raptor 1 were late. *Very late.*

It was a bit of a standoff, and while it was only a matter of time before they got off a lucky shot and actually hit the fucker, the amount of noise they were making was a bit of a concern. Sooner or later, authorities would show up. It was with extreme reluctance that he called up Avicenna on his radio, screwing his index finger into his other ear to cut out the noise.

"Hello. Hello?"

"What?"

"Hello! Avi!"

"Behruse? Where's your com?"

"We're trying to raise Blue Team 1 with it," Behruse shouted.

"What!? Where the hell are they?"

"They were bringing the rocket launcher," Behruse said. "Listen, Avi, we have the fuckers trapped, and they're bleeding. I just need the rocket launcher."

"What the fuck happened to Blue Raptor 1?"

"I dunno."

"Red Hawks 1,2,3, and 4 are not answering either."

"What?"

"The entire fucking color red is not answering!"

"That can't be right, Avi. That's the whole eastern quadrant."

"Five teams are out of communication, you stupid fuck," Avicenna screamed through the phone. "Get Salemi out there. *Someone is fucking killing our men there.*"

"I got the Lion pinned right here, boss," Behruse said. "I can see him moving around."

"How many of them?"

"The Lion and one other guy," Behruse said. "It's the old Republican Guard guy Salemi was looking for."

"Is he the man who got Salemi's son?"

"Er, no."

"Then where the fuck is that fucker?"

"What?"

"Where is the fucker who killed Salemi's son?"

"Er, not here?"

"Could he by any chance be *in the fucking eastern quadrant killing all our birds?*"

Blue Raptor 2 was a four-man team of Mukhabarat enforcers-turned-gangsters, well experienced in running down miscreants and dealing back alley justice. Each of them having been drummed out of the service for excessive brutality and corruption, they had found shelter under their old godfather, the Old Man known in dark corners as the founder of all things secret.

Their loyalty was huge, the devotion of desperate men, and if their courage did not quite make up to the same figure, at least they had a numerical advantage. Their approach into the eastern quadrant was stealthy and cautious. Had they been paramilitary or Republican

Guard, they would have fanned out and taken flanking positions and tried to reach the high ground. The Mukhabarat training did not cover urban house-to-house combat, however, and their own training in petty enforcement made them believe that moving in a pack was the safest method of maintaining their advantage.

The eastern quadrant was marked out as the corner of a dilapidated building that housed a sweatshop making textiles. Having been ordered to make a meticulous search for the intruders, Blue Raptor 2 started on the ground floor and worked their way up, slapping their way through dozens of cowering women and children. They gained entry to the roof by a rusty door and found it covered in wire lines of drying laundry.

Making their way through these rows of abayas and billowing shirts, Blue Raptor 2 began to feel slightly foolish. There were no signs of the enemy. Rather, it was a peculiarly innocuous night with a three-quarter moon and a slight breeze. Up here the resonance of gunfire was faded and harmless, sounding like distant fireworks. They made their way through the laundry, poking left and right with the muzzles of their guns.

They had their orders but were not in a hurry. It seemed to them that if the enemy were to be found elsewhere, it would be no bad thing. They had made it all the way across the roof when the leader, upon turning, found his company shortened by one. He opened his mouth to call out when the unfortunate individual staggered into view, pulling down an entire clothesline. His throat was lacerated, a gaping red necktie looking obscene against the whiteness of his shirt.

Blue Raptor 2 opened fire in all directions, fingers convulsing against their automatic weapons. The laundry was duly slaughtered and the wounded man, who might have had several minutes longer to live, found his existence cruelly shortened by a rip of bullets. When they had exhausted themselves, the leader raised his hand and looked around. They had hit nothing. The enemy had disappeared, like a ghost.

The Lion could take a hit. Hamid had to give him that.

"In the old days, they would have charged us," the Lion said.

"They don't need to," Hamid tapped toward the opposite roof, where the fat man had set up shop. "He's bringing up heavy armaments. They'll just blow us out of the sky."

"We should get out of here then."

"It might be a bit late for that," Hamid said. "Can you still move?"

"I've been known to recover from mortal wounds," the Lion said. "Do you think the others still live?"

"I think we'll see a big explosion when they die," Hamid said.

"I gave the watch back to Dagr," the Lion said.

Hamid stared at him.

"I want him to look after it if he survives."

"What, you're retiring?" Hamid asked. "No more grand quest?"

"Let someone else do it. I used to think Avicenna was the devil, but nowadays, the whole world seems to be like him. It seems he's multiplied and I've reduced."

"Yeah, now he probably wouldn't even make the first deck."

"What?"

"You know, the cards the Americans made for the top villains."

The Lion laughed, startled with the irreverence of the image. For a moment, he felt completely carefree.

"Shall we get on then?"

"Toward the fat man or the imam?" the Lion asked.

"You want to flip a coin?"

Hassan Salemi saw them hurtling toward him, jumping the gap between roofs amid a cacophony of bullets. It did not faze him. He had faced down countless men with the same cold courage. He pushed his soldiers forward and let them take the brunt of the attack. The larger man was swinging his rifle like a mallet, flattening skulls, mowing men down with brutal strength. The other one was *shooting while in the air.*

With the phlegmatic nerves typical of the imam, Salemi allowed them to approach, dropped to one knee, and shot the giant three times at point blank range. He staggered and incredibly kept on moving. *What manner of devil is this?* He let the giant pass him and then shot him again, spraying his back with bullets, until the man went down from sheer volume of fire. The hammer of his gun, having exhausted its store, continued to click for several minutes before he could lift his finger.

He felt a shadow over him and turned. The infidel torturer burst through his guards to reach him. He was grinning, a crazed blood-stained mirth that Salemi could not understand. He was almost dead. *Almost.* He was on fire, hands dripping napalm, touching everything like a demon child, screaming defiance and heat in that tight space. Even as bullets pounded into him, he spun into Salemi and grabbed hold in a tight lover's embrace until they were cheek to cheek and spinning across the roof.

Salemi felt hard round bars pressing into his chest: *explosives. There were explosives tied to the man's vest.* He tried to struggle out of that iron grip, felt the burning man laughing against him, a terrible, haunting sound, a slow-pitched whine that leached the strength from his limbs. Then there was a great noise and the world turned red.

"He's dead then?" Avicenna could scarcely hide the eagerness in his old voice.

Behruse stood over the mutilated body of Afzal Taha, the last disciple of Al-Hakim, as it still stirred with the stubborn remnant of life.

"Not quite. It's remarkable," Behruse shouted into his walkie talkie. His ears and nose still bled from the explosions. "He's been shot eight times, so much that he looks like a beggar's sock. He's also been blown up, burnt to a crisp, and then tossed down eight stories. Yet his body still moves."

"Cut his head off!" Avicenna screamed.

"I am doing so now," Behruse said. He was, indeed, sawing through the neck of the Lion. "God, his spine is massive."

"At last, the devil is dead."

Behruse hoisted up the head and looked around at the carnage. Hardly any of Salemi's men had survived: The explosives had destroyed the entire roof, besides flinging the Lion's body to the ground. Salemi himself was gone, vaporized along with Col. Hamid, formerly of the Republican Guard. Still, it was over. They could leave this place now, and his master would once again fade into obscurity for the next hundred years.

"Are you holding up his head?"

"Yes," Behruse said. "His blood is dripping down my elbow."

There were noises of glass and drink. "I am now drinking to your health, with this cognac that comes from the stores of Napoleon himself."

"Well thanks, boss, but I'd rather have the drink myself," Behruse said.

Just then their communicators cracked to life on the secure channel, and a torrent of panic burst forth.

"Raptor 4 to Bear 1! Blue 4 to Bear 1!"

"What? What? This is Behruse!"

"Abort! Abort!"

"What the hell are you talking about?" Behruse shouted. "Where is Blue Raptor 2?"

"Dead! Dead, everyone here is dead!"

"What?"

"Blue Raptor 2 is down! Blue Raptor 3 has disappeared! I repeat. They're all down! He's killing everyone. Even civilians. These buildings are full of dead people. It's a fucking mausoleum!"

"Blue Raptor 4! This is the Mountain," Avicenna said. "Listen to me. All hostiles in other quadrants are down. I repeat. All other hostiles are down. We are sending reinforcements. I command you to track the assassin in the eastern quadrant."

"No, no, this place is full of hostiles," Blue Raptor 4 moaned. "It can't be just one man. It's barbaric. I'm not staying here."

"How many men do you have?" Avicenna snapped across the line.

"No one. They're all gone. He's killed *everyone*."

"Raptor 4!" Behruse said. "Get your ass back there!"

"Fuck you, Behruse. I'm not dying here for your fat ass. I'm getting   outta.   Aargghh   leavemealoneIwasleavingIsurrender! Isurrenderaaaahhhhh…"

"Behruse, what the fuck just happened?" Avicenna asked.

"Er…"

"Hello?" A new voice, breathing hard.

"Hello!" Behruse said. "Who the fuck are you? What have you done to Blue Raptor 4?"

"Blue *Raptor*? Is that what you call him? Really?"

"Who is this?" Behruse asked. "Listen to me. You're the arms dealer, right? Kinza, is it?"

"Yes."

"Well your boss the Lion is dead," Behruse said. "I've cut his fucking head off."

"Oh?"

"And the other fucker with him is dead too," Behruse said.

"How did he die?"

"He blew himself up."

"Alone?"

"He got Salemi," Behruse said. "Listen, you had beef with Salemi, right? Salemi is dead. He's rain in the gutters. You couldn't pick him up with a teaspoon. This is over. You're surrounded. Just come in and we can talk."

"Yes, I'm coming."

"So you're going to lay down arms?" Behruse asked, dubious.

"Not quite."

"What the fuck do you want? You want to walk? Go ahead."

"Not really, no."

"We have no fight with you. Just walk away, man."

"You're the fat man Behruse, right? I'll be seeing you."

"No, I'm Ahmed! Ahmed!"

"He's hung up, you fat coward," Avicenna said after a minute.

"What the hell does that guy want?"

"He wants to kill us, you moron!" Avicenna said. "Round up your men and get back here! And don't forget to bring the head."

The Lion tried to move, and the searing pain from every nerve ending told him that this was not possible. Things were broken, things pierced, skin destroyed, charred black into a sludge, mixed with the debris of the other fallen, hiding him in masonry and mangled flesh. Ayn Sawfar flashed through his mind, when the Druze had fallen in thousands to Janissary guns, and he had hidden in a hillock of corpses, in the peculiar claustrophobic space between life and death until the immortal clockwork had pulled his body back from the brink.

He saw the fat man looming near him and shut his eyes for the coup de grace, yet the fool moved on, rummaging around some other destroyed body. The machete glinted, blood sprayed from disgusting hacking noises, the thwack of a butcher's blade beating bone, and the fat man stood up triumphant, holding up the wrong head.

The Lion started to wheeze with hysterical laughter.

The gunship hovered in the air like a hesitant moth, the two passengers bickering in the back while the pilot repeatedly thumbed the red trigger button, almost lasciviously, hoping he would finally be permitted to unleash the hellfires. Sabeen and her men were across the street, firing a variety of ineffective long range weapons at them. It was a stalemate of sorts. The Apache had withdrawn somewhat, but the looming shadow of its black form still discouraged Sabeen from charging.

"We just have to soften her up a bit," Hoffman said.

Mother Davala snorted. "Clearly, your time in confinement has broken you. Were you raped by the dog boy? You are completely delusional about this woman."

"It's the bastard Behruse's fault," Hoffman said. "He's poisoned her mind against me."

"I've got things to do, you know."

"I have a plan," Hoffman said, tapping his head.

"If it doesn't involve blowing that bitch up, I'm going to be seriously disappointed."

"Pilot, come in pilot!"

"Sir?"

"Release the box!"

"Er, the one you left on the seat?"

"Yes."

"What's in it?"

"What do you mean what's in it?" Hoffman asked, incensed. "I'm giving you a direct order!"

"Sir, quite frankly your orders have sucked, and I'm gonna have to check what's inside the box."

"I forbid you to open the box!"

"Er, there appears to be leaflets inside the box."

"I forbid you to read them!"

"It appears to be poetry. 'She walks in beauty like the night.' Someone called Byron," the pilot said. "Addressed to someone called Sabeen, from someone called You-Know-Who."

"I forbid you to repeat any of this to anyone!"

"Sir, this is the craziest shit I've ever done. I'm afraid I'm gonna have to tell everyone I know."

"Oh well, then just remember, my real name is Captain Fowler."

"Right, sir," the pilot said. "You want me to dump this stuff from the air now?"

"Yes."

"Over the lady's position?"

"Yes."

"Ok, done."

"Now let me down somewhere safe with the rest of my suitcases."

"Hoffman?" Mother Davala demanded. "What is happening?"

"Don't worry," said Hoffman. "I got this."

Behruse was making his way back down the street, swinging the severed head to and fro when it began to rain leaflets. It made him pause and look up. His men saw the ugly maw of the Apache gunship and quite naturally ran for cover. Behruse, somewhat literate, was drawn to the pink hearts and swirly writing on the leaflet, which appeared to be atypical of the propaganda normally raining down on Baghdad.

A closer scan made him put down the severed head and burst out laughing. The mirth rolled out of him in gigantic waves, making his belly shake and his eyes tear. He was doubled over when he saw the brief shadow behind him. He tried to turn, but the US marine lurking behind him was fast as a snake. Something like a screwdriver plunged into his neck with a hot gush of pain.

He staggered a few steps until his legs gave way. Sprawled on the street, he looked up and saw the marine Ancelloti looming over him.

"I gave you good weed," Behruse gasped, confused.

"Hoffman says hi," Ancelloti said. He stuffed a leaflet into Behruse's open dead mouth and walked away.

"I can't see," Mother Davala complained. "What's he doing?"

"He's got the white flag out," the pilot said. "I think he's surrendering. Ok, he's definitely surrendered. They've disarmed him. The girl has him kneeling down. He's talking a lot."

"He'll probably make us surrender too," Mother Davala said bitterly. She had never before employed such an unsatisfactory servant.

"Wait. One of the thugs is giving him a last smoke," the pilot said. "Now he's passing around a bottle. The girl is getting pissed. Wait. He's got his suitcase open. He's handing things out. Oh shit! He's got all the colonel's bourbon! Fuck! He's giving it away. Ok, Goon 1 is walking away with an armload. The other suitcase is open now. It looks like Skittles. Goon 2 just loaded up his pockets. Ok, Goon 3 is drinking bourbon with his Skittles now. Wait, they're making him get up."

"Hopefully they'll shoot him now," Mother Davala said.

"No, they're hugging him. He's passing around joints. Ok, he's got out a pile of cash. The girl is super pissed. She's waving her gun around. Goon 4 is walking away. Goon 5 just kissed him on the cheeks and took the empty suitcases. Um, pretty much all the goons are gone. Ah, he's wrestling with the girl. He's disarmed her. Ok, he's kissing her now. Aaaand, he's walking back. I can't believe this. He's actually disbanded the entire enemy unit using bourbon and Skittles."

"What's the woman doing?"

"She's just kind of standing there. I can't read her face. It's like she's smiling."

"Put me down," she ordered. "I'm getting out."

Dagr walked slowly, like an old man afraid of breaking his hip. He had taken a bullet squarely in the chest and cracked ribs now made every breath an agony. The Kevlar was deathly hot and heavy. He had dropped all his weapons but one, a single glock tucked into his waist. They had finished all their bullets.

Kinza moved beside him a few feet away, slinking along the walls. He was literally coated with blood, some of it his own. He had taken wounds, perhaps mortal ones, but the Mukhabarat were broken. The last of them had run. Kinza's communicator, appropriated from Blue Raptor 2, had ceased to cackle with commands and countercommands. The last panicked screams had faded to silence. The enemy was no longer trying to find them. Kinza had killed *everyone*.

They walked now through an empty street. Far away the Apache thumped overhead, waiting. The house at the end of the cul-de-sac was unassuming. A single arch hid an ivy-covered door that was bolted. They forced it open. If there had been guards here before, they had run away.

They heard noises in a back room, a man desperately trying to raise someone on the phone. He ceased when Kinza opened the door. It was an old man, drinking brandy, surrounded by CCTV screens.

"You are the arms dealer?" The old man said. "I am Avicenna."

"Yes," Kinza said.

"Please, both of you, take a seat," Avicenna said.

"That's not why we're here."

"I understand that you've met Afzal Taha?"

"Yes."

"Then you know his story."

"Yes."

"You also have the watch?" Avicenna asked.

"My friend does," Kinza said, nodding at Dagr.

"Well, the long story of Al-Hakim the Druze is finally over," Avicenna said. He raised his hands in mock prayer. "You are no longer required. Give me the watch and go your way. There will be no further retaliations from me."

"Retaliations. Hmm."

"Afzal Taha is dead," Avicenna said. His voice was calm. "It's over."

"So I've heard," Kinza said. "It's not over for *me*."

"I don't know what you're fighting for, you pup," Avicenna said. "But your insolence is more than I can bear. I will kill you. I will rape your mother and your sisters. I will sell your family into slavery. I will erase from this earth any human who harbors any memory of you."

Kinza smiled.

"He is smiling," Dagr said, "because he has no mother, no sisters, no lovers, no one at all."

"Then you, professor," Avicenna said, something twitching in his eyes. "I know you. I will beat your wife to death. I will throttle the breath from your child. I will kill your friends and their friends. Do you think I have not done worse in the long years of my life?"

"My daughter is dead," Dagr said. "My wife is dead. I had two friends. One blew himself up killing your dog Hassan Salemi." He started to laugh and then choked because it hurt so much. "You'll be taking fuckall from me."

"Do you want gold then? Money?" Avicenna asked. "I have the wealth of a hundred kings buried in the desert."

"That's not why I'm here," Kinza said.

"Life then?" Avicenna asked. "The secret that gave Taha his powers is the same that has kept me alive this long. Give me the watch, and let us become immortal!"

"No."

"Die then!" He leapt from his chair, far faster than humanly possible, something sharp darting out of his sleeve.

Kinza snaked forward. The spring-loaded knife tip took him in the throat, severing all the arteries. Poison flooded his mouth. The edge of his blade crashed into the old man's outstretched wrist, taking it off. As they both fell, Kinza's second knife slashed upwards, scoring along Avicenna's belly, ripping up everything.

"Dagr," Kinza whispered. "Run."

Something in his bag began to beep.

★

EPILOGUE

HOFFMAN OPENED A THERMOS AND POURED SOME COFFEE. HE fished out two tin mugs from somewhere, filled them, and offered one to Dagr. The helicopter thumped the air, clawing up with brute force. Kinza, in the end, had settled his accounts with an explosion that had rocked the entire city. Avicenna's house was gone, the bodies of the dead vaporized in a gaping crater. The fire had spread, and the outer buildings, rigged with explosives, were starting to blow up like fire-crackers on a string. The heat from the blasts rocked the helicopter. Far below, hapless policemen and firefighters were trying to come to grips with the madness.

"You alright, man?" Hoffman asked.

"Numb," Dagr said.

"Me too," Hoffman sighed. "Love is hell. This is not how I thought it'd play out."

"Me neither."

"So," Hoffman said. "Where d'you wanna go?"

"I don't know," Dagr said. "What about you?"

"Sabeen ran off," Hoffman said. "And I don't even want to know where the witch went. I'm thinking we should get out of here before someone comes to look at the mushroom cloud."

Dagr looked out of the window to the east. The gray of dawn was lighting up the sky. He looked at the watch on his wrist and then the wad of paper Hamid had given him.

"I still have the Druze watch," he said finally, putting the paper away.

"Yeah?"

"It gives directions to some place," Dagr said. "You want to see where it goes?"

298   SAAD Z. HOSSAIN

Hoffman tapped the helicopter pilot's shoulder. The insubordinate bastard rolled his eyes. "I'm still telling everybody I know," he said. "Whenever we get back."

Hoffman gave a little whoop, and then the helicopter shot out, over the clouds of discharged ordinance, across to the great river, rolling with barges and boats, crossing toy bridges filled with little cars, all of it matchbox from up high, everyone moving along in a new day as if nothing much had happened, and perhaps nothing much had.

Down below, Mother Davala sat alone in the center of the wreckage, the last of the furies, wispy hair framing a halo around her disheveled bald head, her enormous smoking revolver tapping against one bony shin. Her boots were knee deep in spilled blood, her body bent against the apocalyptic wind, but she chewed on her half-lit cigar with gusto, and her eyes glinted like the desert sun. In her arm, she cradled an earthen amphora, etched with the patterns of ancient Babylon.

"And so passes one more of our enemies. Our work continues, dear one. I'll speak the names of the victims," Mother Davala said to the amphora. "And you will scour the world looking for the oppressors. You will be the hand of vengeance. You will be retribution. They will tremble before our names. Is that not a glorious fate?"

"Fuck off," said the voice within.

THE END

GLOSSARY

AL-HAKIM: King of the Druze, Fatimid caliph who disappeared mysteriously one day at the age of 36 after evening prayers. Occultation is the technical term for this kind of disappearance. He was an important figure in Ismailism and considered the imam of the Druze.

'AS SAIQA' SPECIAL FORCES: Part of the much-vaunted Republican Guard of Iraq, which, in the balance of things, did not contest very well against the American regime change.

BAKLAVA: A dessert of many layers of pastry, honey, and almonds, which is so good that almost every country from Greece to Persia claim ownership of it.

DJINNS: In Islam, there are three sapient races: the djinn, humans, and angels, of which djinns are made of fire and humans of mud. Both humans and djinns enjoy free will, although the djinn appear to have a lot more power. A bit unfair, really.

DRUZE: Secretive ancient sect of mystics within Islam who follow a number of esoteric beliefs that are known only to their sworn elders. Although small in number, the Druze enjoyed periods of power disproportionate to their size. The Druze are currently a closed religion. They do not proselytize, and it is not possible to join them. Apologies to all Druze, by the way, for all the liberties taken in this book.

THE GREAT LIBRARY: The great library of Alexandria, which was destroyed. First by Caesar, then by other brutish Romans.

THE HOUSE OF WISDOM: The great university and library of eighth century Baghdad, the highest seat of learning in the world at that time, destroyed by the Mongols. It is thought that the contents of the Great

Library of Alexandria were preserved in the House of Wisdom. The library contained in the house of the blue door is part of this ancient collection.

IBN SINA: Famed scientist and the father of modern medicine, he was by no means a villain and became so by accident in the course of this novel. It is possible that he discovered the key to eternal life. Latin name, Avicenna.

IED: Improvised explosive device. By all accounts, one of the chief weapons used by insurgents, rebels, bandits, and other people bent on violence. These were essentially homemade bombs often cunningly disguised as everyday objects. Most of the casualties suffered by US–Coalition forces during the insurgency were caused by IEDs.

JABER IBN HAYYAN: Geber. Famous chemist, mathematician, scientist, alchemist, and philosopher. A towering genius. He wrote some of his alchemical works in code to prevent random people from reading it. The word gibberish might come from his name. Sometime after his alleged death, another body of work came up in Latin, attributed to him. There is some dispute as to who the author is, so he is referred to as "Pseudo Geber." The answer, however, is clear. Obviously, Geber the master alchemist owned the secret to immortality and continued publishing works well past the length of a normal human life.

JAM: Jaish Al Mahdi, or Mahdi Army. Not to be confused with other Mahdi armies, of which there are many. This particular one was set up by the Shi'a cleric Muqtadr Al Sadr (see later entry), who was active in Baghdad politics during the US occupation of Iraq. The JAM was set up in 2003 as his paramilitary force and fought in the uprising against US coalition forces, menacing everyone. They were eventually put down in 2008 by the Iraqi national army for being too good at what they did.

KA-BAR: US marine combat knife, a multipurpose tool suitable for any operation from opening cans to actually stabbing someone. The origins of the name appear to be from 1923, when the Union Cutlery Co. of Olean, New York, branded its knives with this logo. By 1944, many of the combat knives being used by the US armed forces were manufactured by Union Cutlery, who continued branding its products with the prominent Ka-Bar logo. As a result, soldiers started referring to all knives as Ka-Bar, regardless of the manufacturer. (Also referred to as K-Bar).

KIBBEH: A kind of kebab. One of the many good things to eat found in Middle Eastern cuisine.

KURDS: A landless ethnic group living on the edges of Turkey, Iraq, and Iran, who've sneakily managed to steal a country of their own from the clusterfuck that is the Iraq war. Their army is called the Peshmerga.

M60: A heavy machine gun used by the US armed forces since 1957, copied from German WW2 machine guns. Often used by a team of three men or a single Rambo-type soldier. It weighs a lot and uses belt-fed 7.62 mm ammo that runs out quickly due to the high firing rate.

MOQTADA AL SADR: Shi'a cleric active in Iraqi politics during the early days of the occupation. At one point commanded his own private army out of the Sadr city area of Baghdad. A most fearsome man.

MOTHER DAVALA: The ancient matron of a safehouse in Baghdad and incarnation of one of the three furies, or fates, of Greek mythology, who are particularly interested in divine vengeance.

NAG HAMMADI LIBRARY: A collection of early Gnostic texts found in Egypt. One-of-a-kind haul, really. Got nothing much to do with the book, just thought it was cool.

SABIANS: Not in the book, but an interesting fact. The Koran mentions three acceptable people who should not be molested: the Jews, the Christians, and the Sabians. The Jews and Christians were easily identified, but no one was quite sure who the Sabians were. Apparently, all sorts of unlikely candidates have and continue to claim to be Sabians to avoid molestation.

SHI'A: The party of Ali, the largest minority in the Islamic faith. Said to contain many sects, some of which are wildly divergent from the orthodoxy.

SOLOMON'S DJINNS: When Solomon—Suleiman—was king, he ruled a bunch of djinns.

SUNNI: The majority, the orthodoxy.

SUNNI-SHI'A CONFLICT: The major schism in Islam from early days, the root is essentially political. The Sunni believed that the caliph— the political and theological head of the Islamic empire—should be from the tribe at large. The Shi'a believed it should be from the family of the prophet, namely, Ali, his son-in-law. This seemingly innocuous disagreement has degenerated into a rabid hatred of each other, especially in the Middle East, where the doctrinal differences are backed up by racial divides between Arabs and Persians. While the rest of the Muslim world looks on in slight bemusement, these sects have shown a marked preference for killing each other, particularly in Iraq, where everything is up for grabs.

TAREQ AZIZ: Saddam-era former deputy prime minister of Iraq, now serving prison term. One of the chief deputies of Saddam. Interestingly, he is a Christian. His employer apparently believed in equal opportunity.

US DECK OF CARDS: Shortly after the US invasion of Iraq, the Americans brought out a deck of cards each featuring a high value target. Those narrowly missing the deck were deeply offended.

ACKNOWLEDGMENTS

I'D LIKE TO ACKNOWLEDGE MY FAMILY FOR MOCKING MY LITERARY pretensions at every opportunity and offering no encouragement whatsoever. Also, thanks to my old friends for being ruthlessly sarcastic and forcing me to waste many hours of my life doing random, pointless things.

Thanks to the members of Writers Block for critiquing large amounts of text with well-disguised boredom and promoting my work at every opportunity.

Many thanks to Chris and the people at Unnamed Press for your fantastic editing and for taking a long shot.

Finally, thanks to Bengal for getting me started.

In the off chance that I should become famous, I shall strive to forget all of you as quickly as possible.

ABOUT THE AUTHOR

Saad Z. Hossain writes in a niche genre of fantasy, science fiction, and black comedy with an action-adventure twist. He was published in the anthologies *What the Ink?* and *Six Seasons Review*. He has written numerous articles and short stories for *The Daily Star*, *New Age*, and the *Dhaka Tribune*, the top English daily newspapers in Bangladesh. He's a monthly columnist for the *Daily Star* literary page, reviews science fiction for SFBook, and lives in Dhaka, Bangladesh.